Marion Zimmer Bradley's
Sword and Sorceress 31

Edited by
Elisabeth Waters

This book is a work of fiction. All characters, names, locations, and events portrayed in this book are fictional or used in an imaginary manner to entertain, and any resemblance to any real people, situations, or incidents is purely coincidental.

SWORD AND SORCERESS 31

Edited by Elisabeth Waters

Copyright © 2016 Marion Zimmer Bradley Literary Works Trust
Cover Design copyright © 2016 by Dave Smeds
All Rights Reserved.

ISBN-13: 978-1-938185-45-8
ISBN-10: 1-938185-45-5

Trade Paperback Edition

November 2, 2016

A Publication of
The Marion Zimmer Bradley Literary Works Trust
PO Box 193473
San Francisco, CA 94119-3473
www.mzbworks.com

ACKNOWLEDGMENTS

"Introduction" copyright © 2016 by Elisabeth Waters
"Sage Mountain" copyright © 2016 by Deborah J. Ross
"Beasts and Monsters" copyright © 2016 by Michael H. Payne
"Tale-maker; Tale-spinner" copyright © 2016 by Pam L. Wallace
"Earth's Daughter" copyright © 2016 by Catherine Mintz
"Pig-Headed" copyright © 2016 by Suzan Harden
"Hot Milk Before Bed" copyright © 2016 by L.S. Patton
"Unicorn Heart" copyright © 2016 by Pauline J. Alama
"The Fountains of Karona" copyright © 2016 by Julia H. West
"Lord Ruthven's Masque" copyright © 2016 by Steve Chapman
"After The Swan Song" copyright © 2016 by Lorie Calkins
"The Sassy and the Naegg" copyright © 2016 by Dave Smeds
"Tears of a Dead God" copyright © 2016 by Jonathan Shipley
"In Her Shoes" copyright © 2016 by Melissa Mead
"Simplicity" copyright © 2016 by Marian Allen
"Shiny in the Shallows" copyright © 2016 by Rose Hill
"Black Dust" copyright © 2016 by Robin Wayne Bailey
"Reading the Future" copyright © 2016 by Laura Davy

CONTENTS

INTRODUCTION   7
by Elisabeth Waters

SAGE MOUNTAIN   8
by Deborah J. Ross

BEASTS AND MONSTERS   23
by Michael H. Payne

TALE-MAKER; TALE-SPINNER   47
by Pam L. Wallace

EARTH'S DAUGHTER   58
by Catherine Mintz

PIG-HEADED   77
by Suzan Harden

HOT MILK BEFORE BED   90
by L.S. Patton

UNICORN HEART   106
by Pauline J. Alama

THE FOUNTAINS OF KARONA   118
by Julia H. West

LORD RUTHVEN'S MASQUE   144
by Steve Chapman

AFTER THE SWAN SONG   163
by Lorie Calkins

THE SASSY AND THE NAEGG *by Dave Smeds*	**173**
TEARS OF A DEAD GOD *by Jonathan Shipley*	**196**
IN HER SHOES *by Melissa Mead*	**218**
SIMPLICITY *by Marian Allen*	**229**
SHINY IN THE SHALLOWS *by Rose Hill*	**251**
BLACK DUST *by Robin Wayne Bailey*	**260**
READING THE FUTURE *by Laura Davy*	**274**
ABOUT SWORD & SORCERESS *by Elisabeth Waters*	**278**

INTRODUCTION
by Elisabeth Waters

When I was reading stories for *Sword and Sorceress* this year, I noticed that I was humming a song from Gilbert & Sullivan's *H.M.S. Pinafore; or, The Lass That Loved a Sailor*. (If you want a good parlor game, see how many subtitles of their operettas you can come up with.) It's the song that starts: *Things are seldom what they seem, Skim milk masquerades as cream....*

I don't think I'm likely to confuse skim milk and cream, but in several of this year's stories, things are not at all what the protagonist thinks them to be—and one story even features an enchanted cow.

One of my favorite lines in the song is: *Gild the farthing if you will, Yet it is a farthing still*. While that's certainly true in the real world, it's not the case in fiction. It's not that fiction doesn't have rules; it does, and they can be rather strict. One complaint of beginning authors on being told that their story is incredible (MZB's rejection #31: willing suspension of disbelief does not mean "hang by the neck until dead.") is "but it happened that way in real life." At that point a patient editor will explain that, unlike non-fiction, fiction has to make sense.

So an author's job can be described as gilding a farthing in a way that makes the reader believe it's *not* still a farthing. It's a strange job, but it can be a lot of fun.

Here is this year's batch of transformed farthings. I hope you enjoy them.

SAGE MOUNTAIN

by Deborah J. Ross

Roseline's thoughtless conduct has caused more problems than she ever expected. She's going to have to travel far and spend a lot of time thinking to determine what to do now.

Deborah J. Ross is an award-nominated writer and editor of fantasy and science fiction. Her most recent books include Thunderlord *and* The Children of Kings *(with Marion Zimmer Bradley);* Collaborators *(as Deborah Wheeler); and* The Seven-Petaled Shield *trilogy. Her short fiction has appeared in* F&SF, Asimov's, Star Wars: Tales From Jabba's Palace, Realms of Fantasy, *and* Sword and Sorceress. *Her work has earned Honorable Mention in* Year's Best SF, *and nominations for Gaylactic Spectrum Award, Lambda Literary Award, National Fantasy Federation Speculative Fiction Award for Best Author, Nebula Award, and inclusion in the Locus Recommended Reading, Tiptree Award recommended reading, and Kirkus notable new release lists. She has served as Secretary to the Science Fiction Fantasy Writers of America (SFWA) and is currently on the Board of Directors of Book View Cafe. When she's not writing, she knits for charity, plays classical piano, studies yoga, and provides a happy retirement for a former seeing eye dog.*

On a sunny spring morning, Roseline snuck out of her father's castle, saddled her pony, and took off for a clandestine rendezvous with the stable boy. The snow that had blanketed the meadow all winter had melted, leaving sodden ground dotted with early wildflowers. Beyond the expanse of new green lay the forested mountains that yielded the meager wealth of the kingdom: timber, furs, and nuts.

On the far side of the meadow, Roseline dismounted at the edge of a stand of fir trees and led the pony through a gap. The light dimmed, cut off by the masses of needles, and the temperature fell. Her heart beat fast with a delicious sense of anticipation.

A hand clamped over her mouth from behind. Adrenaline jolted through her. A hot breath brushed against her cheek and a masculine voice murmured in her ear, "Now I have you in my power."

Roseline clawed the stable boy's fingers away from her mouth. "Audric, you scared me half to death, sneaking up on me like!"

Fists on her hips, she faced him. They were almost the same age and her clothing was in no better shape than his, although her boots were of finer quality.

"Come on, can't you take a joke?" Spots of color darkened his cheeks.

"You could have been a bandit, an outlaw—anybody!"

"I'd never let anything happen to you—don't you think I can protect you?"

Her irritation faded at his bantering tone. She answered him in the same manner. "Maybe *you're* the one I need protection against."

"I didn't imagine that you liked it."

Roseline liked being kissed by him, but she wasn't entirely certain whether what she enjoyed was the kiss itself or the delicious sense of doing something her father would disapprove of.

"I might need a reminder... Of course, you'll have to catch me first." With that, she darted around the pony, putting the beast between them.

Audric lunged after her, but she danced away. When he changed directions, so did she. Back and forth they went, until they were both laughing, anticipating each other's next movement as if they were partnered in a Solstice Festival dance. Finally Audric grabbed hold of the pony's saddle and vaulted over its back. He landed on his feet in front of her.

When he reached out, she allowed him to draw her into an embrace. Unlike when they'd first kissed in the hayloft last summer, she knew what to expect. His lips felt dry at first, then wet. She closed her eyes, the better to focus on the sensation. His mouth moved over hers.

Audric drew her even closer and slipped one hand around the back of her neck beneath the heavy coil of her hair. The touch sent shivers through her. Her own breath quickened. She held him as firmly as he did her.

"Oh, Roseline..." Audric burrowed his face in the side of her neck and kissed the tender skin there. He was now breathing as fast as if he'd just run all the way here from the house. One hand caressed her breasts and the other moved to cup her buttocks. "How wonderful it will be when we're wed."

Wed? Blessed Mother, is he asking me to marry *him?*

In a flash, Roseline perceived that was exactly his meaning. How could she have been so stupid not to have seen it? He wanted her in bed, certainly, but the bed he wanted was her own, in a warm room in the house instead of the stables, with soft woolen blankets, meat at dinner, a fine knife to carry, boots of good leather, and maybe a horse to ride instead of simply mucking out its stall.

Why not? At this rate, she was going to end a spinster, living off the charity of her family. She was pretty enough, and willing to work hard, but nobody wanted a penniless bride. Nobody who could bring any benefit to her family, that is.

And she would be forever known as the daughter who married a stable boy because she could not control her impulses. It would break her father's heart. And for what? She and Audric could barely hold an ordinary conversation of more than a few sentences.

"I must return home—now." Without waiting for his answer, she jerked free and started across the meadow.

He caught up with her, marching alongside. "Roseline! Slow down! I didn't mean anything wrong by it! I thought you *liked* me!"

"I never should have allowed what happened. I'm sorry, I really am."

"Sorry? After the way you led me on—"

"I made a mistake, that's all. The best thing is to end it now.

To never speak of it again."

"You just can't walk away from everything we had." He grabbed her arms and held her in a grip like iron. "Everything we did."

Roseline's temper flared. She hated being manhandled this way. "Let me go!"

Audric glared at her, an angry flush suffusing his features. He looked like a stranger. "All I have to do is tell your father what we've been doing, and he will *make* you marry me."

"What are you talking about?" she cried, now truly alarmed. "I may have been indiscreet, foolhardy even, but I have done nothing wrong!"

"So you say, but I will tell him that you already spread your legs for me. And unless you wish to be poked and prodded by a midwife, with your whole family and everyone on the estate knowing why, you will have no way of proving my story false. He'll make you marry me to cover up the scandal."

Roseline was so appalled that she jerked away with sufficient force to pull free. "Say whatever you like, my father will not believe you. You are an utter idiot if you think he will place your word above mine." Even as she spoke, she felt a growing uncertainty. The accusation itself would be enough to ruin her.

He must have seen the hesitation in her face, for he stepped closer to her. His eyes gleamed with triumph. "I can produce proof."

"How can you, when we never—never—"

"Last fall, you left a ribbon in the hay."

"A ribbon. It could have been anyone's."

"A fine satin ribbon, too costly for a milkmaid's? A fine *scarlet* ribbon?"

Roseline felt blood drain from her face. She did indeed own a scarlet ribbon, but it was for her hair, not her undergarments. The ribbon had gone missing—she was not sure when she'd first noticed it. At the time, she'd thought it had come off while she was out riding. But it could just as easily have been while they were kissing.

Who was the idiot now, Audric with his stupid attempt at

blackmail, or she herself for thinking she could escape the consequences of her dalliance?

Audric stepped back, leaving her a clear path to the pony. "Go on home. I'll give you a few days to convince your father. And then you'll be mine."

The part of Roseline's mind that had gone numb with the impossibility of her situation now woke up. She needed time to figure a way out. "Two days isn't nearly enough. My father takes longer than that to make up his mind what color to dye his socks. I need at least six weeks."

"Six weeks? That's ridiculous!"

Roseline lowered her eyes, hoping that she now looked demure and unthreatening. "You have more confidence in my ability to persuade Father than I do, but I will try. Give me a month."

"Three weeks, not a day more."

"You swear by your mother's grave that you will not say anything until then?"

"Only if *you* swear not to steal the ribbon."

Roseline did not trust herself to speak, lest she crow aloud. She had gained a small respite, but that did not mean she was safe. She had no idea how she might get herself out of Audric's clutches, but she might come up with all manner of solutions in three weeks.

She scrambled on the pony and booted it in the direction of home. The beast willingly leapt into a full out gallop toward its snug, dry barn.

By the time Roseline clattered into the courtyard, she was truly furious. How dare Audric put her in such a position? If he went to her father with the ribbon, her life was over. If *she* accused *him*, her life was over. Even if she gave in and agreed to marry him, that would not solve anything. Her father would likely throw both of them out.

The only way her life would *not* be over was to somehow make the wretched scoundrel go away. For about two seconds, she considered bribing him to remain silent. She didn't have much wealth of her own, just a few pieces of simple jewelry, not worth much. He would still have the power to ruin her life and would likely would be after her for the rest of her days with one demand after another. No, she needed a permanent solution.

The next morning, Roseline still hadn't come up with a strategy, but there was one person who might know: the mystical, reclusive, and all-knowing Sage of the Mountain. She saddled her pony, tied on the saddlebags stuffed with as much food and warm clothing as she could manage, and set off.

The sun shone warm and bright, her pony was fresh, and her hopes rose. She said sang as she rode, and by the time afternoon's shadows were lengthening, she envisioned herself a warrior woman on a grand quest. Eventually, however, the day turned chilly and she realized she had not given proper thought to where she would spend the night.

Thinking that perhaps she could find a cave in one of the hillsides, Roseline began searching for one. The trail had taken her downhill into a valley by a swiftly running stream. She smelled the icy, metallic tang as the water rushed over its stony bed. Although the light was fading fast, she spotted the entrance to a cave in the side of the hill.

Roseline had read enough stories about caves and the creatures who lived in them to be suspicious of this unexpected luck. After dismounting and tying the pony to a bush, she managed to find a thick, short branch that would serve as a cudgel.

As silently as she could, she tiptoed into the cave. A fire pit in the center of the floor gave off a sullen red glow, barely enough to see by. Surrounding it were chunks of charred wood, splintered bone, and piles of extremely smelly rags. Roseline whirled back toward the entrance, but before she got there, a large, hairy, smelly, half-naked body blocked her way.

The troll bent over to peer at her. "What you do here?"

Roseline had heard stories of people eaten by trolls, but she had never heard of a troll who initiated the process by asking a question. Without thinking, she blurted out, "I've come to ask you for help."

The troll was so startled, it sat on the ground with a loud thump, thereby effectively blocking the entrance to the cave.

For lack of anything any better idea, Roseline assumed her most trusting expression. That had always worked with her father and, come to think of it, with Audric as well. The troll night be persuaded to sit on Audric and squash him into jelly, and that would solve her problem.

"I'm in terrible trouble," she said. "There's no one else I can turn to. I have always heard that trolls are fearless," which was perfectly true, although not necessarily in this context, "and so I came all the way here too beg for your assistance."

The troll blinked at her. Being begged for assistance was undoubtedly outside its previous experience. "What you want?"

"There's this horrible boy who is forcing me to marry him. He has threatened to tell my father all kinds of lies if I don't. Please help me!" She did not elaborate further, for fear of confusing the troll with too much information.

The troll scratched its head. "Eat boy?"

"That's all very well for you," she said. "*You* are big and powerful. I, on the other hand, am only a weakling human girl. Besides, the boy would object to being eaten. He'd much rather kiss me. Can't *you* do something?"

The troll sat for so long, digesting this question, that Roseline begin to fear it had gone to sleep. Then the troll shook itself. "Have answer. Give girl troll egg. Girl swallow. No more boy want to marry."

This sounded promising, but she knew better than to take the troll at its word. "How exactly will that solve my problem? What happens when I swallow the troll egg?" she added, to make sure the troll had understood her question.

"Girl kiss boy. Girl turn to stone. Problem gone."

That did not sound like an acceptable solution to her problem. Not one little bit. "Suppose I got him to swallow the egg? Would that switch the turning-into-stone bit?"

"Boy here?"

Roseline explained that the boy was still at her father's castle. She'd have to come up with a way to bring Audric here, one that most likely involved pretending to agree to marry him and proposing they elope in this direction. This approach struck her as entirely too fraught with things that could go wrong. She'd likely end up married to him anyway.

The troll scratched its armpits. "Egg not match to boy who not here. Egg match to girl who here."

Roseline gathered that the troll egg would somehow imprint on the first person who handled it. "Couldn't you just sit on the boy?"

"Boy here?"

She rolled her eyes. "No, boy not here." Heavens, now she was starting to sound like the troll.

"Sit on girl? But bony bits not nice for troll backside. Better get egg."

She wondered if she would have to thwack the troll with the cudgel to get it to move out of the way so she could escape, or if that would even work. The troll, however, seemed to think she had accepted its help, for it trundled to the back of the cave, where it began rummaging in one of the larger, smellier piles.

Roseline did not linger to find out what troll eggs looked like.

Several days later, Sage Mountain was considerably closer, but Roseline was somewhat the worse for wear. She had been cold, sleep deprived, hungry, thirsty, bruised, scratched, sunburned, and saddle sore, although thankfully not all at once. The hillside here was dry and almost barren, except for a few spindly pine trees here and there. Platter-sized stones, many of which were broken or blackened, littered the ground. The pony dragged its feet, and when she kicked it, hoping to stir it to a more brisk pace, it arched its back and threatened to buck. In the end, she got off and led it.

Although the sky had appeared clear, unbroken blue, she spotted a filmy cloud that seemed to come from the hillside. She went on a little farther, thinking that a change in perspective would reveal its origin. The closer she got, the less it looked like a cloud and the more it resembled a plume of vapor. After tying the pony to a bush, she clambered up the hillside. There she found a cave. Of course, another cave. It was her fate to find caves on this quest.

Unlike the troll's cave, which had been dark and more than a little damp from the river mists, this one was quite dry and bright. Roseline knew a dragon's cave when she saw one. The dragon was curled up, apparently asleep, and its body gave off a steady red-orange glow.

She was about to tiptoe back down the hillside when the dragon opened one amber eye.

"Well," said the dragon, "or rather well-come. How delightful to make your acquaintance. I don't get many visitors up here, it's such a dreadfully long way from civilization. I do hope you'll stay to dinner."

Meaning, Roseline thought, *that I am going to be dinner.*

The dragon was either telepathic or understood her terrified expression, because it hastened to reassure her. "Fear not, gentle maiden. I have no intention of harming you in such a barbaric manner. I am not only a being of great age, wit, and taste, as you can plainly see, but I am also a vegetarian. Meat gives me terrible indigestion. I suspect it's too rich, or perhaps it lacks the necessary balance of etheric elements. I have a lovely parsnip stew that should be ready to eat now. I don't suppose you brought any crackers to eat with it?"

In short order, Roseline sat down with a dragon over crackerless but otherwise delicious parsnip stew. As they ate, she explained her problem.

"I quite understand your predicament," the dragon commented as it set aside the metal bowls to char them clean later. "If an appeal to enlightened morality and reason proves fruitless, then you may have to resort to a strategy that does not require your suitor's cooperation."

"That was my thought exactly. He's not going to give up, not when he thinks he has a chance. Could you please fly down there and incinerate him?"

"By the Flaming Egg, what an outlandish notion! If I am ethically constrained from the consumption of flesh, *of course* I cannot go about *incinerating* people!"

It seemed she would have to go all the way up the mountain to ask the Sage for advice. Clearly, neither trolls nor dragons were of any use in solving her problem.

"On the other hand," the dragon went on in a silky voice, quite different from the one it had used only a moment ago, before she brought up the topic of incineration, "I might be of assistance to you. All you have to do is permit me to *breathe* upon you. Bathe in the vaporous essence of my dragon fire."

"That sounds rather painful."

"Oh no, not at all. Not for *you*. I've been informed it is a rather an exhilarating experience. You will be quite well until you confront this reprehensible young man." The dragon's amber eyes narrowed, giving it an expression of slyness and cunning. "Then you kiss him, or allow him to kiss you, it doesn't matter which. The labial interface will ignite the dragon fire, incinerating the object of your displeasure. And incidentally turning you into a dragon, but that must be deemed an advantage. You could move into the next-door cavern and we could hold the most delightful conversations. And you would make a most enchanting—um, attractive—female dragon."

As the dragon spoke, Roseline found herself coming under its influence. It words, combined with the hypnotic tone, cast a spell. Becoming a dragon would be a wonderful thing. She'd be able to fly, and create intricate fiery designs with her breath...and never, ever be at the mercy of the likes of Audric. In her imagination, her white-hot flamed engulfed him. She heard his screams rising and then dying away. Then her vision failed her, as she recoiled at the thought of his strong body, his familiar face with the lips she had once loved to kiss, turning black and charred. He would never soothe a restive horse or dream of a better life, or find a girl who would be happy to marry him. As much as Roseline did not want to be that girl, and as much as she had once been willing for the troll to squash him or the dragon to burn him up, she now found that she truly did not want that fate for him.

The dragon had sidled very close, looming over her with an intent expression. There was no point in trying to run away; it would be upon her in an instant.

Roseline scrambled to her feet, drew herself up, and addressed the dragon in the same tone she'd heard her eldest sister use. "Stop right there! If I came all the way up here so I wouldn't have to marry Audric, who in retrospect is a perfectly nice if misguidedly ambitious boy, I'm certainly not about to turn into a manipulative, self-serving worm like *you*!"

She half expected the dragon to breathe on her without her permission or envelope her in flames, but the dragon responded with an expression of long-suffering acceptance, undoubtedly a reflection of its philosophy.

"I quite see your point," the dragon said after a few moments of deep abdominal breathing, accompanied by the barely-audible intonation of a calming mantra. "You humans have a most peculiar perspective on such things. But if you will not take my help, I suppose you had better go and consult the Sage of the Mountain."

"That's where I was originally headed," said Roseline.

"Then what did you ask me for?"

Not trusting to the temper of an irate vegetarian dragon, Roseline took her leave.

The wind turned colder and wilder, and the terrain got steeper and rockier. In places it threaded between piled-up boulders, the opening so narrow the pony could barely fit through. At the entrance to the next such passage, the pony set its feet and refused to take another step. Roseline acknowledged the wisdom of proceeding on her own. She left the saddle and bridle beneath an overhang of rock, shouldered the saddle bags, and gave the pony a farewell pat.

Within a short distance, she was clambering with both hands as well as her feet. She considered turning back, but managed to talk herself into going a little further. Just around the bend, just to the next resting place. And then, when there seemed to be no end to scrambling up slopes and squeezing through clefts, she emerged onto a gently rising meadow encircled by standing stones and luxuriant groves, the like of which she had never seen. The wind died into a soft, warm breeze. Inhaling it, her aching muscles relaxed and the abrasions on hands and knees stopped stinging. In the very center of the ring, a tiny, white-haired woman sat cross-legged on a flat stone.

Roseline approached the stone, let her saddlebags slip to the grass, and bowed.

The Sage gave not the slightest reaction. She continued to sit, eyes lowered but not closed, a faint half-smile on her lips, her only movement the slow rise and fall of her chest. So profound was the Sage's stillness that Roseline choked back her prepared spoken greeting.

After a time, and not knowing what else to do, Roseline climbed up on the flat rock, folded her cloak, sat on it, and did her best to assume the same posture as the Sage.

Time slipped by, marked by the slow and slower beating of Roseline's heart. The sun seemed hardly to move, until she noticed how the shadows had lengthened. Her legs had gone to sleep, and despite the padding of her cloak, her bottom was sore. She was thirsty and hungry as well. She got to her feet, stretched, walked around the meadow, and drank a little of her water. In all this time, the Sage had not moved or showed any discomfort.

Roseline sat back down. After another long period of time, most likely several hours, during which time her mind drifted, half awake, she woke up to a bowl of steaming noodle soup in front of her. The Sage sat in her place, calmly sipping her own soup.

With sunset, the temperature fell. Roseline wondered if they were going to sit here all night, but apparently this was not the case. The Sage got to her feet as fluidly as if she had not been sitting on a hard rock all day, and led the way to the densest grove of trees. Roseline grabbed her belongings and hurried after her. Within the grove was a hut, so skillfully constructed that it appeared to be part of the surrounding trees. Inside was a kitchen with a fire pit and iron cauldron, a table and two stools, and two pallets made up as beds. The cauldron contained an herbal brew that gave off the aromas of chamomile and honey. The Sage dipped out two cups, handed one to Roseline, and sat down to drink her own, all without a word. They finished their tea, washed in a basin, and went to bed.

When Roseline rose the next morning, the Sage was already sitting on her rock. Feeling she ought to contribute, Roseline washed the tea cups and swept the floor before joining the Sage outside. Twice more during that day, bowls of food appeared, although she never saw the Sage place them there.

This pattern went on for long enough that Roseline realized that the Sage was never going to say anything. In her mind, she rehearsed how to explain her problem and pose a question to the Sage. She remembered how the troll had offered to solve her problem by turning her to stone. She didn't want to be stone, she wanted to be alive. How would harming herself help anything?

The dragon's solution was even worse. Audric might be a nuisance, but he wasn't evil. All he wanted was a comfortable, secure place in the world. She disapproved of his methods, but she could not fault his dream of a better life. And to be the one who destroyed those dreams—she felt ashamed to have ever considered such a thing. How would she have lived with having countenanced murder? No wonder the dragon had turned to meditation and a vegetable diet, even if it couldn't help being dragonish at heart.

Roseline found herself thinking that it would be better to give in, marry Audric, and spend the rest of their lives as penniless outcasts. At least, he would have a life. She might be miserable, but she would survive, and she would be able to sleep at night. Yet she was not ready to resign herself to that fate; she had come all this way to find another solution, one that offered a remote chance of a happy ending.

She meditated on this dilemma for several weeks, perhaps a month, while sitting silently facing the Sage, surrounded by mysterious stones, sunshine, and trees. Why not stay here? Why not leave her old life for this simplicity? The answer surprised her as much as her insights about Audric's motives. It would be unkind to both him and her family to simply disappear. She still did not want to marry him, but she could no longer tolerate the burden of his threats. One way or another, she must resolve the current situation.

After bowing to the Sage, Roseline made her way back down the mountain. The pony had not wandered far, and somehow it had found ample forage. When she saddled it, the girths were tight. She took an unexpected pleasure in how well the pony had fared.

Upon arriving home, Roseline went first to the stable. Audric was mucking out the stalls, whistling as he worked. He scowled when he saw her.

"It's about time. Have you made up your mind to marry me, then?"

Roseline shook her head. "You deserve a wife who loves you, a helpmeet in life. That isn't me, and we would make each other miserable. I'm going to tell my father everything. I will try to convince him to keep you on as a stable boy, and someday a groom or some other better position, but I can't promise he will agree. If you don't want to hang around to find out, you'd best get a head start."

She left him, looking astonished, and headed up to the castle. As she neared the gate, one of her older brothers, training with a pair of men-at-arms, noticed her with relief and excitement, then anger that she'd had them all worried. By the time she'd reached the front doors, half the servants and all her other brothers and sisters came rushing out.

Although it would have been easy to concoct a story to explain her absence, Roseline could not bring herself to exaggerate. The truth was that she had been so wrapped up in her own conundrum, she had given no thought to how distressed everyone else must have felt when they discovered her missing.

"I'm very sorry to have given anyone cause to worry," she said. "I had a pressing problem and sought the advice of the Sage of the Mountain."

From their expressions, she imagined them thinking, *Wandering around the countryside, and now going off to see a mythical personage? We always knew she was odd, to say the least.*

Roseline did not disabuse them of this notion. After all, they were right. "Now I must make amends to my father, whom I have offended most of all with my wayward behavior."

She found her father in his library, bent over his favorite book of military history. He looked older than she remembered, and careworn. When he looked up, she saw it in his eyes how worried he had been about her.

Roseline knelt on the floor beside him and told him how badly she had behaved with Audric, and how Audric had been led to believe that he might improve his lot in life by marrying her, his attempt to force her to agree, and how she understood that her reputation had now been tarnished. Audric was not to blame, and surely deserved a chance to improve his lot in life by hard work and merit.

Her father was very angry. She had expected nothing less. He did not protest when she told him she was going away. He could not tell her that he loved her, he was too prideful for that, and he would not listen if she said the same. Somehow, that did not matter. Nothing here, in this castle or the lands around it under her father's rule, did. No wonder she had flirted with Audric. The castle folk were right: she *was* odd, a misfit here.

She did not see Audric in the stable as she saddled her pony and rode away. She wondered where he was, and what sort of life he would make for himself.

The Sage was still sitting calmly on her rock.

Roseline settled on her folded cloak, closed her eyes halfway, felt her face soften in response to the sun and the fragrance of the wildflowers, and took a deep breath.

Then the Sage spoke. Roseline was so startled, it took her a moment to recognize the single word.

"Apprentice."

Smiling, Roseline sat.

BEASTS AND MONSTERS

by Michael H. Payne

Cluny is a powerful wizard, but, being a squirrel, she is somewhat handicapped by the need to pretend that her human familiar is the wizard. That, however, is just the everyday problem. As they start their sophomore year, she needs to find a wizard for a new familiar—both because she likes him and because Raine, the headmaster's familiar, wants her to. She doesn't dare disappoint Raine, who monitors the bonds between all wizards and familiars, but the incoming freshmen find Jorvik just a bit intimidating. This problem is going to require a very creative solution.

Michael H. Payne's novels, The Blood Jaguar *and* Rat's Reputation, *are currently available from Sofawolf Press, and he's both bound and determined to eventually get the first eight or nine Cluny short stories conglomerated with a bunch of new interstitial material into a whole novel thing chronicling her first year at Huxley College. He is a library clerk, church musician, college radio host, webcartoonist, and fanfiction curator for several My Little Pony websites. Y'know: the usual. Check his site hyniof.livejournal.com for particulars.*

"—reared up on my hind legs, slammed him hard into the wall, and gave him the *big* grin." On the carpet in front of the fireplace, Jorvik cocked his head, pulled back his lips, and crossed his forepaws almost daintily. "A rather effective look for me, I've been told."

Cluny's tail frizzed at the sight, but Shtasith, perched just inside the fireplace, gave a hissing laugh. "Ah, yes," the little dragon said. "The value of proper dental care."

Crocker laughed, too, but Cluny couldn't quite manage it. Jorvik was scary enough just lying there, all smoke and shadow and those glowing red eyes, but when the barghest let himself solidify into a big black canine with far too many teeth, she had to struggle with her squirrellier parts not to scramble from the nest of blankets she'd made for herself at the foot of Crocker's bed to their dorm room's highest bookshelf. "But," Crocker was saying, holding up a finger from his desk to the right of the fireplace, "you were polite about it, right?"

Jorvik touched a paw to his chest. "Sure, and that's truly the mark of a gentle soul, is it not, Terrence, my lad?" He shook himself, the long, thick fur flapping around his broad shoulders, before he puffed into his less-substantial form. "I politely informed Master Donovan that he'd become grotesquely delinquent in his child-support payments, and that if he valued the connection his left arm currently enjoyed to the rest of his body, he would accompany me forthwith to the offices of Tassel, Rend, and Gavor to speak with the attorneys there." He nodded to Shtasith. "So it's as you said, young sir: being fearsome in a good cause is much preferable to the alternative."

The firedrake nodded, and Cluny found herself just plain astonished by how much her life had changed in a mere twelve months. At the end of last year's Welcome Week, she'd been both heartbroken and furious that every one of the students in Huxley's incoming class of frosh wizards had seen her only as a squirrel rather than as the familiar she'd so desperately wanted to be. And now? At the end of *this* year's Welcome Week?

She snuggled deeper into the blankets. Now, she was a wizardry student herself—in secret, of course, since Magister Gollantz, Huxley's headmaster, continued to insist that the world wasn't ready for something as completely unprecedented as an animal wizard. She even had two familiars of her own—*another* secret since the history of wizardry showed quite clearly that madness and horror followed in the path of those whose power drew more than one familiar. Add to that the way that one of her familiars was human, and she had multiple reasons to hide the truth.

Which was perfectly fine with her. She'd learned an incredible amount during her first year at Huxley, and as long as they let her stay and keep learning, she didn't mind anything else.

Still, becoming friends with a monster who turned her whiskers to icicles every time she looked at him—

Jorvik blew out a wintery breath. "'Tis the main reason I gave up my glamorous life as an interdimensional goon-for-hire: one seldom gets asked to exercise one's power for what a sane mind might call a beneficial cause."

Cluny aimed an inner scowl at herself for letting the word 'monster' cross her thoughts a moment before. She and Crocker and Shtasith had been in the right place at the right time when the barghest had begun considering a change of career, and he'd happily joined the incoming class of familiar candidates at the beginning of Welcome Week. But since he was here instead of out mingling at one of the many social events Huxley's various residence dorms held to allow the frosh wizards and familiars to get to know each other—

"So!" Cluny tried to keep her voice sprightly. "Any promising wizardry students catch your eye so far, Jorvik?"

His smoky ears drooped. "They're a fine bunch to be sure, Mistress Cluny. But, well, they're all so *young*, aren't they?" He gave another sigh. "And haven't I just had cause to mention the effect my sweet and pleasant smile has upon even the most stalwart of individuals?"

Those grouchy feelings about shortsighted novices stirred in Cluny's chest again, but before she could make a comment, Crocker was waving a hand. "Are they nuts?" He shot Cluny a look. "Not that there's anything wrong with nuts, but, I mean, any frosh who isn't interested in you instead of some old cat or fox or owl, well, they need to think long and hard about what they're doing here."

"Indeed." Shtasith spread his leathery wings, caught the updraft from the fireplace, and drifted across Jorvik to settle on the wooden footboard of Crocker's bed just above Cluny's blanket pile. "Perhaps you should challenge one of them to single combat and allow yourself to be defeated: that proved quite effective for *some* of us."

Leaning back, Crocker cleared his throat. "Is that what

happened, Teakettle? You allowed yourself to be defeated?"

Shtasith puffed steam through his nostrils in Crocker's direction, then swung his head back around, green flecks flashing across the black depths of his eyes. "Or better yet, Jorvik! Attach yourself to one of the professors! I'm certain that dozens of them would happily trade up from whatever common animal they currently employ as a familiar to someone as accomplished as yourself!"

Cluny couldn't stop a gasp at the thought, and the growl that rose from Jorvik's curled lips showed that he felt the same. "Poaching, one might call that, mightn't one, Shtasith?" Each word fell as sharply and precisely as a master assassin's dagger thrust. "And mightn't such an action be considered more than a bit impolite?"

"I—" Shtasith seemed to shrink, the claws of one front foot clutching his chest. "I meant no disrespect, sir."

Jorvik remained looking as scary as Cluny had ever seen him for another half a heartbeat, then he closed the embers of his eyes, smoothed the shadows of his neck fur, and nodded. "I know you didn't. You're just, well, as I said before: nearly everyone here is so young..." He surged to his paws, shook himself again—half solid muscle and fur, half wavering smoke and mist—and bowed. "As it is, however, there's one last mixer this evening at Mayfield House, and I'd best make myself available to any of those novices as might develop spine enough to form a partnership with a tattered old soldier. As always, Mistress Cluny, I thank you and your fine familiars for your hospitality."

She scrambled to her paws to bow back. "You're always welcome here, Jorvik." But she couldn't help adding: "I'll just ask you to remember that, for the record, *Crocker* here is the wizard when it comes to our little group."

"Of course, of course." He turned a slightly less horrifying version of his grin toward Crocker. "Rest assured, sir, that you'll be Master Terrence should ever we meet in public. I am, after all, more than accustomed to the importance of the judicious fib." He gave another bow, then whisked away like wind-blown fog.

Cluny settled back into the tangled blankets, gave a sigh, and looked at her familiars. "We don't know anyone in the incoming class we can talk to about him, do we?"

Crocker snorted. "The way the frosh look at us when we're walking around campus, I'll bet we cause more nightmares than Jorvik does."

"What?" Cluny sat up, her neck fur bristling.

Shtasith's head swayed on that long neck of his. "Recall, my Cluny, the reputation we have gathered this past year." He waved some claws at Crocker. "After stopping a would-be mass murderer, an insane professor, and certain machinations of the Ifriti Ranee, our simian is thought to be as powerful and unbalanced a wizard as Huxley has ever seen. I'm no expert in the field of human relations, but I believe that to be the sort of thing that makes for wariness rather than offers of friendship."

Clasping her front paws, Cluny looked from the firedrake to Crocker. "I didn't— I haven't— I mean, I guess I've been so busy studying, I never even noticed that anyone was—" Leaping to the top of the footboard, she activated a brief levitation spell and sprang across the stretch of carpet to land in Crocker's lap. "This is terrible! I don't want people to be afraid of you! How can we fix that?"

His snort this time was more a laugh than anything else. "It's fine, Cluny. The people who matter know I'm not a monster. And, well, the sort of people who'd be interested in getting to know the me we're pretending I am aren't the sort of people I'd be interested in getting to know." He blinked. "And I swear that sense made in my head."

"No, no." Cluny smiled up at him, his magic always as warm as flannel around her. "It makes perfect sense."

That got a snort from Shtasith, and she scampered around to give him a smile, too. She couldn't keep it in place, though, her thoughts turning back to Jorvik. "It's just too bad we don't know anyone who needs a familiar." Further thoughts made her fur prickle. "I remember when I first came here, everyone said that familiars who don't find a wizard by the end of Welcome Week usually wash out by the time midterms roll around." She balled a front paw into a fist and smacked it against the open palm of her other. "We've got to make sure that doesn't happen to Jorvik!"

"Great!" Crocker clapped his hands. "Any idea how?"

Having no answer, Cluny let herself flop back against Crocker's stomach, but a flutter of wings drew her attention to Shtasith rising into the air. "Perhaps," he said, wafting over to his usual perch, stretched along the back of Crocker's neck from shoulder to shoulder, "we can forgo worrying about that and worry instead about arriving late for our regular Friday meeting with Magister Gollantz?"

"Eeep!" Cluny spun, scurried up the front of Crocker's robe, and slipped into the big pocket she'd sewn for herself over his heart. "Thank you, Shtasith."

His black and golden scaled tail snaked over to tap her shoulder. "You'd be lost without me."

Riding down the three flights of stairs and out into the October afternoon sunlight, though, Cluny couldn't keep the problem out of her mind. The bond that formed between a human and a familiar was intrinsic to the theory and practice of wizardry, but Cluny's studies this past year had shown her quite clearly that no one really understood how or why any individual connection got made. If only there was some way to—

A sigh from Crocker. "She's worrying about Jorvik."

Shtasith's sigh gusted warm and damp across the top of her head. "She'd not be our Cluny otherwise."

"Fine, then!" Sagging into her pocket, she folded her front paws across her chest and didn't even try to keep her ears up. "For the rest of the day, I'll be nothing but the sweetest little ray of sunshine!"

Crocker gave one of his big laughs. "OK, now that's got *me* worrying."

"Fear not." Shtasith gestured toward the west. "Dusk is but half an hour away, and by her own pledge, at evenfall our dear, fretful Cluny will once again make her appearance."

More laughter from Crocker, then they were coming into the campus's central plaza, the marble spiral of the Admin Building curling up to a point in the center. Cluny organized her mental notes while Crocker climbed the front steps and carried them all into Magister Gollantz's suite, Janice at her desk in the outer office just smiling and waving them on to the inner office door.

And for once, the meeting went well. Yes, the magister gave out his usual dire warnings about the chaos that would arise should anyone ever find out about the three of them, but he also approved Cluny's research plans for the upcoming year: "The bond between wizard and familiar," he said with a nod, "continues to be not only a fertile area of study but one which an outside observer will see as natural for Crocker to pursue."

"Thank you, sir." And as much as she'd tried to banish all thought of him during her presentation..."But, umm, speaking of wizards and familiars, I was wondering if you'd been observing Jorvik's progress this week at all."

Magister Gollantz arched a brambly eyebrow, and Cluny quickly held up a paw. "It's nothing bad, sir! He just, well, he's having a hard time—"

"Yes, yes." He jabbed his pen into the ball of ink that floated just above the open bottle on his desk. "It's always difficult for non-traditional students entering as frosh. But if he truly wishes to be here, I'm certain he'll overcome his reticence and begin making connections." Signing Cluny's advisory card with a flourish, he flicked a finger at it, and the paper vanished with a puff of sparks. "I think you'll find that Magistrix Ippolitov has some thoughts of interest."

Cluny's ears perked. "On Jorvik?"

The magister rolled his eyes. "On your chosen area of study, Sophomore."

"Eeep!" It took some effort for Cluny not to sink into the depths of her pocket. "Yes, sir. I'm sorry, sir."

His scowl softened. "Never apologize when you're showing concern for a fellow creature, Cluny. Jorvik's quite the canny campaigner, though: he merely needs to discern how he and his particular talents fit in around here, and all will be well." He gave her another nod. "Now, I've a particularly unpleasant meeting of the Academic Senate I must prepare for, so I'll bid you good evening, hope you have an productive first week of classes, and see you next Friday."

Crocker rose, and Cluny clung to the hem of her pocket as he bowed to the magister, pushed through into the outer office, closed the door behind them, and stopped with a gasp.

Rattled out of her thoughts, Cluny blinked, looked ahead, and saw Magister Gollantz's familiar Raine lying stretched across the carpet, the big she-wolf's hind paws resting against the wainscoting and her nose touching the edge of Janice's desk. Janice typing away at her word processor effectively blocked any exit around the back of her desk, and considering how tense their interactions with Raine had been this past year, Cluny found herself wondering if trying to step over her might be a bad idea.

The way Crocker had frozen in place made her sure he was having similar thoughts, but Shtasith, perched above and behind her, cleared his long, long throat in a grumbling fashion. "Such a pity," he said, "to find unsightly detritus blocking the roadways even in so fashionable a part of town."

Raine's ears flicked, and she looked up. "Ah, Sophomore Crocker...and ensemble." She rose into a sitting position and yawned, her sinuous grace and muzzle full of teeth making Cluny's squirrelly parts shiver almost as much as Jorvik did. "How fortuitous." Her yellow eyes narrowed, and Cluny found herself suddenly looking directly into them. "I was hoping I could speak with your squirrel for a moment or two."

"Me?" Cluny squeaked, her mind flashing back to spring break last year when Raine had very nearly deduced the truth about her and her familiars. It had taken the intervention of Lady Hesper, the unicorn who was interim dean of Huxley's Healing Arts Department, to mislead Raine then, and Cluny had done her best to remain out of the she-wolf's sight ever since.

When Raine rolled her eyes, she looked so much like her master, Cluny couldn't help staring. "I've put the past behind me, Cluny," she said. "I'm hoping you'll be willing to do the same." Her tail lashed the wall, and her scent, usually so firm and commanding, tickled uncertainly at Cluny's whiskers. "I just want to talk."

Again, it took Cluny some effort not to dive into her pocket, but the motion of Crocker folding his arms across his chest made her glance up at him, a frown looking very out of place on his round face. "And this is something you can't share with the rest of the class?"

About half a growl escaped Raine's lips, and the uncertainty in her scent spiked even as her power began stirring to form what felt to Cluny like a teleportation spell. "Fine," the she-wolf snapped. "Never mind."

"Wait!" Cluny scrambled from her pocket down Crocker's robe and leaped to the carpet in front of Raine. "I mean, yes, of *course* I'll talk with you." She looked back at her two familiars, their eyes wide. "You and Shtasith have studying to do, Crocker, so I'll send you a message spell when we're done."

Crocker's brow wrinkled. "You're sure, Cluny?"

She nodded. "I'll see you later."

Both his and Shtasith's power poked jaggedly at her, but Crocker returned the nod. She watched him start for the outer office door, but then everything was swirling around her, a very efficient teleportation spell whisking her away to a dim and damp-smelling cavern, stone and dirt cold under her paws.

A growling sort of sigh puffed out behind her, and she turned to see Raine settling beside a glowing pool, ripples of blue light dancing up the jagged wall of rock surrounding them. "You've been well, I take it, Cluny?" Raine asked, her gaze focused on the pool and her ears still lying close to the grayish-black fur of her head.

"Yes, ma'am." It didn't take much pretending for Cluny to put a quiver in her voice.

Raine winced, something Cluny was sure she'd never seen her do before. "I mean you no harm, child." She motioned with a paw. "Come, sit, and allow me to apologize, if you'd be so kind."

"Apologize?" Cluny scurried across the rocks and squatted closer to Raine's outstretched paws than she really wanted to. And while she could've made several suggestions as to things Raine should apologize for, she decided to keep her innocent woodland creature face on. "For what, ma'am?"

"Please." Raine's muzzle wrinkled. "That you aren't the wizard I once thought you were, I will readily admit. But neither are you an idiot, and I'll thank you not to insult my intelligence by behaving as if you are."

For an instant, Cluny considered maintaining her mask, but instead she let herself relax a bit, even gave a smile and bowed her head. "That may be the nicest thing you've ever said to me, ma'am. So I'm assuming you want a favor."

Raine gave a panting little laugh. "Ah, the cynicism of the young. But you're right, of course." That same salty wiggle of uncertainty came back into the she-wolf's scent. "I know you've no reason to give anything I say a fair hearing, but you— That is, I— That is—" Her head slumped between her forelegs. "I've no one else I can turn to."

Cluny deployed every passive detection spell she could think of, but they all agreed with her gut instinct: Raine was honestly and deeply disturbed about something. Taking a breath of the cool, subterranean air, Cluny blew it back out. "If I can help, ma'am, I will."

Something dripped from the cave's ceiling into the pool, and Raine raised her head with a sigh. "Jorvik," she said, and the name seemed to echo slightly in the blue shadows.

"Jorvik?" Cluny couldn't help repeating, her tail jittering and speculations blooming in her mind.

One paw went to Raine's chest. "It must be three-quarters of a century since I've had these sorts of feelings for a male." Her attention sharpened on Cluny. "And if you breathe a *syllable* of this to anyone—and I very much include your precious Sophomore Crocker and that damned reptilian familiar of his—I will track you to whatever hollow tree you've climbed into and gladly relieve you of your ears and tail."

"You're—" Cluny stopped and searched for a word that might not get those lips to pull back from those teeth. "—interested in Jorvik?"

Raine's snort was more laugh than growl. "Full marks, Cluny. I've had few opportunities to speak with him this past week, but having dallied with many a charming cur during my rather extensive lifetime, I find him to be...well, the less said about all *that*, the better." She straightened up and became once again the authority figure Cluny had come to know and avoid the past year. "Suffice it to say that I would very much like to see Jorvik continue on the familiar track at Huxley. As you pointed out, your master has his studies to see to, but since he's become friendly with Jorvik, I'm assuming you have as well. Therefore, I'm requesting that you devote your attentions to finding Jorvik a permanent place here."

Five or six responses ranging from *"What?"* to *"Wouldn't you be in a better position to do that, ma'am?"* flashed through Cluny's mind, but she pushed them all away. That Raine was coming to *her* of all beings could only be a sign of desperation, and the more calculating parts of Cluny's mind couldn't help but think how much more pleasant her second year at Huxley might be if the Magister Magistrorum's familiar didn't actively hate her. So Cluny gave a nod. "Y'know, ma'am, I've been considering exactly that matter all day, and I'd certainly appreciate hearing any thoughts you might have on the subject."

"I?" A lupine smile curled Raine's muzzle. "The only thoughts I've had concerning Jorvik are not any I'd care to share with an innocent youngster such as yourself." Her eyes narrowed and fixed their gaze on Cluny so intently, Cluny had to fight the urge to leap backwards. "Perhaps you have no sensible sort of magic about you, Cluny, but you have an undeniable cleverness and a survival instinct second to no sapient animal I've ever met. Consider this, therefore, either a challenge or a threat, whichever will motivate you more: find a way to keep Jorvik at Huxley. That is all."

Raine's eyes flared white, and Cluny's whiskers shivered again at the rush of her teleportation spell. The cave swirled away, and before she could take another breath, she was blinking at the door of her room, the faded gray carpet of the dorm's hallway almost as cold and rough as the stone she'd just been sitting on.

The door flew open, Crocker there with Shtasith wrapped around his neck. "Cluny!" he shouted. "You're OK!"

Forcing a giggle, Cluny scampered between his feet and up onto his bed. "What, you were expecting Raine to eat me?"

Shtasith leaped from Crocker's shoulders to settle on the headboard. "She has proven herself no friend of ours in the past," he hissed.

She's just lonely, Cluny almost blurted out, but swallowing the words, she offered instead, "She wanted to apologize." Not a lie, technically: yes, she hadn't actually apologized for anything, now that Cluny thought about it, but she'd more or less said she wanted to. "I think maybe she's finally realized that we're not going away and that she might as well make the best of the situation."

"Really?" Crocker closed the door and turned to face her with his arms folded. "That's the story you're going with?"

"It is." Cluny pointed a claw at him. "Now I'd like to see the work my familiars did while I was away."

Shtasith snorted. "Mostly, your simian lunged back and forth across the room with many a loud and inarticulate howl while your firedrake wondered if you'd forgotten our dinner meeting with Lady Hesper."

"Eeep!" Leaping to the bed's footboard, Cluny stared at the clock on Crocker's desk. "That's *today*?"

Crocker cleared his throat, and Cluny heard more there than any words could've said. "I know, I know," she said, letting herself fall back into the mess of blankets. "I'm getting carried away, overscheduling things, and running myself ragged." She rolled up onto her hind paws. "But after tonight, I promise I'll settle down and concentrate on our studies." As well as the whole Jorvik problem, of course. "Besides, Hesper's the only unicorn familiar in the whole of Pel Laugos, and talking to her about how she and Evantrue came together will provide vital data to understand the process of—"

"Yes, yes, yes." Shtasith spread his wings. "But perhaps we could not keep the lady waiting?"

Again, Cluny scrambled up Crocker's robes, Shtasith taking his place; a quick flick of her whiskers popped them across campus to the faculty housing on Hobb's Hill and the little cul-de-sac at the end of Berryman Drive where Hesper's cottage nestled among the pines and jacarandas in the gathering twilight.

Crocker started toward the cottage, but Cluny couldn't stop a shiver at the thought of how their first visit here four months ago had ended with thunder and lightning and Magistrix Evantrue shrieking madly. Cluny still had nightmares about the gibbering Wild Magic that had channeled itself so explosively through her in order to stop Evantrue from gaining control of its supposedly uncontrollable power; the magistrix herself had ended up a hollow, smiling shell, and Hesper, her bond as Evantrue's familiar broken, had taken her former mistress's place as dean of Healing Arts on campus.

Which had led to *another* series of problems, a loud and influential portion of Huxley's faculty and alumni complaining about a familiar holding that prestigious chair even on an interim basis. Cluny had found herself smack dab in the middle of that conflict as well when she'd helped stop Princess Alison's personal sorceress from killing Hesper over the summer.

Cluny rubbed her eyes. Had she really only been here a year?

A knocking startled her, and she blinked to see that they were standing on the cottage's front porch. "It's OK," Crocker muttered. "I mean, it *will* be OK as long as Lady Hesper hasn't started making Magistrix Evantrue's chili."

"Indeed." Shtasith's breath washed warm over Cluny's shoulders. "I've had boiling pitch more digestible."

Cluny had to grin, her tense muscles loosening just a bit. Then a golden glow was surrounding the door; it swung open to reveal the fawn-slender figure of Hesper looking up at them, her mane and expression both slightly frazzled. "Oh, Cluny! I'm so sorry! I forgot all about dinner! Can we postpone till, well—" Her ears drooped. "After what's likely to happen tonight, I doubt I'll still have a place here on campus, but—"

"What?" Cluny said at the same time as Crocker, and Shtasith burst into the air with a cry of, "My Lady!"

Hesper rubbed a front hoof at the base of her horn. "It's just—Oh, come in, please. This is all awful enough without giving the neighbors a show..." She turned and headed into the house.

Crocker stayed standing on the porch till Cluny jabbed a claw through the material of his robe; he jumped a little, stepped inside, and closed the door behind them.

The decor, a style Crocker had once called "post-modern fairy tale," all rounded corners in lace white and cornflower blue, hadn't changed as far as Cluny could tell even after Magistrix Evantrue had gone into long-term care. But the chair by the fireplace had been replaced with a large red satin pillow, and Hesper was settling into this as Cluny let her magic sail her across the room to the coffee table. "How can we help?" she asked.

The unicorn gave a sound that Cluny would've called a snort had it come from any other creature. "There's apparently only one remedy for what ails me, and I doubt even the peculiar talents you three have manifested in the past would be enough to turn me into a human."

A groan behind her, and Cluny looked back to see Crocker drop onto the sofa. "Don't tell me," he said. "The Academic Senate again, right?"

Shtasith's wings beat so quickly as he hovered beside Crocker's head, they blurred the air. "By all the foul and pustulant—"

"Now, now." Hesper shook an unshorn fetlock at him. "Only *half* of them are foul and pustulant. Or perhaps just over half." She sighed. "And therein lies the root of my dilemma."

"But how—?" Cluny had to stop and swallow against the anger that tightened her throat. "How can anyone on the faculty honestly say that a unicorn isn't qualified to be the dean of the Healing Arts Department?"

Sparks flashed in Hesper's eyes. "Magister Watts is quite eloquent on the subject, in fact." She touched her chest, and her voice roughened into a fairly close approximation of the scarecrow-like professor's nasal tones. "'How can this institution call itself the finest in the world when we allow familiars to stand in places of authority over wizards? How can we ask serious humanoid students to attend the words of beasts and monsters?'"

"Humanoid." The usual warm blanket of Crocker's power

around Cluny felt suddenly itchy, and she could almost hear his teeth clenching. "'Cause we wouldn't wanna insult the dwarves and elves and pixies we so magnanimously allow to teach us the secrets their ancestors spent their lives coaxing outta the rocks and the trees and the clouds, now, would we? No, no: they get to be honorary humans! And I'm sure they're just thrilled about that!"

Shtasith was sounding more and more like a swarm of wasps with each passing second. "I take it then, my lady, that this old and tired argument has somehow gained new strength of late?"

Hesper leaped from her pillow and started pacing in front of the empty fireplace. "Watts and his cronies managed to wrangle just enough votes to call the question: when the Senate meets this evening, I'll have to present a defense of my place here. And yes, I'll have Gollantz and Ippolitov and quite a number of colleagues on my side, but—" She stopped, and even though she looked as dainty as a baby gazelle, when she stomped her hoof, the whole house shook. "By the absolute most literal reading of the Huxley Charter, Watts is right! I am technically not a wizard, and I'm therefore unqualified to hold this position!"

The clock on the mantle chimed five, and Hesper heaved a sigh. "So while I would much rather enjoy a leisurely supper with three of my dearest friends and discuss the lovely days before Evantrue went insane, I instead have to appear in the well of the Senate and try my damnedest not to call them all knaves and bigots." Golden light shimmered around her horn. "I'll stop by your room later this evening to let you know how things turned out." A pale smile washed over her muzzle, and she vanished.

The silence in the room jabbed Cluny's ears. "No," she managed to squeeze out.

"That's...that's crazy!" Crocker sounded just as stunned. "I mean, crazy isn't a crazy enough word for this!"

"The fools!" Shtasith whooshed down to hover in front of Cluny, his eyes almost as fiery as Jorvik's. "Give the command, my Cluny, and I shall unleash as molten a swath of destruction upon this wretched place as the Material Realm has ever seen!"

"Wait." Holding up a claw, Cluny let ideas crash together in her head. "That's it," she said, the fur tingling along the back of her neck. "Because that's what makes a wizard a wizard, isn't it?"

Shtasith blinked. "The ability to unleash a swath of destruction?"

Crocker snapped his fingers. "No! The ability to command *her familiar* to unleash a swatch of destruction!"

"'Swath' is the word, simian." Shtasith's mouth went sideways. "And you're making meaningless distinctions: as our Cluny's research has shown, the bond between wizard and familiar is entirely fundamental to the concept of—" His eyes whirled to a stop, the dark reds and oranges bursting to a golden-white. "Of course!" he bugled. "We much find Jorvik at once!"

Cluny had already cast her locator spell. "He's between Mayfield House and the temporary familiars' dorm." A twinge of sympathy tugged at her—he must have struck out with the frosh wizards yet again—but she pushed it away. "Crocker? Take us over there."

"Me?" Sourness spiked into Crocker's scent, and Cluny looked up to see him looking down. "Umm, I mean, sure, I *can*, but—"

"You have to." Cluny swallowed. "We've got to be really, really careful with this, or we're likely to expose ourselves to the entire Academic Senate." She reached up a paw and patted his chin. "You're our wizard, so you take us to Jorvik."

He nodded, but the sourness only faded rather than disappeared. "Shtasith?" he asked. "Little help here?"

The firedrake swooped back onto Crocker's shoulders, and Cluny gently shifted the collective flow of their power to center around Crocker instead of her. Nodding again, Crocker stood, and for all that Cluny couldn't help thinking of an amateur potter trying to spin a ball of clay into a vase, he made the motions, whispered the words, and popped them with a shower of sparks from Hesper's living room to a stretch of Tenebrous Road on the other side of campus.

Under the trees around them, shadows were starting to

deepen, and a deeper piece of those shadows turned two spots of fire toward them. "Master Terrence?" Jorvik asked, solidifying partially into black smoke. He cocked his head. "Is something amiss?"

Cluny couldn't keep from leaping to the ground in front of him. "We've found your wizard, but getting the two of you together is going to be tricky." She clasped her paws to her chest and focused on his widening eyes. "Do you trust us?"

Jorvik's ears folded, then straightened. "More than any beings I've known for hundreds of years." He bent down and touched his nose to the top of Cluny's head. "Lead on, and I shall follow."

Warm and cold at the same time, Cluny forced her shivering squirrelly parts aside, turned, and scrambled for her pocket. "Shtasith! Where does the Academic Senate meet?"

"Founders' Hall on North Campus," the firedrake answered, the link between him and Crocker flaring. "I will guide your spell, my Crocker."

"Go." Crocker drew on Shtasith's power, a sensation that always got Cluny grinning—she'd worked long and diligently so an observer would think she wasn't involved in this process at all—and the world flickered yet again as the oldest section of Huxley College melted into place around them.

Founders' Hall, the school's original administration building, slumped against the side of the hill ahead, its moss-covered walls making her think of an abandoned warehouse. One thing Cluny had learned early on, however, was how much the structures on North Campus seemed to enjoy appearing run-down. Lights glowed behind the dusty windows, for instance, and the power that hummed from its walls prickled her whiskers.

Jorvik's whiskers seemed to be prickling as well, his nose raised and sniffling. "I *am* picking up quite the interesting scent here." He looked up, his teeth flashing white. "We're to be inside, I take it?"

Cluny was still sorting through the defensive spells surrounding the place. "Well," she began.

But Shtasith spoke over her: "We are. And we must let

nothing stand in our way."

"What?" Starting to crane her head back, Cluny was jostled sideways by Crocker moving jerkily forward, Jorvik rushing past him and up the building's worn front steps to the door. "Wait!" Cluny called.

But a shape was already forming in the doorway, Magister Gollantz's office manager Janice appearing. "I'm sorry," she said, a nimbus of fire crackling the air around her. "This meeting of the Academic Senate is closed to the public due to the personnel discussions taking place." She smiled, and something about her teeth made Cluny shudder almost as much as Jorvik and Raine did.

So when Jorvik smiled in return, the combination pretty much dried Cluny's throat completely. "You'll forgive me, madame," the barghest said, his brogue lilting even though Cluny couldn't keep from hearing the rumble of distant thunder there as well, "but I'm told my wizard's within. And I've been rather anxious to meet that individual since my arrival at your lovely institution a week ago."

Janice's face clouded, but then just as quickly cleared, her jaw dropping. "You mean—?" Her gaze came up to Cluny's and continued past. "Sophomore Crocker? Do...do you honestly think this'll work?"

Crocker nodded, and Cluny somehow managed to get some moisture back into her mouth. "Please, Janice," she said, digging her claws into the edge of her pocket instead of leaping across to grab the human's lapels. "We have to try."

Another long moment inched by, and Cluny started thinking they might still have to force their way in. But then Janice stepped aside, the doors creaking open and her smile becoming something much less panic-inducing. "If anyone asks," she said with a wink, "I'll tell them you overwhelmed me with your cuteness."

"Thanks," Crocker blurted out, then he was pushing inside, Jorvik a shadowy blur beside them.

Torches flickered low in sconces along the walls of a small, shabby atrium, identical dim hallways leading left, right, and straight ahead. But pricking her ears brought Cluny the scritch-scratch of someone speaking from their left; she gestured, and they all started in that direction.

Double doors stood closed at the end of the passage, and the closer they got, the clearer the voice became: Magister Watts saying, "—isn't a question of Lady Hesper's abilities at all! But the practice of magic is concerned with the interplay of subtle relationships, and no relationship is more important than that of wizard and familiar! And many a study has shown that the humanoid body is the one true shape for containing the powers essential to true wizardry! So how can we possibly allow—?"

He kept going, but Cluny stopped paying attention, her claws and whiskers guiding her own power out to deflect, cut, and disable the wide variety of defensive spells strewn and stretched across the corridor. Sweat starting to form on the pads of her paws, she opened her mouth to ask Crocker to slow down before they all ended up tangled and immobilized, but a snort from Jorvik stopped her. "Enough of this," he growled, and the wave of cold darkness he blasted from his eyes froze and shattered every bit of magic in their way. Lunging forward, he slammed his shoulder into the two big doors.

They bulged inward, then smashed open, Cluny clinging to her pocket as Crocker scrambled to catch up. "Sorry!" he shouted, stumbling past the barghest into the space beyond. "Really! It's just we have to—!"

"Sophomore Crocker!" Magister Gollantz's voice cut through the torch-lit air, and Cluny didn't even try to stop herself from sinking into the folds of Crocker's robe this time. Every professor she'd ever had—or had ever even *heard* of—seemed to be seated in what looked like bleachers around the outer walls of the room with their familiars beside them. Lady Hesper stood at one end in a white puddle of magelight, Magister Watts at the other end behind a podium, Magister Gollantz rising from the front row of seats directly ahead—

And all of them were glaring directly at Crocker.

Even from this distance and in the uncertain light, Cluny was sure she could see Magister Gollantz's eyebrows bristling. "This is a closed session," he said, enunciating each syllable.

"Yes, sir!" Crocker's voice managed to crack three or four times just in those two words. "But we— We brought— This is—" He waved toward Jorvik.

In the stillness of the room, Cluny heard a sound so quiet, it made even the silence seem loud. Whiskers bristling, she looked down and saw Jorvik, wreathed in smoke and darkness, staring across the room at Lady Hesper, all white and golden and shining. Hesper was staring back, too, her ears spread and her eyes wide.

It took Cluny some effort not to leap cheering into the air, but instead she simply called out, "Lady Hesper's familiar Jorvik!" at the top of her miniscule lungs.

The stillness became for an instant that of a held breath, then every voice, both human and familiar, exploded throughout the room with a force that hit Cluny like a blast of cold water. "Impossible!" Magister Watts seemed to be shouting the loudest. "Familiars having familiars?? It's a violation of all natural and man-made law!"

Across the room, Magister Gollantz's right hand shot out; a gnarled wooden staff appeared in it, and he slammed it against the floor. Sheer invisible force smashed out, driving every sound away like a wind storm blowing away gnats. "This meeting," Magister Gollantz said into the suddenly regained silence, "will come to order."

A flicker to her left drew Cluny's attention to Hesper, still standing in the light but with a more confident smile on her snout than Cluny thought she'd ever seen there. And beside her, as black as a moonless winter night, stood Jorvik, towering over the unicorn in an unmistakably sheltering manner.

"Indeed!" Magister Watts was shouting. "I have the floor, and I will be heard!" He pointed a shaking finger at Hesper and Jorvik. "This abomination cannot be tolerated! *Will* not be tolerated! The Huxley Academic Senate is much too august an assembly to ever be hornswoggled be such obvious tricks and falsehoods, and I—!"

Jorvik didn't move, didn't even breathe so far as Cluny could tell. But the menace he suddenly radiated seemed to catch Magister Watts around the throat, his words choking off.

"Point of order?" a voice asked into this patch of silence, and Raine stepped from the shadows beside Magister Gollantz, her eyes glinting in the torchlight. "As senior familiar here on the Huxley campus, it's my duty to monitor the bonds between all wizards and familiars among our students, faculty, and staff." Looking toward Hesper and Jorvik, she narrowed her eyes, her nose twitching. "And this before me now, I will testify, is as stable and true a bond as any other in this room." She gave the two a slight nod, and they nodded back, an interesting sort of smile, Cluny thought, curling the barghest's muzzle.

Raine then turned to Magister Watts. "Don't ask me to explain it, sir," she said, "but the aura cannot be falsified."

Magister Watts had been getting more and more red-faced; Cluny found herself feeling concerned that he might actually be choking, but then he began shouting again: "Impossible! Humans are the only beings capable of true wizardry and are therefore the only beings capable of taking familiars!"

Several loud coughs drew Cluny's gaze to the section of bleachers to Magister Watts's right, Magister Scuttle and the other gnome and dwarven professors glaring at him with folded arms, the various terriers, stoats, and canaries around them also glaring.

"Humanoids, I mean, of course!" Magister Watts waved a hand at them, then pointed it at Hesper once more. "But for an animal to claim a familiar is unheard of!"

"Point of order?" a soft, musical voice asked, and Magistrix Dellamori rose on orange and black butterfly wings from the pixies and elves seated to Magister Watts's left. "It's been a mere six centuries since the last county in Pel Laugos outlawed its annual pixie hunt. Of course—" The air around her shivered, and the curvaceous blonde wrapped in a green leafy gown became something almost entirely insectoid. Her compound eyes still managing a glare, she spread her upper and middle pairs of legs before settling back onto the head of her iguana familiar Tetsuko. "Once we learned certain illusion spells, things became much simpler for us all, didn't they?"

The corner of Magister Watts' left eye twitched, but when he didn't say anything, Magister Gollantz cleared his throat. "So," he said, the staff he'd summoned vanishing when he let it go, "I believe I will be calling for the vote." He snapped his fingers, and two glowing orange boxes appeared in the air above the center of the room. "The matter before this assembly, let me remind you, is *not* who should or shouldn't be considered a wizard. We're merely voting on whether Lady Hesper is qualified to remain the interim dean of our Healing Arts Department. I will *further* remind the Senate that Magister Watts himself just this evening praised Lady Hesper's abilities in no uncertain terms."

"Point of order!" Magister Watts shouted, gripping the podium as if it had become something precious to him.

"Too late, Cyrus." Magister Gollantz gave a thin smile. "The boxes are open. Senators have one minute to cast their ballots." A tiny lightning bolt sizzled from his finger, arched across, and struck the box on the left, one mark appearing in there.

Magister Watts opened his mouth, but then it pulled shut again. Scowling, he flicked a hand dismissively, and a mark appeared in the right-hand box before he turned away and took a seat among a group of similarly scowling professors.

More bolts and bubbles shot and soared upward, Cluny unable to keep from biting a claw as marks accumulated pretty much evenly on each side. She wanted to ask Shtasith how many members the Academic Senate actually had, but she didn't: the three of them had already attracted *way* too much attention to themselves tonight without muttering and whispering as well...

"Ten more seconds," Magister Gollantz announced after what seemed to Cluny like ten minutes, and when that time had ticked away, a few magical flashes arriving just before the boxes snapped over from orange to purple, Cluny couldn't tell which one had more marks in it.

Magister Gollantz wasn't scowling, though. "The final tally is 50.7% 'aye,' 49.3% 'nay.' The ayes have it, therefore, and Lady Hesper retains her post as interim dean." He gave a nod and an actual smile to Hesper and Jorvik. "Thank you for your time, Lady Hesper, and congratulations." His smile faded, and he turned to look directly at Cluny. "I'll ask now, however, that all non-members please vacate the chamber."

Cluny clamped her paws over her mouth before she could let out the "Eeep" she felt forming there, and Crocker, bowing, shuffled backwards into the hall. Hesper came trotting through the doorway then, her head and tail high, Jorvik padding along like a storm cloud behind her—

And a whispered chuckle stroked Cluny's ears; glancing up, she found herself meeting Raine's gaze. The big she-wolf dipped her head, the tiniest of smiles touching her snout, then the double doors clanged shut.

Hesper spun in the hallway, and Cluny would've sworn that sparks swirled in her wake. "Cluny! Crocker! Shtasith! How did you—? Where did you—?" She stopped with her mouth open, her head tilting back till she was looking up into the barghest's shadowy face, his tongue lolling out in a canine grin. "Jorvik," Hesper said, her eyes wavering, "I'm very pleased to meet you."

Jorvik bowed. "Likewise, Milady." He jerked his muzzle toward the double doors. "I gather from all that palaver that we've a bit of work ahead of us."

"We do." Hesper touched a hoof to her chin. "But I'm guessing you've *done* a bit of work in your time."

"Well, now." Once again, Jorvik's lips pulling back from his teeth made Cluny's every hair leap upward. "I can honestly say that I have, Milady."

"Good!" No sparks followed Hesper when she spun this time, but she had a definite spring in her step as she headed for the front door. "Cluny? Crocker? Shtasith? If you're still free, perhaps you be so kind as to join Jorvik and myself for a bit of a celebratory dinner?" She looked back over her shoulder. "Not boiling pitch, I promise you."

"Ah." Jorvik shook his shaggy head. "A pity, that." He shrugged, then trotted after her.

"Of course!" Cluny just about crowed. "Thank you!"

But Crocker didn't move; Cluny looked up to see him

watching them go with his brow furrowed. "Now, wait," he said. "Does that mean they kind of think she's a wizard?"

Cluny couldn't keep her ears up. "Not really. Magister Gollantz said at the end there that—"

"Ha!" Shtasith puffed steam, his head stretching down from behind Crocker's right ear. "Gollantz has always been a timid fool! The fire we've started here tonight will spread as only true immolation can, and those who do not fans its flames will be consumed by them!" He touched claws to his chest. "For I am the expert in these matters, am I not?"

"You?" Crocker's lips pursed, and he poked Shtasith's leathery side. "You're a teakettle."

"Insolence!" Shtasith started to expand—

But Cluny reached up to touch his nearest paw. "A step at a time," she said, smiling at both of them. "That way, we can maybe not consume anyone or anything too much."

Shtasith seemed to quiver in place, but then he collapsed back across Crocker's shoulders. "If that be your will, my Cluny."

Crocker gave a little shrug. "Except, y'know, dinner, right? When it comes to consuming, I mean."

Slipping back into her pocket, Cluny gave a giggle. "Not if we keep standing here all night."

"Eeep," Crocker said in a deep, rumbling voice, and Cluny giggled some more as Crocker hurried the three of them after Hesper and Jorvik.

TALE-MAKER; TALE-SPINNER

by Pam L. Wallace

Magical swords sound wonderful—until you find one and discover that it owns you as much as you own it, and you can't get rid of the wretched thing. If you are very lucky, you may someday find a use for it other than killing people.

Pam Wallace is a little bit of this and a little of that, but the sum of her parts can mostly be described by one word: family. Her stories can be found at Daily Science Fiction, Every Day Fiction, Abyss & Apex, Shock Totem, *and* Journal of Unlikely Entomology, *among others. She is one of the badgers at* Shimmer Magazine.

Definitely a human figure, sprawled on a slight hillock of reddish brown desert sand some three hundred paces to the east. Mereen studied it for several minutes, but saw not even the slightest of movements. Someone ran afoul of a sand rattler, most likely. If they weren't dead yet, they soon would be.

Hot, dry winds tugged at her caftan, pushing her southward. She eyed the figure again as she angled away from it. Still no movement. A waste of time to check. One hundred paces more, the familiar thud of Tale-maker between her shoulder blades her only company. Her hand crept under the soft leather wrap covering the sword's distinctive hilt. She'd come this far south to live a quiet, obscure life, where no one knew of the magical sword and the Hero of the Cataverigan Wars. Hero, indeed, she thought with a mental snort. Dealing death at every turn was not something to boast of.

She halted, looked again at the motionless figure. With a heavy sigh, she changed her course.

A few steps shy of the figure, she crouched down to study it further. Sprawled face down and covered by a long dark caftan and headscarf, it was impossible to tell its sex. She nudged a foot with her boot. No twitch of movement in answer. A smooth motion brought Tale-maker from its scabbard. She cupped the pommel, a blue sphere of marble, and waited for the familiar spark of magic. A barely-glimpsed flicker of light shot up the blade's length and into the black quillions. A faint whiff of sulphur stung her nose; the hairs on her arms lifted as the sword answered. Swirling energies flowed from the hilt into her veins.

No danger here—but plenty ahead.

Mereen lifted the headscarf with Tale-maker's tip. A woman's delicate features were revealed. Across her forehead was an intricate tattoo done in bright purple ink.

"Gods' breath!" A Tale-spinner. And by the color of the tattoo's ink, one of the King's own, to boot. Mereen may not have been in this backwater desert kingdom long, but she'd quickly learned about their Tale-spinners. So powerful were their words, they were forbidden to speak except when telling a story, for listeners became spell-bound, forgetting who or where they were. Only the ending of the tale released them.

Mereen pressed her fingertips against the Tale-spinner's windpipe. "Piss-ants! Still alive!"

She sat back on her heels. What in the halls of Hell was a Tale-spinner doing this far off the caravan path and the resting oases? And by herself? Tale-spinners were protected by law, and always accompanied by an interpreter and at least two Royal Guardsmen. "I suppose I'm honor bound to deliver you to Al-Massour now," she said with a grunt. The only saving grace here was that it would not take her far out of her way.

She rolled the Tale-spinner over. No snake bite or other visible wound, nor any bloodstains on her caftan. Given that a bejeweled dagger, easily worth a prince's ransom, was belted to her waist, she'd not been a victim of thievery.

From her waterskin, Mereen dribbled water onto the Tale-spinner's headscarf. She swabbed the woman's temples and wrists before laying the damp scarf across her brow. The bejeweled dagger tucked into her own waistband, Mereen settled in to wait.

From the direction the other woman faced and a few faint scuffles the desert winds had not yet obliterated, Mereen conjectured the Tale-spinner had come from the east. According to the maps she'd studied, it was a four-day journey from the caravan crossroads to the eastern kingdom, and they were yet some ways from the crossroads. A treacherous journey to make alone and without supplies.

The desert sun slowly burned its way to the horizon and the relief of cooler night air. The Tale-spinner's breathing eased and settled into a more natural rhythm. Soon after, her cheeks began to regain color and she stirred, murmuring under her breath and restlessly moving her head. With a soft cry, she jerked upright, glancing wildly around.

Mereen held herself very still, slowly raising her hands to show she held no weapon. "No harm here, milady," she said in a low voice. She laid the waterskin on the ground and pushed it forward. "Drink. Slowly now."

The Tale-spinner scrabbled back, her hand stealing toward her belt and the dagger. Fury tightened her face when she found it gone.

"I'll give it back, if you swear me no harm," Mereen said, taking the dagger from her waistband and offering it hilt first. The Tale-spinner snatched it away and settled back on her heels, her expression stormy but wary.

"A present from your king?" Mereen asked, gesturing to the dagger.

After eyeing her for several heartbeats, the Tale-spinner gave a half nod. She licked her lips, gaze darting to the waterskin before her. With a visible struggle to swallow, she snatched it up and drank, going too fast and losing some of the precious liquid down her chin.

"Slowly now," Mereen cautioned.

The Tale-spinner wiped her chin with her hand, leaving streaks in her dust-stained face. From her guarded posture, and the way she kept an eye on the surrounding desert landscape, Mereen wagered the woman was running from something—or someone. "Are you hurt?" she asked.

The Tale-spinner shook her head.

"Where are your guards?"

A dismissive shake of her head, her face set in a stony expression.

"Were you attacked?"

She nodded.

Mereen bit back a curse. She'd never realized how difficult it was to try to question someone not allowed to speak. "Did you recognize them?"

The Tale-spinner's lips compressed into a tight line and her eyes grew stormy. Her irises were dark brown as cedar tree bark, shot through with golden highlights. Mereen's attention was drawn away from those expressive eyes when the Tale-spinner's hands began to move in signs.

"Whoa, milady. Slower now. I've only a rudimentary knowledge of hand-speak." Mereen had never dreamed a face could be so expressive. One corner of the Tale-spinner's lip pulled into a fleeting half-sneer as she rolled her eyes, making it plain her thoughts on Mereen's intelligence. Mereen bit back a chuckle. It'd been a long while since she'd been treated with disdain, and it felt infinitely more honest and refreshing than unadulterated hero worship.

The Tale-spinner switched to a combination of more primitive signs coupled with mime-like acting. It was a testament to her story-telling talents she was able to get as much information across as she did.

"You. Two others plus one. Your guards and an interpreter?"

The Tale-spinner nodded.

"Someone followed, surprised your party while sleeping, and killed the others. You crawled away and made yourself small—hid." Mereen scanned the surrounding desert. "How long ago?"

The Tale-spinner held up two fingers.

"Two days? Thieves?"

The Tale-spinner's expression grew guarded. Her eyes hooded over. She nodded, but it was plain she was keeping something back, if not lying outright. Mereen's hope for honest dealings evaporated as quickly as sweat on the dry wind.

Dusk had settled; the moon cast a white glow over the countryside, shadowing the Tale-spinner's face with sharp angles. "We should move on. Can you walk?"

A nod, quickly offered, answered her. She rummaged through her pack and handed a chunk of dried meat to the Tale-spinner. Mereen set out, not looking back to see if she was followed. She led a smart pace, impressed she only had to wait twice for the Tale-spinner to catch up.

When daylight lightened the eastern horizon with a blue glow, Mereen called for a halt. The Tale-spinner dropped to the sand. Mereen offered dried dates from her pack. She adjusted Tale-maker's position to alleviate the weight on her shoulder. The Tale-spinner chewed with a narrowed expression, staring at the hood hiding the sword's pommel. She gestured toward it, a question in her eyes.

That was a tale too big to tell, especially to a Tale-spinner. "Sand. It gets into everything," she said.

The Tale-spinner's hands spun signs in the air. Mereen pretended to not understand. The look of disgust returned to the Tale-spinner's face. She turned her back and stared off into the distance. Eventually she lay down and slept.

Mereen kept a close watch on the countryside, but her gaze kept rounding back to the Tale-spinner. Her eyelashes were a dark half-moon against the sun-gilded bronze of her cheeks.

Heat waves rose from the sand, shimmery and restless as Mereen's spirit. The responsibility of traveling with another weighed heavily. Another two days, perhaps, and she could continue on her solitary journey.

She came to her feet, intending to water the sand beside a small uprising of rock several feet away, when she felt the change in the air.

Tale-maker hummed, rising to the high-pitched whine that signified danger. By the time she made it back to the Tale-spinner's side, four camels with riders appeared over a ridge to the east. Her hope that they were traveling nomads evaporated as the lead rider shouted to his comrades, pulled a scimitar from his belt, and spurred his camel forward.

Tale-maker practically leapt into Mereen's hand, its hood quickly tucked into her waistband as she roughly pulled the Tale-spinner to her feet. The desert offered little in the way of hiding places. The best Mereen could manage was the small rock uprising. She shoved the Tale-spinner down against it.

Tale-maker's blue orb swirled with silver sparks as she ran to meet the approaching riders. Surprise registered on their faces as she bore straight for them. The camels hissed and balked, shying away as their riders cursed. All the men wore green head-coverings, marking them from the same desert tribe, but the fourth and last was more richly dressed than his compatriots, sporting golden chains and girdles.

The lead rider reached Mereen first, swinging his scimitar in a wide arc at her head. She ducked under the swing, grabbed the man's leg, and pulled him from his mount. Tale-maker whirled and sliced into his neck. Warm blood spattered her face.

The second rider rushed in, his mount braying and spitting. Mereen stood her ground. Tale-maker sliced through the camel's hamstrings, and the animal fell to its side. While the rider tried to extricate himself from five hundred pounds of screaming camel-flesh, Mereen turned her attention to the remaining two riders.

The one with golden chains struggled to control his camel, kicking and cursing as the animal balked and refused to move. Mereen leapt to pull the third rider from his mount. They both rolled to the ground. In one fluid movement, she rose and stuck Tale-maker into the man's left eye. A twist of the blade quieted the man in mid-scream.

The second rider kicked out from under his downed camel and stood with drawn sword.

He beckoned Mereen in.

"The more fool, you," she said, and closed in with Tale-maker raised. The man met her with an ululating desert cry.

The swords rang, steel upon steel. Lightning flashes of light splintered up Tale-maker's blade. Strength flowed into her arm. She forced the other blade down, coming nose to nose with her opponent. She stared into his eyes without flinching, pushing against him, until his pupils widened with a slight sting of alarm. Quickly, she reversed her movement into an upswing that cut into her foe's underarm and continued through to the bone. The man crumpled, his lifeblood ebbing away.

Mereen turned to Golden-chains. He'd dismounted and was headed for the Tale-spinner, who had crawled from her hidey-hole and crouched with her pretty, jeweled dagger ready. The man charged ahead, sword readied for a swinging cut that would likely cut her lithe form in half.

Mereen would never reach him in time. With a flick of her wrist, she sent Tale-maker spinning through the air, trusting in the sword to find its mark.

Golden-chains hesitated, his left arm reaching toward his back, where Tale-maker buried itself halfway to its hilt. He stumbled two steps forward, feebly swinging his sword at the Tale-spinner's head.

In a fluid, dance-like move, the Tale-spinner ducked away, twirled, and slashed the man's throat open. Blood spurted, arcing toward her. She continued spinning, her caftan billowing about her, catching drops of blood in a crazy-quilt of crimson splatters.

Golden-chains gurgled a last breath.

Mereen pulled the sword from the man's body and wiped bright blood from the gleaming blade. The wounded camel thrashed on the ground, screaming hoarse brays. Spit flying, it tried to bite and kick her as she dealt it a death blow.

Would the carnage never stop? It didn't seem to matter how far she roamed, to the streets of Cathay or this backwater desert country, death and destruction always found her. And all for what?

The Tale-spinner looked up and met Mereen's eyes, glanced to the sword, then back to Mereen.

Mereen saw bewilderment and awe in the Tale-spinner's expression, the same thing she'd seen a thousand times before—in friends and strangers alike. A look in their eyes, acknowledging her as not a mere warrior, but one who strewed death as casually as most picked food from their teeth. After this acknowledgment, always, a step back, an involuntary move to keep from physical contact.

The Tale-spinner did not hesitate. She stepped forward, raising both hands. Mereen stumbled back, fear rising for the first time since she'd laid hands on Tale-maker all those years ago.

The Tale-spinner's fingers were long and lithe, slim and expressive as her face. She swept them through the air, as if she were pulling invisible threads and weaving them together. Circles and spirals, oblique twists and turns, her fingers created a dance Mereen could not pull her eyes from, even as a part of her brain began to register what the Tale-spinner was doing.

"No. No," she stammered. But it was too late. The hands stopped, the capturing done. She knew Mereen's story.

The Tale-spinner assumed a formal stance, shoulders back, fingers steepled before her. "I shall tell you a tale," she said in a rich, velvet voice, much deeper than one would suspect on a woman of such slight frame. It was melodious as a song, demanding to be listened to.

"Seventeen years and eight months ago, King Maneen came to this earth, chosen ruler of the land of Al-Massour. Two months ago, as he was about to come into his majority, he learned his Uncle Vasfoure, in the land to the east, was to be married for the fifth time. This humble Tale-spinner was sent to entertain the wedding guests."

Mereen was rooted to the sand, her vision filled with images of people dressed in rich colors of a desert sunset, feasting at a long table under a bright red and gold tent.

"Many days of celebration followed. On the last night, all the nobles assembled for the wedding feast. The palace was alive with lamps and the heady aroma of sandalwood and myrrh. The guests were entertained by dancers from Marakah, flutes from Wanorbi, puppets from Shanarrae. Exotic dishes were served—eye of peacock, hummingbird hearts, kraken soup—the number of courses almost out-numbering the guests.

"This Tale-spinner told story after story until her voice was numb. She finally stole away for a respite. Outside the tent of Vasfoure's guards, she overheard a nefarious plot to overthrow her young King. Treachery, from a supposedly loving uncle! She grabbed up her guards and made haste to return home to warn her king.

"But they were followed. All were killed—except this Tale-spinner.

"She wandered through the desert and fell. But luck was her glory and her savior appeared, a magical sword in hand. Tale-maker, they call it in the heathen lands, carried by a dark-eyed hero who wields justice."

"Death, perhaps," Mereen said. "Justice is not such an easy matter."

The Tale-spinner sputtered to a stop, her mouth dropping open. She stared at Mereen, her eyes rounded with amazement. "You spoke!"

Bemused, Mereen replied, "While I'm aware you think little of me, milady, you did hear me speak earlier."

The Tale-spinner waved both hands in the air, as if shooing away a gnat. "No one interrupts a Tale-spinner!"

Mereen shrugged. "I'm already damned. Your king is welcome to flay my sorry flesh for my sin."

"No. Not that." Stunned, she held her hands out before her. "My magic should keep you in thrall, unable to speak." She wiggled her fingers. "I feel it within me." She shot Mereen an accusing glare. "Even now, you should be lost in my words."

Mereen frowned, considering. "I cannot explain it, milady."

The Tale-spinner looked Mereen up and down, her gaze coming to rest on Tale-maker. "Unless..." The blue orb yet shone and pulsed with remnants of magic. "Toss your blade away!"

Mereen gave a hoarse laugh. "As if it would do any good. Countless times, I've tried to leave it behind. Since the day I climbed to the Caves of Fossorinth and claimed the sword, it's been my siren—the death of my soul."

The Tale-spinner waved off Mereen's words with a flick of her wrist. "Pah. Toss it away. Quickly now!"

Only to prove her wrong, Mereen threw the sword. The blade landed out of sight over a jagged rise of rock.

"Now. Why did I bade you so?"

Mereen could only stare at the woman's mouth, waiting for the next word to fall from those regal lips, robbed of all movement or even the desire to move. Her only need was to hear that voice again. And again. May it never stop.

With a wry smile, the Tale-spinner trudged across the sandy terrain, Mereen following like a pup anxious for a scrap of food.

Something was thrust in Mereen's hand. Tale-maker. The blue globe swirled, spitting sparks. Reason returned as her grip tightened on the sword.

The Tale-spinner dared to touch the sword's hilt, a look of awe on her face. "I was five when my magic was discovered and I was taken from my parents to be trained. Since that day, I've not had a normal conversation. Not a chat about the weather. Or dresses. How to wear my hair. Whether this life is what I wanted. I am looked upon not as a person, but a—a thing."

Mereen knew well the feeling. How many times had she cursed herself for not listening to Da? She should have stayed on the farm and never gone off adventuring. When she claimed the sword, she'd been full of foolish dreams of wealth and glory. All she'd found was a never-ending parade of swordsmen trying to win Tale-maker by besting the best. If she could, she'd gladly hand it over, but there was no resisting the blade's battle call.

Once Tale-maker claimed her, she'd walked hand-in-hand with Death. Young toughs, believing until their blood leached into the ground they had a chance to defeat her. Seasoned fighters, dying with surprise they'd been bested writ across their faces. Faces, hundreds and hundreds of faces, each one scalded into her memory, slack in their death throes. Some innocent youths full of promise, others perhaps a boon to society for them to be gone. But all remembered and recorded. Honored as best she could. Each one a further weight to her soul's burden.

The Tale-spinner waited, a silent pleading in her expressive eyes. Mereen couldn't bring herself to answer truthfully. It was best to remain alone and uninvolved. She was a statue, cold and dead inside.

Tale-spinner chewed her lip, while sweat beaded at her brow. Slowly, the hope in her eyes faded. Her shoulders sagged. "Well.

TALE-MAKER; TALE-SPINNER

My duty is to warn my king. I must return to Al-Massour."

When she turned away, Mereen felt herself falter, as if she teetered on the verge of a cliff. One word would release a landslide. But risking that word would take more courage than Tale-maker had ever lent her.

The Tale-spinner walked away, headed west. The desert suddenly seemed even more desolate.

Tale-maker vibrated in her hand, warming with a subtle hum. Hadn't she always said the sword had never been wrong?

"Milady," she called out.

The Tale-spinner turned, her expression guarded.

Mereen struggled to swallow, her mouth dry as sand. "I—I do know what it's like to not be seen as a person. I'm weary of fighting. Weary of senseless challenges that end in death. This sword has been more curse than blessing."

A smile spread across the Tale-spinner's dusky features, lighting her eyes. "But it's a blessing to *me*. Its magic negates my magic. I can talk to you and you hear *me!* Me—not a story."

The Tale-spinner offered her hand. "I find myself in need of a new guard. My king is young, but he is a just ruler. If you'll help me be more than a story-teller, perhaps I can help you be more than just a story."

A dry wind kicked a swirl of sand in the air past the Tale-spinner. When it closed on Mereen, it twirled into a graceful dance around her feet. Each grain of sand sparkled, moving in concert with the others. How had she never noticed the small things before? Perhaps there was still beauty to be found in unexpected places.

Mereen shoved Tale-maker into its scabbard. "Da always said I should learn to listen." She chuckled, mostly to herself. "Let's get you to Al-Massour."

She took the Tale-spinner's hand.

EARTH'S DAUGHTER

by Catherine Mintz

"Know thyself" tends to be an ongoing project—and never more so than for this young woman.

Catherine Mintz has published over sixty works of fantasy, science fiction, and horror, including novels, graphic works, short stories, poems, and video scripts. She has served as both SFWA's Eastern Region Director and Secretary, and hosted one Nebula. She likes Chinese cooking, jazz, and the sound of rain on leaves.

Eyes dazzled by the rising sun, Rosinel lost her balance when she sat back on her heels and the well-tilled garden soil unexpectedly yielded underfoot. Falling, she put one hand to the ground to hold herself upright a moment longer while the other completed the protective gesture she had begun and so must finish. Then, letting herself collapse in a sprawl of skirts, petticoats, and bare white legs, the herbalist laughed.

As a child, she had preferred places on the margin between the wild and the cultivated, had squatted beneath the wide leaves of the bristle-bane or huddled up in the crotch of a wild apple tree, watching the world around her grow, flower, and fruit. Now she loved a garden.

Still sprawled, still smiling, Rosinel drove her fingers into the warm earth and gripped a fistful, feeling the wind tease her hair and eyelashes, cool her teeth and tongue. This was the best time, with new plants to be coaxed to grow sturdy. When the harvest came, everything must be turned into the medicines and dry herbs that she bartered for whatever she needed and could not grow or gather herself.

But nothing was ready for harvest yet, although the sun shone for long golden hours, almost conquering the winds off the ice on the mountains. *There is work to be done*, she reminded herself, yet she turned her face to the light and air, willfully idle for just a moment longer. Eyes closed, she felt the striving plants as if they were part of her, and got up to tend to them.

Her feet and fingers earth-stained, Rosinel moved down the rows, crouching here and there, looked at the curling tendrils, the twining vines, the clustered petals. All healthy and as they should be, strong enough to benefit from the encouragement she could give them. Her breath barely stirring the nearest leaf, she whispered into her cupped hands, urging the bean plants to unfold more quickly—

"Rosinel?"

Her shoulders hunched: a visitor, and so early in the day. Careful to first say the invocation's closing clearly, the herbalist rose out of the shelter of the foliage-heavy poles. Lips smiling, hands cleaning themselves on her apron, Rosinel came back from the still center she sought when conjuring power. "Herve," she said in recognition and started for the house. No need to talk after all.

The man stood at her side, waiting, while Rosinel measured and packed the salve he required. The herd-ward's smooth, guileless face might conceal deep thoughts or none at all, depending on the wind and the weather, but whichever it was he seldom spoke more than was necessary and, the herbalist suspected, preferred the company of the beasts to that of men and women.

In all seasons when the pair of them traded—his milk and cheese for her herbs and medicine—scarcely a dozen words passed between them. This time of year, Herve needed salve for the cuts and bruises of active animals just moved to pastures so high they were still the first tender greens of spring, even though the herbalist's garden had already blossomed into early summer.

Rosinel tied the salve jar shut with a running loop of cord that passed under the clay straps on the lid and sides; pressed the top into the soft wax around the rim of the jar. They walked back through the bee-loud forest of the beanpoles, until, coming to the end of the row, she said, "Here," and handed the salve to the man, who silently tucked it in his waist-pouch, and started back up the mountain.

"Good fortune!" called Rosinel, and watched his back for a moment, well-wishing, as custom required. She'd see him again when the first cheeses were firm enough to bring down from the milk house. Her mouth watered at the thought. She'd eaten the last of her aged cheese some while ago and it was not yet time for the new.

I should wash and sun my storage shelves, she thought. I'll need clean straw. She rubbed her hands together as she thought. The head-sized lump of beeswax must be melted, skimmed and strained, too, for the ripened cheeses would need protection. And cord, she would need more cord.

The herbalist looped a bucket's rope handle about her wrist, and went to draw water from the stream. She needed to clean her hands, for the salve had a pungent reek and made the lips and tongue burn if it touched them. With the animals this was an advantage: they left it alone.

Hands scrubbed, Rosinel decided that since she had been interrupted, she might as well go down into Wassen Village and pay the potter a visit before she resumed her work with the beans. She was almost out of the smallest-size jars. It could take weeks for Oren to fill her order if he had none in stock.

Besides, much as she valued her solitude, it was wise to keep up with the news and gossip. It had been eight days since she had gone down from her mountain and she needed to know what was happening among her potential patients. Half of an herbalist's job was guessing what the source of the trouble was, who was sad, who angry, who had simply drunk too much, or eaten too little. Who needed a change, excitement, or rest.

The potter was a comfort to a silent woman in a different way than closemouthed Herve. Hands gloved in red clay slip, foot thumping as he pumped the wheel, Oren talked continuously and without prompting, providing enough conversation for three or four, instead of just two.

He made no distinction in the importance of his information, that Susen had dropped one casserole on her hearthstone and bought another, just the same, just the same; that Devet's cat had three male kittens, likely mousers all; and that Taren's boy Yuset had stormed out of the house, this time perhaps for good, since he had the promise of a job from Brume, whose boat was tied up at the gravel bar below the village, loading already-out-of-season berries and vegetables that would go all the way to Fastness—

Ears ringing in the silence after Oren's storm of words, and burdened with all the small jars the potter had in stock, Rosinel stopped at the one point where the trail was higher than the roof of her own house. She sniffed the wind, rich with the scents of growing things.

Far below, the cultivated land rolled away, fields stitched and patched by darker hedges and woodlots, the whole cut by the curves of the river. *It may be the finest growing day of the year*, she thought. If her beans promised to crop early, she would put in an extra planting of the meaty speckled ones from Klath. Thoughts busy ordering her day, Rosinel hurried.

The herbalist was a dozen strides from her door when she saw a glittering flaw in the air, a flaw that moved against the breeze that shredded the leaves and stripped the petals from the soris flowers.

A wind-eye.

She took a deep breath and flung her arms wide, seeking focus, heedless of the crash of dropped pottery. Tiny though it was, a wind-eye meant death to them all if it could not be closed.

What must I do?

Humming, the nascent wind-eye drifted like some near-invisible bee seeking pollen for its hive. Hands knotted together, Rosinel sank to her haunches, not hearing the crunch of broken jars, not feeling the shards beneath her bare feet.

What must I do?

There was no answer, yet something must be done and she was the one who must do it. Her trembling hand rested on the smooth curve of an unbroken jar fallen into a tussock of grass at the side of the trail, recalling a time when she was five, almost six, and had caught a—

Silly, she thought. Better she run, get someone to keep of track of the thing's location as it drifted and grew, locate one messenger to go to Fastness and others to begin warning the villages that another flaw in the walls of the world had appeared.

Nonetheless, eyes on her prey, she cradled the unbroken jar in one hand, found a lid that was only chipped with the other, then stalked the thing that hummed above the blushing spires of never-care until, like a child capturing a fire-fly, she could clap top and bottom together and trap it inside. The pottery droned in her hands, thrummed against her chest, as she ran for the stream, fleet with terror.

Wind-eyes were fire and air; maybe they could be defeated with earth and water. Even as Rosinel released the jar, it fell inward on itself, vanished, leaving nothing but a palm-sized dimple in the rocky bottom and a fierce current tearing at her hands.

She pulled her hands free. *I could have died*, the herbalist thought. *I could have lost my hands.* Handless, Rosinel would have no power. Nothing but chance she had released the jar before it was destroyed. The young woman watched the wind-eye whirl in the milky glacial-melt, hollow the surface of the stream as it pulled the water into itself.

It must be marked, confined. With four cobbles she made a hasty cairn on the graveled bank. Then, stone by stone, she built a dam around the fist-sized whirlpool, trying to make it act like some natural thing, an eddy, a backwater. Back and forth she went, using fear-augmented strength to lift heavy stones and roll those still heavier.

The sun was a hand's-width lower in the sky before Rosinel turned from the water. As she did, the upstream wall of her dam collapsed, its stones tumbling into the whirlpool, vanishing. Raw fingers knotted into fists, eyes filled with tears of frustration, she bent to do it all again a second, harder time, for all the nearby stones had already been used, and the wind-eye had taken them.

She stopped and stared.

The drowned wind-eye had become smaller.

Rosinel took a single smooth pebble, dropped it into the whirlpool. It, too, vanished but the flaw seemed unchanged.

Fingers groping behind her, she found a larger cobble, dropped it in. The thing might have contracted. Might have. Testing stones, clods of earth, twigs, she crouched and thought. Rocks worked best, perhaps because they were the densest.

Time, she needed to gain time to run for help.

When Rosinel was ten, she had been to Fastness, seen the Battle Tower, watched a rift-defense. She had traveled home with other pilgrims singing, "—of the ending of days there is no end." There was no way that she could imitate the mage robed, masked, and veiled, enveloped in wind and fire, battling the ravening hole between here and there.

Desperate, she toiled on, entirely in the moment.

When she finally looked up, the changing light made it plain she must act now to see the success or failure of her plan and still have time to reach the village for other help before dark. Rosinel tossed the four stones of the cairn into the wind-eye, thrust a branch into the coarse shingle of the bank to mark the place, and ran.

She needed one of the small rain barrels Herve had bound with rope handles so they could easily be traded between the downspout and the kitchen. Pouring out the soft water on the doorstep she ran back the way she had come, barrel banging her side.

Please, she thought, watching water disappear into nowhere, as she tore off her apron, dress and petticoats, leaving her clad only in the thin modesty of her shift. *Please let this work.*

If Brume had decided to stay the night with his cousin, leaving hot-blooded Yuset to cool his temper by loading the produce alone, then there would be a boat to Fastness. If her idea worked she would need the boat and the boatmen. If it didn't, and if she escaped, she would need them anyway: the Esen River was the quickest way to Fastness.

Water-smoothed stones rolled under her feet. She fell, cracked one knee, and pulled herself up. Blind with pain, her hands anxiously felt over the barrel. It was in one piece; she hoped that it was still sound enough to hold together. It would not matter if it leaked.

At the edge of the current, Rosinel knelt, placed the barrel on its side, breached her wall of stones downstream, and watched the whirl of water slide into the dark interior. *Now*, she thought, *if I keep it centered, away from the staves, I may be able to move it—*

She dragged the small barrel to deeper water, where it floated upright, humming, rim rising and falling beneath the surface, allowing water to feed the hungry maw of the wind-eye. Tilting the container would insure a steady flow as she towed it.

Rosinel hooked the fingers of one hand into a loop of rope, began wading downstream. The stream gradually grew deeper, reaching to her shins, to her knees. The water was gelid, already the herbalist's teeth chattered, and she had a long way to go.

The current sucked and pulled at her, nearly as hungry as the thing in the barrel. She fell into a routine, stroking, checking the wind-eye, then swimming again, murmuring warding spells to count her time.

Rosinel saw mist, floating above the cascading water. Wherever it was, the water was a few degrees warmer than the fresh glacier-melt of the central flow and less rough. Stroke by stroke, she made her way downstream, dragging the wind-eye behind her in its barrel.

The mist cascaded down shallow falls, drifted above pools, beckoned her on, a wraith of the river. Its features were not visible, but she knew it was haggard with care, with eyes gray as storm clouds. Rosinel swam harder. A moment or two more and she would see the real face within the hood of the cloak of spray—

The water dropped from under her. Slithering down the chute she cracked her injured knee, and was jolted back into full consciousness by the pain. The barrel vibrated and roared, torn inside by the wind-eye as she lost control in the boil at the foot of the falls. Desperately embracing the thrumming barrel, Rosinel floated out into the warmer waters of the Esen.

"Help," she cried, sounding weak even to her own ears. "Brume!" she cried and felt the current pluck and pull her toward the swifter flow at the center of the river. She was tiring rapidly now, but drowning was still the least of her fears. If she lost the barrel, she would only be the first of many sucked into the wind-eye. "BRUME!" she screamed, "HELP ME!"

The gold light of a lamp rippled out across the dark water and Brume, mouth still full, stood in his open doorway, peering into the darkness. From his stance, he could not see her and might not be sure he had heard anything. "Yo!" he yelled, lifting the lamp high. "Who's there?"

"Here!" Rosinel called. "Help me," then gasped and sputtered as a wave washed over her chin. She coughed, lost her stroke and went under, ears filled with the underwater drone of the barrel. Treading vigorously, the herbalist forced her way up to the surface again.

Once there, she could hear the thud of boots on the dock as Brume ran for his rowboat, the splash of the oars as he sent the craft out into the flow. "Yo!" he called, oars cocked up, still as he listened.

"Here," she said again, not sure she really spoke or only wished that she had.

But the rowboat loomed next to her, its side high and solid, and Brume's muscle-corded arms stretched toward her. "Rosinel? What happened?"

"No," she said, splashing out of his reach. "Let me—hold to the side. Don't let—the barrel get away." The herbalist clung, suddenly too tired to speak, watching Brume, a black shape against the starry sky, stand and use one oar to pin the barrel against the boat.

Barrel, oar, and rowboat vibrated on one low note.

"What is it?" he asked in a whisper.

"A wind-eye," she said. "A small one. I think."

He was silent, then, "What did you do?"

"I found it," she said.

"Ah." He did something with rope. "It's secure."

"Water has to flow in," she said. "Make sure of it." Her legs had gone numb, and she knew her hands held only because she could see her white-knuckled fingers in the light of the prow-lamp.

Brume didn't answer her, just bent, gripped, and heaved. She rolled on the bottom of the craft, knee a knot of incandescent pain. He began rowing, slowly, as she closed her eyes. The whole craft droned to the hunger of the wind-eye, searching, seeking prey. She focused upon it—

Rosinel came back to herself on the dock, lapped in coarse blankets that smelled of smoke and tar, hearing Brume call orders. She tried to sit, and was pressed back down, not unkindly. "Lie still," said the boat master. "Water's flowing into it. I made sure."

"We must take it to Fastness," she said. "We need the mages."

He grunted agreement and strode off.

The whole dock roared beneath her. Thinking it was the wind-eye, the herbalist sat up abruptly, head spinning. But it was only Dov, Brume's crewman, rolling a barrow of crates up the two planks set side by side that served as a gangway.

"Get the other," said the boat master, shoulder and arm through a coil of rope. "Then wake her."

"I am—awake—"

The drink Dov held to her lips was bitter, made barely palatable by several spoonfuls of honey. She recognized one of her own concoctions. *I must do something about the taste*, she thought, and forced one swallow, another. At least it started a welcome glow in her stomach, and eased the pounding in her head.

A fierce whine came from the barrel: the wind-eye was at the staves again. "Stones," she said, and tried to rise. "Add stones." Brume hooked one hand through the hole in a discarded anchor block, questioned her with a glance, then gave it to the barrel, peering in to watch the result. Then he added three cobbles in quick succession. "It'll do," he said dryly.

The wind-eye slurped and Rosinel shivered.

"Now," said the boat master. "We need to know how you found this thing." Brume and Dov squatted before her. Yuset crouched behind the other two, eyes rimmed with white, kept from running only because he was too scared to stand.

Poor boy, she thought. For all his hot temper, Yuset and the rest of his family were fainthearted, not the sort for adventures. Better it had been Benni or Sult—

She wanted to think of anything but the fact that all of them might die in an instant, without warning, if her warding failed.

Blankets hooded over her head, she told the three everything she had seen and done in as few words as possible. "I think I can keep it from growing, but we must take it to the mages—" she concluded, "—to the mages, as quickly as we can."

"They'll know what to do with it," said Dov, but his tone said that this was a hope and not a belief.

Brume nodded, pursed his lips, considering. "We might make it," he said.

"We should send another messenger, by the road—"

Brume stood. "In case something goes wrong. I'll see to it." Then to Yuset, "See she's fed, has something dry to wear." Then to Dov, pointing, "Watch that. Don't take your eyes off it. Yell if you need help." He went off, in haste, but not running.

Yuset was already gone. Rosinel hoped he thought of bringing something hot to drink. She was shaking uncontrollably, and would need all her strength on the voyage to come.

Listening to the slop and gurgle of the river, shuddering in her wet shift despite the dank and heavy blankets, Rosinel listened as Brume's crewman went back and forth, gathering cobbles, adding another stone to the barrel whenever it began to hum and vibrate loudly.

Yuset didn't come.

Work would warm her. One blanket wrapped around her, the herbalist staggered up, took a basket from a pile at the side of the boathouse, and began prying more cobbles from the paving along the shore, wishing the workmen had done a poorer job in setting the stones.

Dov nodded thanks as she limped up, tumbled her first load out beside him. "We'll need some for the trip," he said. "Leave them in the baskets, so we can shift the weight."

Rosinel moved cobbles until there were no more containers left to fill, then sat on the dock, back against a mooring post, painful leg doubled against her. There she fell into a doze, hands bleeding in her lap, too tired to speak, listening to the droning wind-eye.

Still no Yuset, no food, no dry clothes.

Although Dov was methodical in tending the barrel, the herbalist was afraid to go and scavenge for herself. Brume came back, but, intent on preparing the boat to leave, didn't comment on her state or Yuset's absence. Houses dark and fires banked, to all appearances Wassen slept, silent in dreams and nightmares.

The end of the world trapped in a water butt and no one to help. Perhaps, thought Rosinel, *Brume had thought the frightened villagers would be more trouble than their help was worth, and had told no one. Surely they would come if they were asked.*

Everyone knew distance would not keep anyone safe from the flaw in the wall of the world. When once a month the wind-eye at Fastness appeared, even the cattle in the highest pastures lowed in fear until the threat had been beaten back once more.

"Time to go," said Brume. Coming fully awake with a jerk, Rosinel half-climbed and was half-dragged inboard. She felt the boat curtsey and bob as Brume poled it out of the shallows and caught a current toward the main channel. They were off, water gurgling into the wind-eye as they went.

Surrounded by crates of strawberries and leeks, she checked the barrel was secure. Her small barrel had been slid inside a larger in which holes had been bored, the jury-rigged whole lashed to pegs fresh-hammered near the prow.

Exhausted, Rosinel placed one hand on the quivering rim of the barrel body. The boat creaked as the main current took it. The shore moved past faster than anyone could walk. Wherever he was, Yuset had been left behind. *Perhaps he's gone with the messenger.*

Eyes dazzled by the lamp on the forked pole at the bow, she settled in for a long night. Dreaming she was awake, she sat, hand on the rim of the barrel, feeling it thrum as the water flowed into it, smelling lettuce and green peas. *All will be well*, she thought, *all will be well—*

—of the ending of days there is no end. Rosinel woke with a

start, feeling the whine of destruction through the wood under her fingers. "A stone," she cried. "Give it a stone!" She fumbled in the basket at her side, too confused to get a good grip with her bruised and swollen fingers.

Brume had hands only for the rudder, but Dov came running and heaved cobbles until she feared the barrel would burst. The horrid sound diminished, and the three of them stared at one another, faces white as new-peeled potatoes.

She lifted the torch from the prow and looked in. The smaller barrel was gone, and the larger barrel's interior had been scoured white and furry where the wind-eye had spun against it. A bit more and the thing would have cut through and been free in the river, uncontained and uncontrollable.

Dov, leaning past her, grimaced in dismay. "That won't hold," he said. He looked around him, considering.

Although the boat was piled high with produce in baskets and slatted crates, they were all made for one-time use, and no stronger than they need be, for they would kindle the kitchen fires of Fastness once their contents were sold.

"We'll go to shore," he said.

"There's no time," she answered.

But Dov had already gone to speak to Brume. Rosinel felt the motion of the boat change. She gave another stone to the wind-eye. She had almost failed, could not risk leaving her post to argue with them. There was no margin for a second failure.

The boat's bottom ground on cobbles, and she heard the quick, regular splashes of Dov's running through the shallows, the thud and rustle of his progress along the bank, and then nothing. Water leaped high at the stern—Brume had dropped the anchor-block—and the boatman came wading up alongside the boat.

"Take a break," he said. "There are dry clothes in the locker, drink and food in the latch-box under the pilot's bench."

She stood, and found her legs would hardly hold her.

Brume, mistaking her motion, said, "I'll feed it stones the while. When you come back, I'll add to the ballast." He stripped the belt from his waist and wound it around the barrel's loosened staves, then began bending and lifting rocks from the bar that they had landed on.

He's saving those already on board, she thought, *in case we have to leave quickly.* She ran a hand along a rank of crates, smelled green onions, parsley, chives. Her stomach knotted in hunger.

"We can throw the cargo overboard, if we must," said Brume's voice—he was a shadow bobbing up and down near the side of the boat—"but going downriver the boat's built to ride best when it's loaded. Current grips the keel, pulls you right along." He grunted, tipped a stone the size of her head into nothingness.

Her fingers found the latch-box, and in it a bottle, still warm to the touch. She held the sweet tisane in her mouth a moment then let the warmth fill her chilled stomach. That gave her the energy to nibble half a thick sandwich of bread and cheese, and then plunder a handful of ripe strawberries from one of the crates.

I should help Brume, she thought. But the boatman had not swum in the icy mountain stream bringing the wind-eye down to the river. She was useless if she could not think and work, and she needed fuel. The herbalist took another handful of sweet, ripe berries and ate, speckling the water with green hulls.

The dry clothes, when Rosinel found them, smelled of sweat and old fish. Nonetheless, she climbed into the baggy pants, back to the man stripped off her sodden shift, and pulled on the loose shirt.

Missing the loose ease of a skirt, she went to help Brume. Neither of them mentioned the still-absent Dov, although, remembering Yuset's terrified face, Rosinel wondered if the young man was coming back. Brume was loading stones and tending the barrel—he would not let the herbalist work, insisting the task would be all hers again once they were underway—did not seem troubled.

So she sat, hands in her lap, listening to the sounds of the river, the "Cloop!" as something small leaped to escape something larger, the wind-eye's chuckle and gurgle, the grating of stones as the river ate at the channel end of the bar. Near the other bank Rosinel could see the glitter of torches on water. *Night fishermen*, she thought. They'd be drawing their nets through the slower current at the side of river, trying for the red-cheeks heading for their spawning grounds upstream.

They'd have no luck tonight.

Everything that lived fled a wind-eye.

In the barrel, the thing growled, and Brume fed it an extra stone. "It's growing stronger," he said. "It takes more rocks to keep it from growing."

"Where is Dov?" she asked.

"The nearest house is two miles upstream," said Brume. "He'll be back when he's got what we need. Besides," the boatman swung a basketful of stones inboard, "we'll need these to finish the run. The rest of the bars are mostly pea gravel and sand." He grunted, and wickerwork creaked in protest as he heaved another basket into the boat. "This coarse stuff drops out early."

They heard Dov before they saw him, oarlocks groaning as he rowed down the stream, followed by a bobbing line of barrels like beads on a string. "You're still here," he said, tying his borrowed craft to the stern. "It took longer than I expected. I thought you might push off." Then, to Brume, "Jehen says, return her when we come back up."

He meant the rowboat, realized Rosinel.

Dov and Brume pulled a fresh barrel over the damaged one by cutting the bottom band, shoving the partially collapsed remains into a new container, then cutting the top band. The flaw screamed as it sucked wood and iron into oblivion, leaving the three of them wide-eyed and shaking.

"We must hurry," said Rosinel. There was no need to tell them the wind-eye was growing stronger and she was growing tireder. They all were.

With deft motions, the two men lashed the new barrel where the old had been. Dov shifted several baskets of stones nearer Rosinel, and then he went to take the lookout at the prow. Brume lifted the anchor block and pushed with his pole. Rosinel dropped a stone into the barrel and put a hand on the rim. The wind-eye droned, tame for the moment.

They were off again.

Gripped by the main current, the boat moved very fast. The river, fed by melting snows, was still well up, although the spring floods had come and gone. The ice, stones, and water from the mountains reshaped the channel every year, and, although this was not Brume's first trip of the new season, the Esen was still changing. It was an old saw that there were very few old, careless boatmen.

Rosinel began counting to a hundred and then adding a stone, afraid to depend on seeing and hearing in the uncertain light and constant mutter of the river. Gradually she fell into a state where she was neither awake nor asleep but fed the wind-eye without thought and without pause, feeling its state with her fingers on the barrel rim.

Presently the power within her stirred, although she had not called upon it. What would have been her waking mind was frightened, but the dreaming half saw mountains too steep to stand without crumbling under their own weight, skies the deep purple of a ripe black plum, things that walked like men but weren't sucking clean air and clean water—

She came to herself with a start, frightened, to find she had not failed her task. The motion of the boat slowed and changed. Where before the half-seen shapes along the riverbank had been the humps and mounds of trees and bushes, now there were the straight edges and smooth curves of buildings. They had come to the great pool of Fastness, bearing a cargo of death and out-of-season dainties.

"What now?" said Brume, as he turned the boat toward the docks.

She had not really thought.

"We must rouse the mages," said Dov.

The two men looked at one another and then at her. None of them looked like anyone a door-ward would admit late at night. Rosinel dropped another cobble into the barrel. Time was running short, for they did not have many stones left.

She was the one who had discovered the thing; she was the one who would have to convince the mages that a village herbalist had found something they would not want to believe was true. Looking at the line of light that marked the place where the sun would rise, Rosinel asked, "Does the hold have a water-gate?"

"By the kitchens," said Brume, throwing the tiller over, letting momentum take the boat back into a swifter current. "For the tradesmen." He paused, and then said no more, having followed her thoughts. There would be servants stirring in the household, even this early, and the least important underling would know what he was seeing once she got him to look. Word would pass swiftly indeed in that place where they battled fire and wind and death.

The mage, in protective robe, boots, gloves, mask, and veil, came down the water stairs near the kitchens. He paused, obviously puzzled by the boat with two men and what seemed to be a woman, though she wore a man's clothes, all three laboring to drop stones over its side.

Wasting no more time, he strode though the huddle of open-mouthed kitchen boys, onto the boat, and looked into the barrel. The mage lifted his torch high. The river flowed into it, as into some great drain. "Rift," he said.

"It grows smaller if you add a stone," Rosinel told him, in a hoarse voice. She took a round stream cobble from the bottom of the boat and dropped it into the barrel. When it was gone the swirl had shrunk just enough so one could tell. "We're running out of stones."

The mage settled to his haunches like any village man. "How small can you make it?" he asked. Rosinel showed him her balled-up hand. "Maybe I can close that," said the mage. "If not," the masked and veiled head nodded at the mages who crowded the stairs, "they're ready."

The three who had brought the wind-eye downriver began dropping every stone left into the barrel as rapidly as they could, turn and turn and turn. When the flaw circled the barrel like a giant bee humming and droning at its confinement, the mage reached in with gauntleted hands, closed his eyes, and closed his hands.

Rosinel closed her own in sympathy.

The mage slowly crushed the thing from this existence. Then he sagged where he crouched, head hanging, exhausted.

"Gone?" asked the oldest boatman.

"Gone," whispered the mage.

"GONE!" called the younger man.

The other adepts went rustling back to bed, resuming the rhythm of their days now that immediate peril was past. There would be councils and conferences, arguments and analysis, but for the moment, warm bed and the prospect of a few more hours of dream-free sleep was a sweet thing in a life often devoid of rest.

Favoring her knee, Rosinel stood lopsided on bare battered feet, lost in a scene gone ordinary. The kitchen boys ran and laughed. The cook, unseen in his lair, bellowed commands. The boatmen were bargaining, intent on getting the highest possible price—

"Come with me," the mage said. When they had passed within the shadow of the gate, he threw back his veil and unfastened his mask. "What may I call you?" he asked with formal courtesy. He, a mage, would be nameless to any outsider. It was a rare gesture that he show his features.

"Rosinel," she said. Limping, feet and hands battered and bloody, nonetheless, she felt dignified.

It had been a well-made but not handsome face, now much marred by the white flecks of tiny scars. The eyes were as gray as storm cloud, and colder. He had crushed the rift into nothingness so easily that it looked like something anyone could do. He was a mage, and powerful. His family, his village had lost him forever.

Rosinel pitied him. Her skill was with the living, with growth and wholeness. His was the reverse. *Of the ending of days there is no end*, she thought, remembering the lament for those who climbed the Tower. It was a lovely song to listen to when a winter fire had settled into glowing coals.

Living it was another matter. Most mages strove against the rift until the day they failed and were taken by it. The lucky ones, perhaps, were those who were maimed and retired to teach and serve. No whole man could hope to reach old age in Fastness.

The mage said, "You must tell me what happened, everything you learned."

Rosinel, whose craft was in her blood, her bones, said, "I will tell you what I can."

"Good," said the mage, and he refastened his mask, lowered his veil. Across the smooth flood of the river, rose pale dawn was bisected by the black bulk of the Battle Tower where mages fought the rift. The adept gathered his robes about himself, and sighed.

He stooped, picked up a rock, looked at it. "You should understand." The mage paused, choosing his words. "The stones didn't do anything to the wind-eye."

Rosinel drew back. "I saw! You saw!"

He bent and put the rock back in place, carefully, then stood. "The stones were a focus. Nothing more."

She looked at the rock he had replaced.

"You have talent. There must be a place for you here."

"No," she said. Even as she spoke, Rosinel felt his thought touch the surface of her mind. "No," she said again.

He bowed his head, concentrating.

"If I hadn't been where I was, what would have happened?" With that, Rosinel turned away. When she glanced back, once, at the tall, robed, masked figure, he was standing, head bowed, still striving.

They had held his funeral the day he left home. *It must be lonely*, she thought, walking very fast, ignoring her painful knee. *If I stayed, who would take care of my garden? My people? Someone must care for simple, necessary things.* Stone rang under her running feet. "Brume?" she called, pain shooting up to her hip. "Brume, it's time to go home."

The boat dipped and danced as she boarded.

Brume gave a great shove that turned the craft into the current, the rowboat dancing behind it. He and Dov poled until they could no longer touch the bottom. Then they set the sail. The rising sun gilded the lowest clouds and the ripples of the river.

"Wind's fair upriver," said Brume. "We'll keep near the bank."

"I saved some radishes," said Dov. "There's new bread and a roll of butter."

Rosinel locked eyes with Brume, who looked away.

"Did they give you gold? Silver?" asked Dov.

"Nothing," she said.

"That's good," said Brume. "That's best."

She looked at him and he at her.

"Yes," Rosinel said. "It is."

She wondered what the mage would tell the others and when they would come looking. *Of the ending of days there is no end.* Rosinel closed her hands, remembering that only yesterday they had been full of good, warm earth and she had been happy.

PIG-HEADED

by Suzan Harden

Talis is having a very bad day. She accidentally turned her brother into a pig. The sorcerers' university examiner is on his way to her village to administer her admission test which she's barely studied for. And then, there's the ogre...

Her husband refers to Suzan Harden as a recovering attorney. She prefers the title of writer. Her latest release is A Question of Balance, *a novel based on the characters that first appeared in the Sword and Sorceress 28 short story "Justice." When she's not writing, Suzan grosses out her teenage son with repeated viewings of* The Walking Dead *and corrupts her husband by hiding the remote control and forcing him to watch* Lucifer *and* Preacher.

"Change me back, Talis! I can't court Melinda like this!" Connor stared up at me, his little porcine eyes red with fury.

"And I told you not to interrupt me while I was practicing," I ground out through my clenched jaw. "Father told you not to interrupt me, too. The university examiner will be here this evening."

I wasn't sure what was worse. My anxiety over my entrance exam, or my brother wanting to marry my best friend. I tossed aside Mother's basic spell book. It had nothing on human transfiguration.

"Change me back, or so help me—"

"Shut up and let me concentrate." I rose and crossed the room to Mother's books lining the walls of her study. Goddess, how I missed her. Her encouragement. Her warmth.

The fact that she would have kept Connor out of the study while I reviewed spells for my university entrance exam.

The rest of the village expected me to live up to her reputation as a sorceress. In addition to the every day things she did like healing potions and predicting weather patterns, they claimed she had been responsible for warding our village against the ogre rumored to be living in the Viridian Forest to the north. Their expectations were so high everyone donated coin for my tuition in order to get a full sorceress back in our village sooner.

Though I did wonder how I would ever match her example if I couldn't master a basic transfiguration spell.

My anger back, I thumbed through one of the advanced books until I found the appropriate counterspell for humans. I closed my eyes and pictured in my mind Connor as he should look. Tall and broad-shouldered like Father. His blond, shaggy hair with the cowlick he could never tame. The twinkle in his brown eyes as he teased me unmercifully. I muttered the counter-spell.

Lady barked from underneath my study table, and my eyes popped open.

Connor hadn't transformed back. He still sat in the midst of his clothing on the floor, his tail straight and his wide ears flat against his skull. All the signs of a very upset pig.

On a positive note, I hadn't accidentally changed my dog into a human.

"Talis..." A low growl emerged from him. Lady growled in return, and she inserted herself between me and Connor.

"It should have—" I turned back to the table and flipped through Mother's beginners textbook. Transfiguration of animals was one of spells I would have to demonstrate to the examiner tonight. Transfiguration of a human should have been far beyond my meager skills. And yet...

My heart hammered and my head pounded as I reread the instructions for the transfiguration spell for the third time. The blasted thing should never have worked on Connor to begin with!

"Talis!"

I pivoted on my chair to face him. "I can't concentrate with you shouting at me. Go sit in the yard until I figure out how to reverse this."

He huffed before he clambered to all four feet. His cloven hoofs tapped out his anger and fear on the hardwood as he marched out of the study and down the hall.

Once he was gone, Lady nosed my skirts. I petted her ebony-furred head as I poured through the pages. It was bad enough that I had a dog as my familiar instead of a cat. If I couldn't fix this, I could wave my admittance to the university good-bye. Using magic on another human without university accreditation was illegal. Even though turning Connor into a pig had been an accident, the king's court didn't have a sense of humor in these matters.

And if I wasn't here to protect the village, Goddess only knew when the university would assign a new sorcerer for the people.

By the time I discovered the proper method for restoring Connor, the angle of light in the study indicated it was well past mid-afternoon. I peered out the window, but there was no sign of a white pig lying in the front yard.

Damn, where did he wander off to?

I strode out of the study and headed for the front door, Lady trotting behind me. Too much of my precious study time had been lost, but I couldn't let the examiner see my brother in the form of a pig.

I yanked the handle and stepped outside. "Connor!"

Late afternoon light reflected off the sorcerer's globe in its holder next to the door frame. I could almost imagine it was lit. But it hadn't glowed since Mother's passing.

"Connor!" I yelled again.

A handful of birds sang in response. Dragonflies from the nearby mill pond buzzed in lazy circles around the reeds. Lady trotted past me and barked an echo to my call while she did her business.

Silence.

If Conner is deliberately hiding, I swear I will kick him in the seat of his pants.

Porcine grunts and squeals mixed with men's voices in the barn. My heart sank. Had Connor tattled on me before I could fix my accident?

"Come," I ordered Lady. She trotted back inside the house. I pointed at the floor. "Stay." She whined, but obeyed me as I stepped outside and closed the door.

I ran to the barn to find Father and Uncle Paddric separating the piglets from their mothers.

"I'm telling you, Andrew, all the grown ones are here and accounted for," Paddric yelled over the high-pitched shriek of the piglet he held. He marked it with berry ink and placed it in a separate pen with its littermates, also with bright purple streaks on their backs. As soon as he released the poor animal, it quieted and ran for the opposite fence.

"Well, then who does that white boar belong to?" Father asked.

My body shook, but Father needed to know the truth. "Are you talking about the pig that was sitting in our front yard?"

He smiled. "Needed a study break, Talis?" My words sunk in, and his smile faded. "What do you know about it?"

I couldn't meet his gaze. "The pig in the yard was Conner."

"Conner?" Even the other pigs, the normal pigs, quieted at his question.

"He came into the study while I was practicing a transfiguration spell on Lady, and..." My fingers twined and tightened until they went numb. I waited for Father's umbrage.

Instead, he and Paddric burst out laughing.

"No wonder he took off for the woods." Father roared even louder and clutched the side of the pen to remain upright.

"With Melinda chasing him all the way," Uncle Paddric wiped at the tears streaming down his face.

"Melinda?" I stared at my father and uncle.

"She brought dinner for us tonight. Between you studying and us preparing the piglets for the market, she knew we wouldn't have time to cook before the examiner arrived." He chuckled. "I think she simply wanted an excuse to spend time with Conner."

"I don't think chasing him through the woods was what she had in mind," Paddric said, which sent both men into another fit of laughter.

The woods. Goddess, what if there were *an ogre living in the Viridian Forest?*

I spun and ran for the stone fence marking our family farm. There was a horrendous ripping sound as I clambered over, but I couldn't worry about my skirts. Not now. I plunged past the raspberry bushes, adding more tears to my clothing, and raced into the woods.

Mother had taken me deep into the forest many times before she died, teaching me the various trees, plants, and mushrooms. What you could eat. What had medicinal properties. What could kill.

She'd also taught me to identify spoor and tracks of various animals. Fortunately, the trail left by one frightened pig and one girl were easy to follow.

Until the growing gloom made the broken branches and scuffed loam difficult to see, and I had to walk slower in order to track them.

A burst of wind whistled by me. I stopped and stared at the tree tops. It didn't make sense. There was no sign of bad weather before I left our farm. If it rained now, I'd lose any sign of Connor and Melinda, but no downpour came.

I'd nearly given up on my search when I spotted the fire glimmering between the trees. I prayed the spell had worn off and either Connor, Melinda or both had resigned themselves to a night in Viridian Forest rather than wander around lost.

But I spotted a huge figure moving around the flames, and I thanked the Goddess I hadn't shouted for Connor or Melinda. The form's head was too irregular, the body was too big, and there was far more hair for the figure to be human.

I eased closer. Melinda was trussed up and propped against a tree, her dark hair mussed and her blue eyes wide with fear. Connor, still a pig, lay next to her in a similar state. From the multitude of cords covering his snout, he'd tried to bite their captor.

The ogre itself whistled tunelessly while he whittled a forked branch as big as my thigh. A second forked branch had already been planted in the dirt on the other side of the fire, and a much longer, thinner straight branch was propped against a log.

A spit.

My heart threatened to choke me in its desire to escape from my chest. All the stories and histories I read said ogres were slow-witted and slow-moving.

And they loved the taste of human flesh. Especially babies.

If I could untie Connor and Melinda, we could outrun it for home.

Assuming the three of us didn't get lost in the forest in the dark.

Well outside the circle of light cast by the flames, I circled toward my brother and my friend as another disturbing thought entered my mind. What if the ogre followed us back to the village?

No, we'd still be safe since the university examiner should be there by now, and he was a full sorcerer. However, if I brought an ogre back with me, I could say good-bye to any chance of attending the university.

I was so busy with my escape plan and my worries I didn't pay attention to the placement of my feet. My heel pressed down on a twig, and it broke with a very loud *CRACK!*

"Who there?" the ogre thundered. His voice was deep and gravelly.

I could run now and save myself, but there was no way I could return with help before the ogre had cooked and eaten his prisoners. My only hope was either outwitting the ogre or convincing him Connor and Miranda weren't worth eating. Clenching my fists, I stepped into the little clearing.

"Greetings, sir ogre," I said. "Thank you for finding my friends and keeping them safe."

He grinned at the sight of me. "Good. More food. Mossrock hungry."

"I'm sure you're very hungry, Mossrock." I glanced down to my right. Both Connor and Melinda stared at me like I'd lost my mind.

Returning my attention to the ogre, I added, "My friends and I are much too old to be tender and delicious for you." To my recollection of Mother's records, no one in our village had gone missing in her lifetime, and certainly none had since her death two years ago. "How long have you been living in this forest, Mossrock?"

"Long time. Many seasons." After a brief pause, he added sadly, "Lost count."

"Has it been more than you have fingers and toes?"

His head dropped. "Don't know." He looked at me again. "Hungry."

He lumbered toward Melinda, and I stepped between them and held up my hand. "No, Mossrock. I won't let you eat them."

He stopped and pointed. "One is pig. Pig not human."

"The pig is my brother," I said. My admission seemed to confuse him. Before he could work anything out, I asked, "Who has been feeding you, Mossrock?"

"Sorceress," he muttered.

I took a step back. The only sorceress in leagues had been Mother. Was that how she really protected our village? By feeding the ogre?

"Sartra?" I squeaked.

"Sartra!" He danced. The noise of his stomping drowned my thoughts, and the ground beneath my feet trembled.

"She died, Mossrock," I shouted. He paused and stared at me. "She died," I repeated. "Two years ago. She was my mother."

He cocked his head. "Mother?"

"The one who gave birth to me?"

He nodded. "Mossrock had...mother. Long time ago." He looked at Connor again. "Hungry."

I actually felt sorry for the ogre. If he had been dependent on Mother, Goddess only knew when he'd eaten last. Would he be hungry enough to make a deal? Or too hungry to listen? "I can feed you like Sartra did."

"You feed Mossrock?"

"Yes. I will bring you the best food."

"Babies. Human babies best," he rumbled.

"No human babies." I smiled at him. "But I can bring you a

baby pig. If you let my friends go."

His eyes narrowed. "Why?"

Now, I was confused. "Why what?"

"Why let friends go? Humans lie." He pointed the forked stick he'd been whittling at me. The one big enough that if he ran me through, he'd kill me."

I lifted my chin. "Did Sartra lie to you?"

"No," he admitted.

"Then I won't either." I stepped past the forked branch and laid a hand on his arm.

And tried very, very hard not to make a face at his atrocious body odor.

"But if I don't take my friends home now, other humans will come. And they won't be willing to feed you. I will bring you a baby pig."

"Three," Mossrock rumbled.

I drop my hand from his arm. "Three?" I struggled to get my outrage under control. "Our deal was for one."

"Three humans go. Three baby pigs come."

It wasn't worth arguing with the ogre if it saved Conner and Melinda. "All right. I'll bring three pigs back tonight."

I reached for my knife and turned to cut the ropes binding Melinda.

"No!" the ogre shouted.

I jumped and whirled to face him, my arm outstretched and the knife quivering in my grip.

He pointed at Conner. "You do. Pig bitey."

I stifled a giggle. No sense in destroying the tentative truce. "You're right. That pig is bitey." I shifted to my brother and cut his bindings. "Don't say a word until we're well away from here," I whispered and waved my knife in front of his snout.

He said nothing, which was much more reassuring than anything else he could have done.

It was full dark when we left the ogre's fire. I led the former captives in the direction I'd come from, my knife still in one hand and the other supporting Melinda. Her legs were numb from being tied up for so long. However, Connor raced in circles around us and seemed to be fine.

Except for being in the wrong form.

I scored trees with my initial every fifty steps.

"What are you doing?" Melinda whispered.

"It's so I can find my way back to Mossrock." An odd sensation rose the hairs on my arms and the back of my neck.

As if we were being watched. But surely we would have heard the ogre if he followed us?

"Are you really bringing back three piglets to the ogre tonight?" Melinda kept her voice low.

"Yes."

"Why?" Fear tinged the single word.

"Because if I want any chance of getting my sorceress accreditation, I have to keep my promise. Our vows are their own form of magic."

"Talis! Melinda!"

Connor was far to our left, his white hide the only reason we could see him in the dark. "This way!"

"How do you know?" I demanded.

He snorted. "Because now that my nose is clear of ogre smell, I can pick up our scents."

"Maybe we could have him dig truffles for a season before you turn him back to human," Melinda said as we headed in Connor's direction.

"Don't even think about it," he retorted.

"I could do the counter-spell right now," I offered.

"No, I am not treading through this blasted forest barefoot! You can do it as soon as we return home." He trotted off, and we followed.

I turned to Melinda, who was walking on her own now. "When did you discover the pig was my brother?"

She giggled. "The moment he took off for the woods. He has that cute little quarter moon birthmark on his right buttock."

"Don't speak about my rear end!" he hollered over his shoulder.

Melinda's giggles turned into outright laughter. "And the more I called his name, the further and faster he ran into the forest."

"Hush, you two!" Connor halted and pivoted to face us. "Just hush! I'm the aggrieved party here! Neither of you got turned into a pig!"

"Then let's get home." All good humor fled from me. Would the examiner even still be there when we arrived? As long as I could return my brother to his rightful form and fulfill my bargain with Mossrock, I didn't care what punishment befell me.

As if to warn of my impending personal storm, a gust of wind rustled through the forest and sent leaves flying everywhere.

Connor's nose led us true. I wanted to cry when I saw the sorceress globe lit at our door. Did that mean the university examiner was still here? We trooped inside...

Only to find Mossrock sipping tea with Father and Uncle Paddric and petting my dog.

It was too much for me after the day I'd had. I stamped my foot. "What are you doing here? I said I'd bring three pigs to your fire tonight!"

Father folded his arms over his chest. "And just where were you planning to get these pigs, Talis?"

I needed to get Father and Paddric out of the house and warn everyone in the village. "Can we talk about this in the kitchen, Father?"

"No," he said sharply.

"I was going to buy them from you above market price," I said through gritted teeth. I didn't know what to do. Everyone I love would die because I couldn't master a stupid transfiguration spell.

"With what money?" Father insisted.

I was so tired, and nothing today had gone right, and I couldn't cry in front of an ogre because if I let him see any weakness, he'd lay waste to our village. "My savings for university. After what I accidentally did to Connor, and with the examiner not here..."

Except the sorceress globe out front was glowing.

I turned to Mossrock. I didn't light the globe, not even

accidentally. He was the only new person in the house. Under the great-room lamps, he looked far more terrifying, yet far gentler, than he had in the forest. "You're not an ogre, are you?"

He set down his teacup. "Talis, I assure you I am an ogre." His voice didn't have quite the gravelly quality it had before. He smiled, showing green, crooked teeth. His clothes shifted from rags to proper university robes. "However, I am also your examiner."

Was it still the night before my examination? Was this simply a horrible dream because of my nerves? "I-I don't understand."

"An examination of a candidate isn't just about their potential skill. It's also about their character."

"Character?" I squeaked.

His smile faded. "The character test is different for every candidate. I arrived early, and your father told me what had happened with your brother. However, I had to discover if your brother's transformation was truly an accident, or if you'd deliberately performed illegal magic."

Connor trotted forward and peered up at the ogre. "It wasn't Talis's fault, Examiner Mossrock! I'm the one who interrupted her after both she and Father told me to stay out of the study. Talis worked all morning and most of the afternoon to reverse the spell, and—" His ears and tail drooped.

"You mean, until you foolishly ran away because you didn't want your lady love to see you as a pig," Mossrock chided. Father and Paddric smirked.

"Yes, sir," Connor mumbled.

The ogre turned to me. "It wasn't just confirming the accident. Talis, I was highly impressed with the courtesy and honesty you displayed while you bargained for your compatriots' freedom. Have you ever dealt with my kind before?"

"N-no, sir."

"So what prompted you to use that tactic?"

The truth may be ugly, but the examiner deserved an honest answer, even if he rejected my candidacy. "I originally was going to untie Connor and Melinda, and run away with them, but when I stepped on that dry stick—" I couldn't stop the tears welling in my eyes. "From the little I read about your people, I knew I could get away, but I was afraid by the time I got help, you may have done something horrible to them."

Mossrock nodded. "But something changed as we talked."

"I thought you were out there alone and starving." I sniffed. "M-my mother always said to treat everyone kindly until they give you a real reason not to. And if I could get food for you, then you wouldn't be starving, and you wouldn't eat people here in the village—"

I clapped my hands over my mouth at the realization of what I just said.

The ogre sadly shook his head. "There're many misconceptions amongst both our races about each other. Something we endeavor to correct at the university. However, I think you have already taken the first step."

He smiled again. "Well then, Talis, I trust you found the solution to your mistake. If you can restore your brother on the first try, we'll forgo the rest of your examination."

Thank you for adding more pressure on me. But I didn't say my impolite thought aloud. Instead, I recognized the second chance he gave me for what it was.

I recited the counter spell for restoring a human to their original form. Light flashed, and my brother stood on two legs.

In his very naked human shape.

Melinda nudged me in my ribs. "Told you. Quarter moon birth mark."

"Talis!" Connor shouted.

Paddric tossed a blanket at my brother. "Your sister wasn't the one prancing around your yard and the forest without any clothes."

Connor sputtered some more while he wrapped the blanket around his waist.

"Speaking of clothing," Father said. "Get some on before you come to the supper table. We have guests tonight."

"What about Talis!" my brother shouted.

I looked down. I'd forgotten about my torn skirt and the punctures to both it and my shirt from the raspberry brambles.

Mossrock rose, his bristly hair brushing the ceiling. "I can fix that." With a gesture and an incantation, light flashed over me. When it faded, my skirt and shirt looked almost new.

"What about me?" Connor said with an outraged expression.

"I cannot repair what doesn't exist," the examiner said innocently.

My brother stomped upstairs. A moment later, his bedroom door slammed.

Mossrock rose and extended his elbows to me and Melinda. "Ladies, shall we?"

We each took a proffered arm. This time, he smelled of crisp autumn leaves and river rocks.

"I hear you are quite the cook, Melinda," the examiner said as we headed for the kitchen. She blushed and murmured her thanks for the compliment.

He leaned over and whispered to me, "Back in the forest, I wasn't joking about being hungry. And I do love a good roast pork. Do you think your father would part with three of his piglets in lieu of a portion of your tuition?"

I grinned. "I'm sure he would, sir."

HOT MILK BEFORE BED

by L.S. Patton

Magic can be a useful thing that makes life better. It can also drive you nuts. And that's the magic, not the magician. Of course, when you thought you were safe because the magician had gone away, and he comes back, then the magician can be a problem as great as the magic.

L.S. Patton dipped her toes into fantasy writing last year, and published her first story in Sword and Sorceress 30. *Since then, she has started several other writing projects, and finished the one you see here. She is hoping to find more time to devote to writing in the next year. She lives with her husband, dog, cat, and horse in Peoria, Illinois.*

It had been a quiet, peaceful couple of weeks. I didn't trust it; if it kept up for another week, I'd be scared of my own shadow. Nellie Peterson hadn't even complained when I'd updated the spell on her mirror; clearly the universe had something bad in store for me, and soon. All that training in the natural balance of things that was drilled into you with your beginning magical studies did nothing to help my natural distrust of all things easy, and had fairly well entrenched my belief that the good times were only there to lull you into complacency before the bad.

Things were going so well, in fact, that I had a dozen extra eggs this week and the time to run down to Karen's inn to sell them to her. Muttering darkly to myself, I set off through the unseasonably warm, sunny evening to the town square.

Karen's inn formed one of the four sides of the square, with a long hitching post along the front and a large painted sign with an elephant on it. There was a large, once-enchanted coffee pot on a pedestal in the center of the square: it had been fused to its stand and even the bedrock below by the magic of its maker's uncontrolled anger, though six months had made the memory of Tom's anger fade enough that people no longer reflexively avoided the new statue. Today, three kids were playing on the ground around it.

"Hi, Clara!" piped Sofia, followed by the disinterested "Heys" of Abe and Serena. Sofia watched me closely for a minute, and, when I didn't do anything overtly magical, was again distracted by their game.

I wiped my boots on the mat and tromped into the inn. Weaving between the tables, I ducked behind the counter and into the kitchen, where I found Karen up to her elbows in bread dough.

"Clara! What brings you out so late? Shouldn't you be brooding over your mirrors into people's guts?"

I raised my basket slightly. "I'm afraid my hens have been overachieving recently. You need any eggs?"

"Sure, put them with the others. I'll take it off your tab."

"The mirrors actually seem to be working pretty well. I think I might even have a prototype to show Doc in the next couple weeks."

"Ahhh, no wonder you're brooding, then, everything seems to be going well. Especially since Tom left on that quest into the Enchanted Forest and isn't annoying everyone anymore. You're probably convinced an asteroid is going to crush the town tomorrow." Karen had known me since I was five, and the people-watching she could indulge in as an innkeeper only heightened her ability to tell what people were thinking.

"Hmph," I replied articulately.

"Cheer up, I'm sure something mundanely horrible will happen soon. Look, you've already managed to get flour on your dress." As Karen had been waving her floured hands around to express her point, I didn't feel that this counted.

"Any mail for me?"

"As if you didn't know," Karen headed up front to the bar. "Your gentlemen friend has been writing quite a lot recently. Alex may start to get jealous." This last was directed more toward Lilly, paying avid attention at the bar, than to me. I had given up trying to convince Karen that nothing was going on with Alex and me. Karen pulled an unsealed, three page letter from behind the bar. Karen didn't believe in privacy between friends, and claimed I never told her anything without her having to drag it out of me. She had long since decided opening my mail was easier.

Unfortunately, in this case, all of her gossip was imaginary. After a recent paper on the use of sympathetic magic in recovering memory, Andre Farington had written about trying to apply the practice to his prophecies, and we had been trying to work the kinks out long distance. I was still pretty pleased that The Andre Farington, Prophet of Codswall, was writing to me, but I'm pretty sure that no one else in the village cared.

The inn was doing a fairly brisk business tonight; unusual for a Wednesday evening. I preferred it when things were quieter, and there was less posturing and gossiping and more friendly chatter. As Karen was busy sprinkling Lilly liberally with the flour to make her current point, I slipped out the door.

I crossed the yard and started walking along the track that led behind the main square and worked its way to the north side of town. As I turned north, I looked off to my left, toward the Enchanted Forest, and wondered, not for the first time, what it would be like to be a widely known magician, like the Prophet of Codswall, and not just a hedgewitch known in a few scholarly magical circles for her publications. The problem, as always, was that my magesight-based magic wasn't very flashy, and I was much too sensible to go out on crazy quests from which I learned nothing and proved less. Small, incremental improvements in everyday magics weren't flashy enough to get the general populace interested.

I'd had more of these thoughts recently, since a wildly rare and intricate magical object had been given to a friend of mine. I pushed open his barn door, and said object mooed at me, correctly assuming that I had brought her an apple. Margot was a magical object of a caliber that I had never seen before, and could make the career of anyone who announced her discovery.

Of course, anything that valuable would bring lots of people who wanted her for themselves, not all of them scrupulous. So far, only her owner Alex and I knew what she could do, but that didn't seem like the sort of situation that could last.

As had become my habit, I made a light globe and stuck it in front of Margot's nose as she ate her apple. The light slowly dimmed, and I watched as it disappeared into the cow. Margot could somehow absorb magic and charms near her, condense it into its pure form, and release it in her milk. Milk which could then temporarily make non-mages into mages, and could increase the power of those already mages. She was the sort of tool people would kill for.

I had been studying her since Alex had gotten her six months earlier, trying to figure out what exactly she was doing, and also how it could be stopped, so that any nearby enchantments wouldn't slowly lost their charges to the cow. I had mostly been working on developing shielding that would prevent magic from being drawn to Margot and was effective at preventing her power from reaching through the shields. Magesight was my specialty; however, I couldn't see anything magical just by looking at Margot. Somehow, her magical powers didn't manifest like those of most magical objects, and her attractive power was likewise invisible. She was a mystery I found irresistible.

I cast my most recent shielding spell, which so far was proving partially successful. The problem was that, since Margot drew magic into herself somehow, she tending to absorb shields as well. I had figured out that I could get around that by using momentum; a series of spinning spirals would not be absorbed, but they didn't cover all the area around Margot, either. They were pretty effective at rebounding spells that were cast at the cow, but did not affect the slow absorption of charms that were just nearby. I would have been much happier with the reverse result, since, other than me, very few people tried to cast spells on Margot, but there were lots of ambient spells that I was trying to protect. I slowly shot a long jet of blue shielding, forming a spiral around Margot, meeting up with the ending of the jet as it wrapped twice around the cow.

Tonight my goal was to try to increase the number of spirals in an attempt to cover more area. The problem was that the more spirals I made, the more of my magic it used, and my skills tended much more toward efficiency than raw power.

About an hour later, I staggered out of the barn into the night, exhausted. I saw that the light was on in Alex's house, so I banged on the window and waved as I started on my way home. I'd been doing this enough that he recognized the signs of a tired and probably cranky mage and merely looked up from his book and waved back before returning to his reading. I had made some slight improvements on the shield, but still hadn't made the breakthrough that seemed to hover just out of reach. Incremental progress: my specialty.

I was out weeding my garden the next day when Mia rushed up to me, looking frantic. "Clara, I think Sofia has gone into the Enchanted Forest." Mia collapsed on the ground next to me and wiped her eyes. Sofia was her five year old niece, and she had been particularly enamored of Tom before he went on his quest to the Forest. "Old Bill saw her on the path in front of his house this morning heading that way, and no one's seen her since." Old Bill lived between the Inn and the Enchanted Forest, and there wasn't anything else out that way to draw the attention of a young girl. "Can you do anything?"

Going into the Enchanted Forest was foolhardy in the extreme; no one (recognizable) had come out of it alive in the past fifty years. Tom had only gone on his quest because it had been discovered that his crowning magical achievement had stopped working, and he couldn't manage to get it working correctly before the news had spread. He felt that he had to do something magnificent to win back his status as a court magician, and apparently couldn't manage anything important enough and had to resort to this crazy quest. I felt slightly guilty for my role in his downfall, but mostly I thought he was still being an idiot. I was also more than half convinced that he hadn't gone into the Forest at all, and was just waiting for his chance to pop out and make some ridiculous claim of having survived against all odds.

There were some places where magic bred more magic; the Enchanted Forest was the most potent of these I had seen. Once a certain magical saturation is reached, there is enough magic forming random shapes that some of them will turn out to be spells, just by chance. The surrounding magic made the spontaneous spells hard to see and avoid, and there were enough of them that any visitor would run into a barrage of them only a few steps into the wood, and their chance-made shapes were very difficult to understand and reverse, as they bore no resemblance to the spells that mages learned.

On the other hand, Sofia was in there. I looked at Mia's face and knew that I couldn't just sit here and do nothing while Sofia might be lost in the Forest. "Well, I should be able to tell if she went in, and I'll do what I can." Mia's face lit up with hope, and I went inside to get my supplies.

A quick bit of sympathetic magic with Sofia's hair ribbon told me her direction: she had entered the Forest. I stood at the edge of the Forest, and looked at the swirling patterns of magic that almost blocked out the trees. I pulled my bag around on my shoulder and opened the flap. I had brought enough food for a couple days, a bottle of pure spring water, a coil of rope, and several packets of herbs. A bump on my shoulder reminded me of the other thing that I had brought, and also why I wasn't as upset about having to enter the Forest as night was falling. I looked over at Margot, and hoped that my assumptions were correct.

While the shielding spell I had developed wasn't working well for preventing the cow from dissolving spells in the regular world, it seemed like it might work well in the Forest. The quick-moving spells that were likely to affect us would be bounced off of the shield, and hopefully any slow-moving spells that affected us would be absorbed before they caused us too much damage. It wasn't a foolproof plan, but it was the best I could come up with on short notice, and it was good enough that I thought I stood a chance. It was a better plan than most people's on entering the

Enchanted Forest. And Sofia was out there.

I carefully set the shield spell around both of us, then practiced walking for a couple minutes to make sure that I could actually lead a cow without either of us stepping outside of the shield. Then I reset it slightly larger and tried again. It turns out it's much harder to stay inside of a shield when you have six legs that don't necessarily have the same goals in mind.

Once I felt like we were as coordinated as we were going to get, I steered us toward the Forest. As we stepped in, a soft pink mist surrounded us. I could see the mist seeping past my shield, but it didn't seem to have an effect on either me or Margot, so, after a second, I kept going. A dark green shape loomed on my left, then abruptly bounced off the shield with a loud crack. I staggered to the right, but managed to stay within the sphere. I realized I hadn't actually felt the impact. I guess the shields were working. Several less well differentiated shapes loomed out of the murk and they also had no effect. I pulled out Sofia's hair ribbon, tied it to a string on the end of a stick and stuck it outside of the shield so the magic tie binding it to Sofia didn't bounce off of the shield. A green line stretched from the ribbon into the murk, pointing the direction to Sofia. With slightly more confidence, I strode deeper into the Forest.

Five hours later, I was still wandering. At least it seemed like Sofia could still walk, because I was pretty sure I had passed the same screaming fern three times now. The magic mist made it hard to judge landmarks, and perhaps I just hoped that these ferns weren't part of the standard Forest flora. My shields had so far managed to keep Margot and me mostly intact, though my skin was currently glowing blue, which was fairly unusual. I was also pretty sure that Margot hadn't had cloven hooves when we entered the forest, but they didn't seem to bother her and I wasn't an expert on cow hooves anyway.

Suddenly, I could no longer see the line from the ribbon stretching off in front of me. I stopped and looked frantically around, only to realize the reason I didn't see it stretching in front of me was because it was now stretching down in front of me. Which meant that the orange sweater marching along the forest floor was probably Sofia. I'd hoped the Forest wouldn't have changed her quite so much, but realistically I expected something similarly drastic.

I followed her for a second, trying to figure out the best way to deal with the situation. It seemed like a bad idea to try to do anything to Sofia's enchantments while we were still in the Forest, but I also didn't want to try to see how her charms interacted with the shield. I really didn't want some piece of the spell to go bouncing off the shield and turning her into a puff of air or something else I didn't think I could keep in one piece. I might have to risk taking the shield down to catch Sofia and take her back with me. While I was thinking, several lumps formed on Sofia's left sleeve and shaped themselves into small golden bells, which started ringing, and I realized I didn't have time to think about it. I dropped the shield, grabbed the collar of the sweater, and put Sofia on the cow's back.

As I was setting her down, the full force of the magic surrounding us hit me. My brain seemed to float, I felt myself being pulled in dozens of different directions to dozens of fates as strange as Sofia's. I fell back against Margot, and the pressure seemed to ease slightly. I couldn't focus enough to put the shield up, but I managed to get one spiral going. As the pressure eased further, I was able to create another spiral, then another, until all five spirals were spinning again.

I leaned against Margot for a few more minutes, stunned and exhausted, before I activated the location charm on the splinter of Alex's barn that I carried with me, then tied it to the fishing pole and stuck it out of the spiral. The line of magic stretched off to my left. I stuffed Sofia the sweater into my bag and started walking back out of the Forest.

I was already exhausted from the walking, and now that I'd been exposed to the unbuffered Forest magic I was dead on my feet. When a dark shape loomed on my right, I assumed it was just another weird charm coming at us and didn't even flinch. A lot of odd, poorly defined shapes had popped out at me over the course of the night. This shape, however, hit the back of my knees hard and I barely managed to stay within the shield. I knew I wouldn't be able to put it back up a third time.

I turned to get a look at what had hit me, and found myself face to face with a goat. Well, mostly. It did have a rhinoceros horn and was wearing pink leg warmers, and something funny seemed to be going on with its tail. I used my magesight to look deeper, and realized that, of course, things could still get worse and that they just had. The goat was Tom, apparently still in the Forest on his quest, and also apparently not doing very well. I considered leaving him. It was his own fault, after all, and he really should have known better. I guess I'm a sucker for terrified bleating though, because I threw him across Margot's back and tied him on with the rope from my bag. I could always decide later to leave him as a goat.

Based on the moon, it was only a couple hours later that I stumbled up to Alex's barn, but it felt like ages. I put Margot back in her stall, cut Tom off her, and left the two of them together. I made it as far as the haystack out front before I sat down for a minute and don't remember anything until Alex showed up around noon with a sandwich and cup of tea.

I blinked at him a couple times to make sure he was real, then realized that the sandwich most definitely was real and that it was far more important than anything else that might be happening. I sat up and grabbed the plate. Every muscle in my body screamed at me, but it was worth it. Tomato juice dripped down my chin and, about halfway through, I realized that Alex was laughing at me.

"That hungry, huh? It looked like you were going to sleep all day, but I thought you probably needed something to eat more than you needed more rest."

On closer inspection, Alex looked decidedly worried. I hadn't told him that I had Sofia with me, so of course he was worried. "I got her," I croaked, and pulled the sweater out of my bag. "I need to try to reverse some of the spells before I take her back to her mother, though." I smoothed out the sleeve without the bells.

"That's Sofia? That sweater?" Alex, who had lived in the

shadow of the Enchanted Forest his whole life and should have known better, looked shocked. "What happened to her?"

"The Forest happened to her," I grumped. "Why do you think no one goes in there? The huge amount of magic in there will twist you until there's nothing left. Sofia is still in one piece, and still mostly Sofia, which is more than anyone could expect. Now, if you'll give me some space, I need to see what I can do to help her." I handed Alex back the empty plate and grabbed the mug of tea.

Alex opened his mouth again, but I waved him away and he went. I was still an exhausted mess, and I knew I didn't have the energy to check out Sofia and argue with Alex. Even if he brought more sandwiches.

Sofia's problem was a set of seven interlocking charms. I managed to remove two of them, so she now appeared to be a hedgehog made out of tangled yarn, but the last five were so intertwined that I wasn't sure they could be removed separately. I was also almost as exhausted as I had been last night. I managed to stagger to my feet and into the barn to see how Margot was faring. I reached for the lantern as I went inside, then realized it was already light in the barn. I was still glowing blue.

I'd expected side effects from the journey, but I'd also expected that I was close enough to Margot that they would have faded somewhat, especially a charm as wispy and diffuse as this light charm. I leaned on the half door of Margot's stall and looked at her. Her udder was glowing with so much magic that I could almost see it with my normal sight. Tom angrily butted the stall door, as much a goat as he had been the day before. Perhaps there was a limit to how much magic Margot could absorb. If so, we'd surely reached it yesterday. Maybe Margot needed to be milked before she could absorb more? I grabbed the stool and went into the stall. Tom continued butting the door, and not me, so I went ahead and milked the cow.

I left the stool by the stall and took the bucket of milk back with me to the hay pile. Sofia was still there, and still looked nothing like a five year old girl. I sat down, flipped back to magesight, and was promptly blinded by the bucket of milk. When I put it behind me, it just looked like there was bright sunlight shining on everything, so that should work.

Staring at the tangle of charms, it looked like there was one junction where all five spells came together. If I could destroy that, then the rest of it should unravel fairly easily. *If* I could destroy that. I had never been a particularly powerful mage, and I was pretty drained as it was. However, I also didn't know what the long term effects of leaving Sofia in a non-living form might be. It would be best to get her living again as soon as possible.

I looked back at the bucket of milk. I knew that drinking it would increase my magical powers, but I didn't know what else it might do to me. And I really didn't want to draw attention to Alex's impossibly valuable magical cow. I didn't want him to get hurt by any unscrupulous power hunters. I hadn't tried it yet, despite my curiosity, but this situation was enough to get me to drink some.

I dipped my finger in the bucket and stuck it in my mouth. I could feel it tingling its way down to my stomach and I didn't feel as tired anymore. I scooped up a handful of milk and drank it. Wow. A zing shocked straight down to my stomach, and I felt incredibly powerful. Like I could do anything. I flexed my power and carefully took another small sip, just to make sure I had enough juice for the job.

The spells on Sofia blazed, and at the same time looked gossamer thin, like I could tear them apart with a thought. Which had been the idea, after all. The scary part was that I felt supremely assured about the whole thing, as if I didn't have any doubt that I'd free Sofia and leave her unharmed. With my new-found confidence, I tapped on the spell junction. All five spells shattered, leaving a dazed Sofia sitting on the lawn in front of me. I could see her brain catch and start up again, and see her body settling more firmly around her. I removed the last dregs of the spells, leaving her looking just fine.

"Sofia? How are you feeling?"

She looked curiously at one arm, then the other, then back up at me. "I was a sweater, wasn't I? It was warm and cozy and restful."

"Yes, you went into the Enchanted Forest and it transformed you. I've removed the spells. How are you feeling?"

"Hungry," her eyes latched onto the bucket of milk. "And sleepy. Sweaters don't ever get hungry."

I decided she seemed mostly normal for a five year old, and dropped her off at the front door for Alex to feed. From his look, Alex seemed to think I should come in and be fed as well. "I'll be there in a second. I just need to finish up."

"Clara, are you sure you're okay? You look a little...spaced out. Come in and sit for a minute."

I still felt like the magic might burst out of me at any second. Sitting was out of the question; conversing without exploding was hard enough. I just waved at them as I headed back toward the barn. I took the milk bucket with me, so it didn't get into trouble, and set it down outside Margot's stall. I looked down at Tom. The charms surrounding him were almost a swirl of magic, there were so many. I could study them and figure out the best way to break them without hurting Tom, but the power sang in my blood and I blasted the charms surrounding Tom into bits of free magic.

I saw Tom's form reappear, naked and streaked with what looked like glitter, on the floor of the stall. He moaned. Since he seemed way more fine than he deserved, I ignored him.

I couldn't just dump the milk bucket, or a new offshoot of the Enchanted Forest might spring up, there was so much magic in it. What do you do to get rid of a giant bucket of milk? The magic sang in my brain, and my thoughts struggled hazily around it. Make cheese? On the heels of that thought, I pushed the milk, forcing it to age and lose water, until it was a hard cheese about the size of my spread hand.

I staggered, exhaustion suddenly pricking my eyes again. The euphoria from the magic was beginning to wear off, and I could tell that it was about to catch up to me in a big way. I grabbed the cheese, used the last of my magic to simultaneously shrink it and coat it with copper, to keep anyone from thinking about eating it, and passed out cold on the floor of the stable.

Half asleep, I started to roll over, and pain shot through every nerve ending I had. I'm pretty sure I'd never felt this awful before in my entire life. I emitted a small, pained sound that I hadn't thought anything larger than a bunny could make, and slowly realized that I was on something pretty soft.

"Awake at last, I see. I thought you might sleep until doomsday." Karen's voice blasted through the room.

I made the pained sound again and wondered if I might not rather be dead.

"Here's your soup."

As the smell drifted into the room, all was forgiven, and I started feebly trying to get up. I eventually succeeded, and was rewarded with a mug of chicken broth.

"So, it looks like you might live after all. You've been the talk of the town. Asleep three days! We weren't sure you'd wake up." She frowned like it was my fault.

"I'm okay. Just exceeded my limits."

Satisfied that my health wasn't in question, Karen moved on to the next most important thing: keeping me up to date on gossip. "Tom's making up some lunatic story about defeating a sorcerer, rescuing Sofia, and saving you from the Forest as well. He's been telling everyone you had a minotaur with you, and he turned it into a cow, and carried you and Sofia out of the Forest. Funny thing is, it looks exactly like Alex's cow, which Ned Williams saw you taking into the Forest the other night. At least Tom backed down on that." Karen shoved another mug of soup at me without taking a breath, "He's also been sneezing glitter at an alarming rate, which doesn't do much for people's belief in his powers. Word around town is that you did the rescuing, not Tom, and people are sure that the reason you've been asleep for three days is because you did something interesting."

Karen, at last, paused, and looked at me expectantly. "Well? What happened? Am I going to have to pull it out of you?" She handed me a third mug of broth, just as I realized I'd finished the second one.

It's nearly impossible to keep a secret from Karen, and if she thinks you have, she'll spend the rest of her life trying to tear it out of you. Years of friendship had convinced me that the best solution was to tell her the first time she asked, so I wouldn't be pestered to death. "I found Sofia by following the connection from her hair ribbon, and ran into Tom on my way out of the Forest. I broke the charms on both of them, but it wiped me out."

Karen looked at me thoughtfully for a second. "Well, that's much more plausible than Tom's story, though it really should include something about that cow. Ned really deflated Tom with that cow bit. Watching him back down was the most satisfying thing I've seen in years."

I felt panic start to well up. "The cow has nothing to do with anything. Really, you need to leave her out of this. We can't have people looking at her too closely."

Karen sighed. "Do you think I'm blind? Of course I know you've got something going on with that cow. I kept hoping it was something to do with Alex, but you both seem hopeless about that. I've kept the rumors alive, just to help you out. I'm sure I'll figure out something about the cow."

As she was talking, it slowly dawned on me that, while I was in a bed, it wasn't mine. I was in a large four poster bed with a blue quilt, not my multicolored checkered quilt. I saw a farm field out the window. I must still be at Alex's.

As if reading my thoughts, Karen continued, "At least he's let you stay in his bed after finding you in the barn like that. Maybe he isn't as hopeless as I thought." She patted my foot and headed back into the kitchen. I fell asleep again mid-grumble.

Two days later, I was feeling almost functional again, and I decided to put myself to the test by taking my extra eggs to the inn. I'd managed to stagger home the day before while Alex was out in the field. Staying in his bed had been surprisingly awkward for both of us, so I headed home as soon as I could manage it. You'd think that two people who saw each other most every day wouldn't get tongue-tied just because they were in a different room in the house.

My success yesterday had made me cocky; I barely stumbled

across the threshold with my basket and collapsed into the nearest chair. "Well, look who it is. If it isn't the magician herself!" Dee announced loudly enough that Olivia and Liam, the only other inn patrons this morning, looked around at me. "Saved Sofia and the great and mighty Tom whatever-he's-called-now."

Dee looked at me expectantly. "Yeah, I guess I helped them out of the Forest." I wasn't used to people looking at me like I might be someone important, not just another town worker doing her job. It was both unnerving and satisfying, which is an uncomfortable combination. I squirmed in the chair.

"Well, we're all mighty glad you got that little girl out of there. And you have to expect her to be a little odd after all that." I wasn't sure exactly what sort of odd Sofia was these days, but I nodded like I hadn't been laid up in bed all week and had no idea how she was. Hopefully Dee was just being dramatic; I wasn't sure I'd be up to checking Sofia out magically anytime soon.

I decided my legs would hold me again, and took my basket back to the kitchen and to Karen, hoping to stave off more of this conversation until I had a better idea of what I wanted to say.

"I wondered if I'd be seeing those," Karen swept in from the yard and scooped my eggs into her egg basket. "I didn't think you'd be able to eat them all, even given how much you've been eating since you woke up." True, I had been ravenous for the past few days. Using magical power really took it out of the spellcaster, and using borrowed power was ten times worse than using your own. The fairy stories about magicians borrowing power to face a common evil and then dying in the aftermath made a lot more sense now.

"Oh, and I've been meaning to give you back this." Karen pulled a copper cylinder out of her pocket, about the size of my palm and two fingers deep. If you looked closely, you could see wrinkles on the surface, like those on the rind of a cheese. "You had it when we found you in the barn. Oh, and don't worry, I've told everyone what happened, so you shouldn't have to explain."

I took the cylinder and felt the power blaze up my arm as I put it in my pocket. Karen patted my arm and bustled out of the kitchen again, heading back to the wood she'd been chopping out back. For the first time since I woke up, I felt a trickle of magic return to me, and it finally hit me. I'd survived the Enchanted Forest. My small, incremental magic had prepared me for something that was flashy enough for people to notice. I patted my pocket, starting to wonder if other breakthroughs had also come about so slowly and painstakingly. Maybe I would do enough to be considered a power in the world after all. I'd have to think about it.

Thoughtfully, I walked back through the common room of the inn.

"Just one more thing," Dee called. I looked up at him. "Why'd you have to bring the cow? We know you're sweet on Alex, but if you needed a source of non-enchanted food you'd think a loaf of bread would be a lot less cumbersome than bringing a whole cow. Just bad planning, if you ask me."

"Oh, I, uh...well, I needed the cow to carry Sofia and Tom back. I couldn't have carried them both."

"Told ya, you idiot," Olivia said. "It makes sense to have something you don't have to carry, and can help with the other burdens. And now she knows Alex will let her borrow anything she wants." She winked at me. "Seems worth it, if you ask me. If I were thirty years younger, I'd be borrowing things from Alex myself. He has those nice shoulders." The conversation veered off into relative ages and shoulder widths, and I made my escape.

I wandered back to my cabin, thinking about the things I might yet do, and about how much I had changed, and was changing, and would change with the confidence and skills I had developed. I glanced over at the house where Sofia lived with her parents, and saw her solemnly serving tea to five sweaters, gently laid over chairs.

UNICORN HEART

by Pauline J. Alama

Unicorns are the companions and guardians of purity. But exactly what constitutes purity?

When she was young and foolish, Pauline J. Alama went to graduate school to study medieval English literature. (It seemed like a good idea at the time.) She escaped the ivory tower with a Ph.D., decreased employment prospects, and the draft of her first novel, The Eye of Night *(Bantam Spectra 2002). "Unicorn Heart" is her ninth story in Sword & Sorceress, and the third adventure of knight-errant Ursula and sorceress Isabeau, who met in "The Damsel in the Garden" (*Sword and Sorceress 28*). Her recent work includes an environmental fable published in* It's Come to Our Attention *(Third Flatiron Anthologies 2016) and a dragon story in* Mysterion *(Enigmatic Mirror Press 2016). She lives with her husband and son in northeastern New Jersey, which has far too many cars to be a good unicorn habitat.*

I listened, bemused, as the troubadour sang his songs in vain to my companion of the road, my best friend and onetime adversary, Isabeau of the Isle. I heard him lilt his love songs to her indifferent ear—not without jealousy, for I have a weakness for minstrels. A man with a well-tempered, resonant voice, whether honey-bright tenor or wine-rich bass, goes to my head faster than mead. At times only Isabeau's disapproving presence has kept me from making an utter fool of myself with a troubadour.

But not every minstrel finds a female knight-errant the stuff of poetry. And this one, it seemed, had a weakness for brunettes, or at least one brunette. In the best troubadour tradition, Ivor mapped every inch of Isabeau's beauty with poetic figures: hair like a clear night sky, eyes like wild asters, lips like rose-petals, skin like may-blossom, neck like a pillar of alabaster, shoulders like fair hillsides under snow...

Isabeau looked up from her embroidery and sighed with annoyance. "Descend any lower on my body, troubadour, and your head will be stuck in your lute's sound-hole."

"I mean no insolence, fair damsel," he said, his thumb still droning the bass string, his eyes still lingering on two well-proportioned hillsides of Isabeau's anatomy. "But your beauty so takes me prisoner that I must proclaim it."

Clearly his ardor needed a bucket of cold water. "Your labor is lost, Ivor," I called to the troubadour from the edge of our encampment, where I curried the horses. "I may have a unicorn painted on my shield, but it's Isabeau who has the very heart of a unicorn."

He faltered and fell silent, looking more troubled by what I said than I thought the comment warranted. "Whatever do you mean, Maid Ursula?"

Ah, me, I was never made for a *trouvère*. One poetic figure and it falls flat. "Only that she is complete and content in singleness, like an anchoress," I said. "Wooing her, you can only annoy her. And as the one honored to share her travels, I cannot let you trouble her." I let my hand stray to the hilt of my sword, though in truth I would scorn to strike an unarmed minstrel. Really, he had more to fear from Isabeau herself, but to the unschooled eye, her wand looks like a mere twig.

"My apologies, damsels," he said quickly. "I don't mean to besiege your fortress of innocence. But it startled me, Ursula, to hear you speak of the unicorn, because just yesterday I heard news of a unicorn in Castirroche."

Isabeau dropped her needle in astonishment. "Really?"

"Unicorns are *real*?" I said. I'd traveled to the Isle of Sorcery, fought a dragon, and ridden away with a sorceress for a companion, but I thought *some* stories were just stories, and I'd been sure unicorns belonged in that category. Whoever heard of a horse that cared if a rider were maiden or married, so long as the hand on the rein was gentle and the manger was full?

"Of course they're real," Isabeau said. "Hildegarde, Aristotle, and Pliny wrote of them, and perhaps the Psalms as well, though the translation is uncertain."

Isabeau can read. It is one of her great strengths, and I sometimes think one of her weaknesses, too. Who was this Pliny that she should take his word for it?

"Who told you there was a unicorn at Castirroche?" I asked Ivor.

"A young lord who fled from it," said the minstrel. "I saw the wound it left on him. He could hardly stay mounted."

Isabeau made a little noise of scorn in her throat. "What was this lord doing to enrage the unicorn?"

"Nothing! Merely trying to court Lady Blanchefleur, daughter of the Count of Castirroche. Neither the suitors approved by her father nor the Count's men nor even her own brothers can approach her. Fatigued after an illness, she retreated to a lonely cottage in the heath beyond Castirroche, and has not been seen since. Whenever a man seeks the cottage, the unicorn attacks with horn and hooves. None can go near the beast. It outruns arrows and outfights spearmen."

"If men are trying to spear the unicorn, small wonder it should fight."

"The beast attacked first, I tell you! It may look fine and courtly on Maid Ursula's shield, but in the light of day on solid ground, it's as ruthless as a leopard."

"Did you see it yourself, Ivor?" I asked.

"No," the minstrel admitted, "but I saw the wound."

I rolled my eyes. Likely the young lord hurt himself in some drunken escapade and invented an outlandish creature to excuse himself.

"Lord Reginald of Surhonnes, the wounded knight, is organizing a hunt for the unicorn, offering rich rewards to the man who brings back its head and hooves. He asked me to spread the word, so all the canniest huntsmen in Logres will join him."

"What folly!" Isabeau said brusquely.

Ivor goggled at her; the poor boy was not used to her abrupt manner of speaking her mind. "Beg pardon?"

"All learned authorities agree that only a maiden can capture a unicorn. Even you admit that men who come near it cannot withstand it. But if a pure young maiden waits near the meadow where it grazes, the unicorn will be drawn to her and lay its head in her lap, meek as a lamb."

I smirked. How could learned authorities believe such an outrageous tale?

"You may laugh, Ursula, but it's well attested to."

Ivor looked from Isabeau to me, light dawning in his face. "You two could do it. You could rid Castirroche of the unicorn and rescue the maiden who lies beyond it, cut off from her family and friends. You could earn thanks and gold from the lord and the count, and be remembered in song—"

"For killing a horse?" I snorted. "What a waste of a spirited animal! What if someone were to tame your unicorn and lead it back in a halter?"

Ivor stared at me stupidly. "In a *halter?*"

"Of course," I said. "It's what one puts on a horse, you know. Or do they do things differently in Castirroche?"

"Maid Ursula," said Ivor sternly, "a unicorn is not exactly a horse, you know."

And my own comrade Isabeau took his side: "Some authors describe it as more like a goat or stag."

"No matter," I said. "We had goats on my father's estate, and I am well at ease with them, too—as much at ease as you can be with the sly creatures."

Ivor clearly did not believe me. "If you come with me to Surhonnes and join the lord's hunting party, you will see for yourself what sort of beast you face."

"No," I said, "I will not join this party. I would rather go to Castirroche and see this prodigy for myself without a crowd of meddling huntsmen. Then we will see who knows how to handle a unicorn."

To my surprise, Isabeau seemed gloomy and discontented when I turned our horses' heads toward Castirroche. "We should be looking for a place to spend the winter," she said.

"Maybe we can spend it in Castirroche, if all goes well there," I said.

She rode moodily for another long stretch of the way before saying, "Ursula, you wouldn't kill the unicorn, would you?"

"What, kill my own heraldic beast? Perish the thought!" I chuckled. "I'd no more kill a unicorn than cut off my own shield-arm."

"What will you do, then?" she said. "It won't come tamely to your hand."

"Isabeau, my friend, I'll bet my saddle there is no unicorn at Castirroche," I said. "I know you trust Pliny, and Hildegarde, and some other dusty old authority."

"Don't forget the Psalms," said Isabeau.

"I won't," I assured her, though all I could tell you of the Psalms was that in the church back home in Révie, the young parson sang them with ravishing sweetness. "But it's not the Psalms who told us about the unicorn, it's not the Psalms who got hurt in the unmentionable, and it's not the Psalms organizing a foolish hunting party of blundering boys to avenge his injury. Most likely we'll find a hot-headed stallion that escaped a vicious rider, or a grand herd of wild horses. Lord Reginald probably got kicked trying to show a steed who's master, and the woman he meant to court took off with another man, so he made up the story of a unicorn to cover his failure."

"Then why are we going to Castirroche?"

"Any horse so fiery sets my fingers itching on the reins," I confessed. "I want to see if I can tame him."

"We don't need *another* impossible horse," Isabeau pointed out.

She was right: neither of our horses were the sort of mild-tempered palfrey that would have suited her, and I'd had to sell a third one that I won in a tournament, having no use for another charger.

"I'll sell him after I tame him," I promised.

"Ha. It was all I could do to persuade you to part with Boreas—and he *bit*."

"Aren't you curious, at least, to see if this wild tale of a rampaging unicorn is true?"

"Well..."

"Wouldn't it be thrilling to discover if Pliny and Whatsisname are right?"

"NO."

"What's wrong, Isabeau?"

"All bestiaries say the unicorn is fierce as any lion, except to a pure and chaste virgin."

"Yes, I heard. The unicorn stabs elephants with his horn, savages hunting hounds, and for all I know spears dragons, but when he sees a maiden, he rests his silly head in her lap, which would make him the only hooved beast God ever made to act like a lapdog. Here we are, Isabeau: two maidens. If the unicorn does what your authors promise, he should be as submissive to us as the tamest palfrey that ever carried a five-year-old child."

"Or he might run me through the heart, if he doesn't find me pure enough," Isabeau said.

"Don't be ridiculous," I told her. "You never even *look* at a man in a fleshly way. "

"Not for my own pleasure. But when I served Lady Ettarre, I inflamed men's passions to lure them to her trap. A virgin I may be," Isabeau said, "but pure? Hardly."

For a time, I was silent, not knowing what to say. Finally I said, "Why were you so anxious to know I wouldn't kill the unicorn, if you fear it?"

"It's a holy animal," she said. "The unicorn betokens the Incarnation of Jesus Christ in the womb of the Blessed Virgin. Its single horn reflects the singleness of truth and integrity, against the duplicity of deceit. When the unicorn dips his horn in any water, however it has been tainted, the water will be pure thereafter. All the other beasts of the field love the unicorn, for it makes wholesome water flow. Even if its beauty is not for me to behold, I will never consent to its killing."

"Listen to yourself, Isabeau," I said. "What purer heart could a unicorn demand?"

At Castirroche I bought provisions and listened to gossip about the unicorn: third-hand accounts of men gored by a single horn, huntsmen who claimed to have glimpsed the beast, rough travelers who bought spears and arrows and asked whether the lord could be trusted to pay what he promised. I filled my saddlebags with the sweetest late-autumn apples and kept my counsel to myself.

A friar preached in the marketplace, and I stopped to listen. Sure, I skip Mass now and then, but these Little Brothers of Saint Francis, who preached to birds and even, some say, to a wolf, are men of God that I can understand. This friar seemed agitated, as if he needed to herd us all into some ark before the storm broke: "So corrupt have we become, that when our land is visited by a sign and a revelation, a unicorn wielding its horn in defense of innocence, all we can speak of is which man will prove his pride and mastery over it, and which man will gain gold by selling its horn and hooves."

That sermon nipped me in a tender spot. I edged away from the crowd and found my way to the fountain where Isabeau waited to meet me. "Isabeau, I've been listening to the talk in town. Maybe I've been wrong. Maybe this unicorn isn't just a drunkard's tale. And if it's real, then who knows what its notion of purity may be? Something only saints can attain? You were right: we shouldn't trespass on its domain."

But she gripped my arm hard, pulled me toward her, and whispered in my ear, "No, Ursula. I was wrong. I've been listening too." She pointed out a party of hunters watering their horses. Among them, a pale and skittish young girl, maybe eleven or twelve years old, clung to a gray pony as if it were her lifeline in a flood. "That girl is the *bait*. Just as I was the bait in Lady Ettarre's trap. Those men will use her innocence to lure the unicorn into sight, to pacify it so it will not fight back. When it lays its head in her lap, they'll shoot it full of arrows or stab it with their spears."

"Sweet holy saints!" I said. "That little girl will be lucky not to be killed in the melee."

"And if she is so *lucky*," Isabeau's voice was heavy with irony, "imagine that child going through life with the memory of wild innocence bleeding to death in her lap."

"Cruel," I said. "What should we do? One of those men is probably her father. If we take her from him, the law will come after us—and she herself isn't likely to count it a favor, being snatched away by two strangers."

"We can stop this hunt if we rescue the unicorn," Isabeau said. "Draw it away from the hunters to a safe place. If I'm not innocent enough to attract it, then you must be."

"I don't know about that," I said. " A handsome man, or a homely one who sings well enough, turns my blood to flame. I was even jealous when silly Ivor preferred you to me, and I've cherished most unchurchly thoughts about a young priest."

"All that hot blood must be Nature's warmth, I suppose," Isabeau said. "I wouldn't know: Nature was twisted in me before I was old enough to recognize it. You hear a man's voice and look for love; as Lady Ettarre's apprentice, I looked for victims, and used Nature's charms to draw men into a trap. You could never deceive so."

"No one I cared about ever asked me to do it," I said. "Well. Neither of us is perfect, but we'll have to do, won't we? Let's go see this unicorn for ourselves—if there really is one."

We stole out of town quietly on foot. I left our horses stabled in town, partly so the avid parties of unicorn-hunters would not notice we'd gone on ahead of them, and partly to avoid conflict between one stallion and another. Cloudmane, the horse I'd ridden from home, was a steady enough character, but Fury, the charger I'd won in a tournament, was as proud and irritable as his name. If our unicorn proved a mere horse—or acted like one—I didn't want Fury fighting to prove himself master. Besides, I wouldn't put it past some of those thick-headed unicorn hunters to shoot my horse by accident.

With no saddlebags, I carried only what I thought needful for the journey.

"You're traveling well armed," Isabeau observed uneasily as we threaded through a copse of scrubby pines in the heath.

"I need the bow in case our 'unicorn' proves to be a rutting stag. They can be quite as dangerous as bears."

"What about the sword?" she said.

"I wouldn't entrust my sword to the keeping of anyone in Castirroche," I said. "Don't worry: I have no desire to harm a unicorn. Imagine if I could tame one! Instead of simply the Maiden of Révie, I could be known as the Knight of the Unicorn. Surely the noble beast would help us defend the innocent—"

"Shh!" hissed Isabeau. "What's that ahead beyond the yew trees?"

There was something moving—something large. It might have been a horse or deer, or perhaps some unicorn-hunter who'd lost track of his comrades. In any case, I didn't want to startle it. I squeezed Isabeau's hand to let her know I'd understood, then drew my first-choice weapon for this hunt: an apple.

I advanced slowly and softly, the apple held out before me, my face turned to one side so I would not seem to threaten the beast with a head-on stare. Through the corners of my half-closed eyes, I scanned the path before me. Isabeau dropped some paces behind, and I ventured forward, ready to shield her in case the creature proved rougher than the legends promised.

It was upon me before I could think, and then above me: a pearl-white arc of motion that sailed over my head and landed in front of Isabeau, its bright horn towering over her like a church spire.

It was not exactly a horse, but it was the power and perfectly timed motion of the horse. It was not a goat, either, but it might have been the leap of the goat. Certainly it was not a stag—emphatically not a stag, for it was manifestly a *she*—but she might have been the stag's swiftness. And her horn was not exactly a horn; it seemed to be made of light, or of thought, or of *direction*. It is nothing to say the unicorn was beautiful; flowers are beautiful, and horses are beautiful, but this creature was more beautiful than anything you could *see*. It was beautiful as a *song* is beautiful. My heart ached in my chest, and I felt certain, as I always do around heart-melting troubadours, that I was likely to do something stupid.

Isabeau dropped to her knees before the unicorn. It lowered its head toward her, which jolted me out of my fog of infatuation. I hastened toward her through the underbrush, a hand on my sword-hilt, because however beautiful or holy the unicorn might be, I would not allow this poem in flesh to harm my best friend. But I could not make headway: vines snared my legs like grasping fingers. Helplessly, I watched Isabeau spread her arms in welcome, baring her heart to the unicorn's horn.

"Isabeau!" I cried.

The light of the unicorn's horn seemed to pierce Isabeau's heart and flow all through her body till it streamed out of every finger and blossomed from the crown of her head. Then the unicorn sprang, quick as a thought, and stood suddenly before me. Isabeau followed close behind, moving with a lightness I had never seen in her before, as if some burden had been taken from her.

Eyes half averted, I held out the apple to the unicorn, who accepted it not as a horse accepts a treat, but as a lord accepts homage. Her breath smelled like clover-blossom, which would be unsurprising in a horselike creature were it not late autumn, past hay-making. Her breath brought back the rich life of summer.

I dared at last to look full-on at the unicorn's face, into a great dark eye like a lake under starlight. I felt I was being searched, searched deeply, yet not exactly judged. At length the unicorn bowed her head and laid her horn on my shoulder, like the sword that dubs a knight. *Knight of the Unicorn.*

"Isabeau is right," I told the unicorn. "You are nothing I could tame, nothing I could ride."

But then the unicorn knelt gracefully down. I had only ever seen one horse do that trick, a great lady's horse that had been trained to give her an easy mount. The invitation—perhaps the command—was unmistakable. I lifted Isabeau onto the unicorn's back and climbed on behind. Then the unicorn leapt as lightly as if the two of us and my armor were no burden at all. We flew past woods and meadows, farther and farther from town.

We landed in a circle of stones on a hill where a simple

cottage stood, a hut really, the sort of place where shepherds might take shelter from thunderstorms when they ventured far afield with their flocks in summer.

A damsel ventured out and laid her hand with fond reverence on the unicorn's mane. Her blue dress was unadorned, yet made of such rich cloth that she was obviously out of place in the shepherd's hut. A white mantle covered most of her hair, but the few wisps that showed around the edges were golden, and her face was as perfect as Isabeau's.

"God be with you. Are you the companions I was promised?" she said.

"Yes," Isabeau said.

"I don't know who made you what promises," I said, "but the unicorn brought us. I am Ursula, the Maiden of Révie, renowned for feats of arms. This is Isabeau of the Isle, a learned enchantress. Are you Blanchefleur, the lost daughter of the Count of Castirroche?"

"Not lost," she said. "Escaped. I feel called to join the Sisters of the Poor in San Damiano, but my father would not hear of it. He insisted I marry a rich lord to gain him allies at court. He set me out like a prize filly to let suitors bargain for me. So I ran away to this shepherd's hut and prayed to Saint Ursula of the Eleven Thousand Virgins to help me escape. In a dream, the saint promised me defense from unwanted suitors and companions for my journey. When I awoke, the unicorn stood over me. She has defended me ever since, running the men off when she could, and wounding the ones who would not cease harassing me."

"With such a defender, do you even need us?" I asked.

"The unicorn cannot guard me in the towns. It belongs with the wild things and the heath," Blanchefleur said. "I am safe here from men, but I've run through my supply of food, and I will need to move before winter closes in. Can you give me safe conduct to San Damiano?"

"Ursula is a mighty protector of travelers," Isabeau said, "and I have some crafts to put pursuers off your trail."

"First, you and I should change clothes," I said. "No one will bother you in a mail-coat and visor—and no one in town will know my face."

Blanchefleur clasped our hands. "Will you be my companions, then—now and always? Will you stay with me, and join the Sisters together?"

I shook my head. "As for me, I'm cut of no such saintly cloth. Knight-errantry is the life for me." But I looked anxiously at Isabeau. Surely, now, she had found a companion who might suit her better than I did.

Isabeau looked long and hard at Blanchefleur. Finally she said, "The unicorn is at home in the wastes and wild places, and so am I. Surely God is not only found within walls. But if you are called to the convent, we will help you follow your calling."

We stole back into Castirroche to reclaim our stabled horses. Then we set off for San Damiano, three maidens together, conscious from time to time of an unseasonable scent of clover, a gleam of pearly light, and the pressure of a starlit dark eye upon us, ever watching, searching deeply, but not judging.

THE FOUNTAINS OF KARONA

by Julia H. West

Sarista was a washer woman, so she was familiar with the fountains of Wismund. She knew they all had words carved on them 400 years ago, one line on each of the city's fountains. But she never gave them much thought until an invading army approached, and the fountains became a puzzle she needed to solve immediately.

When I request author bios, I tell them that if it is not turned in by the deadline I will make something up. Occasionally an author takes that as a challenge. I did not make this one up; this is what Julia sent me. Last year.

Julia H. West lives in an idea-rich environment consisting of thousands of books, too many cats, a plethora of penguins (mostly plushies), and three other members of her family who also write science fiction and fantasy.

Most of the short stories Julia has had published in various magazines and anthologies are available as eBooks from Callihoo Publishing (http://callihoo.com). Her website is http://juliahwest.com.

All the washer women at Karona Square's fountain looked up as a man, haggard and bloody, staggered up the steps that led into Wismund city from the eastern gate. He wore torn trews and a puffy-sleeved tunic—from Salbe village, perhaps, or maybe Dettin, farther down the mountain.

Sarista slapped her armload of wet clothing back into its basket and rushed to catch the man before he could collapse to the cobbles. "Warn the Countess," the man gasped as Sarista helped him to lean against the fountain's stone curb. "An army, hundreds of soldiers, maybe even thousands."

"Take a moment," Sarista said. She pulled her headscarf off, dipped it into the water, and dabbed gently at dried blood on the man's forehead and left cheek. "It won't do to have you collapse on Her Excellency's fine tile floor."

Sarista's friends—stout Romene, Olie, and young Alizisa, left their laundry and gathered around the man. "Here, drink this," said Alizisa, pressing a cup to his lips.

"You look like death itself," said Romene. She took bread—her midday, no doubt—from her pocket. "Eat this, but not too quickly."

"The Countess—" the man said, but the women cut him off.

"The Countess has waited what—two days?—while you climbed the mountain. She can wait a few more moments while we help you get presentable." Sarista continued laving the man's face as her friends fed him bites of bread between sips of water.

"Must warn the Countess," the man muttered.

Sarista took a horn comb from her skirt pocket and combed the man's hair. "Better now? Feel like you can walk again?"

As Olie washed bloodstains from the man's sleeves, and mud from his knees, he pushed himself up to a sitting position. At that moment the rising sun limned the words carved deep into the back wall of the fountain, over his head. *The Folk Of Wismund Will Be Free.*

Sarista gasped, and the other women looked up to see what she saw. At their sudden intake of breath, the man, too, turned to gape at the words glowing in the stone.

"We wash here every day," said Olie, "and it's never done this before."

"A sign!" Romene whispered. "From Karona herself!"

The man pushed himself to his feet. "A sign that I must take my message quickly to the Countess."

"Do you know the city?" Sarista asked. When the man shook his head, she said, "I'll take you to the palace, then. I know the quickest route." She turned to her friends. "Can one of you—"

"I'll take your laundry home with mine," Romene volunteered quickly. "I'm off now, to warn the neighbors."

"As am I," Olie and Alizisa echoed.

"Come, then," said Sarista. She rinsed her headscarf in the fountain, wrung it out, put it back wet over her hair, then set off up the steep road that led straight to the palace built into the mountain's peak, in the center of the city. Exhausted as he was—and not used to the thin air at the mountain's top—the man struggled to keep up with Sarista.

Wismund's circle road spiraled up the mountainside gradually, cobbled for the convenience of cart and burden beast. But the road Sarista took led more-or-less straight up, and was often little more than a stairway, fit only for foot traffic. Sarista stopped often to let the messenger catch his breath, standing in doorways of shops or homes to let others pass.

The mountainside had been hewn away in a great flat terrace just below the palace, and another of the city's fountains, cut straight into the stone, stood there. The messenger gasped in relief when he saw flat ground and water. Sarista led him into Lord's Square, where he joined the line of women filling jugs. When he reached the fountain's spout, he filled his cupped hands with water to drink and splash on his face.

Like the fountain in Karona Square, this one had a flat backing wall from which water spouted, and a basin beneath—although this fountain was much larger, and more ornate. The bas-relief carving above the fountain's basin was of an armored figure—some great lord, perhaps, in ages long past.

As the messenger drank, Sarista read the words above the statue. *We Fight Against All Foreign Lords.* That may have been true when this fountain was built, back in Countess Karona's time, but the people of Wismund had been peaceful for generations now. Yet an army climbed the mountain toward the city. Why?

Sarista led the messenger up the last steep road to the Commoner's Gate of the palace, and introduced him to the guard there. "Thank you," the messenger said to Sarista as the guard beckoned him in. "Your life and those of all your friends may hang on the news I bring to the Countess."

The descent from the palace was quick, but harder on Sarista's calves and knees. All those stairs. People in the street murmured, "An army coming to Wismund?" Some spoke with fear, while others scoffed. "Why would the plainsfolk come to Wismund?

There's nothing here for them. They can't even breathe the air!"

Sarista stopped at Romene's house to retrieve her laundry. In Wismund, everything was up and down. The buildings in the part of the city where Sarista and her friends lived were three to five stories tall, often built into the mountainside. Each housed hundreds of people. When most of those people were gathered in the courtyard between buildings, talking so as to be heard above their neighbors, it was deafening.

"Here's Sarista," called Romene.

"What did the messenger say?" called someone from the crowd.

"Did you see the Countess?" Others shouted questions until she could distinguish nothing in the babble.

Sarista flung her hands up to get everyone's attention, and as they quieted called, "I dropped the messenger off at the Commoner's Gate. I did not see the Countess. I know no more now than we did at dawn."

"Why invade Wismund? We have nothing those plainsfolk would want. We have *never* had anything." Romene's voice quavered.

"That is for the Countess to discover, not for the likes of us," said Sarista.

"The Countess is ten years old," grumbled Olie, and there was uneasy laughter from the crowd.

"Her advisors, then," someone called.

"But even they know little of war. Does anyone in the city know how to do more than fist fight?" said Romene.

"The constables." Alizisa stood on the edge of the crowd balancing her basket of wet laundry on her hip.

Romene frowned. "And the constables will fight hundreds or thousands of plainsfolk soldiers? There must be...oh, fifty constables. There are hunters, with bows and spears, but they're not soldiers. Even the guards at the gates have never fought."

"Have you forgotten so soon?" Sarista asked her friends. She turned to the crowd of Romene's neighbors. "Did Romene tell you? Karona gave us a sign! She knew this day would come."

"We've heard those stories. Everyone Lairin taught heard

them." Lairin was the woman—elderly when Sarista was young, ancient now—who taught letters to the children of the poor folk of Wismund.

"But what does the sign mean? How can it help us now that an army marches up the mountain?" came a voice from the crowd.

Sarista took a deep breath to answer, and realized she didn't know what the sign meant. "We all know the saying, 'The Folk of Wismund Will Be Free.' But that—" she cut herself off, suddenly remembering the inscription on the fountain in Lord's Square. She continued, "But that isn't the only saying Karona left us. Every fountain in Wismund has Karona's words carved into it."

"What does that matter?" scoffed someone. "An army's coming up the mountain, and Karona died 400 years ago. She can't help us now."

Out in the street, a young man in the Countess's golden livery ran up and stopped where everyone in the courtyard could see him. They quieted and turned toward him. "Hear the words of the Countess," he cried formally. "Every family must prepare to go to the caves. Inform the constables of any infirm who are unable to help themselves." As gasps and whispers started up again, he ran off down the road to repeat his message.

The crowd broke up quickly, and soon Sarista and her friends stood together in the empty courtyard. "Come get your laundry," said Romene. "If there's a city tomorrow, your customers will want it. If there isn't..." She shrugged, and started toward the staircase leading up to her third-floor rooms.

Sarista followed, her unease about the possibility of an invading army battling with the certainty that the sign from Countess Karona was important.

In Romene's crowded room, drying racks competed for space with benches, a table, a single large bed, and children's toys. Sarista's laundry basket had been set on the bed.

Romene was directing her eight and ten-year-old sons, "That bag. Put clothing for everyone in it. Yes, for the baby too. Don't forget Papa's shirts."

Sarista glanced into her basket, assured her washboard, laundry paddle, and soap were there, then told Romene, "If you wait until Ulrid and Gairid get home with the donkey, we can carry all your baggage as well as ours."

"Your poor donkey! Can he bear that much?"

"Berhar carries stone or enormous baskets of goods up and down the mountain every day. Even four families' baggage won't tax him."

Romene pushed straggling hair back under her headscarf. "Thank you, then. You'd best hurry home and pack for your family."

As she settled her basket on her hip, Sarista said, "I'll tell Alizisa and Olie on the way." She paused, then said tentatively, "What do you think of Karona's sign?"

Romene shook her head. "Maybe the Countess knows what it means. I certainly don't."

The streets between Romene's building and Sarista's were full of hurrying people carrying bundles and crying children. Panic was thick in the air, with whispers of, "Thousands of men, mercenaries from overseas, ships full of soldiers coming up the Alten river." *What did Karona leave in place for this?* Sarista thought. *She was a wise woman, some say a sorceress. Does the Countess know? What should we, the people of Wismund, know—but have forgotten?*

The founding of Wismund County was a story everyone knew. Karona and her brother Vinfric had been given Elteden mountain and the plains at its feet as their inheritance, to be split between them. Vinfric had won the toss for first choice of land, and of course chose the plain, with its lush farm land and broad river. He told Karona he would grant her a portion of plains land if she and her people tithed to him. She had refused his magnanimous offer, choosing the mountain for her inheritance, and declaring the line carved into the back wall of the fountain: *The Folk Of Wismund Will Be Free.* She had taken the tiny village at the top of the mountain to be her home, and built it up into the fine city it was today.

If the tales were to be believed, Vinfric and Karona had never been on the best of terms, so it was natural that the folks from Vinfric's plains county of Gerbig and Karona's mountain county of Wismund should squabble from time to time. But soldiers coming up the mountain? What were the plainsfolk thinking?

When Sarista got home, trudged up three flights of stairs to her family's room, and dropped her basket near the drying racks before the fire, her nine-year-old daughter Jordith put down the book she was reading and jumped up. "Mama, are bad men coming?"

"I don't know, love," Sarista said. "I've heard stories, but have no real news."

"Will we run? Will we hide? I was studying, and Manden yelled it up from the street...and it scared me." She ran to Sarista and flung her arms around her mother, burying her head in her mother's chest. "I'm scared, Mama."

"The Countess will take care of us," Sarista comforted her. "Help me pack our things. We're going to the safe cave."

"Then we *are* going to hide."

"The Countess sent a messenger telling us to." Sarista stood and, hands on hips, surveyed her home. She could pack only what they could carry—food, blankets, clothing. Perhaps sewing supplies, the little kettle, a lamp and oil. The caves were dark and cold, though all the safe caves were dry.

Sarista was rather dismayed at the size of the two bundles she and Jordith assembled. Maybe four families' baggage *would* be too much for poor Berhar to carry.

"Bring that book and your copy book," Sarista told her daughter. "Lairin would never forgive us if we let one of her precious books get lost, and you can study when we get to the cave."

"Oh, Mama."

Lairin should know about Countess Karona's promise to her people, if anyone did. In the chaos out in the streets, could Sarista find the teacher?

Sarista and Jordith's two bundles were almost more than they could carry down the stairs. In the courtyard behind the building, as far from the privy as possible, Romene and her boys sat enjoying the summer sunshine. Their bundles were even larger than Sarista's. Sarista wondered how her friend had got them, and the baby, through the streets.

Sarista greeted her friend, then told her daughter to stay here with Romene while she went to fetch Alizisa and Olie.

Jordith wrinkled her nose, but settled down in the sunshine and was playing cat's cradle with the boys when Sarista left.

First Sarista helped Olie and her elderly mother Marcene, then Alizisa and her baby, to carry their belongings to the courtyard behind her building. She wished Ulrid and Gairid would hurry home with the donkey. Had the Countess's messenger not made it to the caves where the donkey was hauling limestone blocks?

While Jordith and the boys chased each other around the courtyard shrieking, the women sat on their bundles waiting for Ulrid and Gairid to arrive. Sarista brought up Karona's promise again. "You all saw it—except, of course, Marcene," she said, nodding at Olie's mother. "That line, the promise, over Karona's head lit up. We all know that's never happened before, even though the sun rises and lights those words every morning. Do you think Lairin would know what it meant?"

"She might," said Romene, frowning. "But she's teaching on the north side of the city today, so they'll send her to the Safe Cave there, not ours to the south."

"What do you think the lines on the fountains mean? Are there sayings on all the fountains? I read the one in Lord's Square while I was up there with the messenger, and it sounds like fighting, not hiding in caves." She recited the line to her friends.

Alizisa shook her head, and her baby grabbed at tendrils of hair escaping her headscarf. "Countess Karona had fighters, but we don't."

"When I was young, I'd go to Square of Bones just to stare up at the skeleton, with its raised sword, carved above that fountain." Sarisa closed her eyes and recited, "'We Pledge Our Very Souls and Bones'—that's what it says over the skeleton."

"I grew up on the west side," said Olie, "where the limestone mines are. Deep Square has a fountain, too, with a carving of a cave over the basin. 'Safe Guarded In The Caves So Deep' is what it says."

"So we know four of the lines. There are eight fountains. What do the other four say?" Sarista beckoned Jordith over, and the girl reluctantly left her game and approached the women. "Jordith, get your copy book and write these lines down."

Obediently, the girl squatted in the dirt and carefully wrote the lines as the women repeated them—Karona Square, Lord's Square, Square of Bones, and Deep Square.

"I've seen the fountain at Freedom Square," said Alizisa. "It's near the caves where Kaydn works." She tilted her head back, pursed her lips, then recited, "'From Death Wismunders Shall Be Freed.'"

Romene sat bouncing her baby on her shoulder, her brow wrinkled in thought. "I've been to Stone Square, south of Deep Square, but the line on the fountain...I can't remember it."

"I know that one," said Olie's mother in a slow, quavering voice. "When Olie was a child, I'd take her to play while I washed there. It's 'Protected By The Mountain's Stones.' The mountainside is all craggy there, you see, and there are more caves than anyone knows."

She would have said more, but Sarista looked up and saw her husband and son, leading Berhar the donkey, struggling to escape the flow of people sweeping toward the nearest safe cave. Ulrid's craggy brows drew together when he saw the women waiting in the courtyard. "You've heard?"

"First of anyone in the city," said Sarista. When his eyebrows raised in surprise, she quickly told the story of the messenger staggering into Karona Square. "Can Berhar carry all our bundles?"

Ulrid gazed solemnly at four families' possessions tied up in blankets, shaking his head. "It will take some doing," he said finally, as the women's eyes opened wide in dismay. "But it may be possible. Ho, Gairid, tie all this onto the donkey, will you?" The women stood up, and Sarista's sixteen-year-old son began expertly tying bundles onto the donkey.

"You tease," said Sarista, hugging her husband. "Worrying us like that."

"Jordith, my pet, what is it you have there?" Ulrid asked the girl.

"It's important," said Jordith. "Mama and her friends remember Countess Karona's magic words, and I write them down."

"Magic words?" Ulrid eyed Sarista sidelong. "Who said they were magic?"

"They must be, if they'll save our city from bad men."

Sarista caught her breath. That was what she was missing. That was what Countess Karona's message on the fountain meant. "It's a spell," she said. "The lines above the fountains are all part of a spell."

Romene murmured something under her breath, but Olie's mother nodded emphatically. "Countess Karona was a great sorceress."

"We have most of them." Jordith showed her father the copy book. "Karona Square, Lord's Square, Square of Bones, Deep Square, Freedom Square, and Stone Square. Two more, since Mama says there are eight fountains."

"I know one," Ulrid said. "I water the donkey at the Horse Square fountain every time I use the Horse Gate. I think Berhar sees himself as the bold stallion carved into the fountain's wall. Let's see if I remember it right. 'Come Faithful Hound and Steadfast Horse.' No, that's not right. The last word is 'steed,' not 'horse.' Steed is another word for horse," he explained to Jordith.

Gairid was having trouble tying all the knobby bundles onto the donkey. "Everything slips around," he complained. "If we don't want things falling out onto the street, we'll need to redo the bundles."

They set to work re-packing the bundles, and to keep Jordith occupied, Sarista said, "Tell me the story of Karona's fountains."

She was sure Jordith knew this one—it was one of Lairin's oft-repeated tales. "The mountain's full of caves, and water seeps down through the stone so none stays in Wismund. Karona built fountains all around the city, and pipes carry the water, and it's free for everyone." She paused for a moment, then said, "It's also why the safe caves and mortuary caves are dry. Do you think she used magic to make the fountains?"

"It's possible, child," said her father, tying the last knot to the huge misshapen mass that was all their bundles. Poor Berhar had nearly disappeared beneath everything he was carrying.

"We'd best go slow, now," Ulrid said, taking up the donkey's lead rope. "Walk around Berhar so nothing falls off—or no one snatches things as they go by."

The party joined the exodus on the circle road, leading around the mountain to the mouth of the nearest safe cave. Sarista wondered if Countess Karona had arranged for the safe caves as part of her defense of the city.

They had a hard time keeping together. People tried to push past in their rush to get away from the threat of an army invading Wismund. Ulrid helped Marcene to walk the distance, and all the women took turns carrying the babies. But at last they reached the cave. Five harried-looking constables stood in front of the stout door blocking its mouth. "No, don't come here," one called whenever anyone approached. "Part of the roof collapsed. There's another cave not far away, just follow the road."

It was hard not to let the panic of people all around her infect her, but Sarista puzzled over the lines on the fountains as she walked. Was it a spell? Could someone who wasn't a sorceress use a spell? Karona must have thought so, or why else would she have had those lines carved above the fountains?

The safe cave, when they reached it, was even more chaotic than the streets. Barking dogs, screaming babies, the odors of urine and alcohol and fried goat meat. Ulrid intimidated a constable into finding the four families a place next to a wall, and letting them keep the donkey with them.

"He'll poop on the ground," one of Romene's boys said with satisfaction.

"Won't be any worse than what's already in here," said Jordith.

Marcene did not like the cave. "We should go home," she stated, covering her ears with her hands.

"There's an army coming!" protested Olie.

"I'll take my chances."

They sat down with their bundles piled in their midst where they could watch them. To take everyone's minds off the noise and smells, Sarista brought up the passages written above the fountains once more. "Don't you remember what Lairin told us, when we were learning our letters? Karona promised us no enemy would ever take this city. Magic, a spell. Part of the Pledge we all swear to."

"That's just a tale. Do you really think Karona had magic?" Alizisa was younger than the rest. Had she not heard the same stories?

"I don't know. How did Karona build this city, at the top of a mountain, where only a tiny village was before? How did she build the fountains we use every day, fountains that never freeze over, even in the dead of winter?"

"She hired plainsfolk to come up and build everything," Romene guessed. "You think she just said a few words and the city appeared? No, she hired stonemasons, and architects, and...oh, everyone else who builds a city."

"Then what about the words on the fountains?" Sarista asked. "Don't they sound like a spell to you? Don't you remember Karona's promise lighting up this morning?"

As they talked, other women Sarista knew gathered around. They were excited when she explained the spell—or possible spell—to them. "We remember Lairin's stories," said a skinny dark-haired washer woman. "We want to help, if there's anything we can do."

"Do any of you know the words on the fountain at Square of Sleep?" Sarista asked. "That's the only line we're missing."

"I do know that one!" said the dark-haired woman. "Let me see. 'Peaceful Shall Wismunders Sleep.' No, that's not quite right. 'In Peacefulness Wismunders Sleep?' That's not it either."

Another of the women recited, "'How Peacefully Wismunders Sleep.' I see it every morning, and wish *I* was the one sleeping peacefully!"

"Well, it won't be in *this* cave that we'll sleep peaceful," said

Marcene. "There's enough noise to wake Countess Karona herself!"

Jordith wrote the last inscription in her copy book, and Sarista passed it around so everyone could see the lines.

The Folk Of Wismund Shall Be Free
We Fight Against All Foreign Lords
We Pledge Our Very Souls And Bones
Safe Guarded In The Caves So Deep
From Death Wismunders Shall Be Freed
Protected By The Mountain's Stones
Come Faithful Hound And Steadfast Steed
How Peacefully Wismunders Sleep

"All the messages sound alike," said Sarista. That was not quite what she meant, but she wasn't sure how to describe that they all had the same feel, the same length. "Here, I'll read them aloud so you see what I mean."

She did, and the other women nodded. "Yes," Alizisa said. "Each one goes 'ta dum ta dum ta dum ta dum.' It's poetry."

"They say such unsettling things," the dark-haired washer woman mused. "I've read the one on Square of Sleep's fountain again and again, and thought nothing of it. But when you put them all together, they're death and bones and stones—"

Romene broke in, "Rhymes! There are rhymes. Bones and stones. Freed and steed. Deep and sleep."

"But no rhymes for 'lord' and 'free.'" Sarista frowned at the copy book. "Does anyone have another piece of paper? I don't want to cut up Jordith's copy book. Lairin would no doubt take my ears off."

On the back of a crumpled piece of paper Marcene had in her pocket, Sarista copied the lines. Then she untied one end of her bundle, found her sewing basket, and took out her shears. She cut the paper into strips, with one line on each strip. "We can put the rhyming lines together."

They were trying the lines in different orders, reading the resulting poem aloud, and then trying again when they were not satisfied, when Ulrid came back from where he had been helping the constables. He put hands to hips, shook his head at them, and said, "What's all this then? We're crowded into a cave, everyone's in conniptions about an army coming up the mountain, and you're getting all poetical?"

"We've tried so many ways, but we're not sure which lines go where."

Ulrid scratched his head, then settled down cross legged on the stone floor next to Sarista to study the slips of paper. "There's something missing," he said.

"How can there be?" said Sarista. "We got the lines from all the fountains."

Ulrid frowned at the papers. "Remember, just before we were married, when there was a great landslide on the north side of the city? I spent days carting rock and rubble out of there. Nobody went back to most of the houses—it wasn't worth trying to fix 'em. But there's a square there—Sword Square.

"Sword!" cried Alizisa. "It rhymes with 'lord.'"

"Was the fountain buried in the landslide?" Sarista asked.

"No, but its pipes broke, so there's no more water. People had other things to worry about than one fountain not working."

"What about 'free,' then?" Sarista asked. "We've no rhyme for 'free,' either. Is there another broken fountain?"

Ulrid shook his head. "Not that I know of."

"Then we should go to Sword Square for that message."

Ulrid put an arm around Sarista's shoulders. "My love," he said softly, "do you really think some spell hundreds of years old will keep an army away from Wismund?"

Sarista turned to meet his gaze, then looked down at her lap. "I...don't know. But we should try. Karona...was wise, and I believe that she could leave a way for her city to stay free."

"Let us go to Sword Square, then," Ulrid said. "Jordith, Gairid, stay with our things, and the donkey. We'll be back soon."

In the confusion at the cave's mouth, it was easy to slip past the constables and into Wismund city's nearly empty streets. Sarista and Ulrid watched and listened for an army entering the city, but heard nothing but a high-flying bird calling, and the wind that whispered perpetually about the city's heights.

Sword Square was north and west of the poorest, most ill-kept part of Wismund, and seeing the piles of rubble and decades-old broken buildings made Sarista realize why no one had bothered to rebuild here. The cobbles of Sword Square had buckled, the square itself was half buried in dirt, and a corner had slid off down the mountainside.

"Here's the fountain," said Ulrid, leading them to what Sarista had thought just another half-broken wall. She knelt on the gritty cobbles, touching the rim of the empty, debris-filled basin. It, like the other fountains she had seen, was worn smooth by generations of washer women. Then she looked up, to see what the inscription on the fountain said.

The bas-relief was an armored warrior in a pose nearly identical to the skeleton on the fountain in Square of Bones. One upraised hand grasped a sword that looked like the flat, useless swords that were buried ritually with every citizen of Wismund.

It must have been because she had not seen this statue hundreds of times, but she noticed that the armored figure held a shield with the number '7' inscribed on it. The saying above the warrior's head read, *We Raise Our Strong Ancestral Swords.*

She had brought Jordith's copy book, so she wrote '7,' then copied the line after all the others.

Sarista blinked, and her heart started beating more quickly. Was it possible that each fountain had a number on it, that the number 7 she had just written meant that the 'swords' line was the seventh in the spell?

"Look, Ulrid," she said. "The number 7 on the warrior's shield."

Ulrid caught her meaning immediately. "So this is the seventh line?"

"That's what I thought. Now we'll have find out if the other fountains have numbers on them. Do you think anyone will remember such a thing?" Sarista asked. She had been so excited about discovering this last line, but now it seemed there was another obstacle in their path. Had Countess Karona expected the spell to be this difficult to assemble?

"We can but ask."

The cave was even more crowded, noisy, and smelly after the peaceful quiet of the summer-lit streets of Wismund. When Sarista and Ulrid got back to their group, Alizisa was leaning close to the other women and saying, "I think I know what the plainsfolk want in Wismund."

She straightened and looked around when Sarista and Ulrid came up behind her. "Oh, you're back," she said in obvious relief. "I thought...did you find it?"

Sarista wanted to know what Alizisa had been saying. She knelt beside Alizisa and asked, "What is it you know?"

Alizisa shook her head—not in negation, but as if to clear it of something blocking her vision. "In the cave where Kaydn works," she said, then dropped her voice even lower, so it was hard for Sarista to understand her. "They've been finding jewels. Strange, fragile things, with bright colors that change within them. The nobles fancy them, and from what I hear, one of the Countess's men sold some down in the plains. What if...if some plainsman knew we had no army, here in Wismund, and thought to come take the jewels?"

Romene made a disgusted noise. "So, after all these years of the plainsfolk leaving Wismund alone because we have nothing they want, now we *do* have something?"

"It's too bad that we all suffer for some plainsman's greed," Olie said.

"That's the way of the world," her mother answered her.

"So tell me," said Alizisa in a loud voice, twisting to face Sarista, "did you find Sword Square?"

Everyone accepted her change of subject. Sarista wrenched her thoughts from horror at how someone's greed could endanger ana entire city back to the puzzle of the spell. "We did. And I discovered something else. The number 7 is written on the warrior's shield. If that means it's the seventh line in the spell—"

"And if the other fountains have numbers on them—" Romene broke in, only to have Alizisa finish her thought.

"We'll know the order of the lines."

Sarista looked from face to face. It was difficult to interpret their expressions in the flickering light of a single lamp set atop their bundles. "Does anyone know the carvings of the fountains well enough to remember if there are numbers on any of the others?"

Alizisa took a deep breath and let it out in a sigh. Her baby, asleep against her shoulder, stirred and let out a thin wail, then settled again. "I don't remember. I just look at Karona, and wonder what it's like to be a countess, not a washer woman."

The talk went around the circle, with no one remembering numbers on the fountains. Then Alizisa's husband Kaydn found the group, and everyone was distracted with the relief in his face at finding his family safe.

"I'll ask my friends," said the dark-haired washer woman. "They don't need to know why."

"I don't care if they know why. This spell belongs to Wismund. Everyone should know it." Sarista was not certain why she felt this so strongly.

Rather than have people disturb the children, who lay asleep with their heads on the bundles, Sarista wandered out into the cavern, flanked by Romene, Olie, and Alizisa. They asked everyone they met—washer women, laborers, even constables—if they remembered numbers on any of the fountains. One by one they found people who remembered: An old man who told them there was a 5 on the horse's saddle cloth at Horse Square; a constable who spent time up in Lord's Square and knew there was an 8 carved into the armored chest of the lord there; and others who recalled numbers on the other fountains, until Sarista had them for all the lines but Karona's. The line with no rhyme.

She and her friends returned to their little corner of the crowded cavern, and lay the pieces of paper out in order.

Safe Guarded In The Caves So Deep
How Peacefully Wismunders Sleep
Protected By The Mountain's Stones
We Pledge Our Very Souls And Bones
Come Faithful Hound And Steadfast Steed
From Death Wismunders Shall Be Freed
We Raise Our Strong Ancestral Swords
We Fight Against All Foreign Lords

Where did Karona's line go? At the beginning, or the end?

"Now what do we do?" asked Romene. "Will it work if we just say it aloud, here in the cave?"

"We can try." Sarista read the spell aloud twice—the first time with the line from Karona Square first, then with that line last.

"How do we know if it worked?" asked Alizisa's husband Kaydn. Someone—probably Ulrid—had told him the whole story while Sarista and her friends were out searching for numbers.

"I don't know. I don't think it has." Sarista still felt the sense of great urgency that had been building in her all day. "I think...I think we have to do it at the fountain in Karona Square."

"Are you mad?" asked Kaydn. "One of the gates opens straight onto that square."

"Not mad." Sarista searched her mind for the appropriate word. "Driven?"

It was frighteningly easy to talk their families into letting them leave the safety of the cave and venture out to Karona Square. Perhaps now that everyone had fled to the caves, the threat seemed less. So it was that Sarista, Romene, Olie, Alizisa, and four other washer women ventured out while the constables were distracted.

The shadows were growing long; it would soon be dusk. The empty streets were eerie—littered with items people had dropped, but empty of anything living.

They were almost to Karona Square when they heard the tramp of feet echoing off mountainside and buildings. The sound came from the south, not the east—the invaders had entered the city through Horse Gate, not the gate onto Karona Square.

Alizisa gasped, but none of them faltered. They ran through the empty streets to reach the square. When had the others become infected with Sarista's urgency?

Sarista climbed to the rim of the fountain's bowl, and faced the bas-relief of Countess Karona. She studied it as she never had before, in all the years she had washed clothing in this very fountain. Cupped in the Countess's upraised hand was the number 9. Was there another saying, or did Karona's words finish the spell? All the other squares were named for the last word in the spell, or one very similar. But Karona Square was named for the countess, and her line ended in 'free.' It was her famous promise. Would there be anything in the spell after that?

There was no need to take the strips of paper from her pocket; Sarista had memorized the lines. There was nothing left to do now but try the spell. Her heart hammering, Sarista glanced up at Karona's likeness, at the Countess's proud upraised head, at her hands held out, palms up, open to her people. Trembling, Sarista stepped straight into the water of the fountain, and stood before the ancient Countess. She threw her head back, raised her arms, and began reciting the spell. With each line her voice gained power, and the meaning of each seemed to sink under her skin.

The other washer women, who had ranged themselves along the bowl of the fountain, recited the words with her. As they spoke, the air about them seemed to thicken and curdle, making it difficult to breathe. Still she forced out the words, until the last 'Free!' rasped from eight pairs of lips.

The sun disappeared behind the palace, leaving the square in shadow. A warm wind rushed through Karona Square, smelling of roses and the odor the earth gives off after rain.

For long moments, there was nothing but the sound of something large and heavy crashing to the ground farther into the city. They glanced in that direction to see smoke rising.

Then a hoarse battle cry sounded, and armored soldiers staggered up the steps that led into Karona Square. If Sarista had thought it difficult to breathe before, it was nothing to the heart-stopping panic that gripped her now. She and the other women had no weapons, and it was too late to run. The soldiers had seen them on the fountain.

To make matters worse, from the north came the sound of many feet, and from the south, hooves on cobblestones.

Sarista stood straight and tall as soldiers rushed toward her, ready to show these plainsfolk that a washer woman of Wismund was no easy prey. "Up on the fountain with me," she told her friends. "Make it harder for them to reach us."

The others clambered into the bowl of the fountain quickly enough that the nearest soldiers couldn't reach them. "Stop right there," one of the men yelled, his plains accent so thick she could barely understand it. The washer women found themselves facing what seemed a forest of swords and spears. No, just four spears and two swords, but it was more weapons than they had, and if there were bowmen behind these soldiers, or one thought to throw his spear...

An army poured into the square from the north, and instead of welcoming it, the plainsfolk turned and ran from the square in panicked flight.

Sarista took a deep breath and turned to see what had routed the soldiers. Her mouth dropped open in awe and horror. She thought of the skeleton carved above the fountain in the Square of Bones, with sword upraised. Hundreds of such—some still bearing skin and hair, some merely skeletons—filled the square.

A line of the spell came to mind, and she recited it softly. "We pledge our very souls and bones; from death Wismunders shall be freed."

Beside her, one of her friends grasped her hand. "So this is Karona's army."

"All who have taken the Pledge."

The army of the dead stopped. Now that the plainsfolk soldiers were gone, there was uncanny silence in the square. No breathing, no coughing, no shifting of weight. The only sound came up the road from the southwest, as a cavalcade of ghostly creatures, more bones than anything else, entered the square. Horses, donkeys, and between their hooves smaller animals— dogs and cats, even a few goats. Some were mummified, with skin clinging to the bones, and half-rotted harness about their heads. One horse even sported a saddle.

A hysterical giggle rose in Sarista's throat. "Come faithful hound and steadfast steed," she whispered.

Sarista knew she must do something; she had summoned this ghastly force. She trembled, unsure how to deal with an army of the dead. But as she stepped down from the fountain's rim, her friends closed in around her and accompanied her as she strode to greet Karona's army.

At the head of the horde was a suit of antiquated plate armor, bones showing through the gaps at shoulder and elbow. It raised a corroded sword in salute, then lowered it and a voice like branches creaking in the wind said, "Where is our leader?"

Sarista took a deep breath, and let it out slowly. "Do you mean the Countess Karona?"

"Our Countess." The sound came from many...not throats. Most of those in this army no longer had throats.

"She did not rise with you?" Sarista asked.

"She is not here."

How would she find the Countess? The real Countess, not the stone likeness above the fountain.

"She's in the mortuary cave north of here, east of the Square of Bones," whispered someone in the tight group surrounding Sarista.

Gulping down another hysterical giggle, Sarista managed to say, "Go, find your mounts. I will seek Countess Karona." She took another deep breath. It was then that she noticed that, although the square was filled with the dead, there was no odor of decay. Just that warm wind faintly smelling of roses.

A path opened in the midst of Karona's army, and Sarista raised her chin and started up the road, looking neither left nor right so that she would not have to see the creatures her spell had summoned. Her friends followed in a tight little group, unwilling to get too near the skeletal warriors.

The mortuary cave at the northeast edge of Wismund city was reserved for the more well-to-do citizens. Braziers at the cave's mouth gave off welcome light and warmth, now that the sun had set. "My Mama told me that this cave has been used since before Wismund was a city," whispered Olie. "That's why Karona chose it. People have been laid to rest here for more than a thousand years, Mama said."

Sarista and the other women each took a torch from the rack just inside the cave mouth, lit them in the braziers, and walked into the cave. The air was cool, but the smell of death lingered here, where it had not with the skeletal army. It was Wismund custom to carry a body as far back into a cave as possible, with the entire mourning party following solemnly behind, sometimes singing or chanting prayers. When Sarista's Mama had died, she remembered what seemed an interminable walk through dark passages, and then her mother had been laid, in all her finery and clutching her rawhide sword, on the ground next to a body that had already mummified.

Sarista shuddered. Was her mother among those marching in that army? But no—those had come from the north. Was there another army—which had of necessity taken a longer route—coming from the mortuary caves to the west?

There was ample evidence of the army having left this very cave. Scuff marks, scattered bits of rotting fabric, but luckily for Sarista's stomach, no bones or other body parts.

As Sarista and her friends moved deeper into the cave, saying very little and staying close together, they began to notice the drip of water, which was all wrong for a mortuary cave. In the torches' flickering light, they could make out fantastical formations, red and tawny gold, flowing down the walls and dripping from the ceiling to the floor. When Olie poked one, she declared it stone.

Abruptly, they reached the end of the cavern. Niches had been carved into the walls—these were mostly empty, but for those at the very back. Stone had flowed down over those niches in incomplete rippling curtains.

"Who disturbs my rest?" came a whispering voice. "Why have my people been summoned?"

The already tight group huddled even closer. Sarista tried several times to get her voice to work, finally swallowing and managing, "Are you the Countess Karona?"

There was a long silence, then a sound like a sigh. "I was she, in life."

"An army has come up the mountain to attack Wismund. I spoke your spell, and the dead rose to protect the city." Sarista stated the facts without embroidering them. "But your knight seeks you to command your army."

"Aaaaah." Another long silence. Sarista found herself shivering from more than just the cold damp of the cave. Huddled closely as they were, she could tell all the others trembled too.

"The stone that protects Wismund's bones has trapped mine, I find. You, brave one, shall be my commander."

"I? I'm nothing but a washer woman! What of our Countess's advisors? Or the chief of constables?"

"Do not question me, brave one. You spoke the spell. You command my army. Your friends shall be your generals. Go with my blessing."

For long moments Sarista and her friends waited, but Countess Karona spoke no more. Finally, they turned and sped from the mortuary cave as quickly as they could. Luckily, the floor had been smoothed for the ease of the mourning parties, so they didn't trip and fall in their rush.

"What did she mean, 'Your friends shall be your generals'?" quavered Romene as they exited the cave into the starry sky of Wismund's night.

"I suppose you'll find out when *I* discover what it is to be commander," said Sarista.

They kept their torches, to light the road back to Karona Square. They got there to find rank upon rank of sword-bearing foot soldiers, with mounted skeletons interspersed among them. Eight skeletal mounts stood eerily silent next to the fountain.

"I think those are for us," said Olie.

"I can't—" Sarista cut off what she had been about to say as the knight rode up to her, oddly quiet for a suit of rusted armor on a mummified horse.

He bowed from his seat atop the horse. "The Countess has spoken. Commander. Generals. Let us begin. The enemy is already within the city." He reached out with his sword and, one by one, touched Sarista and her friends, each on the right shoulder.

A feeling of utmost confidence filled Sarista. She marched back to the fountain, taking the reins of the nearest mount. "Why, it's old Dedel," she said. When Dedel died, she and Ulrid had left their beloved donkey—who had served them faithfully for so many years—in the animal's mortuary cave like nobles did, rather than selling his carcass for meat. Sarista climbed up the fountain's rim once more, then settled onto the donkey's skeletal back. It did not feel bony—rather, it was warm and hairy, and smelled pleasantly of donkey. When Dedel took a step, she felt muscles shift under her thighs just as when she had ridden him in life.

With the others also mounted, Sarista and her generals rode into the city, followed by an army of the dead.

"We don't want to kill anyone unless they force us to," Sarista called to her generals. "Have your troops drive them through the streets. I know exactly the place to imprison the invaders. The safe cave where the roof collapsed. It has a strong door—built to keep invaders out, but now it can keep them in."

Romene, atop a skeletal horse, nodded, and a horde of the dead followed her west on the circle road. Each of the other generals led part of the skeletal army away from Sarista, seeking the invaders wherever they were in the city.

Skeleton hounds sought out the enemy, and drove them screaming toward Wismunder dead armed with the flat rawhide swords left with them when they were interred.

All through the steep roads of the city, and then along the branching trails down the mountain, the Commander, her seven Generals, and the army of the dead swarmed that night. They took the plainsfolk by surprise, for the Gerbigen thought the Wismunders had no fighters. When the plainsfolk saw what they fought, most screamed and ran, as Sarista had hoped. A few put daggers to their own throats, unwilling to fight adversaries that could not be killed, for they were already dead.

Sarista, riding her dead donkey, as if in a dream because of the sheer impossibility of what she was doing, led her undisciplined horde as they drove the plainsfolk toward the cave she had chosen. When they arrived, she dropped from Dedel's back and approached the two terrified constables who had stayed to direct Wismunders away from the cave. "You will need to act as jailers," she said. "The Countess must deal with this army sent to invade Wismund."

"Y-yes," said one. The other merely stood and gaped out at the hordes of dead surrounding the invaders they had herded through the streets. Then he turned and took a large key from around his neck, unlocked the door, and opened it wide. Sarista and the two constables stepped aside, and her skeletal horde drove the invaders inside. As the dead retreated, Sarista slammed the door with a satisfying thud. "There will be more," she said. "Please stay here and take care of them." Silently, one of the constables helped her back onto Dedel's back, and she led her troops out into the city once more.

Just at the time the sun's light would be touching the bas-relief of Countess Karona above her fountain—though, of course, Sarista was not there to see it—the Wismunder dead turned back toward the mortuary caves they had left hours ago. There was nothing orderly about them, just hundreds of the dead returning to their resting places. At the fountain the Commander and her Generals dismounted. Sarista gave Dedel one last loving pat, and their eight skeletal mounts joined those returning to the animal cave.

The knight approached Sarista and her friends where they stood dazed with sleepiness and the inconceivable task they had just undertaken. He knelt, and just as he had done before, touched each of their shoulders with his sword. "All Wismund is in your debt," he said in that creaking, rasping voice. "The Countess Karona thanks you."

"Y-you did it all. You and all the...dead people. We didn't even fight. We had no weapons." Sarista was too exhausted to be tactful or diplomatic—had she even known what to say in a situation such as this.

"We could not fight without your leadership. You were fearless—all of you. You did not shrink from us, nor from the enemy. You are true heroes."

The knight raised his sword in a last salute, and followed the dead who straggled off to the north, back to their niches in the mortuary cave.

Another mob of skeletal forms moved westward, returning to the mortuary caves there, Sarista noted through exhaustion that threatened to pitch her straight into the fountain.

She clasped the hands of each of the other washer women. "Thank you all. You did not have to stay with me. You did not have to be part of...this."

"I think we did," said Romene. "We helped with the spell, and it caught us up too."

"Let us, then...let us go home, and find our beds." She hugged the others, and watched as they set off.

Sarista trudged home through empty streets. Buildings had been smashed or burned, and in places blood stained the cobblestones beneath huddled bodies. What tales would be told of this battle, and the rout of the plainsfolk army by the dead of Wismund?

The door to her building had been smashed open, but thankfully there was no blood, nor any bodies, on the stairs. She opened the door to her room to see all as she had left it—and then, remembering that her family was in the caves, with all the food and blankets in the house, she started laughing, very softly.

LORD RUTHVEN'S MASQUE

by Steve Chapman

Princess Shada has always leapt from one battle to another. But then she killed her godfather, and was maimed by a necromancer. She has learned a new style of fighting to compensate for the missing finger on her sword hand, but she hasn't yet dealt with her real handicaps: guilt; and the loss of the confidence that carried her through her previous adventures.

Steve Chapman is a learning science professional who writes genre short fiction and novels in his somewhat elusive spare time. He lives with his wife, daughter, and sailboat at the New Jersey shore. This is his seventh appearance in Sword and Sorceress.

"Tall, bald. Horrendous nose." Petra shuddered at the memory. "He was just as you described. I'm sorry I didn't believe you before."

Shada was sorry, too. A whisper of support from Petra Ruthven, the beautiful, terrifying daughter of the wealthiest man in St. Navarre, and the past months might have played out differently.

Shada knew the necromancer Pitch was loose in the city. Its people were in terrible danger. And none of them believed her.

But now Petra had seen him. Petra, the last girl Shada had expected to have on her side.

"Coming down here was stupid, I know." Petra led Shada into a maze of streets in the shadow of the city walls. Passersby grew scarce as the sun sank. Dried leaves scuttled across cobblestone. "Ansel wanted privacy. He's in love with me, you know."

Every girl at Court knew Ansel Arabount was wrapped tight around Petra's expertly manicured finger. Rumor had it they'd announce their engagement on her seventeenth birthday, a union between the two beautiful, horrible children who'd caused Shada endless grief in classrooms and ballrooms.

"What will you do if we find them?" Petra glanced at Shada's right hand, her ring finger an ugly stump. "You can't fight with that hand."

"I can fight." Shada tucked her right hand into her left. "But not with a sword."

She'd developed, by her sixteenth year, one the best sword arms in St. Navarre. But that was before Pitch maimed her. For months she'd retrained herself, short sticks and ju-jitsu, close-fighting techniques that didn't rely on her ruined hand.

Those techniques wouldn't matter to the necromancer. His cloaks could paralyze at five paces. So she carried a prepared spell, crafted by the College of Mages. It should—*hopefully*—bind Pitch.

"Where did they go?" Shada asked.

Petra pointed to a pedestrian bridge, ahead in the gloom. "That's where the necromancer took Ansel."

"If he's alive I'll bring him back." Hands shaking, Shada drew the blue gemstone that held her spell. This was her chance to set everything right.

"Good luck," Petra whispered as Shada slipped into the darkness beneath the bridge.

She heard only the drip of broken cisterns, barely discernible above her pounding heart. Then, movement; she pulled tight against the wall. A tall silhouette soaked out of the murk. She brought the gem to her lips; her breath would activate its magic.

Dim light hit the figure. It was no necromancer, but Petra's brother, Markus, followed by his friend Damien. A footfall, behind her...

She whirled to face Ansel Arabount.

Petra hadn't seen the necromancer. Her story was a lie, a lure. Ansel, Markus, and Damien; Shada had humiliated them all in proving ground training. Now that they believed she couldn't defend herself, they wanted payback.

Curse Petra Ruthven. She no doubt couldn't wait to tell the

entire Citadel about how her awesome boyfriend took Shada down.

"Shada." Ansel grinned like a cat in mid-canary swallow. "What's an august personage like you doing in a neighborhood like this?"

They triangulated, blocking every escape route.

"Three on one?" Shada shifted left, getting the wall at her back.

"You said you were good as any five of us." Ansel was the ringleader. If she took him out the others might crumble. But he hung back.

Markus and Damien flanked her. She worked out angles, timing. Markus would punch high; it was all he knew. She'd duck, chop his throat and hook Damien's ankle as he tried to pin her arms.

Her breath caught in her throat. What was she doing? She was *crippled*. She couldn't fight one boy, let alone three. Her missing finger throbbed.

"Please." Her fists came apart, palms out to protect her face, wet with tears. "No."

Four hours later Shada sat staring at the swords on the walls of her chambers. She was physically unharmed. The boys had no interest in beating up a weeping girl. Ansel had actually offered to walk her home. He could afford to be magnanimous; the story would sweep through Citadel halls like autumn wildfire. Shada would never again be able to show her face in public.

Flushed with shame, she reran the moments in her head. It didn't matter that her body could still fight. The necromancer had taken more than her finger; he'd stolen her confidence. Without it she was, apparently, useless.

She couldn't just wait for Pitch to strike. But was there any point hunting him? When she burst into tears the necromancer was unlikely to offer a walk home.

Shada's sister Sienna marched into the room in a sheath of a dress that appeared to be made entirely of vines.

"You're supposed to be a tree?" Something about a costumed

ball flickered in Shada's memory. "Possibly a bush?"

Strands of emerald silk coiled to give the illusion of live greenery. Tiny violet gems dangled from Sienna's ears, were wrapped about her wrists and ankles. As much as Shada hated to admit it, the costume was pretty great.

"Talia the Trickster," Sienna said. "And you were supposed to be Alyah the Lost Princess—twenty minutes ago."

Lord Ruthven's Autumn Masque; in the tears and trauma, Shada had forgotten. "Not going."

Sienna marched into the bedroom and returned with a white doublet and tights, threaded with gold. She threw it at Shada. "Going."

Shada flushed with anger. "You've no idea what I've—"

"You let Petra Ruthven bait you into a beatdown which you cleverly escaped by crying like a small child. I'd congratulate you on that tactical masterstroke, but I worry I'd get hit."

Shada understood that Sienna was joking, but somehow the joke was always on her. "It wasn't funny."

"You must admit that it *sounds* funny." Sienna handed Shada a pair of white slippers. "We represent the Crown tonight."

"It's at Petra's house." Shada stared at the flimsy tights. "I'd rather wear plate mail."

"The Alyah outfit comes with weapons." Sienna shoved a box at Shada. "You'll be the belle of the ball."

Inside were two short dolu sticks and a sling, Alyah's traditional weapons in the violent children's stories that had been among Shada's favorites.

"We need Ruthven," Sienna said. "Put on the damn costume."

Shada picked up a dolu stick and counted silently backwards from ten. It didn't lessen her anger but gave her something to do other than shatter her sister's kneecap. "The only way I'm leaving this room for the rest of my life is wearing a mask."

Sienna passed her the final piece of the costume: a glittering white domino. "Your lucky day."

Edward Ruthven, the richest man in St. Navarre, wore a stuffed raven atop his head. Feathered cloaks hung from his shoulders and a glittering black domino obscured his features as he brought Shada's hand—with admirable delicacy, given her missing finger—to his lips.

"Princess Shada." He grinned. "Or rather, Alyah. The Raven Lord welcomes the Lost Princess to our revels."

Ruthven always played the Raven Lord, mythic herald of the dying season. He was as famous for his lavish parties as the fortune that made those parties a political necessity. Shada disliked dressing up, dancing, and politics. She would have given much to avoid this evening. But in the recent civil strife Ruthven hadn't chosen a side.

Her father's advisor, known as the Consul, had tried to usurp the Crown. He'd recruited the necromancer Pitch and rallied Houses to his side.

And then he'd vanished.

Some said the Consul was dead. Others claimed he'd fled. Shada knew the truth. To save her own life she'd killed him.

Her father needed Ruthven's support because the Consul's necromancer had yet to make his move. So for an evening she could smile and dance to the best of her limited ability.

"And Talia, the sylph so clever she talked the oaks into giving up their leaves." Ruthven pecked at Sienna's hand. "The trickster and the warrior princess; lovely and apropos. Wouldn't you say, Petra?"

Petra, an air sprite in ruffled pink, smiled with tortured politeness. It took much of Shada's self-control not to test her sticks against that elegant jawline.

They all entered the enormous ballroom. St. Navarre's best and brightest preened in costumed finery as a small orchestra organized itself.

The Baroness Arabella, red hair tumbling over an emerald domino, bowed to Sienna. "A single exit, two more upstairs." She looked up to the balcony and then to the crystal ceiling, afire with the light of the setting sun. "The situation is acceptable."

Shada's heart sank. For all their disagreements, it was Shada who had Sienna's back at public events. Arabella was only here because Sienna no longer trusted Shada to keep her safe. Shada felt tears threaten as the orchestra struck up a waltz. She turned away, her mask hiding the worst of it.

Ansel Arabount, dressed as a Ramacian duelist, bowed. "May I have the dance?"

As the sun set an enormous, mandala-shaped chandelier ignited, a wheel of fire burning in the twilight. Shada felt like she was in an enchanted castle, the masked revelers creatures of dream, caught in the romance of the dance.

Then she remembered she was dancing with Ansel.

He'd no doubt told everyone about her breakdown. Now, to complete her mortification, he stepped perfectly through the dance, his fingers at her elbow, then her hip. Any refusal would negate her goodwill mission. She could do nothing but complete the steps.

It was surprisingly difficult. The floor was ragged and uneven.

The music stopped; the dancers halted. It was only a momentary relief. Shada had to finish the set with him.

"I remember that tale of Alyah," Ansel said. "Where she returns to her kingdom to find Death himself has usurped its throne? You see parallels to your necromancer?"

Shada touched the weapon on her hip. "I saw that this costume came with sticks."

The music struck up again. Ansel extended his right hand. "I might be frightened if you hadn't collapsed in tears at our last fight."

"That was *so* clever, having Petra lure me into the ambush." She met his right hand with her left. They walked a four point pattern, fingertips touching. "Know what was cleverer?"

Ansel stepped clockwise and raised an eyebrow.

"Crocodile tears." Shada followed his lead. "A bit of dirt in your eye and ambush becomes escort."

He stumbled on the tricky floor. Shada made an unlikely mental note to thank her sister.

But the smile returned. "Then how about a few rounds now? Just you and me."

It was what she wanted. One on one, she could take him. Or rather, the girl she had been could have. This new Shada, the cripple, was a question mark.

She took courage from the beauty of the firelight above. "In the middle of the dance?"

"This is Pet's house. I know where we can find some privacy."

The Ruthven family crypts were unlikely to draw many guests. The flickering light of Ansel's torch illuminated sculpted specters and gargoyles overseeing generations of decomposing Ruthvens.

As they'd descended two stories down a tight, circular stairway Shada felt her courage fade. If things went badly no cry for help would be heard. But pride wouldn't let her turn back.

Ansel lit the wall tapers and set down his sword. She put her sticks aside. He stepped forward. Her arms rose. He was stronger. She'd need to be faster. Unpredictable.

The understanding came suddenly: she'd lost the confidence to let instinct guide her moves. That unpredictability had driven her swordplay. Now it was gone and Ansel Arabount was going to kick her sorry ass.

He reached toward her. She chopped his arm away.

He looked confused. "We're not really going to fight. Are we?"

"Why else are we down here?"

Ansel grinned. "Privacy."

She didn't follow—and then he was inside her guard, his face inches from hers.

"I heard you wouldn't look twice at a guy who couldn't give you a fight."

Understanding battled with the absurdity of what was being understood. "Getting your buddies to beat me up was your idea of *flirting*?"

"I figured you'd knock them down and then I'd give you a run. A few blocks, a few falls. Good fun. You know: prove myself worthy."

Tears vied with laughter. But if Shada allowed either, she'd never stop.

"That is *not* the preferred approach, I'm guessing now?"

The intensity of his stare disarmed her. Instead of dodging, she told the truth. "Ridiculous as it sounds, that might have worked last summer."

He looked to her hand. "Before you were injured?"

She'd told no one, not even Sienna, how *undone* she had felt. No one could know. But she nodded.

"At the bridge—you weren't faking."

She didn't bother denying it. "I'm useless, now."

The moment hung between them.

"I'm an entitled prat." Ansel took her right hand. "I've no claim to wisdom. But that's crap. You are who you are. The rest is just technique. Everyone's talking about the amazing hand to hand stuff you're doing with Miss Delerium."

If Shada could imagine anything more mortifying than her tearful breakdown it might be Ansel Arabount giving her a pep talk. He seemed sincere. Boys who wanted to kiss you often did. Yet she hadn't shoved him away. At this point she'd apparently take whatever encouragement she could get.

"Shada, you stopped Vander deGroat from destroying the Moon Pool. You killed the Enchantress Rionach. You're a hero."

She felt panic. Nobody outside the Citadel knew about her misadventures. "That's absurd."

"And a terrible liar. Seriously: we *know*. It's why you intimidate people."

"I don't intimidate—"

A footfall echoed across the tombs.

"Oh." Petra stood at the base of the stairs, torch in hand.

Ansel dropped Shada's hand as if it were on fire. They couldn't have looked guiltier if they'd planned it.

Petra slumped for only a moment before recovering her regal bearing. "I suspected your true purpose before. Making me an accomplice was low, but it's not as if I just met you."

"Pet." Ansel reached for her.

"However," Petra drew back, "We are now in my father's house. Continue to embarrass me and you *will* suffer."

"Not that I owe you anything," Shada said, "but I only came down here for the violence."

"I came looking for my father." Petra curtly changed subjects.

Shada felt a shiver of dread. "He's missing?"

"A servant couldn't be found. He went looking—an hour ago."

Shada grabbed a taper and moved into the tombs, sculptural specters throwing shadows. Petra pointed at a stone coffin, similar to the others, but with a pipe extruding from its side, running up and into the near wall.

Shada's light revealed a fresh layer of debris beneath it. "This is new?"

"It's outrageous." Petra pushed the lid. It didn't move.

"Why? Who's buried here?"

"This was an empty crypt." Ansel had followed them. "Prepped for the next Ruthven to die. Ghoulish, if you ask me."

"No one did." Petra glared. "A family tradition. That someone has felt free to desecrate."

Ansel tried to open the coffin. "It's locked from the inside."

Shada touched the pipes. They were ceramic, unlike the ancient stonework. She'd seen similar coffins in necromancy books, but those conjurings required blood and death. From where in Ruthven's house would the blood come?

"Is this tradition, too?" Ansel's torch revealed a jester's costume and mask, hung in an alcove.

"That's hideous." Petra removed the hanger and gasped. Behind it a black-robed man lay in a pool of blood.

"So much blood," Ansel said. "How did he die?"

Shada found the bloody stump of a neck. "Decapitated."

"Who is he?' Petra's voice trembled.

Ansel stood. "We'll know when we find the head."

"We have to get everyone out," Shada said. The necromancer had his blood supply, and half the government of St. Navarre was dancing upstairs.

"Father will know what to do."

"If we can find him," Ansel said. "But—maybe he's in on it."

"You hate Father," Petra spat.

"I don't trust him." Ansel replaced the hanger, blocking Petra's view of the corpse. "Ruthven was planning to back the Consul."

Shada felt a surge of anger. "You Arabounts were the Consul's biggest supporters."

"My dad," Ansel said. "Not me."

"Ansel and his father disagree about *everything*." For a moment Petra sounded like herself. "It's *riveting*."

Shada hated politics. She could never keep track of it. "The Consul didn't do this. He's dead."

"You can't be sure," Ansel said.

"I killed him."

"Really?" he chuckled.

"You believe I killed an immortal enchantress." Shada's voice broke. "He was my godfather; I loved him. But he gave me no choice. And I'm not sorry."

"Then—"

"The necromancer is in this house." Shada felt queasy just saying it. She had to find her courage. She had to think. Someone upstairs must be Pitch's target.

A large, bearded man wearing the emerald colors of Ruthven's Guard appeared in the torchlight.

"Damien," Petra said. "Thank goodness. Is Father with you?"

He was just feet away when Shada saw the terrible wound running from hip to shoulder. His eyes were ovals of pure white.

White eyes were the sign of a wight; corpses animated by necromancy.

It reached for Petra with blood-soaked hands.

Ansel leapt between them, sword up. He blocked a blow and drove his blade through the monster's chest.

Petra let out a peep of joy.

"Ansel!" Shada shouted. "Don't—"

It's the mistake everyone makes fighting a wight. You don't get that your opponent is already dead.

The wight slid forward along Ansel's steel. Its hands clamped around his head.

Petra screamed.

You can't stab a wight to death. Drive your sword through its heart and you've only given it an opening.

The dead man pressed its thumbs into Ansel's eyes and wrenched his head back to expose the flesh of his throat. Yellow jaws reached for it.

Shada couldn't breathe, couldn't move.

Petra shoved the dead man. Ansel broke free. The wight turned, broke the arm off a stone gargoyle and swung at Petra.

Ansel threw himself in front of it. The weapon smashed into his hip, the crack echoing across the crypts.

Petra grabbed a taper from the wall. Fire could destroy a wight. The dead man hesitated.

Shada's only option was the stairs, to bring help. But the taper sputtered. It would die, and then Petra would. Shada didn't leave people to die, even if she didn't like them. She didn't run from danger. But she was no longer a brilliant warrior. She was a cripple.

The taper faded.

Shada leapt forward, driving her shoulder into the wight. It sprawled, its club rolling into darkness.

"Run!" She shoved Petra toward the stairs.

The wight's hand snagged Shada's ankle. She lost her balance, hit the floor.

The wight rose, moving between her and the stairs.

Shada scrambled to her feet. She was trapped by a walking corpse.

The wight had strengths and weaknesses like any opponent. It had been a trained warrior. In death it was slower but stronger. It could not be killed. The only way to stop it was to burn it or chop it into pieces.

Everyone's talking about the amazing hand to hand stuff you've been doing, Ansel had said. She had to use it.

The wight shambled forward.

Shada slid backwards, arms up, hands open. She ducked a pulverizing blow, creating an opening into which she threw a high kick.

It grabbed her leg and flung her like a doll into the side of a crypt.

Her ribs took the worst of the impact. Air rushed from her lungs. Then she was on her knees, blinking her vision clear. Arms closed around her head, lifting her to expose her throat. The wight's jaws opened wide.

Shada grasped its arms and shoved back, pulling her legs up. She locked her ankles behind its head, crushing its throat between her knees. Yet it was still moving, yellow teeth snapping at her calf.

She'd fallen into the same trap as Ansel. Her attack would have killed a living opponent but barely inconvenienced the wight.

Even a small bite could turn her into a thing like itself. Panicking, Shada rocked her hips, trying to break its neck. Vertebrae snapped. The grotesque head lolled—it couldn't bring its teeth to bear.

In response its massive arms squeezed tight about her head. Pain erupted between her temples. It meant to crush her skull. Shada couldn't get her hands inside its grip. Her eyes watered, her vision blurred...

The pressure eased. She dropped to the floor and looked up.

Petra was beating on the wight with a torch. She kicked a dulo stick to Shada.

Shada slammed the stick into the wight's kneecap. As it dropped to all fours she straddled its back, grabbed Petra's torch, and forced the flame into its greasy hair. She held the wight down as fire spread to its clothes and flesh and its struggling ceased.

"Did it bite you?" Shada stood, every muscle in her body trembling.

"No." Petra wiped her eyes. "Damien. I don't understand—"

"He was murdered, turned into a wight." Shada tried to clear her head. "Put here to kill someone at the party. It's the only reason to do this tonight."

"Ansel." Petra approached the sealed coffin.

His left leg was bent beneath him at an impossible angle, but Shada couldn't see past the bloody bite on his neck.

Ansel gaze met Shada's. He understood. "Stay back."

"He's bitten." Shada forced back tears. "He'll turn."

"Sorry, Pet." He tried to grin. "Shada, will you do the honors?"

She could snap his neck. He wouldn't feel a thing. But the necromancer was *here*. She had the spell. If she could kill him before Ansel turned, might that save his life?

"Only if I can't find a better way." She pulled Petra toward the stairs. "Hang on."

Two guardsmen were sprawled in the foyer, blood splattered across the marble floor. The ballroom doors were sealed, a steel chain soldered to the handles. Inside, Shada heard screaming. There was no help here. This was a nightmare, and she would never wake.

"The balcony—how do I get up there?"

Petra just stared at the dead guardsmen.

Shada shook her. "There's a wight in the ballroom. With your father, my sister, and lots of other people. If we don't help them, they'll die."

Shada sprinted up a stairwell in back, small enough to be overlooked. The balcony was empty, but the ballroom below might have been the third circle of Hell.

Half a dozen wights slashed at panicked partiers. Survivors had retreated to the near end of the ballroom, behind a line of defenders: Arabella and Ruthven's surviving guardsmen. Sienna was at their center, directing them to plug gaps in the line.

Swords penetrated wights to no effect. Slain comrades rose as enemies.

Shada's blood ran cold. With just a handful of wights and a locked door, the necromancer was murdering everyone who ran St. Navarre.

"This is unacceptable." Petra, white as a sheet, surveyed the mayhem. "I'm an excellent hostess."

Shada pointed to lines of scarlet crisscrossing the ballroom. "What's that?"

"The new floor was a disaster," Petra said. "Long gouges cut across it. We didn't have time to order another. Those gouges are filling up with blood from *my guests*."

Viewed from above, the scarlet canals formed a five pointed star, leveled so that liquid flowed toward a single spot on the wall—the mouth of a pipe—which must run into the sealed coffin below. Shada had assumed the headless corpse was the sacrifice, but now multiple deaths were feeding whatever nightmare Pitch was conjuring. She'd underestimated his ambition. This massacre wasn't his endgame but fuel for something greater.

Shada was hurt and exhausted and wouldn't come close to turning the tide. But if she couldn't save Sienna, she couldn't abandon her, either.

She threw a leg over the rail.

"Where are you going?" Petra grabbed her wrist.

"To save them."

"You've an outsize opinion of your abilities. I count eight wights. You needed my help to kill *one*."

"So glad I saved your life."

"I understand you're overcompensating for the finger—really, you and Ansel would get along splendidly—but maybe we could *think* for a moment?"

"What do you suggest?" Shada fumed.

Petra admired the draperies behind them. "Acadrian silk. Strong as steel, much more expensive, and—long enough to reach the floor."

Shada understood: a lifeline up to the balcony. It could work—if Sienna's fighters could hold off the wights long enough to evacuate the ballroom. But the struggling line was besieged as new wights rose. Without fire, it seemed hopeless.

And then Shada realized she was staring at an enormous mandala of burning oil.

"Get the drapes down." Shada unscrewed a bronze sphere from the rail and placed it in her sling.

Petra prepped the curtain. "The wights will see it. They'll try to cut our people off."

Shada was counting on it. "Sienna!"

Her sister turned to see the curtain unfurl from the balcony; survivors ran towards it. The wights understood as well, and surged forward.

Shada spun her sling, eyes on the target.

The sphere smashed the latch securing the mandala chandelier to the ceiling. Everyone looked up, including the wights who'd just advanced directly under it.

The chandelier fell.

Four wights were crushed beneath it. The rest staggered back as burning oil poured across the floor.

"They burn!" Shada yelled to Sienna.

The first of the survivors clambered up the curtain. The wights were trapped behind the firewall, Sienna's fighters creating makeshift torches.

"He's not here, is he?" Petra said.

Arabella set a wight ablaze. Ruthven, raven still perched atop his head, made his way to the curtain. There was no sign of the necromancer.

Pitch must be downstairs in darkness, making use of all the blood and death flowing there.

"I've got this," Petra said. "Find him. Save Ansel. Make this stop."

Shada, torch in hand, stepped back into the crypts.

Whatever Pitch was doing here was more important than the upstairs massacre. And she'd left Ansel, crippled and helpless, with him.

Stealth was pointless with the torch. The necromancer could certainly kill her without revealing himself. Shada was betting that he wouldn't. He was prideful. He'd want her know what he'd done. He'd want to terrify her before he killed her.

So she had to act like she wasn't already terrified.

She approached the sealed coffin and waited to be struck dead.

The coffin stood open, empty but for a residue of blood. The jester's costume was gone.

Ansel crawled from the shadows. He looked terrible, feverish. The change was starting. "Something came out of the coffin."

She was too late. The necromancer had his new monster. "There are wights upstairs. Petra's getting her father and the rest of them out of the ballroom."

"I don't think she is." Ansel held a skull. It was slick with blood; the head severed from the body in the alcove. The skin and hair had been stripped away, leaving only gristle and bone. "Found this, behind the coffin."

Necromantic ritual required blood and death, not skin and hair.

Ansel turned it to reveal a black bird's feather stuck to cranium. "Because *this* is her father."

The ballroom doors stood open. Stunned survivors shuffled out. Fires blazed within, the remains of burning wights. Ruthven stood beyond the wreckage of the chandelier, arguing with Sienna.

Petra fell in beside Shada. "Did you find the necromancer?"

"I did." Shada nodded to the Baroness. Arabella drew her blade.

"Lord Ruthven thinks we should surrender," Sienna said.

"The necromancer's here." Ruthven was black and blue about the eyes, his voice hoarse. "He doesn't need wights to kill us. We've no choice."

Shada grabbed Ruthven's headpiece. His hair and face came away with the bird. Beneath this second mask laid the pale, bald visage of the necromancer. Pitch had worn the hair, and face, of the man he'd murdered an hour ago.

Petra gasped.

"Leave these people be." Shada drew the gemstone. "And deal with me."

"You'll be dealt with. Last." The necromancer's voice deepened as he dropped the performance. "Like dessert."

The raven cloaks undulated like a mass of black tendrils.

Shada leapt backwards and brought the gemstone to her lips.

"Attempt magic and the girl dies." Pitch's cloaks wrapped about Petra. Frost spread across her skin at their touch.

Shada recalled their chilling grip all too well. She nodded to the Baroness. Arabella and the guardsmen ringed the necromancer with blades.

"I could kill you all," Pitch said.

Shada didn't think he could. The cloaks were nasty against a single sword but they couldn't handle six. That had been the point of the wights. The necromancer could be ended by a blade that slipped past his cloaks.

"Your plot's failed," Shada said. "What do you want for Petra's life?"

"Safe passage."

"So you can return to attack us at your leisure?"

"Precisely."

Petra's gaze found Shada.

"Decide." The necromancer ran his black tongue across Petra's cheek. "Or I start taking bits of her as I did you."

Petra wrenched her head around and bit down on his nose. As he screamed, the cloaks released her.

Shada blew on the gem. Silver sparks arced toward the necromancer.

The cloaks shifted into a defensive cocoon. Two lashed out, knocking down guardsmen. Pitch broke through the circle.

"Block the door," the Baroness called.

Pitch didn't require a door. Shada had seen him disappear before. She was on his heels as he reached the shadows at the end of the ballroom and vanished, leaving her facing a blank wall.

He was gone. And with him any chance of saving Ansel. She kicked the wall in frustration.

A masked jester entered the ballroom, his arm around Ansel.

Shada's blood froze; this was the monster created in the coffin. She leapt bits of burning chandelier to get between it and the others.

"Shada." Ansel raised his hands. "It's okay."

The jester removed his mask.

"I've healed the boy," the Consul said. "He won't turn."

The world slipped sideways.

Shada had driven her godfather's dagger into his heart. She'd watched him die. It was the worst thing she'd ever done.

"We thought you dead," the Baroness said. "Some said Shada killed you."

The Consul set Ansel down. He looked younger, tanned and vigorous. Shada wondered if she would scream or attack. Instead she stood frozen as he hugged her.

"Rumors," the Consul sighed. "Whatever my issues with her father, I will always love the princess like a daughter."

His cheek was smooth against her face. He smelled like a newborn baby.

Shada understood; the Consul *was* newborn. Pitch had harvested enough blood and souls to fuel his master's reanimation. Only luck and Petra Ruthven had prevented the massacre of all who might oppose him.

"I know what you are." Her hand went to his knife.

He caught her wrist with unnatural strength, without disturbing their apparent reunion.

"Killing me won't work twice," he whispered. "You can't imagine what I've become. What I've been through. Perhaps, in time, I'll return the favor."

Shada heard fury in his voice. The Consul was back, and far more dangerous than before. But she found she wasn't afraid. She realized it wasn't her finger, or her confidence, or her unpredictability that had been taken from her.

It was her certainty.

She had done wrong. She had killed her godfather. In self-defense, yes, but in her own eyes that made little difference. She should have found another way. If she'd been the warrior she imagined herself to be, she would have.

It was unforgivable.

Now his bottomless ambition had rescinded her sin. The guilt lifted from her shoulders. She felt whole, even without her sword arm.

The Consul had bought himself new legitimacy with Ansel's life. Courtiers fawned about him. Fair enough; she'd take that deal.

Shada returned her godfather's hug. She could play this game, bide her time, unravel his schemes.

Yeah, okay: the Consul was back.

But so was she.

AFTER THE SWAN SONG

by Lorie Calkins

Derianne regarded being turned into a swan as her destiny; being changed back to human again was a curse. Of course, her mother took the opposite view. And when the swans she had lived with returned, they weren't happy about it either.

Lorie Calkins has short stories in numerous publications, including Sword and Sorceress *anthologies 19 and 28, and* Beyond Centauri Magazine, *as well as a children's SF novel,* The Terrarium Dragons, *available on Amazon or from White Cat Publications. Besides writing and reading, she enjoys many hobbies, including, but not limited to: carving, painting, mosaics, woodworking, quilting, and welding. But most of her time is spent crocheting for her grandkids, baking cookies for her grandkids, or playing with her grandkids. Lorie and her husband, Guy, live in Western Washington with Magic and Chaos, their Miniature Schnauzers.*

The swans attacked from above. Derianne shrieked and dove into the brush. Like a pack of flying wolves, they came at her from all sides, nipping with their pointed beaks, clawing at her arms and face with the sharp claws on the end of their webbed toes, pulling her hair and tearing her clothes. Hissing and bugling, they came at her again and again, driving her deeper into the thicket. Sharp dead twigs stuck out from the crowded copse of little trees, gouging the skin of her hands, scratching her arms and poking her face. They caught in her hair and pulled, each in a different direction, tearing out strands as she tried to push her way deeper into the tightly clustered branches, blindly retreating from the fury of the swans.

And why were the swans attacking her, anyway? She loved them, and she thought they knew that. She had waited hungrily for their return, visiting the pond as often during the day and evening as she could get away from her mother and sisters unnoticed. And from Elston, the suitor who wouldn't take no for an answer. Magda, her mother, continued to encourage him, while Derianne herself told him she wasn't interested. But Magda wanted her to marry and have children—"Before it's too late!" she'd say, as if seventeen were the age of death's door. Her sisters, too, nagged her to marry Elston and get it over with. "Time to get out of here and start having a life," Sharra said. "Doesn't matter who you marry. The men of this town are all the same. What matters is getting out from under Mother's thumb, so you can do what you want, run your own life." But Deri knew that what Sharra wanted most was for older sister Deri to be out of the way, so Sharra could marry her own suitor.

She had been watching for the swans this afternoon, hoping the V-shaped flock would appear in the sky. It was spring at last, and time for them to return to the pond, where she expected them to break her heart again every time she saw them floating in stately beauty. Better that heartbreak than to be bereft of them altogether. Her breath had caught when she spotted a distant V. She had stared until her eyes stung and watered, eager for any hint that these were *her* swans, and not some other flock, or some other kind of birds. When they had come close enough for her to recognize Argonne's peculiar wingbeat, with the slight tremor from that old injury, when she could hear the sound of Balgur's distinctive bugle, when she could see the little patch of black feathers on Orthur's flank—her heart reached out to them. They were home! And so was she.

Derianne cried out as the coarse cloth of her dress caught on a broken branch and tore. Her apron was long since gone, snagged and pulled away. "Stop, stop!" she shouted, finally too terrified to care if her family discovered her with the swans or not. "Why are you attacking me, Dalrain? Rhymthus? Argonne? We were...are...friends!" She shrank back, protecting her eyes against their vicious beaks. "Please! Have you all gone insane?"

With great effort, the huge birds broke off their assault, one by one taking hold of their emotions and pulling back from

Derianne. They moved back only a few steps, forming a ring of impenetrable scorn about her. They panted and looked exhausted, as well they should, ending a day of migration with a wrathful battle, but still the cold fury of betrayal filled their eyes. As soon as they had seen her standing there by the pond, waving and smiling, they dove, pecking and jabbing with their beaks, driving her into the underbrush, farther and farther from her mother's house. Now, they glared with eyes full of menace. "What? Why?" was all she could think to ask.

"Ah," Dalrain barked, in her low growling voice. "Did you not think we could know of your suitor?"

Orthur hissed. "You thought us too far away to see you dallying with the dark human. But others saw, and others gossiped."

"I knew you would return to your human life," Balgur said, almost matter-of-factly. "In fact I was surprised you waited so long to take a human mate and leave your mother's nest."

Dalrain stretched out her long, sinuous neck until her beak was close enough to peck. "But Almore believed in you," she spat. "Almore, the fool, thought you would never love another."

"Now he lies in the marsh, waiting to die," cried Argonne, her voice gone sharp with bitterness. "He would not come with us, and would not have us stay."

Rhymthus voiced his usual calm logic, so different from his recent fury. "We told him to behave as if you had died, and take another mate," he said blandly, and Derianne was surprised how deeply the words cut her.

That she still understood their language didn't surprise her at all. It never had, even on that first day, when her mother had cut her own hand to draw blood, dripping it onto Derianne where she struggled in the fishing net, and chanting the spell that ended the curse and changed her back into a human. Even then, it had only seemed right that she would still understand the language of the swans. If she had thought about it, she would have realized that she had always understood the swans, at least on some level. Just as she had always known she would become one of them.

As long as she could remember, she had known that she

would turn into a swan when she grew up. The talk in the village had always hissed around her as she walked through with her basket, whether to buy or sell, visit or work. Someone always pointed her out and whispered that she was the one, the cursed one, Magda's eldest daughter, who would turn into a swan at the sight of the first full moon of her sixteenth year. But to Derianne, it was never a curse. It was her destiny. And it had never occurred to her that her mother would seek out a way to get back the daughter she had never seemed to want in the first place.

"Almore," Derianne said, her voice gone wooden with disappointment. "Almore is not with you?" All the swans began to hiss and snap in reply, a babble of sound. "Take me to him," she said quietly, and there was silence. "It is not by my choice that Elston—the human male—courts me. I would rather be with Almore."

"You cannot go there, a *human* maiden, alone. What would your *mother* say?" Dalrain hissed cruelly. "She who owns you as the farmer owns the geese with the clipped wings."

But Deri had already decided. There was no life for her among the humans. No happiness she could imagine as the wife of Elston, though he was kind enough and good. She would miss her sisters, perhaps. But it was Almore she had longed for these months, Almore and the clear waters beneath her as they floated peacefully, concerned about nothing but the plucking of tasty water plants beneath them, fresh and abundant. Handsome Almore, the clean white of his feathers, the smooth line of his strong beak, the elegant curve of his powerful neck, and the great span of his tremendous wings. "I will sneak away tonight. Will you meet me at dawn, where the roads cross south of town?" There was silence, as a dozen swans stared at her, deciding. "Please," she said. "Let me go to him. Perhaps I can persuade him to come back with you and...and...take...a new mate." Derianne didn't know how she got the words out, they stuck so in her throat. "And if not, at least we will be together. I will stay with him." This she knew. No matter what Almore decided—and she truly hoped he would move on to a new life with a new mate—she would not return home. Home. A strange word. Her mother's house, where she had grown up and spent most of her life, was no longer her home. Her home was the sky and the ponds and lakes along the migration route, from spring to fall and back again. The ache of homesickness clenched at her heart. She wanted to go home, to Almore. "Please."

There was much discussion and bickering among the flock, as well as a few more pecks at Derianne, but in the end, they agreed. Dalrain rose up to her full height, her head nearly level with Derianne's eyes, and her wings outstretched to their full majesty. She barked, "Argonne and Orthur alone will lead you. They are old, and the least likely of the flock to propagate viable young this season." Deri's breath caught, and she looked down at the muddy earth beneath her bare feet. Dalrain's frank assessment of the birds was meant to hurt Deri, and it had. She had not considered the effect of a delay in nesting. She was asking them to risk the future of the flock on a human whim. They had already accepted the loss of Almore, for the good of all. Now she was asking them to risk nesting losses the small flock could ill afford. Worse, she was challenging their leader's decision. Dalrain went on, "Be no later than sunrise, or they will return immediately to us. We will all move further north." With the final sounds of her edict, Dalrain launched into the sky. Twigs and reeds crackled under the push of her legs. The others followed, almost as one bird. Gusts from their powerful wingbeats blew Derianne's hair wildly as the birds took off. And they were gone. Before Deri could make her way out of the thicket of saplings and brambles, the swans had flown from her view, beyond the tall trees to the north.

She took some time to rinse away blood from scratches and nips, and fashion a story to explain the mud and the marks. Bruises from the bites would not show up until morning, if she was lucky. Twigs crackled somewhere behind her. She whirled, but saw no one. Did she hear footsteps trudging away? Or was that her imagination? The breeze rustled last summer's reeds, now dry and dead. Ducks on the pond laughed and squabbled, as a drake proclaimed his success at mating. Such braggarts, the mallards. Suddenly the air was full of bird calls and moving water and sighing wind. She hadn't noticed any sound but the swans' words, as she tried to make her pact with them. Now, trying to judge whether footfalls were real, and whose they might be, she couldn't disentangle the noises. It didn't matter. She had no choice but to go ahead with her plan, and be alert for whoever might try to stop her.

The day seemed to last forever; her mother's scolding—Magda was an expert at undercuts and laying on guilt. Her sisters' snide remarks—they had seen the swans arrive and guessed she had gone to them. They had not been fooled for a moment by her fiction of trying to save one of the neighbors' chickens from a hawk. They couldn't have known what happened, but they had accurately deduced the birds' lack of welcome for her. "You need some friends who don't *bite*, Deri."

"Not good enough for *birds*, eh Deri?"

Sharra enjoyed her sister's misery, but Nessie, the youngest, meant well. "Elston is not a swan, Deri, but neither are you, anymore," Nessie told her as they turned the earth for the spring garden. "And he loves you." Deri sighed. Wherever she went, whatever she did, someone was hurt by it. But she had made her decision.

When the other women of the household were all finally sleeping that night, Deri collected her warmest shawl, Magda's hand-me-down shoes that she had worn for the winter, and a few items that she had slipped into pockets during the day. She fairly flew down the road through town, as soon as she had escaped the house. It wouldn't do to be seen passing through in the dark. She wrapped the shawl about her in the chill damp of the pre-dawn, but carried the shoes in her hand. Running barefoot was quieter.

At the crossroads, she put on the shoes and huddled in bushes near the road, knowing she was early and hoping for a bit of sleep before her journey began. It was a good plan, but it was not to be.

"I've come to ask you to reconsider."

The voice startled Derianne so much that she leaped up, yelping. "Wha—? Elston?"

The young man came closer, so she could recognize him in

the moonless dark. "I heard you," he said simply. "I heard you talking to the swans. Don't go. I admire your loyalty, but you are no longer one of them. Marry me and stay. Or marry someone else, if you must. Or don't marry at all, if you choose. But stay with us. We love you, too. More than they do, it seems."

"Oh, Elston," she said. "I can't." She sighed deeply. "How can I explain?"

"You don't need to," he said, with a sigh of his own. "I would do the same, and I knew you would answer thus. Yet I had to try." He took off his pack and sat down near where Deri had huddled in the bushes. "I will see you safely to him."

No threat or argument would dissuade him from going along, just as none would make her stay. In the end, he agreed to keep out of sight when the swans came for her, and then come out when they took to the sky again.

"Almore!" Deri cried when she finally saw him stretched flat among the cattails, barely alive. She sat by him, ignoring the mud. Lifting his head gently, she settled it in her lap. "You must not give up on life, Almore. We cannot have the life we wanted together, but there are enough good things left to be worth going on."

The swan butted her hand with his head, saying, "Not for me."

"Yes," she insisted. "There is the blue of the sky, the breeze from the ocean, tender new shoots that taste like spring, the wind out of the south, the sun on your back as your feet dabble in clear water." Speaking of the things she so sorely missed hurt her, but she hoped they would stir as much in Almore's heart as they did hers.

"Lovely memories," he said. "Not enough to call a life."

"Then choose another mate and make more of it," she said. It came out much harsher than she meant, for she'd had to challenge herself to say the words aloud.

"Even if I could bear to do that," he whispered. "It's too late." He lifted a limp wing and let it drop. "I am too weak to rejoin the flock, even if I knew where to look for them."

"Then I will carry you," Derianne said. "I will not let you give up and die." She took off her shoes and waded into the cold waters of the marsh to find some food for Almore. "There," she said, laying the tender plants next to his beak. "You must eat and grow strong again."

"And if I refuse?" he sighed.

She stamped her foot. The sharp edges of the dry stalks underfoot made her wish she hadn't, though she couldn't say so. But the sting added emphasis to her words. "Then I will chew them myself, and poke the paste down your throat with my fingers, you stubborn bird!"

"And I will nip your flank until you swallow," Argonne added, coming out of the reeds and touching Deri softly with a wing tip. "We—" she glanced at Orthur for agreement, but went on without waiting for it, "Will wait for you to grow strong enough to fly, so that we can lead you back to the others."

"No, I will carry him, to make sure he goes."

"Then we will lead you there," Orthur added, sidling up to Argonne.

"I will guard you both, lest someone think to rob you for an easy meal," Elston said. Deri's breath caught as Elston parted the thick forest of cattails and came to stand by her side. But the swans only looked him over curiously.

"You're not angry to discover that he came with me?" Derianne asked.

"We have known since we smelled him at the crossroads," Orthur said. "And how could we be angry," Argonne added, "when he is as faithful to you as you are to Almore? You humans are difficult to fathom." She turned toward the woods a little way off. "Will you not now acknowledge the other human who has followed from your home?"

With a pang of fear, Deri turned toward the trees. "Someone followed me? Who? Is it *Mother*?" Magda would just as soon kill the swans, as give up her daughter—her possession—to them again.

Deri ran to the trees, fearing the worst, but ready to defend the swans however she had to. The woman she startled in the trees was not her mother, though. "Nessie!" she cried. "How did you get here?!"

"I followed you, of course." The girl was completely unapologetic. Now that they knew she was here, she wasn't going to back down. "I came for Elston, actually. I knew you would hurt him in the end, and I wanted to make sure he came back."

Derianne smiled. All the comments of the past months, and Nessie's angry disapproval of Deri turning Elston away again and again—it finally all made sense. She hugged Nessie and led her back to meet the swans.

Derianne nodded at Argonne and the others, her faithful friends. The swans didn't understand the concept of thanking. One did what one did, and one coped with what others did. It was a simpler society.

"It is late," she said, taking charge. "We will camp in those trees tonight." She pointed to the woods where she had found Nessie. The others went to set up camp and find food.

"Almore," Deri said when they were finally alone. "will you think about taking another mate? I would not like to see you remain alone."

"No," he replied right away. "If it pleases you, I will go on living, perhaps with the others, or perhaps alone. But I will not have another mate. You were meant to be mine. Only you."

She hugged him sadly, and stroked his long neck. After a while, she spoke. "There is a way, Almore," she said hesitantly. "I told Anela, the village witch, that I wouldn't even ask you, but now I see..."

"What is the way? We must do it. Can you become a swan again?"

Derianne sighed, and the tear finally slid down her face. "No, that is not the way. I asked the village witch for a spell to change me back. I begged. I bribed. I threatened. But she only looked at me with sorrow and pity in her eyes. She said the magic will not work twice on the same person. When I was changed back to a human, it was forever."

Almore's body fell limp with loss of hope. "But you said

there was a way."

"There is," she said, "but you must think very hard before you accept it."

And so, as the full moon rose, Derianne scored her own hand with the knife she had stolen from the kitchen. In that moment, she came to understand her mother a little better. Perhaps there was more to Magda's love than possessiveness. Deri dripped her own blood onto the beautiful white feathers of Almore's strong wings. She chanted the spell that had once cursed her, and bade Almore look at the moon. He turned out not to be as handsome a man as he had been a swan, but it mattered not, for he was her Almore.

They would live in a little cottage by the pond, where they could welcome the swans in the spring and bid them safe journey in the fall. Elston would likely find solace with Nessie, who truly loved him, though he would have to wait at least two more years for her to come of age. Sharra could get on with marrying her suitor.

The walk home was slow. Almore had to learn a great many things before they reached the village. But Derianne would have her Almore, and perhaps, someday, Magda would have her grandchildren. Derianne frowned, wondering what they would look like.

THE SASSY AND THE NAEGG

by Dave Smeds

Claeri was feeling confined by life in the safehold, but when she wanted something from the Wild, she sent the boy who was with her. When he didn't come back, however, she had to go into the Wild herself and deal with the consequences.

Dave Smeds is the author of novels such as The Sorcery Within *and* The Schemes of Dragons. *His short fiction has appeared in myriad anthologies, including fifteen previous volumes of* Sword and Sorceress, *and in such magazines as* Asimov's SF, Realms of Fantasy, *and* F&SF. *His next major upcoming release is* The Wizard's Nemesis, *the conclusion of his "War of the Dragons" trilogy.*

Claeri could get a boy to do anything she wanted. Her mother said it was her curse.

With some boys, she didn't even have to try. Of those, Gannen was the worst. He would follow her around like a new-hatched duckling if she'd let him.

One morning Claeri wanted to walk along the west trail. She hoped it would help her mood. Salt Dell was not as confined as some safeholds. It stretched three leagues north to south, and even wider west to east. It was home to over five hundred plainfolk. It had brine fields and mills, farms and berry brambles, and two separate villages. The river was a joy, from the five-tiered waterfall to the huge mill pond where she'd learned to skate when no taller than her father's knees. But by now Claeri was the better part of twenty years old and it seemed as though she had seen behind every stack of hay and climbed every tree and knew every single person in the enclave. She was corseted by familiarity, and on that morning the laces were drawn too tight.

At least when she walked the west trail, through the woods and the mushroom mounds, she was at the verge of the Wild. She could gaze over the low stone fence and contemplate the unbounded world.

She could not walk the trail alone. Custom did not allow it. And so she asked Gannen to walk with her. She knew he would.

Gannen did not try to get her to talk. Wise of him. He simply walked beside her, half a step behind so as not block her vantage of the Wild.

The woods were quiet, the dew still so heavy the moisture dulled the echo of their footfalls. She inhaled until her chest could expand no further, savoring the crispness of the air. Only the shadiest spots cradled any unmelted snow but the breeze was still northerly. She loved winter. Summer was an ordeal of workshifts in the fields, gnats flying up her nostrils, sweat touching her too intimately. Winter was perfect for leisurely strolls. It was all going so well until they spotted the elk.

"Look," Gannen said.

She frowned, annoyed because she had already noticed them for herself, and because at the sound of his voice, the animals realized they were not alone.

A stag was standing just inside the safehold boundary. A calf stood next to it. The sentry charms that kept out inimical beings had not prevented their entry. Elk were welcome to pass through—particularly when they lingered long enough for hunters to fetch their bows. The cooking sheds never smelled finer than when fresh hunks of venison were turning on the spits.

The stag made a huffing sound that declared its reluctance to be observed. It turned around. A quick hop and it was across the barrier. The youngling leaped over with even greater ease. Two cows and two more calves greeted them on that side. Together the little herd turned and began heading back the way they had come.

Their way led through a natural passageway in the trees. The stag lowered its head, but its left antler grazed a branch.

Claeri blinked. Had she seen what she had seen? Yes. The

antler that had struck the branch was now dangling beside the stag's neck, clinging to the skull by a shred, on the brink of detaching.

"Gannen," she murmured.

"I see it," he whispered back.

Lifebone. The bone that needs neither death nor bloodshed to free it. Found when fresh, and coaxed with the right incantations, it could cure the pox or turn a barren womb fertile.

"Can you believe our luck?" she asked.

"Our *bad* luck, you mean? 'Tis the wrong side they're on."

"It's on *this* side they'd be if you hadn't spoken."

"I'm sorry."

How many times had she heard him utter those words?

"Never mind," she said. "Follow them. The ancestors will smile on us, make no mistake. The antler will fall off and you can come right back."

"But..."

"You'll be the talk of the safehold." She smiled at him. "Proud of you I'll be."

She reached out and took his mittened hand, closing it inside both of her own. He was so startled he almost pulled it back.

She already knew he would do it. He had to straighten up, wipe the branch-drip from his forehead, and gaze at the elk tails disappearing between the boles of the trees before his faith rose to the level of hers. He slid his hand free, eased over the stone fence, and was soon gone from her sight.

She waited where she was, expecting him back at any moment given how tenuously the antler had hung.

He did not return. Not while she stood there on the west trail. Not for the rest of that morning. At noon, she mustered the courage to tell the elders what had happened. The searchers went out, protected by fetishes, fortified by elixirs, and armed as well as the plainfolk knew to arm themselves. They did not find him, not even with his brother's dog to sniff along his track. Spring came and went before any denizen of Salt Dell learned what had happened to Gannen son of Ayn.

-oOo-

One humid morning, not long after Claeri had started her shift at the loomhouse, her father sought her out. "You're to go to the elders' keep," he said. "It's about the boy."

"There's news?" she asked.

Her father shrugged. "I expect it's you who'll be telling me, come supper time."

She hurried off at once, so distracted by the possibilities she tripped on her way across the rope bridge and nearly tumbled into the river. Her hair was matted with sweat by the time she marched up the slope to her destination.

The elders' keep stretched as long as four barns—the largest structure in all Salt Dell with the exception of the festival lodge. Even so, the audience was overflowing the gallery of the main council chamber.

So many faces, and all regarding her. And the only one with any sympathy was Maerea, her mother's aunt.

A burly young man stood off to one side, his red hair standing out sharply above the horizon of grey-haired and white-haired heads. She knew him well. Ollsos. The woodchopper. One of Gannen's friends.

The way was cleared and Claeri proceeded forward to stand right in front of the dais, facing a half-circle of elders seated behind their heavy table of oak and sigil tile. In the center chair sat Dame Haddah. Spindly as a skeleton she might be, as well as blind in one eye, but no person in Salt Dell had shown surprise when she had been reelected as speaker of the council for the fourth year in a row.

"An emissary of the Eyeless appeared at the west gate at dawn," Haddah said. "They have Gannen. They have offered to return him to us alive and unharmed. All they demand is an item coveted by one of their warlords."

Claeri's breath caught in her throat, trapped. She wanted to cry out in joy that Gannen was not dead, and at the same time, the anguish she had struggled to dampen for five months was now rekindled. A captive of the Eyeless?

"Wha—What do they ask for?" she stammered.

"They want *this*."

The speaker's voice was deep and male. Out of the crowd emerged a figure in work leathers and heavy boots that said he had come straight from his forgeworks to the gathering. He carried a sword.

Embruss was his name. He was Gannen's uncle.

The blacksmith was a hale man, still active in his craft, but the creases in his face had deepened to canyons, and he held his burden with a profound unsteadiness.

Embruss had made many swords in his time. Most had gone to customers outside the safehold. Blades were among Salt Dell's most important trade goods. Once and only once, Embruss had made a sword for himself. No other piece contained so much of his essence. He had been offered great sums for it in times past. He had always said no.

Embruss placed the sword on the council table, unsheathed. Five heartbeats later, he let go of the hilt.

"This is to be taken to Gibbet Rock and bonded to the warlord," Haddah said. "When all that is done, Gannen will be released. We have decided the duty falls to you, Claeri."

Claeri lowered her glance to the floor. "I understand."

"And you accept?"

"I do," she answered.

"Good."

"When is it to be done?"

"Tonight. Before the sun sets, out the gate you'll be."

"Oh."

"Revered elders. If it please you, I will go with her."

Claeri's head darted to the side. Ollsos had taken a step forward and, wrists crossed in official supplication, was awaiting the reply.

Her heart began to race. To not have to face the ordeal alone—that was honey on bread, cool water on a hot day. She nearly rushed over to hug the woodchopper, no matter that the last time she and Ollsos had spoken, he had called her names and spat at her for encouraging his friend to cross into the Wild.

Haddah shook her head. "The Eyeless are oathbound not to harm our envoy, but treachery is as common to them as dung in a pasture. Better to risk one of our number than two."

Ollsos picked up his ax from where he had left it in a corner and he exited the keep. Despite the frown on his face, Claeri knew that was that. The elders had spoken, and Ollsos was not the sort to defy their judgment.

Haddah set a knobby hand upon the table beside the sword. "We will spend the afternoon teaching you the ritual and supplying what advice we can," she told Claeri. "Take an hour or two now and go say your farewells to those who matter most to you. If all goes well, you will see them all again tomorrow. But best get it done, for their sake."

The expressions on her parents' faces tore at her heart, and it was nearly as bad with the others she chose to seek out. Agonizing as the process was, she was almost relieved when the agreed-upon hour arrived and she had to journey back to the elders' keep.

Her great aunt was waiting for her at the threshold.

"We'll prepare you the best we know how," Maerea promised.

"Helpless I'll be," Claeri warbled. "And hopeless, too. I've never even learned to set a snare or bait a hook. I can't even run all that well."

"Who's to say, that may give you an edge. The Eyeless won't be on their guard with you—certainly not the way they'd be with Ollsos. And you make friends easily."

"I've no wish to be *friends* with the Eyeless," Claeri objected.

Maerea clucked her tongue. "Hear me with your good ear, not the one you've stuffed with straw. I am saying, child, look to your strengths, and don't forget what those strengths are."

The old woman gave Claeri one last hug, then urged her through the doorway.

Claeri departed through the south gate late that day and set out along the wagon ruts of Traders Way, soon entering a rolling terrain of scrub, woodland, and breeze-bared hilltops. The sun set not long after she veered off onto the footpath she'd been told to take, her route winding a little toward the west now, not strictly toward the south.

The brightness of the horizon faded, the sky giving way to twilight, and then to dusk. It felt to her as though she was being covered over by Death's cloak, but a gibbous moon hung behind her to her left and she had no difficulty seeing where to place her feet. She had a small glowstone with her. Should clouds appear and hide the moon, she would use it. For the moment, she did not need it. In fact, she could see so well that when a small creature crossed the trail a hundred paces ahead and disappeared down the bank of a small creek, she could tell from the white striping it was a skunk even before its stench wafted her way.

No, it was her mood that was dark, and so it should be. All manner of Other Folk roamed the Wild, and now that she was away from the safehold, if any decided she would serve as a meal or as entertainment or as property to be seized, there might be little she could do to thwart their designs. Brutal her luck would be if she had to deal with something worse than the Eyeless tonight, but when she considered the odds, dark her spirits remained.

She trudged on. She knew she was climbing, but the increase of elevation was so gradual her legs felt no more taxed than before. Mostly the change manifested in the disappearance of boggy spots, and in the speed with which the rivulets trickled along the creases of the landscape.

Gradually she became certain she was being followed. She had heard nothing. When she turned, she saw nothing. It was more a matter of her hair stiffening at the nape of her neck, and goose pimples rising from her wrists toward her armpits.

At the end of another hour, she understood the cause, and was embarrassed it had taken her so long to puzzle it out.

She pulled the glowstone from her pack, cupped it so that its light was steered toward her right, where clumps of summerdrop heather formed a natural hedge.

"If you want to sneak around after me like that, you should try doing in some other form," she called out. "As it is, I smell you every time you catch up."

The skunk appeared in the gap between two leaning shrubs

and ambled to the center of the path. It stood up on its hind legs and started to shiver. Or at least, shivering was what it resembled at first, but the disturbance evolved in an odd manner. Eventually Claeri began to wonder if her eyes had forgotten how to remain steady in her head. All she could be certain of was that the newcomer was getting larger, and then larger still.

Finally the shape was man-sized, and indeed, what stood in front of her seemed to be a man in fact—a gnarled, hairy, and very naked man. Quickly she put the glowstone away. Moonlight gave her as much of a view as she cared to be granted.

At least the smell was fading.

"That's close enough," she told him.

He made no move toward her. But then, his sort would not, so she had been schooled. With his sort, it was what you said that would ruin you. Or save you.

He smiled. For all the scruff and dirt that adorned him, his teeth gleamed white and straight and were perfectly intact. His breath was blossom-sweet.

"Now what would a maiden such as yourself be doing so far from her warded glen all alone on a night of woe and portent?"

She put her hands on her hips. "It's a maiden I've become? My! They say the Wild will change a person. Quick it is about its business, I must say."

Her companion laughed. "A sassy you are, then. Good. That's some protection, at least. I will not describe what happened to the last virgin who wandered this—"

"Was it my safety on your mind?" Claeri interjected. "And why should that be your concern?"

"Considerate I am," he said. "The kindest of fellows, to those I like."

"So you say. A moment ago you were a skunk."

"And a *kind* skunk I was. Naeggs may take a thousand shapes, but our natures are as fixed as stone."

"I've heard much talk of the nature of naeggs," Claeri said. "So...is it my escort you've made of yourself? Will I have your kindness beside me the rest of my journey?"

"A little way, perhaps. Who do you think is keeping that

shadow man over there at bay?"

Claeri almost turned to look at the spot the naegg indicated, but she caught herself in time.

"There's no shadow man there," she stated.

"A poor and desperate thing my eyesight is tonight," complained the naegg. "I suppose next you'll be telling me *you're* not really here!"

Claeri sighed. "Unfortunately, I *am* here. Much as I'd prefer to be back in my warded glen, as you put it."

"Well, you're here, then, and I'm here. Let's get to the important matters. Have you any five-fold leaf in that belt pouch of yours?"

"Maybe. Maybe a pipe as well."

"*Salt Dell* five-fold leaf?" the naegg added with eagerness.

"What other kind would I have?"

"Oh, and it's a cruel wench you are, to put me on the brink of begging."

"I liked 'sassy' better than 'wench' if you must know. And anyway, now hardly seems like the time to be lighting up a pipeful."

"Any evening's a time for five-fold leaf! And what better occasion than on your way to likely doom and torment?"

"Are you a seer as well?" she asked.

"It's to Gibbet Rock this trail leads. You're not on the way to a midsummer dance, are you now?"

"I am not."

She rummaged through her pouch and brought out her pipe. She tossed it to the naegg, who cradled it reverently. She uncorked her bottle of leaf, poured a measure into the bowl, and poised the striker.

A spark. The naegg inhaled. The longer he held his breath, the more peaceful his smile became. When at last he opened his mouth, only a whiff of vapor was left to escape his lungs.

"Ahhh," said the naegg. "If ever I'd a mind to work, I'd labor in the fields, and this would be my crop."

"No food?" Claeri asked.

"No. I would share this, and my friends would set their

baskets in my larder and their kettles of soup in my fireplace, and I'd get by very well."

"You've a house and a larder and a fireplace?" Claeri asked.

"And so I would have, were I a farmer. To go with the fields and the barn."

Claeri took a long draw. It was ordinary leaf by her measure, but she was willing to concede her perspective was different than a being who owned no pocket and carried no pouch. She handed the pipe back.

"Your first time beyond the boundary?" the naegg asked, voice squeaking as he held his breath.

"When I was sixteen I went in a caravan to Wheathaven. For spring carnival."

"And how was that?"

"Different boys. That was nice. Alas, not different enough."

"Isn't that the way?"

"I wish I'd gone again this year," she said. "Might have been my last chance."

"And why is that?"

She couldn't ken why his questions didn't strike her as nosy, but they did not. It wasn't just the leaf—though goodness knows a bit of leaf was known to bring out the garrulous side of her nature. It was something about *him*. In any case, as they walked on, continuing to smoke, she told him the whole account of Gannen's capture and the task she'd been assigned.

"Well," he said when she was done, "'Tis quite the nettle patch you're in."

"Isn't it, though?"

"Do you know what I heard through all that?" the naegg commented when she was done.

"What did you hear?"

"You didn't blame the boy. You didn't blame the elders. You didn't even blame the Eyeless."

She scoured the dregs out of the pipe and let the bits fall to the ground. "If I think that way, where does it stop? Should I blame my mother for giving birth to me, or my father for the glint in his eye, nine months before?"

"Some might," the naegg said.

"Could be. I suppose I'm not made that way."

The path was beginning to curve. Claeri recalled that as one of the signs to indicate she was nearing Gibbet Rock.

"I'll take my leave now," the naegg said. "You've listened well and given back better. Most plainfolk tire of my blather, and rude they are in telling me so."

"Whereas I am sorry we are at the end," Claeri responded. "The conversation was a kindness. A distraction from what lies ahead."

"And what lies ahead? Doom and torment did I say? Well, meet me early of a night, and it's a pessimist you'll find. Meet me later, and it's an optimist I am. Go forward, young lass. Perhaps all will be well."

"Not everything changes as readily as do you," she said. "I set out on a path to peril and it's to peril I'm goin' still. You've been good company. That was a bounty I'd not expected, and I thank you for it."

"A joy it is to know you," the naegg declared, and he stopped in place, and held entirely still. "I grant you the favor of a wish."

She turned. He remained where he was, more steady of form and motion than he had been since he'd emerged from the hedge as a skunk.

"I've heard about shifters' wishes," she said.

"They are as dependable as we are," cackled the naegg. "But may come a time when you've naught to lose. If so, wish away. Keen my ears will be."

The naegg resumed his characteristic jiggle and wag. Soon it developed into the peculiar shiver she had witnessed before. When her vision settled, she found her companion had become a treefrog. He bounded away with astonishingly robust leaps.

Her dread stretched the remaining journey in her heart and mind, but when she rounded a shoulder of a hillside and saw Gibbet Rock looming in front of her, the moon was straight overhead. That meant it was still well before midnight.

The formation looked nothing like a gibbet. It was prominent in the landscape and possessed a flat top. When the Eyeless or the shadow men wanted to leave a morsel dangling for the crows, that was where they would do it. Nothing stood up there at the moment, the plain folk having torn down the most recent butcher's tree, but she could sense the lingering miasma of death. When the Eyeless themselves emerged from the shadow of the rock and ambled out to meet her, they seemed to bring the mephitis with them.

They had arms and legs, faces and hands, but the Eyeless would never be confused with the plain folk. Horns grew from their head, curling down like ram's regalia. Their chins came to points. Their skin was grey. Their knees bent backward.

They weren't actually eyeless, but Claeri saw at once how they had acquired the label. Their eyes were uniformly black—pupils, irises, and sclera—and so the sockets appeared empty except when they stood close.

Unfortunately they soon were all too easy to see clearly. They did not come to a halt until they were only a few paces away. There were five of them. The one in the center stood slightly taller, though all of them were too tall to suit her. He wore the most accessories, including a necklace of what appeared to be severed fingers. He took another two steps forward, leaned in, and studied her.

They *were* severed fingers. She was glad that at least they were grey, clawed fingers, clearly taken from his own kind. She did not let herself tremble. She stared straight back at him, no matter that it felt like she was staring at holes in his skull.

He did not touch her. The bargain did not allow that. But he was so very close. Her nose filled with the ripeness of his body, the ripeness of his breath.

And still she did not let herself tremble.

He smiled.

"I am Hadren."

"Is it to you the blade will be consecrated?" Claeri asked.

"Of course," he replied.

She reached behind her back and drew Embruss's masterpiece from its scabbard. She held it level at the height of her chin, letting them get a good look at the folded steel and the intricate roping of the hilt.

All five stared at it with an intensity she could only call ravenous, and yet they all, even Hadren, kept their distance. Iron was poison to the Eyeless, as it was to so many of the fey. That in part was why they craved iron weapons—the better to kill enemies among their own kind, for any cut might be fatal, even a small slice on an arm, or a jab into a thigh. That was why she could be certain she would live at least a few more minutes. She still had to complete the ownership enchantment.

"I've shown you the sword," she said. "Now show me my compatriot."

Hadren shrugged. "In due time."

"Now."

He mocked her with a laugh.

She slid the sword back into its scabbard, folded her arms, and glanced off to the side and upward, barely keeping Hadren in her field of vision.

Hadren ignored her. A bat fluttered across the face of the moon. It had already fluttered back the other way before he spoke.

"As you wish."

He raised a hand and gestured. Two more Eyeless emerged from the shadow of the rock formation, bringing with them a human figure in tattered winter garments. His hair was matted, his face dirty, his shoulders were bowed rather than broad and even, but she recognized him as soon as the moonlight struck him. It was Gannen.

Tears brimmed on her lower lashes. She almost spoke, but then she saw the vacancy behind his eyes. He walked between the escorts like a cow plodding from one stack of hay to another, too pasture-dazed even to raise its tail and give its flies a slap.

"What have you done to him?"

"He was being uncooperative. We took the fight out of him. There's nothing awry with him that your wisefolk can't mend. See for yourself. Have we bled him? Have we broken his bones?"

She went to him. He gazed straight ahead as if he did not see her, but his eyes were open. His chest filled with each breath. She pressed and prodded and found no indication of wounds or bruises. He was unbathed and had lost weight, but not to a degree any worse than could be explained by the deprival for five months of a roof, a hearth, and his mother's kettle.

"You have him. Now fulfill the bargain. The moon is high. It's time."

Claeri swallowed the temptation to keep him waiting. After all, she wanted to be on her way back as soon as possible.

She unlaced the scabbard and lifted it and the sword from her back.

"Where is it to be done?" she asked.

Hadren led the way around to the far side of Gibbet Rock and slightly farther up the ravine. From the tenth step onward the sound of falling water grew more distinct. They came to a waterfall the height of Claeri's waist. A rock shelf permitted a person to walk right up to one side of the feature. Near the spot stood a bucket adorned with the glyphs of the Cloudwalkers.

The place had the necessary conditions.

"Begin," demanded Hadren.

Claeri fully recalled the steps the elders had drilled into her that afternoon, but how she would have loved to introduce a "mistake" in the ritual. She dared not. Hadren was observing her carefully, and she had no doubt he knew the required elements even better than she.

With the bucket, she filled a granite hollow some twelve to fifteen paces from the waterfall. It took several trips until the water was deep enough that it would cover the sword, assuming the sword was laid down flat.

She gestured to Hadren. He placed a forearm over the puddle and cut a slice in his own flesh with his obsidian blade. His blood dripped into the puddle. She took a wand of rainwood from her pack and stirred the blood until it was thoroughly mixed with the water, then threw the wand away.

She drew the sword, set the scabbard aside, and went to the waterfall. She turned and tilted the weapon until every part had been rinsed in the torrent, then she did it again. All the while she murmured gentle incantations of release beneath her breath. She felt the bonds that had dedicated the artifact to Embruss weaken and one by one, slip away. Finally none remained.

She walked back to the puddle, where Hadren waited, his sneer now gone. His eagerness was obvious from the way he leaned forward, gaze following every move she made.

She saw the puddle was not quite ready. Four transformative attributes were required: Water. Blood. Moonlight. And finally, stillness.

Hadren bared his teeth, as though about to growl at her, but apparently he understood the need for the delay. Gradually the water finished settling. When it was mirror smooth, she opened her mouth and said, "Hadren." Immediately thereafter she bent down and set the sword down in the water, submerging it completely.

She let go of the hilt and straightened up. Her part was now done.

Again the wait. She feared she would chew the inside of her cheeks raw before the water grew still again. Finally, for the second time, the water became motionless.

Hadren grabbed the hilt and lifted the sword out. He did not writhe in pain. His hand clutched its prize steadily. No tremors. No odor of burning flesh.

He cut the air. Smiled at the swishing noise it made. His companions, though they eased back to a safer distance, regarded him as though he had become one of their gods.

Claeri went to Gannen, took him by a wrist, and tugged. He moved in the same desultory manner as before, but he did enough that she would not have to drag him all the way back to Salt Dell. She set off along the trail with him.

"No, no, no." Hadren chuckled. "It's not really my sword until I've spilled blood with it, is it my girl? Your blood will do nicely."

"You are sworn not to harm me," Claeri exclaimed.

"Nor will I. It's the sword that will harm you."

Hadren sauntered three steps forward. Claeri retreated, pulling

Gannen along.

"So quiet you are," Hadren jeered. "This is usually the point where your ilk tries to throw a curse or two at me. By all means, give it a go."

Claeri had been supplied with a chant verse and had rehearsed the words and the activating rhythm, but she could see by Hadren's cocksure pose that she was unlikely to inflict harm. He might well be enough of an adept to reflect the assault back on her.

The bat fluttered past again. Strange how it lingered. Bats tended to like places where insects hovered. Stagnant puddles. Sedge ponds. Slivers of meadow. All of which she had noticed on her way up the ravine, but none of which existed here near the waterfall.

Bats, she considered, have keen ears.

"Nothing to say?" Hadren cut the air again. "How disappointing."

"If it's words you need, you shall have them: *I wish I had a horse.*"

Hadren tried to charge, but the bat swooped in, expanding so rapidly it was a stallion by the time it reached the ground. Hooves flashed in Hadren's face, and he back-pedalled so suddenly he fell back on his rump. The sword bounced from his grip and clattered away in the direction of the puddle.

The horse lowered itself down. Gannen stood there dully, as if nothing was going on, but Claeri shoved him forward and he ended up draped over the horse's midsection. She vaulted into place behind him, grabbed his belt with one hand, and a fistful of mane with the other.

The stallion surged away. Claeri thought she heard Hadren cackle in triumph, but perhaps terror alone put the noise in her ears. In any case, her back was not split open, nor did the horse scream. She didn't look back to see how close their escape had been. She put all of her concentration into hanging on to Gannen and keeping the both of them atop their saddleless mount.

An arrow whisked by, then another, but then they were around Gibbet Rock, and not long after, around the curve of the hillside.

The whole way along the ravine and through the scrubland, retracing her outward route in reverse, she worried that formerly unseen members of Hadren's band might rush out of hiding places, but they covered the distance without further attack. The most frightening aspect of the journey came from another source entirely. The naegg apparently was not accustomed to being a horse. Twice he skidded on muddy ground and at other times, his hooves landed poorly and kicked up small rocks. Claeri was sure they would all tumble over in a gigantic somersault. Much as she wanted to go quickly, she was relieved when he ceased the gallop and fell into a brisk but stable trot.

At last the brush and brambles and trees vanished to either side, leaving only grass and clumps of wildflowers. Claeri realized they were on the Traders Way and were at the verge of the buffer zone just outside the south gate.

There they stopped.

"Oh my achin' back. Heavy as boulders, you two are." The body beneath Claeri and Gannen was still that of a horse, but mouth had transformed, and the naegg's voice came from it as distinctly as a bard from a stage.

Claeri dismounted. She wasn't certain how she was going to get Gannen off without making a mess of it, but all at once, he slid off of his own accord. Her breath caught. Was he freed of his affliction? Unfortunately, once his feet were on the ground he just stood there, staring at nothing and showing no further indication he was in command of himself.

Meanwhile the presence beside her was no longer a large animal drenched with horse sweat. It had become a hairy naked man drenched with horse sweat.

"Thank you," Claeri told the naegg.

"The pleasure was mine," he replied. "Been wanting to give that fellow grief for ages now."

"You certainly did that."

The naegg's amusement put a bounce in his limbs and a lilt in his voice. "Hee. That I did. That I did." He waved her onward. "Now off with you. Tend to your friend. He is only half-rescued."

"I will."

"And come back, of an evening, and tell me how he fares."

The naegg shivered and shrank. She blinked, and by the time her vision cleared, a bat was fluttering off toward the midge meadow.

Claeri could not get Gannen to do more than stumble a few steps forward at a time, but as her wits returned, she realized she did not need to deal with the matter at all. She pulled out her glowstone and waved it back and forth over her head. It wasn't long until four strong sentries arrived from the direction of the gate. Two picked up Gannen and hauled him off. The other pair bracketed Claeri as she followed.

Claeri was sure some calamity would befall her at the last moment, but everyone moved efficiently and carefully and soon they had crossed the threshold to safety. Just inside the gate, she dropped to the greensward and kissed the grass.

They were taken at once to the elders' keep. Despite the hour, many of its denizens were still up, including Haddah. When Gannen was laid out on a bench, the woman limped over and studied him carefully with her one good eye.

"Many a trick I've known the Eyeless to play," she muttered. "And here is another to add to the list."

"What's been done?" Claeri asked.

"His spirit has been untethered. In his present state, any restless ghost could force its way into his body and nevermore would Gannen be free of it."

Haddah was trying to be kind, but Claeri knew perfectly well that restless ghosts were the least awful thing likely to seize the opportunity.

"Can it be un-done?"

"Yes. But quick we must be about the task, or Gannen will know suffering worse than any the Eyeless might have caused him on their own."

Haddah beckoned to others who had just entered the council chamber. They carried sticks of spirit incense and bottles of trance brew.

A hand settled upon Claeri's shoulder. It was her great aunt.

"This will take many hours. Meanwhile you will come with me."

"I want to be here," Claeri objected.

"No. Your presence will be a distraction, and in any case, you need cleansing. You were among the Eyeless. No one returns from that untainted."

"They did not touch me."

"Glad am I to hear it, but you're to come with me nonetheless. Don't make me pull you by the ear."

The cleansing was a matter not only of magical ritual, but of soap and hot water in the crones' tub room. Maerea kept Claeri company, but it was a trio of white-haired sorceresses that tended to her. Between that ordeal, and the soporific effect of the bath, and the exhaustion stemming from her encounter with Hadren and his cronies, Claeri lacked the energy to argue she should be allowed to return to Gannen's side. Barely minutes after she had been shown to a bed, sleep reached out and snatched her.

She woke to Maerea's hand on her upper arm.

"What's the time?" Claeri asked at once. "Is it done?"

"Nearly noon," her aunt replied. "And yes, it's done."

"Did they save Gannen?"

"That they did."

To Claeri, it was as though a breath she had been holding for five months could finally be released.

"He'll need to be left in peace at home for a time," Maerea continued. "No busy-bodies asking him lots of questions about things he'd rather forget. His father has come to fetch him. Get dressed and come to the council chamber. You've just enough time to say the words you need to say."

Maerea went on ahead. Claeri followed in short order.

Her footsteps echoed from the far corners of the chamber, a startling emptiness compared to the day before. Those in attendance now consisted of not much more than the elders who had performed the ritual upon Gannen, along with some of the attendants who had assisted them.

Claeri smiled to see Gannen on his feet, standing next to Ayn. He turned as she entered, and she could tell by the alertness of his glance that he was "there."

She opened her mouth and was on the verge of blurting her apology—about to make a tangle of the careful words she had rehearsed—when his hand shot up, palm toward her.

"Say nothing to me."

She froze in place, mouth open. Then, reading his expression, she did just as he requested.

He looked away from her and began walking toward the door. His father stopped him halfway there.

"Son. Whatever else, 'twas she who rescued you."

Gannen turned his head only halfway, not enough to face her. His mouth contorted one way and then the other, and finally two sullen words came out: "Thank you."

Ayn let loose his hold, and together father and son left the building. Gannen did not look back.

So many times in the past few years, Claeri had wanted less devotion from Gannen. Now there was not a trace left, and already she missed it.

She turned back to the council. Two of those who had participated in the re-anchoring of Gannen's spirit were heading away, their stumbling gaits and lowered chins showing they could not remain awake any longer, but a small cluster of others including Haddah and Maerea sat down in the common area, away from the dais. Haddah gestured Claeri to approach.

"Tell us the tale, child. What did you see, and how did you make it back to us?"

The elders never passed up the chance to learn more about their neighbors in the Wild. It was not as though they could obtain that knowledge routinely.

Claeri gave a summary of the whole excursion from the first glimpse of the skunk to the moment when the four sentries came out of the gate to ferry her and Gannen back inside. To her surprise, she described more of the seemingly idle conversation with the naegg than she expected she would.

"I'm grateful it went so well," she concluded. "And humble I am to know I had such luck. I'm unhurt, and Gannen is no longer lost."

Not one of the elders smiled at that assessment. Haddah wore a particularly somber expression. Gradually Claeri caught up to their thinking.

"I haven't seen the last of this matter. Have I?"

"Certainly not the last of that naegg," Haddah said.

"I understand. He granted me a wish, and now I owe him."

"For the wish? From what you've told us, that was freely given, was it not?"

"Well. Yes. I suppose it was."

"Then you owe him nothing for the wish. 'Tis the other thing."

"What other thing?"

"You owe him for saving your life."

"Um. Wasn't that part of the wish?"

"You wished for a horse. Did you wish for a *brave* horse?"

"I didn't specify."

"Then it was his choice to be the sort of horse you needed."

"I see," Claeri said. "But—if I'm to ever save his life, I'll need to..."

"You will have to frequent the places where he is to be found."

"Oh, dear."

"Yes. Oh, dear, indeed."

Shapeshifters were fey folk, and no manner of fey folk were to be found at any time within Salt Dell. The sentry charms were not refined enough to allow an exception, not even when the individual in question was trustworthy. The ban was absolute. Claeri was facing at least one more excursion into the Wild, and probably many.

"You've much to think about, child, but plenty of time to weigh and ponder and plan." Suddenly Haddah was overtaken by a huge yawn. "As for me, I'm off to bed before I'm reduced to curling up right here next to Bluebell." With her toes, she nudged the dog sleeping beneath her chair.

The other elders rose with Haddah and began limping and wobbling toward their rooms. They waved away Claeri's fumbling attempts to thank them all over again. Soon she was making her own way from the council room, and from the keep itself. Maerea walked beside her as they took the path that led to Claeri's home.

She contemplated what she was facing. A few months ago she had been aching for the chance to venture beyond the boundary, but this was far from what she had been after. Her situation was not unlike a sentence of exile, and exile was the worst punishment a condemned member of the safehold could suffer.

"How do I begin?" Claeri asked her aunt.

"Do you like him?"

"Who? The naegg? Not well enough to be his mare, if that's what you're getting at."

"What I meant was, did you enjoy the time you spent with him? Was he good company?"

"I've had worse," she admitted.

"In that case, you know that plot of five-fold leaf your father is tending?"

"Yes."

"Tell him that when harvest comes, he should hold onto a reserve. You won't want to run short."

"I see. I'm to keep the naegg in a good mood."

"It's always a good idea to keep a shapeshifter in a good mood," Maerea replied, "but it's not just him I'm thinking of. It's you. Takes steady nerves to be out in the Wild. As you learned last night. And frankly, you're better company when you're relaxed."

Claeri blushed. Her aunt made it all sound straightforward—something within her means to accomplish. But she knew perfectly well it would not be anything like that. On the contrary, she was quite certain she had managed to mire herself in a destiny.

"I may die," she said plaintively.

"Child," Maerea said. "We all die, sooner or later. On the way to that moment, while you still bide among the living, I think you will find there are worse things than getting to wander the Wild, with a naegg as a friend."

TEARS OF A DEAD GOD

by Jonathan Shipley

Jonathan Shipley's seventh appearance in Sword and Sorceress is another tale about Jenna the exorcist who this time is faced with a dead god—something completely beyond her scope that forces her into new territory. Often with a series of increasingly exotic stories—like Jenna's—the challenge is "what comes next?" This year's "Tears of a Dead God," however, has already generated possibilities for the next two stories. Such is the power of a dead god.

Jonathan, a Fort Worth fantasy writer, has sold another baker's dozen of stories since Sword and Sorceress 30, ten of which are futuristic science fiction. He maintains a web presence at www.shipleyscifi.com where you can find a full list of his published short stories.

The afternoon sun was low on the horizon when the gray walls of the Commandery appeared around the next turn of the forest road. "Never thought I'd be so glad to see the old barracks," Jenna sighed, heartily sick of the saddle after a long week on the road. And it had started to drizzle again. She kicked her mare into a trot toward the gate.

Beside her, her Knight-Guardian Trayn urged his mount to keep pace. He had been unusually quiet on the journey back from King's City, but events had given him a lot to think about. Then he gave a sudden shudder. "I do believe our dead dwarf has awakened," he muttered. "I'd recognize that chill breath on my backside anywhere."

Jenna glanced over and saw he was right. Dwarf—centuries dead and now their ghostly traveling companion—had appeared on the horse's rump right behind Trayn's saddle. But "appeared" was too generous a term. Even to her exorcist's Sight, Dwarf was only a pale shadow in the sunlight.

"What kind of swamp dung have I landed in now?" Dwarf demanded in a gravelly voice.

"We've arrived at the Northern Commandery of the Knights of the Holy Retribution," Jenna answered. "It's our home base when not on assignment."

"Not much to look forward to," Dwarf snorted and faded out again.

Perhaps there wasn't much cause to celebrate a squat, gray fortress, but it was secure lodging with no lack of food. That was something to look forward to after traveling rations and struggling to keep dry in the rainy season. Trayn had the look of a drowned rat with his generous mane of hair soaked through. "Dwarf isn't impressed by the Commandery," she translated for Trayn. He could only hear one side of her conversations with Dwarf.

"Only because he's too dead to appreciate a hot bath and a change of dry clothes," Trayn retorted. "Gods, this has been a long road back."

Jenna winced, hearing in his tone all of his frustrations with his family. He wanted to be as far away from Castle Harebridge as the borders of the kingdom allowed. And with cause. The potentially deadly conflict of his older brothers over the heirship was nothing if not grim.

Through the main gate, they crossed the courtyard into the smaller stableyard. Her brother Herrin met them with a big grin. They were all three young for their roles, but Herrin was the youngest, a seminary student cast in the role of priest by the necessities of the hinterlands. "Glad you're back, Jenna," he said, then more coolly, "Trayn." For multiple reasons, Knight-Guardian and priest weren't so comfortable in each other's company.

"I'm off to the baths," Trayn said, handing over the reins of his post horse to a stableboy. "Don't expect to see me before dinner."

"Sir Knightly Horsely is as gracious as ever, I see," Herrin murmured as Trayn retreated to the keep.

"These have been hard weeks for Trayn," Jenna explained quickly. "In-fighting in his family. Let him be for once. He doesn't need bickering right now."

Herrin's thin face momentarily took on a stubborn cast, but then he shrugged and let it go. "Whatever you say, Jenna. You're the exorcist."

"Indeed, I am," she agreed loftily as she gathered her saddlebag and followed him into the keep. "And that and a pile of gold will buy you a good-sized castle." Her profession didn't make her popular company. Anyone with a ghost problem was certainly glad to see her come, but equally glad to see her go.

At the stairhall, they turned toward the barely habitable Cold Wing. It was heavily haunted from old deaths in the dungeons directly below, but Jenna and her brother kept rooms where no one else wanted to sleep. Lots of space but not much comfort. Still, she had her exorcist tricks to keep the ghosts out of their parlor.

"Any rumors while I've been away?" she asked as they walked the frigid corridor. She meant rumors of hauntings, of course. In a kingdom rife with unquiet dead, an exorcist's job was never done.

"Always this and that," Herrin shrugged, "but the biggest new problem is Godshead Spring."

"Something more than the spring's healing properties continuing to fail?"

"It's getting worse. The spring's become erratic and hurts as often as heals. Of course the Commandant gets an earful and keeps saying you should be doing something to protect the pilgrims."

"I was summoned by the Exorcist-General to King's City," Jenna reminded him. "The healing properties of Godshead Spring have nothing to do with haunts anyway."

"Oh, I agree. But people hereabout are used to you fixing Otherwordly problems. So even though it has nothing to do with ghosts, you're likely to get pushed into this. And soon. The spring only flows once a month when the sun and moon are opposite in the morning sky. And the next Pilgrims Day is..." He counted on his fingers. "Why bless me, it's tomorrow."

She gave a long sigh. "Wonderful. An immediate problem completely beyond my scope. I don't even know which god is associated with the spring." She gave her brother a pointed look.

"How would I know that?"

"Because it's a god and you're a priest. Didn't you learn things like that in seminary?"

"No." Herrin looked scandalized. "This isn't a Church god, it's one of the Old Gods that no one even remembers anymore. We're taught in seminary not to call them gods at all, just malignant spirits that have attached themselves to certain places." He brightened suddenly. "Maybe a spirit is in your jurisdiction after all."

"Wonderful," she repeated. At least Godshead Spring was relatively close, only an hour or two at a steady trot. She wasn't up for another lengthy journey after King's City. But her thoughts caught on something Herrin had just said: *no one even remembers the Old Gods anymore.* She had a suspicion that "no one" might not include a long dead dwarf. And that brought up one of the two awkward points of this reunion.

As they reached the parlor, warmer within the protection of a perimeter salt line, she took a breath. "We picked up a companion in King's City," she said, making it sound as matter-of-fact as possible. "In order to escape a haunted locale, I promised to show a bit of the modern world to a dead dwarf."

Herrin's eyebrows quirked upward. "Is that a joke? There's no such thing as dwarves."

"Not anymore," she admitted. "Apparently they existed once upon a time, and our new companion is a relic of that time."

"So he's a dead relic of a mythical race."

"Yes, a dwarvish ghost under a magical curse."

Herrin grimaced. The Church rooted out magic wherever it found any hint. "Old High Magic?" he said as though the very words were bitter on his tongue. The Church especially hated the residue of the wizard-lords from a few centuries earlier. Powerful cursed artifacts were uncovered from time to time that the priesthood had to deal with.

Jenna nodded. "Cursed by a wizard-lord to linger beyond death." They'd run into cursed ghosts before, just never cursed dwarvish ghosts. "Please be civil when he's around and no fanatical rants."

Herrin gave a disgruntled shrug that she took as agreement. At that moment, she made up her mind not to bring up awkward point Number Two, also Old High Magic. Trayn had brought a very dangerous sword back from his home at Harebridge.

"So is this dwarf-thing here now?" Herrin asked. He didn't have the Sight as she did.

"No, probably in the barracks with Trayn. I'll introduce you at dinner."

He rolled his eyes. He was the brother of an exorcist and part of their exorcism team, but for all that, not so fond of the dead.

Dinner came an hour after sundown when most useful work ceased for lack of light. It was the one time when the knights at the Commandery gathered as a group. Mostly that meant nothing to Jenna and Herrin, who weren't part of their tight society, but it was still a good idea to go and eat with the assembled knighthood. They might sit at the end of the long refectory table distanced from the discussion, but at least they were there. By contrast, Trayn was always in the center of the table, carrying on two or three conversations at a time, and that was just the way it was. He was a good friend and an excellent Knight-Guardian, but he liked his "knight time."

Tonight, however, he was looking distinctly unsteady, well on his way to getting drunk. "Not good," Jenna muttered under her breath, but she understood. It was one way to deal with his family coming apart.

The air grew abruptly colder, and suddenly a squat, bearded figured materialized by her side. "He started drinking in his bath," Dwarf told her in a gravelly voice. "Mark my words, he'll be sloshed before dessert."

Jenna frowned. "Why were you spying on Trayn in the baths?"

Across the table, Herrin gave a start. "I wasn't...I swear."

"No, that was a question for Dwarf," she explained quickly.

On the road, Trayn had gotten used to this, but now she had to initiate Herrin into her one-sided conversations with thin air. "Dwarf, the young man in the cassock is my brother Herrin."

"A good-for-nothing, mealy-mouthed priest," Dwarf snorted.

"A seminarian," she corrected. There were so many times when she was glad that no one else could hear the other side of the conversation.

"Do you have a name, Sir Dwarf?" Herrin asked in his most polite tones. He was obviously trying.

"Mealy-mouthed *and* rude," Dwarf huffed. "You don't just up and ask something like that. Your kind wouldn't be so keen on names if they could be used to trap you."

"No, just Dwarf," Jenna supplied. "The name was a casualty of the centuries. I was thinking Dwarf could help with Godshead Spring..."

Dwarf snickered. "Just arrived and already you're whining for my help."

"...by sharing some background on the god of the spring."

"They're not gods," Herrin pointed out. "Just very old spirits."

"The priestling got that right," Dwarf nodded. "Places might be inhabited by Gods of the Wood or Old Stone Gods, but those were just names. These things were ancient and faded even in my time, but we always gave them wide berth. Nasty lot, according to legend, especially the Old Stone Gods. And not people-like in any sense of the word. Creatures, more like. Big, nasty creatures."

"Yet they were worshipped," she pointed out.

"They *weren't* worshipped," Herrin protested.

"Oh, maybe by the mentally deranged," Dwarf added. "But I'm guessing they've mostly faded out by now."

"But the sites themselves could still have power?" Jenna persisted.

Dwarf gave a yawn. "Boring dinner talk. I'm heading up the table for raunchier stories." He vanished, and the temperature returned to normal a moment later.

-o0o-

The next morning, Jenna assembled her pack at first light. Normally salt, bread, and blood were the substances that attracted the dead, but that was the human dead. A divine spirit, faded or not, might be something entirely different. She included her silver-handled ritual knife because silver was the primary mystic metal, but she also took a gold coin and a copper bracelet as additional options.

By the time she finished, Herrin had completed his morning prayers in the chapel and stood at the front door, dressed to travel. "No Trayn?" he asked as she joined him.

Jenna shrugged. "I'm not expecting much from this first visit. Mainly this is to find out what we're dealing with, and the spring isn't far. I didn't even mention this morning excursion to him."

Herrin gave her a narrow look. "I thought you and Trayn were close. Did something happen between you two in King's City?"

"No...yes." She shook her head. "His family problems colored everything. They still do." She pulled open the door and led the way to the stable court...and stopped cold.

Trayn was waiting with three saddled horses. He looked a little bloodshot in the eyes but gave her a cool stare. "Perhaps we should revisit the definition of a Knight-Guardian, Mistress Exorcist."

"I thought to spare you a routine trip. Herrin and I will be fine."

"Dwarf thinks otherwise."

Jenna frowned, working that through. Spirits picked up all sorts of information because they could walk invisible among the living, and Dwarf was no exception. But Trayn couldn't see or hear Dwarf. "How do you know?" she finally asked.

Trayn grimaced. "Ever tried to sleep with a block of ice sitting on your chest? It was clear he wanted me awake and once awake, I had only to ask the stableboys to find out you had ordered horses for early morning. The rest I'm assuming. But you can always ask him directly."

"I would if he were here." Dwarf seemed to be strangely absent. She gave a sigh. "Good morning, Trayn. Would you care to accompany us to Godshead Spring?"

He gave a short laugh. "Dwarf and duty compel me." Then he stepped closer and lowered his voice for her ears only. "I'm not that fragile, Jenna. Whatever is happening between my brothers is half a kingdom away, and I intend to keep it that way." He cupped his hands for her. "A leg up?"

She accepted because he offered, even though she could ride passably enough. Then she watched Trayn swing effortlessly into the saddle and Herrin do the same with less elegance. As they passed under the portcullis of the forward bastion, she kept craning her neck for some sign of Dwarf. But nothing.

They rode straight through, not stopping until the forest gave way to more open hillocks. Twenty minutes beyond that, they approached the pilgrim gathering ground with its cluster of wagons and tethered horses. "We should leave the horses and climb the rest of the way on foot," Trayn said, already dismounting.

"Approaching the spring on foot is traditional," Herrin added, also dismounting.

"To hell with tradition," Trayn snorted. "I'm more worried about a horse breaking a leg on that steep path."

"No worry about *our* legs, I'll wager," Herrin shot back.

The bickering, at least, was normal, Jenna thought as she shouldered her pack and started up the path. And she didn't believe for a moment that Trayn wasn't fragile just now. How could he not be with his brothers on the verge of a duel? Distance was no deterrent to that type of worry.

"So what's the plan?" a gravelly voice demanded in her ear.

She spun and nearly lost her footing on a loose stone. "Finally you're here. I was afraid you'd deserted us for a warm bed this morning."

Herrin opened his mouth to respond, but Trayn touched his arm and shook his head. "She's not talking to us."

"Deserted you?" Dwarf spat. "That's the thanks I get for trying to help out on this foolhardy mission. Let the Old Gods be, I tell you, but since you won't, I thought you'd want some of the lore that's floating around."

"Floating around where?" Jenna asked. The look on Herrin's

face was priceless.

"The Otherworld. There are spirits out there older than me, and I went asking what they knew."

"Ah," she nodded. She was aware that spirits brushed up against each other and sometimes knew things about each other, but this trolling for information in the Otherworld was something new. It probably took a spirit as strong as Dwarf to hold to a purpose like that. The faded human spirits she dealt with didn't even know they were dead half the time. "What did you learn?"

"Not one of the Old Stone Gods, and that's a blessing. Likely a nature spirit of Water, Wind, and Woods. Pleasanter to deal with, but don't be surprised if it wants a human sacrifice."

"A human sacrifice?" she repeated, startled.

"That *is* why we brought Herrin," Trayn responded archly. Herrin's mouth dropped.

"No, that's nonsense," she said quickly. "We're offering no human sacrifices this trip. Dwarf was merely warning me that the god of the spring may *want* a sacrifice."

"Not a god," Herrin muttered sullenly and trudged on.

Godshead Spring appeared as a shallow pool between two stony banks, overlooked by a cairn of rocks higher up. There wasn't much of it, only forty feet or so of mud, but there were scores of gray-robed pilgrims crowding its banks. Some of them poked at the mud with their fingers, but mostly they just waited.

"I thought you said the healing properties had failed," Jenna murmured to Herrin.

"Not failed as much as become wildly inconsistent," Herrin replied. "One handful of water may heal while the next may the scald the skin."

Trayn muttered some response under his breath and began unpacking the saddlebag he was carrying.

"Well, it's all wrong for an exorcism," Jenna said. "Bright morning light, crowds of people, running water—all things that spirits avoid."

"*Human* spirits," Herrin reminded her. "We have no idea about pre-human spirits."

They found a patch of grass away from the crowd but still

with a view of the spring, and hunkered down to eat the travelcakes and watery wine that Trayn produced from his saddlebag. And wait. Jenna was perplexed and anxious. All of this was so different from her normal mode of working that she doubted she could accomplish anything. And yet it was expected of her. She took another swig from the wineskin, then glanced up with wide eyes as a low moan rattled her bones.

"Is it here?" Trayn demanded, drawing his sword. A plain, utilitarian blade but still cold steel. He set a second scabbard nearby on the ground. Jenna grimaced and looked away from it.

"I see nothing, but hear loud moaning," she said. "I assume no one else does."

"No one," Herrin nodded and glanced at Trayn's blade. "That's a different sword. What happened to your old one?"

Trayn tensed. "Broken on the return from King's City."

"And this one?" Herrin persisted, nudging the second scabbard with his toe.

"Don't touch it!" Trayn snapped, pushing Herrin away.

"What's the matter with—"

"I'm starting to see something," Jenna interrupted. From the cairn above the pool, diaphanous wisps emerged and congealed into a huge, attenuated form. The shape was huge and unnaturally thin, with long arms and long questing fingers that clawed restlessly at the air. Not male, Jenna noted immediately. But not all that female either. Maybe there were other options for gods.

She focused her will. "I come in peace," she said in her calmest voice. "I heard that something is amiss in the spring and have come to offer my aid."

But the great, wispy shape just seated itself on the cairn and began sobbing. Tears trickled down the sides of the rock and into the muddy pool. Tears and more tears.

A cry went up from the crowd on the bank as the water level rose. People pushed toward the bank to dip their hands into the pool. At least one person fell into the pool. The whole of it was a cacophony of cries and screams and songs of thanksgiving.

Jenna wrenched her eyes from the spectacle back to the figure on the cairn, still sitting but no longer sobbing. Then the form raised its head, turned an eyeless face in their direction, and pointed an impossibly long finger at them. "*Uthala uṗ!*" it cried and faded a way.

Jenna felt her stomach lurch and the world spin as she collapsed onto the grass.

"Jenna? Come back. Jenna?"

She opened her eyes to see Trayn hovering over her. The sun was low in the sky and the afternoon was ice-cold, even though a makeshift campfire was crackling near her. She shivered and tried to sit up. All her joints ached.

"She's back—bring tea," Trayn called over his shoulder and Herrin came at a run.

"Back from where?" she managed to ask, though her lips felt wooden. "Why so cold?"

"Here, drink this," Herrin ordered, pushing a battered tin cup at her. "It's root tea and should do you good."

She drank. It tasted foul but warmth surged back through her body. When she finished, she repeated, "Back from where?"

"From the Otherworld, most likely," Trayn said, squatting to rub her arms and back. "You collapsed and the air around you turned cold as death. I took it as a sign not to move you."

"A sign from Dwarf?"

"Who else?"

She glanced around. "Dwarf?"

No stocky form appeared, but she heard a gruff whisper. "Not here—too close."

She glanced at the empty pool with the cairn of stones at its head. The crowd of pilgrims had departed, but two bodies lay on the bank, either unconscious or dead. A fleshless skeleton sprawled in the center of the mud. So a human sacrifice after all. No, this was not a safe place. "Help me up," she said. "We need to move farther away...maybe down by the horses."

They doused the fire, and with Herrin supporting one arm and Trayn the other, she managed to make her way down to the foot of the hill where wagons were being readied for travel. She sank into a pile of leaves with a solid tree bole at her back and took a deep breath. "Far enough, Dwarf?"

The stocky figure slowly materialized, looking ragged and faded.

"What happened to you?" she demanded.

"Same thing as you. Thought I was being tricky and invisible, but the word of a creature like that rips through everything. Managed to fall on top of you, and Stupid and Priestling got the message. Dangerous to move a body when the spirit's been knocked out of it. The spirit wouldn't know where to return to."

"My spirit was knocked out of my body?" Jenna repeated. She knew about spirit travel from her grandmother, but that wasn't one of her gifts. So it wasn't a word that the creature spoke; it was a Word. Had to be a Word of Power to cause that much effect. Then other images flooded back to her. "Was that what happened to those pilgrims?" She grimaced at the memory of the skeleton.

"Uh, no," Herrin answered tentatively. "If that was addressed to me, that is."

"No predicting who's she's talking to these days," Trayn shrugged. "Just jump in when it suits."

"Like a talking stump," Dwarf snorted.

"Herrin, continue," Jenna directed, ignoring the last comment.

He nodded. "The spring's been running strange for a while with healing and harming all mixed together. But no one's died before. This is much worse."

"And yet the pilgrims keep coming," Trayn muttered.

"Dwarf," Jenna said to be clear. "Do you know what we are facing here?"

"Already said—old spirit of Water, Wind, and Woods."

"But it was sobbing. What does that mean when a god sobs lethal tears that kill?"

"Bad day at the temple? Look, I'm weak and tattered. Save the stupid questions for later and give me some blood so I can heal myself."

Jenna looked up at Trayn. "He needs blood."

"Always the blood," Trayn sighed, but pulled out a hunting

knife and drew the blade lightly across his palm. Dwarf leaned closer and lapped up the blood as it welled up. When the bleeding slowed, he faded out.

Herrin frowned. "Keeping company with an accursed spirit and feeding it with your own lifeblood. You know that's how the Exorcist-General would view this, Jenna."

"The Exorcist-General is the least of our worries at the moment," she retorted. "We have a dead god simultaneously healing and killing people with its tears. How do we begin to stop this?"

"Is that question for Dwarf?" Herrin asked.

"No, for myself," Jenna sighed. An answer from anyone would have been welcome, but she was supposed to be the expert.

"Unless you have answers for yourself," Trayn said, "I recommend traveling as soon as you feel strong enough so we can have the light for the journey back." He glanced up at the sky. "And it looks like more drizzle." When Jenna didn't respond, he turned. "Jenna?"

"I heard," she said. "I'm just not sure what to do. According to Herrin's calculations, the next Pilgrims Day will be a month distant."

"Directly after the full moon," Herrin nodded. "When the sun and moon are opposite each other in the morning sky. That's the only time the spring flows."

"Then we have a month to work through the problem," Trayn said. "There's no more to be done today."

Jenna shook her head. "I'm not convinced of that. From what I've seen today, Pilgrims Day seems to be the worst time to intervene when the god is at full power."

"Not a god," Herrin murmured doggedly.

"And by that same logic," she continued, "the hours following the tears may be the god at its weakest. Perhaps the time to act is right now."

"To do what?" Trayn prompted.

The sense of helplessness descended again. In the distance, she could hear the subdued chatter of pilgrims returning home, a mix of joyful and mournful. "Those who died this morning may know," she said suddenly. "Surely their spirits are still lingering." She fixed Herrin with a firm stare. "I need you to retrieve the skull of the skeleton in the spring. Bring it here so I can find out what it knows on the Other Side...and give the poor spirit release, of course," she added when Herrin looked unconvinced. He might see disturbing the bones of the dead as sacrilege, and maybe it was. But it was what she—they—did. The only difference in this case was that these were very recent bones. "Yes?" she prompted him.

"Very well," Herrin nodded and started back up the hill.

Trayn waited until her brother was out of earshot. "You haven't told him about this, I gather." He tapped the scabbard at his hip.

"How can I? He's still dealing with Dwarf as an 'accursed spirit.' And to that I add an accursed magical sword?"

He gave a long sigh. "Accursed, aye. But surely Herrin will see that I would use it only for good, not evil."

"I wouldn't use that particular argument," she advised. "The Church's stance on using accursed objects to do good is well documented. It is said to be a slower path to damnation, but the destination is still the same. But I have no answers," she added to forestall an argument. "I claim no special insight into magical swords."

He gave a snort. "Then perhaps I should—" Trayn fell silent as Herrin appeared between the trees, carrying a skull. He held it gingerly, but it looked sturdy enough, just cleaned of all flesh.

"Where?" he asked and deposited the skull on the ground where Jenna indicated.

She traced a circle around it with salt from her bag and placed a lump of bread at each of the cardinal points. She would try this first without blood. With the very recently dead, there should be enough lingering energy to make the connection.

She focused. "Wandering spirit, wrenched but recently from this your body, come and speak to me. Tell me of the force that ripped you asunder."

The cold welled up around her almost immediately, and a

well-detailed apparition formed over the skull. "What—who calls me?" it whispered.

A man of some wealth, she noted. Pilgrim's robe of fine linen, but with a crutch under one arm. "Tell me your story," she prompted.

"I was maimed when my horse rolled over on me," the spirit answered. "I have heard that Godshead Spring will heal the afflicted, and so I have come. The first time didn't work, so I shall wait for the next."

He doesn't realize he's dead, Jenna thought with a grimace. "Did you notice anything at the cairn while the spring was flowing? Any strangeness?"

"I did," he nodded. "Right at the end I saw a pale giant sitting up on the rocks. It was crying into the pool."

"How did it feel to you when you saw it crying?" Jenna asked carefully. "Angry?" Angry enough to kill, it seemed.

The spirit shook his head. "No, miserable. I could feel the sadness even before I noticed the crying."

It was easy to assume that tears that killed pilgrims were born of anger or vengeance. But emotions shone more brightly in the Otherworld, and the state of one spirit could easily be seen by the others. If this spirit thought tears of sadness, then it was probably so. "Do you see any other pilgrims lingering close by?"

The spirit turned and stared upwards in the direction of the spring. "Yes, two more by the bank."

"Call them over. I have things to say to all three of you." A moment later, two more pale shapes joined the first. "Welcome, pilgrims," Jenna said formally. "I have news for all—your trials are at an end. You all sought the spring that it might heal you, and it did indeed free you from your afflictions. However, there was a cost. All of your lives were forfeit. Look around carefully, and you will see that I am right. But do not linger in your past. You need to accept eternity and move on."

There was only silence in answer, but after a moment the spirits faded and the coldness as well.

"Nicely spoken," Herrin commented. "I take it that was an easier transition of souls than most."

"These were pilgrims seeking a miracle," she reminded him. "And to those in pain, death can be a miracle. But this was only an aside to our main purpose. That, I fear, will not go as easily." She glanced over where the pilgrims were engaged in their travel preparations. "Probably the families of the three spirits need support as well. If you go to them and speak of the sacrifice of their loved ones, it could lessen their grief. Especially coming from a priest."

"I'm only a seminarian," he reminded her.

"But you're robed like a priest and with a Knight of the Holy Retribution at your side, you'll be sufficiently impressive."

Herrin gave a quick nod, beckoned Trayn, and the two of them headed towards the pilgrims.

"I hoped you're recovered enough for a conversation, Dwarf," she said softly as they disappeared.

His squat form wobbled into view out of thin air. "Perhaps a short conversation. You got rid of Priestling and Stupid deftly enough, I note."

"This isn't a conversation either of them would be comfortable with. We need to talk about Words of Power."

"Ah."

"That was a Word of Power that the god-spirit used, was it not?"

"No doubt."

"But I'm thinking that wasn't an actual attack, even though encounters with Words are usually threatening and dangerous. Am I right?"

"Might could be," Dwarf murmured.

She gave a sigh of exasperation. "Why are you suddenly so reticent?"

"Because there are consequences with Words of Power. And frankly, I know too much about them, and you know too little. No happy ending there."

"Well, there's no avoiding this discussion when they're part of this situation. And since we're being frank, let me say that I heard the Word uttered quite clearly, and could utter it myself if I had to."

"You daft wench!" Dwarf growled in his throat. "You don't go spouting a Word of Summoning just because you heard it once. No telling what you'd get. In my day, wizards studied for years to learn exactly how to hold their mind to control a Great Word. Otherwise the Word controls you."

"Which is why I need your counsel. You obviously have knowledge."

"I was slaved to a wizard-lord. It would be strange if I hadn't heard some Words along the way. Does me no good now, though. All the Words in the cosmos don't mean diddly once you're dead in the Otherworld."

"But the spirit of the spring spoke—"

"Well, there's dead and there's dead, and who knows which that spirit is. Thing is, these Old Spirits may not be gods with the Power of Making and Unmaking, but they all kept company together at the Beginning and used the same language. Bits and pieces of that language became our Words of Power."

"And it was summoning something when it bespoke?"

"Summoning is what we do with that word. In every day use, it might just be asking for help."

"Asking for help," Jenna murmured and sat down to think. What kind of help and from whom? From her...because she was the one with Sight? Or from Dwarf because he was a fellow old spirit? They were the only two who could hear and see what was happening.

"What does a god want when it asks for help?" she finally asked, but Dwarf had already vanished.

When Herrin and Trayn returned from their errand, the afternoon sun was sitting low on the horizon. They found her staring at nothing.

"Jenna?" Herrin asked softly, seating himself beside her. But he was careful not to touch her in case she might be in trance.

She gave a sigh. "I'm fine, just thinking. Did you find the right pilgrims?"

Trayn nodded. "Yes, and Herrin calmed their grief with his words. A good thing to do while you and Dwarf were hatching a private plot."

Trayn knew her too well. "Not a plot—not even a plan, unfortunately. Just a short talk about what we're up against. The god used a Word of Power to knock me cold, and apparently it was a Word of Summoning. I may have to return the favor as we move forward."

She heard Herrin suck air. "Jenna, the Church burns people with any knowledge of Words. They're all gone now, burned at the stake with their lips stitched closed, and you dare not start—"

"I know, I know," she sighed. "But it's the language of the gods. I may not have a choice in this case. You two should probably keep your distance this time. You don't need to hear the Word. Dwarf and I will confront the god."

Trayn crossed his arms stubbornly. "I'm coming with you. A dead Dwarf is no protection from a dead god. But I have this." He drew the cloth-covered sword from his second scabbard and unwrapped its hilt to reveal a pommel set with ruddy gemstones.

Powerful gemstones. Filled with Old High Magic. Something clicked at the back of her head.

"What is that?" Herrin demanded. "It looks like—"

"Herrin!" she snapped. "Don't argue, just go to the pool and shoo the last of the pilgrims away...and don't ask questions when you won't like the answers."

He glared, but kept his mouth shut as he stood up and walked back to the path.

"This may be pushing the priest in him too far too fast," Trayn murmured.

"That's for later," Jenna sighed. "We'll worry about Herrin after we've survived the next minutes. I think it's like this." She caught and held Trayn's eye. "The spirit wasn't asking for my help or Dwarf's. It was pointing at us because it sensed what you were carrying. It wants *your* help."

"To do what?" he asked warily.

"To—" And she had to stop to let her thoughts catch up with her gut feeling. She knew almost nothing about gods, but this was a very faded god, a ghost of a god, and she did know what ghosts wanted. Completion and release. Sometimes vengeance, but that was really only the mechanism to completion, just as completion was the means to release. And in those terms, what would a sobbing god-form want from a hero bearing a magical sword? She gave a firm nod. Definitely not vengeance.

"We need to climb up to the cairn," she said. "And probably quickly. Once the sun goes down, the energies will be different, and we may not be able to rouse the god until the sun and moon align again." She started toward the pond. "And Dwarf—are you there, Dwarf?"

The squat form materialized by her side. "I'm not your servant."

"But you're part of my team, and I need you with me. In a moment, I'll need one of your Words of Power to talk to the god of the spring."

He gave a snort. "Told you that kind of power doesn't work after you're dead."

"Yes, but you can whisper a Word in my ear, and I can speak it."

"What is this—Arbessian roulette? If the Word doesn't burn you, then the god will smite you. Don't want any part of that. Don't want to be anywhere near that Old Spirit."

"It's not roulette, but there's no time to explain. Give me a Word that says 'we bring you release' and you can keep your distance from the god."

They reached the top of the cairn right at sundown, and their shadows stretched long behind them. "You have to trust me," she told Trayn and tapped the palm of his glove. "Feed the sword and get ready to strike."

Part of the price of wielding this magic sword was activating it with blood. Much like feeding Dwarf and for much the same reason—blood was the great lifeforce for all things supernatural. They had yet to discover if there was a price behind the price. Trayn had blood-right to the sword through his family lineage, but that might or might not mean he was immune to it. She kept her eye on Trayn as he removed his glove and pressed the palm of his hand briefly against the blade until it was stained with a trickle of blood.

She waited until he had a good grasp on the hilt with his bloody hand, then gave her full attention to the empty cairn around them. "*Uthalaüþ,*" she intoned, forcing the strange sounds from her throat. The wind whipped her words into oblivion and the sky rumbled overhead. "V*rim-tal lenya þuindath!*" she finished at a scream.

The sky suddenly clouded over. *If the Word doesn't burn you*—Dwarf's comment came chillingly to mind, but she pushed it away to concentrate on the first pale wisps rising from the cairn. The great form slowly solidified, looking more transparent than earlier, but the featureless face turned unerringly in their direction.

"It's here—raise the sword," Jenna ordered Trayn, and saw the large face nod once and twice. She stepped forward until she was only an arm's length from the spirit and held out a hand to touch it. Not cold as death, but wet like water. "Go in right above my hand—now!" she called over her shoulder.

Trayn lunged, driving the sword into thin air, then gave a cry. The red gemstones on the hilt blazed forth like sudden fire. The great, pale form shook violently and slowly faded from view. As the last wisp disappeared, a bolt of lightning shot down, knocking them both off their feet.

Jenna took a few deep breaths and raised her head. A patch of charred stone lay right in front of her. She looked to the side and saw Trayn pulling himself to his feet. He was cradling one arm. "You're hurt." She got to her feet to help him. She felt rattled, but he looked worse.

He gave a grunt. "Something—maybe the lightning—traveled right up the sword." He tried flexing his arm. "It's going to be sore for a while, but look—the sword's gone. If the lightning burned up the damned sword, well worth it. What about the god?"

Jenna extended her senses, looking with Sight as well as sight. "I think it's gone for good. It has found release."

He gave her a curious look. "How did you know it wanted to be stabbed?"

"Release is what all trapped spirits want. And this spirit was very desperate because it was immortal—faded over the centuries, but still immortal. Perhaps no hope of ever moving on." She turned for the climb down the cairn, then frowned. "Bad news, Trayn."

He looked where Jenna pointed at the edge of the dry pond where the ornate sword lay in the glow of red gemstones. He shook his head but said nothing then, or on the climb down. At the bottom, he wrapped the hilt in leather again and with obvious reluctance, sheathed it at his hip.

As they started down the path, Herrin joined them, his eyes locked on Trayn. "An accursed sword?" He whirled on Jenna. "When were you going to tell me?"

Jenna gave a long sigh. It was going to be a long ride home.

It was a very long ride home. Two hours in morning light translated into more than three at a snail's pace in the dusk and dark. And the drizzle that had been holding off finally arrived. At least they were too sodden to argue. All their attention was on the road.

Finally they reached the gray walls of the Commandery. Leaving their mounts to the stableboys, they entered the keep and split in the entrance hall, shedding wet cloaks as they went. But as Jenna and Herrin turned toward the Cold Wing, she saw a page hurry across the hall to Trayn and hand him a message scroll. Expecting bad news, she paused and watched him read through the message. His clenched jaw told all, and she immediately backtracked to join him.

"How bad?" she asked.

"Lanyer killed Aryn," Trayn said woodenly. The younger brother had killed the older. "And Father as well. Lanyer is now Lord of Harebridge." He gave a bitter laugh. "But that's half a kingdom away and nothing to do with me." He walked off quickly.

Jenna stared after him, knowing he was in pain but not knowing what to say. For all their fears, neither of them had seen this double murder coming. Herrin came up beside her.

"I heard," he said. Then after a strained silence, he added,

"With such a brother, perhaps Trayn should be thankful he has a 'special' sword as protection."

A huge concession from Herrin. "He should be indeed," she nodded. "The more so because his brother Lanyer has the matching blade. If it comes to it, Trayn is the only one who can stop him. Just as he stopped a god."

"Not a god," Herrin murmured but without conviction. He'd seen too much today.

IN HER SHOES

by Melissa Mead

I love the story of Cinderella. Like most fairy tales, you can do so many different things with it. In fact, this is the second version I've bought from Melissa in the last four volumes of Sword and Sorceress.

Melissa Mead lives in upstate NY. She loves messing with fairy tales, and wrote Daily Science Fiction's Twisted Fairytale Flash series, among others. Her somewhat-dusty web page is at https://carpelibris.wordpress.com. You can also find her on Facebook.

Ella and Nan were already awake and sitting on Ella's hearthside mattress when the first rays of daylight stole into the kitchen. Ella had buttoned up the back of Nan's dress for her. Nan helped Ella into her battered shoes, worn in the odd pattern of somebody who "walks" on her knees, dragging her feet behind.

While Ella straightened the bedding, Nan circled the kitchen, checking the iron nails she'd placed on the kitchen windowsills and refreshing the trickle of salt across the doorway.

"Do you want your crutches, Ella, dear?"

"No, thank you. They're more trouble than they're worth on this stone floor, sometimes."

"You'll wear your poor knees to powder," the other girl protested, but Ella knee-walked to the table anyway. She climbed onto a chair, washed her hands, and set to work peeling apples. "No nails missing, Nan? No fairies got in?"

"Now, don't tease. With His Majesty hosting that ball tonight, there'll be more Good Folk about than ever. Wouldn't they love to play their tricks on some high-and-mighty Duchess or Earl!"

"It's just superstition, you know," Ella said. "You'll look ignorant if you keep saying things like that."

"It's common sense, Miss Eleanor," replied Nan in her very mildest voice, while she fired up the old iron cookstove. "If the Good Folk are real, you don't want their eye on you, and if they aren't, where's the harm?"

"Oh, don't be angry and start calling me Miss Eleanor. I didn't mean that you're ignorant, Nan. I just don't want people thinking you are because you follow those old habits."

"Your stepmam'll believe I'm a halfwit even if I start reading and writing in three languages."

"Then she's ignorant. Just one language will do. I'll give you another lesson if we have time before Stepmother and the Dreadful Duo wake up."

But just then Stepmother and her daughters all jangled their bells at once, and there was no more time for talk.

After luncheon, while Nan was busy with her upstairs work, Ella scrubbed pots and thought. It really was too bad how people underestimated Nan. She was more than bright enough to work in Mr. Greene's shop, or be a companion to old Mrs. Waterby, or...anything that got her away from Stepmother's slaps and insults. If only she could read. And didn't persist in braiding a rowan twig into her hair every morning, or dropping one of her hard-earned pennies down Coldstream Well every Midsummer, or following any of the dozen or so superstitions that marked her as uneducated.

"But she won't stop as long as she believes that fairies are real." Ella's glance fell on the old nails on the windowsill. "Only one way to prove it to her, I suppose."

She fetched her crutches from the corner, swept the salt away from the doorway, and removed the nails.

"There! Now when no fairies show up, she'll realize that they aren't real."

"Excellent plan, my dear. Except for the fact that we are real, of course."

Ella leaned hard on one crutch and swung the other at the stranger confronting her. An ordinary intruder would've gotten a painful smack in the shins.

Ordinary intruders didn't appear out of nowhere. The woman in front of Ella hadn't been there a second before. Yet there she stood, just out of crutch range, smiling as though Ella hadn't just tried to pummel her.

"Oh dear. I shouldn't have startled you. I forget that I'm a stranger to you, for all that I've been watching over you since you were born. Such a tiny thing! Your father, rest his soul, was sure he'd be burying you along with your mother. But what's the point of having one of the Folk for a godmother if we can't make things right once in a while?"

Ella blinked and sat down hard on her work stool. This was impossible. This woman couldn't be here. But she very much was. Her shimmering dress dazzled Ella's eyes, and a faint fragrance hung about her. Roses, with an undernote of something sharper.

The stranger broke a bit of crust off of a cooling apple tart and nibbled at it.

"See? Quite real. And you make lovely tarts, my sweet goddaughter. I'm sorry to have neglected you all this time! I would have come sooner, but, well, your friend Nan means well, but she's terribly suspicious."

"If what she believes is true, you're here because you want something. And she was right about the salt and nails. Why are you here?"

"Why, to make up for lost time, of course! To grant your wishes."

Ella felt her heart thump against the back of her throat. "Can you bring my parents back?"

"Oh, my sweet, not that! But I want to give you something wonderful. And make you believe in me. I see that look. Half of you still wishes that crutch had connected. Let me prove myself. I'll send you to tonight's ball."

Ella felt herself flushing. "I apologize for the crutch. But really, balls aren't for me."

The fairy godmother smiled. "You don't think so? Watch."

She drew a slim crystal wand from her sleeve and traced patterns in the air with it. Colors swirled in Ella's vision. If she hadn't already been sitting, she would have fallen.

"Steady! I forget how magic affects mortals, especially when they're not used to it. How do you like your dress?"

Ella looked down. Instead of flour-dusted homespun, she wore heavy silk in shades of blue that rippled and flowed like water. Silver lace spilled from the neck and cuffs.

"It's...it's amazing."

"It's beautiful, and so are you." The godmother produced a hand mirror from nowhere and held it up. Ella reached a tentative hand up to touch what she saw: her hair curled and styled into an elaborate crown, starred with lobelia and forget-me-nots.

"But you're barefoot! That will never do."

Indeed, Ella's feet were bare beneath that fantastic dress, and cold on the stone floor.

"Now for the best part." The fairy godmother smiled. Her smile looked triumphant. The wand twitched. Something cold flowed around Ella's feet. Ella barely noticed.

"Did you hear something? A thump, or maybe a crash? From upstairs?"

"No! Never mind that. Look at the shoes!"

Ella looked. She could almost see her feet through the glittering footwear.

"Are they...glass? They'll shatter!" Forgetting what her uninvited guest was, Ella glared at the fairy. "If this is some sort of joke because I don't dance, it's not funny."

"You do now." The fairy, her gestures grown impatient, poked the wand at her. "Try it! Stand up!"

Ella opened her mouth to protest, but her "godmother" no longer looked so benign. The air around her crackled with unseen lightnings. Ella leaned on the table and pushed herself to her feet.

She didn't fall. Her knees didn't buckle. Her muscles didn't ache from the unaccustomed strain. She took her hands off the table and lifted a foot.

She still didn't fall. She moved the foot forward, set it down, lifted the other...

...and kept going. Out the kitchen door. Up the scullery steps.

Across the grass. She spun in circles, the incredible dress rippling around her, and laughed.

"You are real! I apologize for not believing in you. I don't know why Nan always seemed so afraid of you. Can you make a dress for her too? Let's call her."

"No, don't!" The fairy's command stopped her cold. "I'm sorry, my sweet. But she's not my goddaughter. My magic won't work for her. And what's the point of parading finery in front of her when she can't share it?"

"I suppose you're right." The dress didn't seem quite as splendid now. Even the shoes...well, the shoes were still wonderful. "I'd still love to see her face when I go running up to her, though. And I'm sure she'd love to go to the ball."

"Your dress has pockets. You can bring her bonbons and whatnot. Chin up; stop moping! The ball's already started, and you need transportation!"

"Oh, I'd be glad to walk there!" A little of Ella's enthusiasm returned at the thought. She had no idea how long it would take to reach the castle, its turrets just visible past the apple orchard. She didn't really care.

"Young ladies don't walk to balls, my child. They arrive in style. And you do have to be home by midnight, after all."

"Why? What happens at midnight?"

"Oh, good girls are always home by midnight. Now: Watch!"

Ella watched, enthralled, as her godmother turned a pumpkin into a glorious coach. Her wonder turned to horror as she watched half a dozen squealing mice stretched and distorted into the forms of horses. Numb with shock, she let the fairy shoo her into the coach and shut the door.

The sight of the palace up close gave her another sort of shock, one that drove thoughts of the poor mice right out of her head. Feeling as though she were sleepwalking, she walked up the steps and into the ballroom without giving her name, dazzled by the light, the color, and the tap of her shoes on the ballroom floor. She found to a quiet corner and tried to remember everything she'd overheard of her stepsisters' dancing lessons.

ONE-and-two-and-three-and-four. This WAS fun! ONE-and-two-and-

"Excuse me, Miss, are you in need of a partner? Or is your dance card already filled?"

Ella shook herself out of her dancing trance and focused on the young man in front of her. A nice-looking young man, with a smile that, while amused, held no hint of mockery or condescension. He held out a hand.

"Dancing's much more enjoyable with a partner. If you'll allow me?"

"Oh, I'd love to! But I've never danced before, and I'm afraid I have absolutely no idea what I'm doing."

"Good. Then you won't be able to tell when I'm making a mistake." Smiling, gently persistent, he offered his hand again. Ella took it. Soon they were in the midst of an impromptu dance lesson, stumbling and laughing, heedless of the staring couples around them.

"This is such fun," said the young man. "Court ladies are so stiff and practiced, it's like dancing with a mannequin."

"Court ladies?" Ella paused, and really looked at her dance partner. His clothes weren't as elaborate as those of some of the other dancers, but his fine dark suit was of excellent material and cut. And all the people who were staring at them were doing it carefully, as respectfully as it could be possible to stare. The young women looked envious. Ella realized that she'd never asked her partner's name, nor he hers.

A suspicion began to form in her mind, but just then the clock chimed. A tremor shot through Ella's legs. Her knees buckled.

"Are you all right?" said the young man.

"Midnight already? Please, I have to go. Thank you so much, but I...I'm not well. Please..."

She ran from the ballroom. With every chime, the strength ebbed from her legs. She fell on the marble steps, tumbled to the bottom, and staggered out of sight behind some bushes while a clutch of uniformed men ran past, calling "Miss! Are you all right, miss? Where are you?"

Oh, she could guess who her partner had been. But the last

chime had died away, and she was scraped, bruised, and bleeding, in her old dress.

And one glass shoe.

Ella put the shoe in her pocket, which still held some sweets for Nan, and crawled home on her hands and knees.

Thank goodness, Nan was still up and working, and opened the door at once.

"What happened to you? Are you hurt? Here's my arm. Here's your crutches. Get inside and wash the mud off, and I'll make you some hot tea."

Once she was clean, changed into one of Stepmother's discarded dressing gowns, and sitting on her mattress, Nan plopped down beside her and thrust a steaming mug into her hands.

"Drink. And tell me true where you've been. I thought the Good Folk had taken you. Did you think I'd not notice that the salt and nails were gone?"

Ella looked at the floor. "You were right. I'm sorry. The Good Folk did get in. One of them, anyway."

Nan went white as Ella told the tale. "She'll want something from you, mark my words. The Good Folk don't just give gifts." Even as she spoke, Nan made her rounds, pouring fresh salt onto her wards. "But you really danced? And with the prince himself!"

"He had to be. The incredulous looks we got—I even saw Stepmother there, with her jaw dropped nearly to her boots. I was so afraid she'd recognize me! But of course, she'd never expect to see me dancing. Oh Nan, I wish you could've been there! It was such fun. I wonder if that's what flying's like? Oh, and I brought you some bonbons."

"Well, you certainly had a better time than I did! I didn't want to frighten you, but since we're both all right now I guess there's no harm in telling. This afternoon the strength went right out of my legs. No warning. I just fell to the floor, with your stepmam shouting at me to get up and stop being such a lazy lump. When she realized I couldn't, she had the gardener's boy carry me down here. It was quite the fright, I tell you, not knowing what happened or how to fix it. Or if your stepmam was just going to leave me there. Then when the church clock struck midnight, I felt my strength come back, and now I'm right as rain. But it was queer."

Ella listened with growing dread.

"Exactly midnight? You got better at exactly midnight? When did you say it started?"

"Late this afternoon, while I was dusting the parlor. Ella, dear, you look ill. Are you all right?"

"Yes. Nan...You said the Good Folk never just give gifts. That they always want something in return. What do they want?"

"Our souls. They have no souls of their own, so they crave ours."

"But a soul is, well, it's who you are! How can that get stolen?"

"You can lose it. By betrayal. Cruelty. Something that makes you not be who you are."

"I didn't agree to any trade! I mean, I danced, but the fairy never demanded payment for it, or told me to do anything for her."

"No. And even the Good Folk can't make a claim where there's been no promise."

"I didn't somehow curse you, Nan, did I?"

"You didn't make a fairy wish, did you?"

"No!"

"Then don't fret. You didn't call her. You didn't promise her anything. All's well that ends well." Nan still looked worried, but she shook a teasing finger at Ella. "But don't you go touching my wards again!"

Ella was scrambling eggs the next morning when Nan ran into the kitchen. "Ella, there's a royal coach out front! With a crest and horses wearing feathers and all. And one of the fellows looks like he could be your young man, and another's carrying a glass shoe."

Ella dropped the bowl of eggs. It shattered on the stone floor.

"Leave it! Ella, you've got to get upstairs before your stepmam runs 'em off."

"She wouldn't. Not royalty. Not if she smelled something to be gotten out of it. I'm the one she'll run off. What's he...what are they doing here, anyway?"

"Something about a shoe. Your stepsisters are trying to cram their feet into it. Ella dear, get up there!"

She went, step by slow step, half fearing that she might be too late, and half hoping that she would be. But there they were in the parlor: her stepsisters squabbling over the glass shoe, her stepmother purple with suppressed rage beneath her pasted-on smile, an affronted servant, and her dancing partner, watching the squabble with an amused expression.

"Ladies, I regret to say that I don't recognize either of you. The shoe's a moot point. If you'll please hand it back to Jenkins, we'll be going."

"Not yet!" Stepmother gasped. "Perhaps one of them might look more familiar if she were properly dressed and wearing cosmetics?"

Ella tried to smother her giggle, but Stepmother heard. "You! Why are you eavesdropping? Get back to the kitchen at once. Your Highness, I most humbly apologize."

"No, wait!" The prince bounded across the room, looking ready to sweep Ella into his arms. Then he saw the crutches.

"Oh! I'm sorry. What happened? Are you all right?"

"Perfectly, Your Highness. Thank you."

"Did you hurt yourself? You said you weren't feeling well. I sent some footmen after you to make sure you were all right, but they couldn't find you."

"I'm sorry for leaving so abruptly, Your Highness. And for deceiving you. I wasn't...well, I wasn't really myself last night."

"Last night?" Stepmother gasped. "What are you talking about? You can't have been there last night. You can't dance! You can't even stand up without those crutches."

"Not usually, no," Ella admitted, watching the prince's bewildered face.

"But...we danced. For hours."

"Yes, Your Highness. We danced." Ella took out the other shoe, ignoring her stepsisters' indignant wails. "Because I had these enchanted shoes. But they only worked the one time."

The prince's face fell. "Are you sure you can't reactivate them somehow?"

"No, Your Highness. I'm sorry."

"Yes she can." With a smell of roses and bitter medicine, the fairy godmother was there, smiling. "Now that both shoes are together again, she can use them any time she wants. All she has to do is put them on."

The prince's face lit up. "Then do it! I officially invite you to the palace for as many dancing lessons as you'd like."

Ella's stepmother and stepsisters started a barrage of protests. The fairy godmother silenced them with a flick of her wand. "Go on, my sweet. Put them on. Your prince is waiting."

Ella forced herself not to look at him. She glared at the eager, smiling fairy. "How'd you get past Nan's wards?"

"They only work where they're placed. In the servants' quarters. But you're no servant, and never have been. Put on the shoes. Your mother and father would be so proud."

Without taking her eyes off the fairy, Ella held out her hand. The prince placed the other shoe in it.

"Thank you, Your Highness." Ella cradled both shoes, remembering. "All I have to do is put them on and they'll work? Permanently?"

"Permanently. The spell will work even when you take them off to sleep."

"And what will happen to Nan?"

"The servant girl? What has she got to do with this?"

"Everything. She's the one who begged my stepmother to let me stay here after Father died. She's the one who does most of the work of an entire household staff. And she's the one who taught me that the Fair Folk never give something for nothing. And that they can manipulate, trick, and deceive, but that they can't give a false answer to a straight yes-or-no question. So yes or no: If I put these shoes on, will Nan lose her ability to walk?"

Lightning flashed in the fairy's eyes. Thunder shook the house. Stepmother and her daughters passed out. Ella stood her ground.

"Yes."

"I thought so." Ella hurled both shoes to the stone floor. They shattered. The fairy howled and vanished in a whirl of broken glass.

Nan dashed into the room. "Ella, dear, are you all right? What happened? The teacups shook right off the...Oh! Beg pardon, Your Highness!" She dropped a curtsey.

The prince looked shaken, but replied with a bow that clearly scandalized poor Jenkins. "So you're Nan. Pleased to meet you. I hear you know something about warding off the Fair Folk?"

"Ah...a bit, Your Highness."

"And Ella's the only person I've ever known to stand up to them directly."

Nan grinned. "You believe in 'em, Your Highness?"

"I have to. They're a potential threat to my parents' kingdom. Ella, why are you blushing all of a sudden?"

"Long story, Your Highness."

"Well, I hope you'll tell it on the ride back to the palace."

"Your offer still stands, Your Highness? Even without the shoes?"

"Absolutely. Will you come?"

"Not without Nan."

"Well, of course I want both of you. You two would be invaluable help with the whole Fae Menace thing."

Nan looked at the unconscious trio on the floor. "Your stepmam'll be in a twist when she wakes up and finds out she's got no servants."

"Yes, she will, won't she?" Ella's smile grew. "Let's get out of here before they wake up!"

SIMPLICITY

by Marian Allen

Pimchan, a Warrior, serves the All-Father—although there are days when she probably wonders why. The All-Father is devious and very fond of getting his own way, and while it's true she needed new slaves, she certainly wasn't expecting anything like the ones he sent her.

Marian Allen traded the mean streets of Louisville, Kentucky for the occasional snake-wrangling of rural Indiana. She writes science fiction, fantasy, mystery, humor, horror, mainstream, and anything else she can wrestle into fixed form. She has had stories in online and print publications, including multiple appearances in Marion Zimmer Bradley's Fantasy Magazine *and* Sword and Sorceress *anthologies. Her latest books are the* Sage *fantasy trilogy, her science fiction comedy of bad manners* Sideshow in the Center Ring, *her YA/NA paranormal suspense* A Dead Guy at the Summerhouse, *and her science fiction short story collection* Other Earth, Other Stars, *all from Per Bastet Publications. She blogs daily at* Marian Allen, Author Lady. *(http://MarianAllen.com)*

It all began so simply.

The Warrior Pimchan sat down to a dinner of noodles, fried pork, and vegetables in a spicy sauce, served in her favorite porcelain bowl. Her cook/housekeeper, Nadia, *clack*ed the matching porcelain spoon down next to it with less than her usual artificial deference.

Then Nadia pushed a sweat-drenched lock of ebony hair away from her eyes and made a simple statement:

"We need some slaves."

Pimchan swallowed her noodles and said, "No."

Nadia settled herself at the table, placing her own wooden

bowl with a solid *plonk*.

"This compound is too big for me to care for all alone. All you see is your sleeping room and bathing area, this eating room, the Chaos garden, and your practice arena."

Pimchan looked up from her dinner. "What else is there?"

"The kitchen! The vegetable garden! The storeroom! The other sleeping rooms and bathing areas! The laundry! The entry! The reception—"

The Warrior waved a hand to stop the recitation. "But there are only we two in the compound, now."

"Yes, so I'm free from cleaning up after Nandan and making sure he doesn't misplace his weapons—"

Unfair, Pimchan thought. Nandan had been an exemplary apprentice, and would serve the All-Father admirably as a wandering Warrior. She only wished she were wandering, too, instead of having the "reward" of protecting the town of Mountain Cloud, bound and domesticated and arguing with a housekeeper over staff.

Nadia was still speaking.

"—so, besides the work he did when he wasn't actually training, he took Tyana with him, and that leaves me with everything to do. And when am I supposed to study?"

Study magic, she meant, gathering up whatever bits and bobs of enchantments she could scavenge in and around Mountain Cloud, cobbling them together into her own particular sorcery.

"Close off the rooms we don't need. Halve the size of the garden."

Nadia served herself a second portion and scooped a radish from her bowl into Pimchan's. Nadia didn't care for radishes. "There aren't any orphans of a suitable age in Mountain Cloud who don't have family to care for them. There might be some in nearby villages—"

"You've been asking? Looking? Without consulting me?"

"But, Mistress," Nadia said, with wide-eyed mockery, "such domestic matters are beneath your notice."

Not for the first time, Pimchan regretted not having beaten Nadia when she was still a nameless slave child, rather than treating her with some amount of kindness and relative respect. Of course, her former Overseer, Tyana, would say that only a servant who speaks freely is fit to serve a Warrior.

"I'll give it some thought," said Pimchan, dismissing it from her mind.

But, of course, it couldn't be *that* simple.

Three days later, deep in the night, the jangling of the entry screen's bells woke Pimchan.

She dressed and armed herself and was lurking in the doorway between the house proper and the entry courtyard by the time Nadia reached the door. It was no small thing to disturb a Warrior's household by night, and no common thing, either.

Pimchan rubbed the Discernment rune on her bald, tattooed scalp, hoping to trigger a helpful insight into what was on the other side of the portal. Nothing came, but she nodded, and Nadia approached the heavy mahogany screen, hung with a hundred tiny brass bells.

Standing well to the side, Nadia called, "Who's there? What's your business with the Warrior Pimchan?"

"Courier from the All-Father," came a muted rumble. "I have a wagon load." He tapped out the code specific from the All-Father to Pimchan.

A wagon load? Pimchan's spirit leaped. *Has he reconsidered? Is he releasing me from my bond with the town, and delivering equipment for a campaign?*

That wouldn't be a wagon load, though. Unless the campaign was so far away, it would require more supplies than she could carry, to a place where she couldn't forage.

Pimchan left the shadows as Nadia lifted the bar; it was hinged and counterweighted, the screen balanced on bearings that made it slide easily—if noisily—open. Nadia closed and barred the screen the instant the wagon's tail cleared the threshold, Pimchan sealing it additionally with a security spell she had learned early in her travels.

Nadia said, "We have nothing to feed your beast, but I can give him water."

"I brought my own feed. Fetch the water."

The dark look Nadia gave the man showed she understood she was being dismissed and didn't like it, but she went.

The bed of the cart was covered with a tarp, which the courier folded back, revealing what could only be called a wooden cage. Inside sat two children, awake and alert. Pimchan's first thought was of Nadia's demand for slaves. Surely, the girl hadn't petitioned the All-Father! No; Nadia was willful, but not a fool, and only a fool drew official notice unless the need was desperate.

"We're here," the courier said, pitching his voice to reassure. "You can speak, now."

They said nothing, though, as he unlatched the door—Pimchan noted the latches could have been easily undone from the inside. Her resistance eased by the slightest of margins.

The front panel of the cage fell forward with a clatter.

"Out, now!" The courier clapped his hands, and the children scrambled out and over the tail of the wagon to stand, in bare feet and blue cotton trousers and tunics, staring at her in the moonlight.

Staring with round pale eyes beneath colorless hair and brows, staring out of faces as white as the moon herself.

Foreigners! She had seen a few of them before, these strange people from across the seas. She knew they came in different colors, some very near to the gold or reddish-brown of real people, others black or—most peculiar—white, like these. Fahrang, real people called them, except for the ones who called them *monsters*.

Nadia returned with a bucket brimming with water, which she put in front of the ox. He grunted and partook with ponderous enthusiasm.

Pimchan and the courier exchanged glances. He nodded, and she gestured for Nadia to join them.

The housekeeper gasped when she saw the children.

"Monsters! Are these young ones, or just little ones?"

The courier rumbled a chuckle. "Young ones." He pulled a folded paper from inside his tunic and handed it to Pimchan. It bore the All-Father's personal seal.

The courier climbed onto the cart, reached behind the cage, and hauled out two boxes bound with leather, one with each hand. He hopped to the ground, carried the boxes to the house, and plopped them down next to the wall. "These belong to them."

Nadia clapped her hands twice for emphasis. "Put them back in the wagon!"

The courier, as was proper, watched Pimchan for his cue, and ignored Nadia when Pimchan did.

Pimchan broke the seal on the paper he'd given her and held it to catch the light from the entryway's lantern. The writing was in the All-Father's elegant, spidery hand.

Greetings, my Warrior.

As your former Male is grown and gone, taking your Overseer with him, and as your presence has permitted your town to be so prosperous it has no unwanted children, I am taking the liberty of sending you two unwanted children from my own compound.

Their parents were advisers to my court from one of the Fahr-ang lands doing business with our Blessed Land. The parents were reportedly killed by footpads when they left our compound to visit the Fahr-ang quarter which has grown up near the docks. Other Fahr-ang are demanding I release these children to them, but I am disinclined to do so.

I present them to you, nameless, as is customary.

"These are the slaves you requested," Pimchan said, rereading the message. "Congratulations: You're now an Overseer."

"I didn't ask for monsters! We can't have them in the house! Remember what happened the last time a monster came here?"

Grimly, Pimchan said, "I'm not likely to forget murder. Nevertheless, the All-Father has given them to me, and that's an end to it." If only she could believe that. "Put them in your and Nandan's old rooms."

Nadia's hand went to the beads she had made from the earth of the compound and had strung on twine woven from flax she had grown herself. After a moment, she grunted and dropped her hand.

"Can they speak? Real language, I mean?"

"They haven't said a word to me," the man said, "but they seem to understand. I'm to move on as soon as I hand them over."

Pimchan lifted the paper he had given her. "I must write my thanks to the All-Father for thinking of me."

"I was told he already knew what joy you would feel, and that I shouldn't wait. If you'll get them out of my way, I'll turn the cart and go."

The children clung together more tightly as Nadia chivvied them to stand against the wall beside their belongings. Moonlight glinted on a few meager tears that escaped from four round eyes and traced the curves of four softly rounded cheeks.

So monsters had natural feelings. Pimchan and Tyana had discussed the possibility, but had come to no conclusion. She wondered if Nadia had noticed.

The monsters did speak, and proved it as soon as the screen had been barred behind the All-Father's courier.

Nadia pointed to the bags and said, "You. Bring." She mimed picking up the boxes.

The girl monster burst into sobs. The boy embraced her and said, "Don't be afraid, Mandy. Mother and Father would want us to be brave."

Pimchan exchanged startled looks with Nadia. Who would have suspected that monsters were civilized enough to revere their ancestors?

Nadia clapped for the children's attention. "You speak the Beautiful Language?"

The boy nodded. The girl swallowed her sobs and nodded, as well.

"Then know that you have nothing to be afraid of. You're now in the service of the finest Warrior and the most generous and just mistress in all the world." It gratified Pimchan to hear Nadia say so, even though she realized Nadia had said it to aggrandize herself, not her mistress. "Her name is Pimchan, but you must always call her Mistress. My name is Nadia, and you may call me that, although you must always speak and behave to both of us with respect. You are slaves. You no longer have the names you were given elsewhere. Here, you're Pimchan's Male and Pimchan's Female. If you work hard and behave yourselves, someday you may be named and freed, as I was. Do you understand?"

The girl, round eyes wide, whispered *yes*. The boy, a flush of something—was it pride?—on his cheekbones, jerked a grudging nod.

Nadia continued, "There are rooms for you. Actual rooms, not corners of store rooms or stables. You're very lucky children."

The girl began sniveling, clutching her brother's hand.

The Warrior scowled. Nadia and Nandan had never mewled so, insofar as she knew. Of course, Nadia and Nandan hadn't been in a land across the sea from their own people, caged and moved secretly to what might as well be the far side of the moon, where they knew no one but one another.

Pimchan said, "I will not be kept awake by a puppy taken before it was weaned. Let them share a room for the rest of the night. Begin their training in the morning, as Tyana trained you."

She strode past the three, down the corridor to her room. From that darkness, she saw Nadia, carrying one of the boxes, directing the girl, who carried the torch, to the room Nadia had used when she was Pimchan's Female.

Pimchan reopened the All-Father's letter and read it again, this time reading between the lines.

Their parents were advisers to my court.... The parents were reportedly killed by footpads.... Other Fahr-ang are demanding I release these children to them, but I am disinclined to do so.

I present them to you, nameless, as is customary.

What was the All-Father dragging her into this time? What had he dragged those children into?

A dimmed lantern floated toward her, and Nadia joined her.

"Will there be anything else, Mistress?"

"Are they settled?"

"Settled and secured. I barred the screen from the outside, just to be safe, although that's probably a wasted precaution. They're asleep already, snuggled together like two ferrets. They seemed bewildered."

"Small wonder." Pimchan handed the girl the All-Father's letter. "Train them within the compound. As far as the world outside our wall is concerned, I live alone with only you to serve me."

Nadia fingered the beads on her necklace again as she read.

"Let the Male and the Female clear away," Pimchan said, when supper was over. "Come with me on my rounds."

"Yes, Mistress."

Once out of sight of the newcomers, Nadia's respectful demeanor melted into her usual familiarity.

"They're doing well, Mistress."

"I need to know more than that." Tyana would have understood what she was saying: Domestic matters were the business of the Overseer; this is why a stationary Warrior needed one. But these were not ordinary slaves, nor ordinary children. Pimchan didn't relish cutting her way through Nadia's impudence to reach the heart of the girl's wisdom.

To her surprise, she didn't have to.

"Their parents were quartered in The Invisible City, far from the All-Father's private compound, of course, but inside the First Wall. Their father wrote a lot, and his writings were collected daily by someone in the All-Father's livery. Sometimes his writing had envelopes with them, but these, also, were collected by the All-Father's people."

Was he writing reports for the All-Father? Explanations of how things worked in the lands of the barbarians? Contracts? Trade treaties? Translations? Was he writing letters to...whoever the proper recipients would be, political or mercantile? Whatever it was, it was with the All-Father's obvious knowledge and under the All-Father's ostensible control.

"Go on."

"The parents went out occasionally to meet with other Fahr-ang. Sometimes they took the children to play with other monster children, sometimes they left the children with their Fahr-ang servant. One day, the servant went out to shop in the Fahr-ang quarter and didn't come back. Someone who seemed important—a real person, not a monster—came to talk with the parents that afternoon. There was a quarrel, and the parents went out without the children that night, leaving them in the care of a woman the children didn't know."

"A real woman?"

"Yes. The children said she was kind, but treated them like animals that were entertaining but possibly dangerous. Which, of course, they are."

"So, with the parents gone, the other Fahr-ang naturally wanted the children released to them. But the All-Father sent them far away and put them under my protection."

"I think," said Nadia, resting a hand on the high garden wall, "we'd better strengthen the wards."

"I think," said Pimchan, "you'd better learn some new ones, too."

The days settled into routine. Pimchan became accustomed to having her tea brought and served by her new Female, and was even able to eat while looking at her. The Female was exceptionally good at making and serving tea, as a matter of fact.

One day, Pimchan allowed her curiosity to overcome her reticence, and quizzed the girl. "Where did you learn the tea service?"

"Mummy and Daddy asked The Great One for a teacher," the girl replied, using the term Fahr-ang were taught to use for the All-Father. The girl blinked back tears. One escaped and she scraped it away with the back of her sleeve.

"My mother and father died by violence, too," Pimchan was surprised to hear herself confide. "I was much older than you and your brother, though."

"Nadia's parents died because they got sick," the Female said, somehow implying that this put Nadia on the other side of a dividing line.

Pimchan didn't like that. Then, again, she did.

One thing Pimchan unequivocally did *not* like was the amount of time Nadia spent with the children. She realized it took time to train them, but the chatter and laughter she heard from the servants' quarters sounded less like training than it did friendship, and she was far from certain that friendship between people and monsters was a good idea.

She was somewhat mollified when Nadia brought her some drawings, after the slaves were in their beds.

"The boy is a clever little monkey," Nadia said. "I've put him to working the garden, and he's made a device to draw water from the well and swing it around and dump it into an irrigation ditch. His people didn't invent the thing, of course, but I could never have constructed one. He did."

Pimchan grunted her surprise. It had never occurred to her the children would actually be useful.

"And look." Nadia handed her several sheets of scrap paper. "He's been drawing pictures for me of Fahr-ang *machines*." She pronounced the Fahr-ang word carefully, as if it might bite the inside of her mouth.

The first was of a wheeled cart with a smoking chimney on it.

Nadia said, "These run on tracks and pull other carts behind them. They go faster than horses, and much faster than oxen, but they can only go where these tracks have been nailed to the ground."

"Inconvenient," said Pimchan.

"That seems to be the way they do things. They think up ideas that only work in a limited way, and then arrange their lives around the limits. They have very strange minds."

There were other pictures, which Nadia explained when they were too outlandish to decipher. One, she held back, passing it to Pimchan with the deliberation it deserved.

It was a gun.

A monster had used one on Pimchan once. Looking at the picture, the Warrior could smell the sharp, smoky odor, could feel the impact against her body, could hear the explosion, like an outsized firecracker.

There were words—Fahr-ang words mixed with real ones—and arrows all around the picture.

"He told you how it works?"

"He did. I couldn't build one, though, and neither could he."

"Why would you want to?"

Nadia looked at her as if she had asked a childish question. "Because the Fahr-ang have them."

Pimchan looked back, not shamed, not angry, until understanding lit the Overseer's face.

"I've been spending too much time with them," the young woman said. "I'm starting to think they make sense." She took the pictures back. "Still..."

Pimchan shared that uncertainty. The gun had made Pimchan's weapons as weak as paper against flame. The gun wasn't a better weapon; it was a weapon of another order, as a sword is of a different order from a fist.

"It's good to know how they work, anyway." Nadia pointed to parts of the gun picture. "They use this finger to pull this thing. That makes this thing hit this thing, and something here explodes. Because it's in here, it comes out very quickly, like a pea in a pea-shooter, only faster and harder."

"Is there magic in it?"

Nadia regarded the drawing as if she could access its reality.

"The Male didn't say anything about magic. They don't seem to believe in magic, so the chances are, there isn't. There could be, of course, the same way as the runes on your weapons."

"Enhancing the skill of the wielder, but not magical in itself."

"Yes. Or possibly increasing the power of the shot by carving runes on the...whatever they call the things that come out and hit things."

"And could magic be used against it?"

"Against the gun?" Nadia shook her head.

"There must be a way."

"Why?"

"If we have no way to defend against this weapon, the Fahr-ang will, sooner or later, use it against us."

"Do you mean 'we' as in 'us' or 'we' as in 'all of us'?"

Pimchan blinked, startled, then snorted a laugh. "Ah...And there we have it."

"Have what, Mistress?"

"The All-Father's reason for sending us something the Fahr-ang want and he doesn't really care about. So the Fahr-ang will come and try to take it—them—from us. With guns."

Nadia's cheeks glowed with indignation. "He wouldn't! He wouldn't let monsters attack us, just to see if we could find a way to counter them. He wouldn't!"

But they both knew he would.

Pimchan said again, "There must be something. Something. And we need to think of it soon. Meanwhile, I'll begin intensive practice tomorrow. You see what magic you can come up with."

She dismissed her Overseer, but didn't drop into sleep, as she usually did.

She was thinking of the gun, remembering the pain and shock of its shot hitting her arm. What sort of person would use such a weapon: a thing with no honor, no matching of wits or skill—what did such a weapon prove? Perhaps it wasn't meant to prove anything, just to master someone.

Then came the day when Nadia returned to the compound with news of strangers in town.

"They're people, not monsters," she said, "but they have the smell of spies about them. A new beggar here, a cousin from down-country on a surprise visit there, a puppeteer renting booth space in the market, a young married couple taking advantage of small-town prices to buy a first cottage...oh, and a mercenary retiring to the quiet life—I liked that one. And those are only the ones I've come across, myself; there may be more."

"Are they asking questions?"

"Of course. They're new in town; asking questions is natural, isn't it?"

"Are they singling you out?"

"No, they're better than that. But regular people are asking me questions, as if somebody else had put me in their minds. They ask how do we manage with just the two of us? Am I still looking for slaves to take the places left by Tyana and Nandan? Are you teaching me the way of the Warrior?"

"And what do you tell them?"

"The truth, of course. We manage. Yes, I'm still looking. No, I'm not a Warrior and don't want to be. But, do you know, I think I'll be very, very careful when and where I walk."

"On the other hand, I'm due to make my visit to the town guard headquarters."

Somboon, the chief of the guards, greeted Pimchan with a low bow. She returned one almost equally low. He had proved to be a good strategist, strong, competent with his weapons and his fists, and unusually courageous for the head of a village brigade. His first thought, always, was for what was the safest course for the villagers, which hadn't always been to Pimchan's advantage. She wondered if it would be, now.

After she inspected the guards, their weapons, and their quick drill, she invited Somboon to walk the walls with her, as she sometimes did.

A lightning flash of exchanged glances, crushed smirks on the faces of guards, a definite responsive scowl flickering across Somboon's brow, told Pimchan her invitation had touched on some subject that had been under discussion.

They climbed the stairs from the guardhouse to the narrow bridge leading to the north wall. When they reached the wall, where they could walk side-by-side, Pimchan said, "What was that about? That silent interchange between you and your troops?"

He waved the question away and said, "A more important question is who's sending people to pry into your business?" He enumerated the newcomers Nadia had detected, adding a few she had missed, missing a few she had noted.

Pimchan added Nadia's to expand his list.

He stopped their patrol. "Do you know what they want? Do you know who they are, or where they come from?"

"I know exactly what they want: something the All-Father has put into my keeping. I don't know precisely who they are, but I know they represent the Fahr-ang. Or, I suppose I should say, some part of the Fahr-ang. Apparently, they have countries and districts and factions, just as we do, and can't all be lumped together."

He flapped his hand in dismissive irritation and they continued their inspection. "We should just keep them all out. Dealing with them is too much trouble."

"The All-Father knows best," Pimchan said, hoping it was true.

"He certainly knows more than I do, that's for sure. Do you think he knows these Fahr-ang agents are here? Don't you think we should let him know?"

"It wouldn't hurt to send him a message—from you, in my name—but I suspect he knows."

"Will..." and this, she could tell, frightened him, "will the Fahr-ang come here?"

They walked silently while she thought this over, moving game pieces on an imaginary board, baffled by the knowledge that she had no idea how a monster's mind worked.

As they neared the end of their circuit, Somboon said, "What I think is—may I say?"

"Of course!"

"I think they're spying on the town more than on you. I think they're trying to see if you have the support of your people—which you do. I think they're investigating whether you can be undermined or betrayed, or your compound walls breached by stealth, or if we'll ignore a breach by force. I think they'll find and report that the integrity of your stronghold is absolute."

A year ago, she would have been astonished at the deep pleasure this gave her. Of course, a year ago, it might not have been true. Once she had pledged herself irrevocably to the town, its relationship with her had changed. Sometimes she chafed at that change. Today, she did not.

She pressed her palms together in gratitude. "And then what? Will they give up? They won't march on us in force. What I have isn't that important."

She felt the gooseflesh rise as she thought of the Fahr-ang, with their deadly explosive missiles, tramping through The Beautiful Land, sending their smoke and stink into the clean, sweet air. No wonder the All-Father was willing to cast children and servants into the monsters' path in hope of learning how to counter that threat.

So swiftly, he must have been mulling over the problem since before it was actual—one mark of a good strategist—he said, "If they know you have the thing they want, and they know your storehouse is beyond the power of gnawing rats, they'll have to come to you openly. If what you have is unimportant, yet they still want it, I don't think they'll risk outright war."

Pimchan smiled. The gambit was classic to the literature of Warriors. "When we're ready, we invite them in where they can exploit what they believe is our weakness. Then we defeat them."

"When you give the word, I'll have my guards round up the spies."

"All of them?"

"I doubt we've identified all of them; we only think we have. Even if we take them all, their reports to their masters will stop, and that will be a report in itself. If you don't have a strange visitor within two weeks, we'll let one of our prisoners go with apologies for the inconvenience."

They clasped hands at the door of the guard house. Somboon's smile stiffened at a smothered snicker from behind him. He dropped her hand, bowed, and closed the door.

Pimchan returned to her compound, bemused at Somboon's misconception that she would be offended by a bawdy joke she hadn't even heard.

Nadia greeted her in the compound's entry court with a wide grin and a dance step. "I have it! It's an enchantment I've been using in the kitchen!"

Pimchan felt her expression go flat and her eyes go hooded as she suppressed her outraged pride. "Kitchen magic?"

The housekeeper presented her palms in apology but never lost her grin and did her dance step again. "Hear me, O Mighty

One, O Giver Of My Sustenance, O Mistress Of My Very Existence, O—"

"Be silent and speak!"

"It was given to me by the butcher, after I mixed an herb packet that eased his headaches. It's called bone-break."

"Bone-break."

"He focuses it on where he wants to chop through a bone and the cleaver goes through it like warm honey through bread."

Could it work? Pimchan saw the Fahr-ang army again in her mind, saw them marching with their terrible exploding weapons, saw their legs buckle, saw them fall, whole ones tripping over the broken ones, tangled and distracted and vulnerable. Chaos triumphant!

"Teach it to me," she said.

"I can do that," Nadia said, "and I can do more, if you'll consent."

"Do more in what way?"

"I can inscribe a rune."

Now Pimchan saw Nadia truly humble, truly offering a service she wanted to give but was afraid would be rejected. And rightly so. Warriors' runes became a part of them, bound to them through ink in flesh. Done badly, a rune could be a waste of time, pain, and scalp; done very badly, it could be a detriment.

"Do it," said Pimchan, without hesitation.

Nadia was good. She was so good, Pimchan didn't have to ask and Nadia didn't have to tell that she had been doing more than collecting herbs and enchantments; it was obvious she had also been studying rune-making and tattooing from the village artist-magician.

Bone-break was long and thin, with sideways spikes like stylized lightning. Nadia inked it in the white and red of bone and marrow. As she worked, she murmured the words of the enchantment, breathing them into Pimchan's flesh and blood and memory.

The Warrior obliged the Overseer and amused the young monsters by practicing her new spell on their sucked-clean chicken bones and barbecued pork ribs. The spell was more difficult than she had expected. By the time the skin of her new tattoo had scabbed, she could snap small cooked bones with relative ease, but fresh ones and thick ones took concentrated effort. Rubbing the rune would have helped, but she knew better than to rub it before the healing was complete.

A month passed, and Pimchan sent Somboon word to arrest all identified strangers and lock them in the cells below the guard house.

Outraged relatives of two of the strangers petitioned Pimchan for their guests' release, but Pimchan did no more than order Somboon to treat those prisoners with respect and as much luxury as a jail could provide. She inspected the cells, herself, when she went to confer with Somboon over the next move in their strategy.

Apparently, the guard captain had been right about the arrests bringing the dogs' master out to look for them: it was ten days after the round-up that another night-time visitor knocked at the compound door screen.

As before, Pimchan rose and dressed and armed herself with a Warrior's swiftness. As before, Nadia stood to one side of the entry and asked for identification.

"I come from the court of the All-Father."

But, unlike before, there was no confirming code tapped on the wood.

This was it, then. The confrontation was now.

She nodded. Nadia unbarred the screen and pulled it open, closing it behind the stranger.

Like most monsters, the man was taller than most real people. His skin was darkened from the sun, and his yellow hair was covered by one of the odd cloth caps becoming fashionable among the gentry, but his blue eyes glowed like ghost fire in the torchlight. He wore plain brown trousers tucked into thick-soled boots and a loose tunic over a shirt with full sleeves snugged at the wrists. Practical and nondescript.

He removed his hat and offered the peculiar, awkward,

lopsided bow the white Fahr-ang used, one foot forward, one hand sweeping the hat to cover his heart.

"The All-Father didn't send you, whether you came from the court or not," Pimchan stated, keeping her tone mild.

"They told the truth, who called you wise," the Fahr-ang said, his accent not nearly as good as his self-satisfied air suggested he thought it was.

"You didn't come all the way from the capitol to pay me compliments."

"No, I did not. May we go in?"

"No." If he looked for courtesy, he looked in vain. Pimchan stood at ease, not threatening or challenging or defying, but not giving anything, either.

He shrugged. "You know what I came for: my brother's children. Why they were refused me, why they were spirited away into the hinterlands, I haven't been told. But the children are blood of my blood, and I will have them."

"What makes you think they're here?"

"Oh, they're here." He turned his head toward the house and shouted, "Amanda! Jonathan!" After a few silent seconds, he shouted for them again.

Pimchan stepped closer to blocking the open house door. She drew her blue-steel saber. "Leave. Now."

But the smoke was out of the stove: Two young voices from inside came nearer, babbling in Fahr-ang talk and calling, "Uncle Paul? Uncle?"

Nadia lunged for the door as if to head the children off, but the man was fast and he had that monstrously long reach. He snagged her and pulled her close to his chest, both of them facing Pimchan.

And there was a gun in his hand. He pressed the end where the explosive pellet came out against Nadia's temple.

The children popped through the door. The boy skidded to a stop, grabbing his sister as she passed, in an unwitting parody of the monster and Nadia.

The boy and the man jabbered to one another. The boy gestured to Pimchan and to Nadia. The girl's face turned red at the man's reply. Her hands turned to fists, she stamped a foot, and the baby tears of helpless rage ran down her cheeks.

The man spoke to Pimchan in true language. "They say they've been well treated, but it sounds to me as if you've used them as slaves. Mandy doesn't want to go home; this barbarous country is the only home she remembers. But they're both coming with me."

Pimchan said, "They both stay here until my superior says otherwise."

The man showed his teeth. "I do say otherwise."

Nadia moved only her eyes, which were wide with terror. She cast a glance at Pimchan's scalp.

Pimchan didn't need the reminder; she felt her new tattoo, its thin, jagged line still fresh in her body. But what would a broken leg—assuming she could manage such a large and living bone—do in this case? Would it cause the gun to go off?

Desperately, she thought of the drawing Nadia had shown her, of the description and explanation the boy had given and that Nadia had passed on to her.

She cast the spell with all the force her practice had built into her.

The man screamed. He fell, eyes rolling, gun flying, collapsing onto the flagstones of the entry court. He thrashed and rocked, grunted, and emptied into unconsciousness.

The children called out and ran to him.

Nadia, whatever her instinct or inclination might have urged her to do, stayed with her charges, examining the unconscious man and reassuring his young relatives.

"Somboon!" Pimchan called in a voice that could carry through a busy battlefield. "Enter!"

The town guards, who had been stationed in shadows outside the compound for the past two weeks, shoved the unbarred screen aside and trotted in, Somboon at the fore. One of the guards squatted next to Nadia and consulted with her on the foreigner's injury.

Somboon listened, then joined Pimchan, who hadn't moved, not even to sheath her saber.

"What did you do to him?"

"I broke his finger."

Somboon said, "All of them?"

"I wanted to break his leg, but the spell is new and I didn't feel I could do it properly. I decided to break his finger: the one that pulls the piece that makes the gun explode."

"I think you did it."

Nadia said, "You broke every bone in his hand, as far as I can tell."

The compound was secured and quiet, and Pimchan sat before her writing desk, but the words she would write to the All-Father wouldn't come. Not the proper words, anyway. Everything she thought of sounded bitter, accusatory, challenging, smug.

For, after all, he had used her—and, what was worse, Nadia and the town—to probe the Fahr-angs' strength and weakness. And they had served their purpose and survived.

The Fahr-ang man now lay, moaning, in a cell below the guard house, tended by the town's chief doctor and by its best medical magician. The children slept, thanks to the tea Nadia had brewed them, barred into one room as they had been on the night they came.

Nadia, for a wonder, was giving Pimchan the peace and solitude she needed, having brought her the writing desk with a low bow of gratitude and a hand-clap of congratulations.

The entry door jangled, the bells set off by a knock too weak to be heard.

Pimchan met Nadia in the hall and waved her back, resolved to break as many bones as she could manage if this was someone bringing yet more trouble.

"Who's there?"

"Lek."

"Who?"

"Lek. The chestnut seller."

Ah, yes, Lek: old and shrunken, once a Warrior's companion, now roaster and seller of chestnuts on the streets of the town.

"We don't want any."

He knocked again, giving the signal the All-Father used for Pimchan.

She opened the screen wide enough for the old man to slip through.

He handed her a paper, folded and secured with the All-Father's seal.

"A man gave me that to give you, and told me the signal knock."

"What man?"

"A man who got through my barred screen in the darkness and threatened to cut my throat if I didn't get up and do what he wanted. His clothing, where it brushed me, felt fine and soft, and he smelled of rich food. That's all."

He held out a palm, but looked at the ground, shuffling backwards as slowly as he dared.

"I'll send Nadia out for chestnuts tomorrow," Pimchan said. "You won't have to haggle over the price."

She let him out and barred the screen behind him. She considered charming the bells—the entire door—to silence, but, after a brief struggle, chose not to.

Once again, Pimchan stood near the courtyard lantern, reading a letter from the All-Father. Once again, Nadia, who had joined her, watched with apprehension.

Greetings, my Warrior.

I congratulate you on your solution to the puzzle Lady Chaos has set our country. I'm told that one of the Fahr-ang generals once said that an army marches on its stomach. That man is a fool, for an army marches on its feet. Not, however, if the bones of its feet are broken. Nor does it shoot guns if it cannot use its hands. No doubt the foreigners will find a way to overcome that attack, but such is the way of warfare. For now, it will do.

Unfortunately, I find it necessary to bring your new slaves back to the capitol. My emissary will fetch them, along with their unlucky relative, and restore all three to their family, who will depart for their own country as soon as it can be arranged.

I await your detailed report.

Pimchan folded the letter.

"Alas for you, Nadia; you're being demoted back to mere housekeeper. Pack the children's things and bring me tea to keep me awake. We'll have another visitor before dawn."

Nadia sighed. "I'll be glad to clear the compound of monsters, although I've grown just a little attached to them, in spite of their peculiarity. These two are more like people than monsters, really. And I've come to rely on them."

"Stop hinting. Look harder for replacements. Send word throughout all seven Circling Sisters Mountains. I want the household complete as soon as possible."

"You mean before a certain someone has a chance to insert more children of his choosing?"

They looked at one another.

Pimchan cracked a smile. "I have little hope of that. Still, you and Nandan were undoubtedly at least approved by him, if not deliberately chosen, and I have no complaints there." Before Nadia could lift a prideful chin, she said, "Not many, at least."

SHINY IN THE SHALLOWS
by Rose Hill

The guy who keeps showing up on the beach where Grace is camping while searching a shipwreck seems harmless, perhaps even a bit naive. But this is definitely one of the "things are seldom what they seem" stories.

Rose Hill lives with her lover and their grayscale pets in Minnesota. She spends entirely too much time building worlds and not enough time petting the cat—just ask him. Rose has been reading Sword and Sorceress *for about fifteen years, but this is her first time being published in it. Her work has appeared in* Beyond the Pillars: An Anthology of Pagan Fantasy *and is forthcoming in* Fantastically Horny! *and* Like a Spell: Erotic Stories of Wizards.

When shadows deepened under the waves, creating too many hiding spots in the sunken ship, Grace decided to call it quits for the day. The sun had sank below the other side of the island and she had to get moving if she wanted to make it back to her camp before dark. Taking a deep breath on the surface, she began her swim back to the fine white sand that the island stretched finger-like into the turquoise ocean. The sand continued beneath the waves to create tricky sailing for ships. Locals could navigate the area, but the shipwreck had not had a local crew.

Lucky for the locals.

She plodded, sodden, back to her camp at the base of the finger, where palm trees leaned over the sand and ferns beckoned in the breeze. Despite the warmth of the water, she was cold from so many hours in the waves. At least the waves were low and mellow today, good for swimming. She had hoped to find the loot today, before anyone else arrived. No such luck. While the bodies had already floated away or been taken by scavengers, the doors remained stubbornly locked and she had located no secret compartments on the areas of the ship she could access in the few minutes of each dive.

Her meager camp offered scant comfort: a tarpaulin braced with a stick to protect her from any showers, a bundle of sticks she would be lighting in a moment, and her pack stashed inside holding fresh water and clean underthings. The beach was still empty at that point, so she ducked into her tent, stripped out of her wet clothes, and put on dry ones. She came back out to start her campfire and nearly jumped out of her skin.

The beach was no longer empty.

A man leaned against a palm tree near her camp. He seemed to be a local, like her, with brown skin and straight black hair messily tied back in a tail. Young-ish, maybe? It was hard to tell. His face bore no lines of age and his hair had no strands of white, but he did not look particularly young, either. He wore only a shirt and breeches, no shoes or vest or coat at all. A line of a chain for a necklace hid under his shirt. She could see no bulge of a dagger in his meager clothes, but he could always have one stashed at his back. Grace had been born and raised with pirates—she knew better than to trust anyone who appeared unarmed.

"What are you doing here?" Grace asked.

He smiled broadly and she could see no hint of malice in his expression. "I came to say hello. Hello!" He waved. Grace continued to watch him warily. His smile faltered. "You seem to be looking for something in the shipwreck," he continued. "Anything in particular?"

"Nothing in particular," she lied. If she could discourage other treasure seekers, she would. The money she could get from the bidding war that amulet would bring would set her up for years.

"Ah well. It's good water to be swimming in, no matter the reason." His smile returned and he looked out to the waves.

Grace watched him suspiciously. He did not seem to be interested in the treasure or the shipwreck, but that could be a ruse. She made a note to keep an eye on him and went back to light her campfire.

More scavengers started showing up the next day, though she did not see the new man among them. By the time she gave up the search for the day and went hunting some clams for supper, most of the beach was covered in makeshift tents and a few had started to pop up on the strand as well. More divers had joined her in the water, but thus far they had left her alone.

That would not last. Once someone found the loot, these sharks would show their teeth.

The new man made brief appearances on the beach that evening, peeking in here and there. He did not try to speak to her again, though he chatted with a few others. Most people either laughed at him or drove him off. They seemed to think him a bit simple. As long as he did not try to take the loot from them, few people would start trouble.

But the loot was proving damned hard to find. She could find no chests, locked or otherwise. Someone had broken the captain's quarters open the second day, but there was no jewelry or coins or gold of any sort there. The rumors of the magic amulet transported among the loot were solid, taken straight from the complaints of the rich man who had ordered the amulet in the first place. The shipwreck had been seemingly untouched when Grace arrived. The amulet had to be around somewhere.

Evening brought more people, their tents stretching out on the strand despite the threat of high tide. Grace slogged out of the water past them. Her skin itched and she would love nothing more than to wash all that salt and sand off, but it would do her little good until *someone* found the treasure. She would much prefer if she found the treasure, but she would take an excuse to bathe at this point.

Once she had changed in to dry clothes and set her wet ones out to dry in the fading light, she sat outside her tent watching the other scavengers. All were heading in for the night, lest they trap themselves in some dark location and drown. No few of the scavengers were drinking—some of them laughing with others, others shouting, a few others muttering to themselves. One trio was loudly discussing what they planned to do with all the money they would earn from selling the loot once they found it.

Fools, the lot of them. Money wasn't money until you had it in hand.

A commotion down the sand drew Grace's attention. Three men cornered the new man, hands on their weapons. Grace frowned. The new man might be hiding something, but he seemed harmless thus far. There was no reason to mess with him. The man in the center jabbed at the newcomer, shoving him back against the rough bark of a palm tree.

"What do you think you're doin' round here, huh?" the center man sneered. "Just hanging around, waiting to steal the treasure from us hardworkin' folk. We ain't going to let you do nothing of the sort." He stepped back and his hand dropped to the blade at his hip.

By the time the first man drew steel, Grace had her cutlass in hand and was halfway there. She kicked sand in their eyes as she reached them, knocking the first man's cutlass up and out of the way. One, clearly a bit more drunk than the other two, fumbled for the weapon at his belt. A slash across the top of his hand made him stumble back, still unarmed. She pointed her cutlass at them, blocking the local man with her body.

"You just leave him alone now," Grace said, voice low and calm. "He ain't here looking for the treasure. There's no need to make trouble out of nothing."

The three men glared at her belligerently. The man's cutlass hovered near hers, then slowly lowered.

"Fine," the man spat. "We'll leave you alone for now. But I don't want to see him poking around here no more." He pointed his blade at the newcomer, then sheathed it and dragged his friends away.

Grace sheathed hers and turned back to the new man. "You hear that? Stop lurking around here, you're making people nervous."

"I will not lurk where they can see me," he said.

She blinked at that phrasing, frowning. "Don't lurk. At all. I can't guarantee I can get you out of trouble again."

He smiled that silly smile from before. "I will not lurk on the island. Will that satisfy you?"

Crazy old coot. If he decided to go fishing in a boat nearby, she could hardly stop him. "Fine." She turned and headed back to her tent. "Stay safe."

But when she got back to her tent, she paused, hand on the tarpaulin. She did not like the look of those three. If they picked on a man who seemed half-daft and harmless then backed down when confronted with steel, they were probably the sort who would come back in the middle of the night to get revenge.

Grace sighed and started packing her things.

Morning found her a quarter mile down the beach, her tent tucked away along the edges of a small lagoon she found. It would be a great place to wash the salt off once she came back from searching and starting farther away would give her a chance to check the ocean floor for any pieces that might have been swept away by the tides. She climbed out of her tent and stretched, enjoying the gentle morning sun.

"You said you're looking for treasure."

Grace yelped and spun. The new man leaned nonchalantly against a tree, in the exact same clothes as he had before. How did he keep appearing like that?

"What treasure?" he continued.

She took a deep breath to calm her racing heart and straightened. Might as well tell him since he probably heard enough sneaking around yesterday. "The ship that sank off the coast had valuables on it. Jewelry, gold, that sort of thing."

"Shiny things!" The man grinned.

Grace eyed him. "Right...Among the valuables was a particularly powerful amulet. It could be sold for a lot of money. That's what everyone's looking for." Though she would be happy with a handful of gold coins at this point. Anything to make this worthwhile.

"You're not going to find it."

Grace cocked her head and considered him. She had assumed that the lack of arrogance in his eyes and tone meant he was not a threat, but she could be wrong. Dead wrong if she wasn't careful. She could not read the tone in his last statement, though his smile hardly dimmed. "How would you know?"

"I just know."

"Are you looking for the treasure too?"

"Nope."

"You don't want to get rich?"

"What would I do with money?"

Yeah, that put him firmly in crazy territory. Grace shook her head. "Look, if you don't want the treasure, just stay out of the way of the rest of us. I don't want to see you getting into any more trouble."

"I will not get into any more trouble," the man said. His smile belied his solemn tone.

The next three days were a blur of diving and searching through sand. She witnessed no few scuffles between the other searchers, though from what she could tell, no one had found a thing yet.

"Where could it be?" Grace kicked sand into the lagoon as she paced along the edge. "There's nothing out there. Nothing at all! That wreck was still fresh by the time I got there. Doors were still locked. How is it completely cleaned out?"

"I did say you weren't going to find it," the man said. Grace shot him a glare. He had taken to sitting on a rock beside the lagoon, watching her come and go.

She shook her head. Her wet black hair stuck to her neck. "Maybe a fish stole it," she muttered.

He grinned. "Maybe an octopus stole it."

She smiled, shook her head, and laughed. "Maybe."

The next morning, Grace was skimming along the sand towards the wreck when the sun hit something shiny out of the corner of her eye. She stopped, hovering in the water. Was...was the amulet just sitting on a rock? But she swam this way every morning. How had she not noticed that?

The "rock" smoothed and shifted colors, turning white with a dark orange pattern across its head and the tops of its arms. An octopus was wearing the amulet they were hunting for. Just like the new man said.

No way.

He had a trained octopus!

It took off back the way she came. Grace pushed off the sand, broke through the surface for air, and dived again, chasing the octopus. She had trained for years and could stay under longer than the average person. The creature scuttled across the ocean floor, pushing with its legs and pulsing its body in the kind of glide only a creature without bones could manage. She shot down, reaching to grab it, and it abruptly burst forward out of her grasp. Damn thing. She pushed off the ground to get more air, and headed down once more to continue the chase.

Over and over she tried to snatch the amulet away, but it always ducked out of reach at the last moment. She came up for breath again and realized she had almost made it back to the lagoon. No matter. She would chase it anywhere to get that amulet.

The octopus climbed over some rocks, and went up and out of the water. Grace broke through the water to see the new man sitting on the rock, grinning.

A variety of thoughts passed through her head, but she went with something polite. "You could have told me you had a trained octopus."

His eyebrows rose. "A trained octopus?"

"*Your* trained octopus." She nodded to the chain still hidden beneath his shirt. "And it brought you the amulet."

"I suppose you could say the octopus is mine."

That was a damn useful pet. She floated in the calm waters of the lagoon, trying not to feel betrayed. He *had* warned her she would not find it. "So, what are you going to do with the amulet? Do you have a seller in mind?"

He cocked his head. "I'm keeping the shiny. It's fun to walk on the sand and breathe the air."

Breathe the...Oh. *Oh.* Not a pet. Not a pet at all.

The local continued to consider her. "I won't give you this shiny, but since you're my friend, you can have another."

She blinked at him. Her mind had stopped at the prior realization. "Another amulet?"

"No, no magic. I've never seen another that does this. But I have other shinies, if you want."

This conversation was full of surprises. "You have other shinies?"

The octopus-man nodded vigorously. "Lots of them. They're very pretty."

The pirate in her perked up its ears. "May I see them?"

He fell into the water, switching back into the octopus seemingly as he hit the water. She followed him deep into the lagoon, down through a small passage. Her lungs ached before they finally came up and broke into air. It was a small cavern, lit by the sunlight from an opening in the roof and the reflected light from the glittering pile. Coins, goblets, necklaces, rings—all sorts of things.

"Where did you find all this?" Grace breathed.

The octopus pulled himself up next to the pile of valuables and turned back into a man crouching beside the pile, a sudden and instantaneous shift. Grace tried not to flinch away. It was less weird with the water as a transition. That would take some getting used to. "From wrecks like the one you were searching."

"And you just...store it?"

"I keep it, I wash it, I look at it." He brushed his hand through the pile, knocking gold coins to the side. "It's pretty. I like the pretty."

Grace smiled. That was a motivation she could work with. But first things first. "What's your name?"

He looked back to her, blinked back to the octopus, and flashed her a pattern of colors she could not follow. Then he changed back and looked at her expectantly.

"That's your name?" she asked hesitantly. He nodded. "I can't do that. Do you have a name I could say? In the air?"

He cocked his head, dark eyes wide, and looked at her. "Why would I need one?"

Like that he looked innocent. Naive. If this octopus was going to keep wandering around as a human, he might need someone to show him the ropes. "So I have something to call you. We're friends, right? My name is Grace. If you say that in my hearing, it will get my attention."

The man shrugged, but his smile acknowledge the gift of her name. "You can pick a name for me."

She considered it for a moment, then said, "How about Sefi?"

His smile grew and he sat back, leaning against his pile of loot. "Works for me."

"All right, Sefi. How would you like to find more shinies?"

He sat up and looked at her. "What do you mean?"

She swam over and pulled herself up on the side of the pile. "We can work together. I find shipwrecks, you get the shinies, we split the loot. Half and half." She reached out her hand to him. "Deal?"

"Deal." He turned back into an octopus and shook her hand. She laughed at the slimy, pulling feeling of the suckers. This might take some getting used to, but she could adjust.

BLACK DUST

by Robin Wayne Bailey

Frost once carried the Book of the Last Battle, while armies fought over it and laid waste to the land. She gave it to a god for safekeeping, and then she died. Death restored her to life. Now his wife wants the book, but Frost has no memory of her previous life—or the book. Unfortunately, Death's wife is not going to accept that as an answer.

Robin Wayne Bailey is a novelist, short story writer, poet and editor. His novels include the Frost *series, the* Dragonkin *young adult trilogy, and the* Brothers of the Dragon *trilogy, along with stand-alones such as* Shadowdance *and the Fritz-Leiber-inspired* Swords Against the Shadowland. *His short work has appeared in various* Darkover® *and* Sword and Sorceress *anthologies, and in two collections,* Turn Left to Tomorrow *and* The Fantastikon: Tales of Wonder. *He's a former two-term SFWA president and a founder of the Science Fiction Hall of Fame. His next big project is an anthology called* Little Green Men—Attack! *co-edited with Bryan Thomas Schnmidt and forthcoming from Baen Books.*

Descending from the high hill country on the border of Chondos, Frost found herself at the edge of an unfamiliar plain. She tugged on her horse's reins, bringing the black stallion to a halt. Rising in the stirrups of her saddle, she stared ahead with a sudden sense of apprehension. The land had a blasted, foreboding appearance, like no place she had ever seen. No blade of grass, no living shrub or tree pushed up from the dead soil, just twisted, tortured limbs and things that might once have been trees. On the far side of the plain, the sharp peaks of an unknown mountain chain chewed at the iron-gray sky.

The stallion snorted as Frost dismounted, then free of its rider, pranced in the last patch of grass. She reached up and stroked its withers.

"That horse is smart," Kipling said. "If the heat doesn't kill us, we'll choke on the dust."

Frost glanced at her young companion on his pale mare. He had traveled with her for a moon-cycle after a street fight in Rhianoth. He had jumped in to help, although she hadn't needed help, and he'd followed her ever since.

Frost walked forward a few paces. The black dust rose up in puffs, covering her doeskin boots. When it twined about her ankles, she jumped back.

"This is not Esgaria," she told Kipling over her shoulder. Her lips pressed into a tight line. "I'm lost."

"We're low on water," Kipling reminded her. "We should stick to the hills." He turned his mare away from the dust. "Let's go."

She wiped a fine sweat from her brow as she gazed upward. The sun, half-hidden in clouds, was unreasonably hot. Bending down, she scooped a handful of dust and let the wind blow it from her hand. She heard a faint moan. "Something has lured us here," she said to Kipling as she stood.

Kipling touched the pommel of the sword he had claimed in the street fight. For days he had cleaned and polished it proudly, sharpened it, his first weapon, but he had barely begun to learn its use. "I don't doubt you," he said, his face almost as pale as his mare. "This place is cursed."

"Cursed?" Frost sensed it, too, but for the boy's sake, she made light of it. "What do you know of the world, Orphan? Cursed is a big word for you."

Kipling tensed in his saddle and pointed. "Then what is the word for that?"

The sky began to darken, and the wind intensified. A bolt of white lightning crackled through the clouds. Another chased it, and thunder shook the air.

Kipling's mare whinnied.

"You may shortly have more than enough water," Frost said as she caught the reins of her stallion and steadied him.

Kipling stared outward with wide eyes. "It's not the storm," he said through gritted teeth. "There's something in the storm!"

Frost swung up into her saddle and gazed where the boy pointed. Lightning flashed again, stinging her vision, and yet, she did see something. Wincing, wiping away tears, she looked again and caught her breath.

Far across the wasteland, a figure approached them with a sure stride. As it advanced, the dust rose up, and in the dust rose faint ghosts of warriors and wizards and dead, forgotten gods with broken weapons and tarnished armor. The ghosts fought as if to impede the figure, but it pushed them away effortlessly and came on.

"Run, Kipling," Frost said. "Ride away as fast as you can."

The orphan shook his head and fought to control his mare. "I'm staying with you!" he cried over the wind as he continued to stare outward. "What is that thing?"

Frost didn't answer. She checked the sword that hung from her saddle, then put one hand on the jeweled dagger she wore. The small blade began to sing in its silver sheath, confirming what she already knew. "Be quiet," she told the dagger, and it obeyed. Then, to the boy, she added, "If you stay, you be quiet, also."

"I will," he answered as he drew his sword. "But with steel in my hand."

"It will do you no good," she promised, "but if it makes you feel brave, do so."

The black stallion shivered, but held steady as she put one hand on its neck. Frost leaned forward. Despite the wind and the dust, the darkness and the ghosts, the advancing figure came on. Cloaked in lightning and menace, it began to laugh. The sound was high-pitched, a woman's laugh.

Another sound almost as loud as the laughter also came over the plain, a rattling and rasp. Frost could not identify it at first, but as another blast of lightning crackled overhead, she saw the figure more clearly. The dagger on her belt began to sing again with a challenging wail.

"It's a woman!" Kipling cried as he fought to control his

mare.

"It's not!" Frost answered. "Stay back, boy."

The figure looked like a woman. It wore a wedding dress, but the color was black and adorned with bones and the veil hung in tatters. A long train dragged in the dust behind, made of skulls. Its bracelets were skulls, and its necklace was skulls, and it wore a crown made of skulls. On each brocaded shoulder, a skull perched. The empty sockets in the ones on her shoulders burned with fire as if they saw ...something.

"I know you," Frost spoke in a low voice, knowing the figure would hear.

The figure continued to advance as the ghosts fell back into the dust. Finally, nearing the edge of the plain, she pushed back the veil, exposing thick white hair that cascaded to her waist. She looked up with empty, lifeless eyes.

"And I know you, Samidar—or Frost or whatever you call yourself these days." The laughter faded. The creature spoke with a voice full of ice and age. "Some people also call you the woman who loved death. Did you think Death's wife would not notice?"

Frost touched the dagger again. The blade understood the gesture and became silent once more. "Did you expect me to care?" she answered. "If you have a problem, take it up with your husband."

Kipling's mare reared in sudden panic. Off-balanced, the boy almost fell. He fought for the reins and waved his sword.

Death's wife raised a hand. Kipling's sword exploded into shining fragments.

Frost also raised her hand. The fragments hung for an instant in mid-air, then reassembled themselves into one blade. "It's the boy's first sword," she said to Death's wife. "Have a heart."

Death's wife smiled. "I can appreciate your sarcasm," she said, "as well as your power, young witch."

Kipling turned the mare in a tight circle, his face full of fear. "I can see what she is!" he shouted at Frost, "but what the hell are you?"

Death's wife laughed again. "Such a good question!" she said to Kipling. "Oh, there is much you don't know about this one." She stopped laughing; her voice turned grim. "You should have listened to her and run away."

Fearing for her inexperienced companion, Frost interceded, steering her stallion to the dust's edge, putting herself between the goddess and the boy. "If your business is with me," she said, "then state it or rattle your ass back where you came from."

Death's wife glared. "You're bold only because you have my husband's favor."

Frost sneered and mocked Death's wife with her own words. "Oh, there's much about me you don't know." It wasn't the wisest course, but she had to keep the attention off Kipling, even if it meant challenging the Queen of Hell. "If you want an apology for sleeping with your husband, then you have it. It's not as if I had a choice."

"No apology necessary," the creature answered. "A philandering husband is my curse, not yours. But somewhere on this plain an object lies buried, and it is beyond my power to find it. I don't believe it is beyond yours."

Frost scowled as she gazed across the wasteland. She thought about the ghosts lurking in the dust. She felt them watching, waiting, and she realized suddenly what the dust really was—the ashes of flesh and bone. "What could I possibly find here that you cannot?"

Death's wife let the question hang in the air as she folded her hands. The skulls on her shoulders seemed to look upward, to fix on Frost as the goddess answered.

"The Book of the Last Battle."

Frost felt a chill upon her heart. "That book was destroyed a long time ago," she whispered.

Death's wife smiled and shook her head. "A grimoire that contains all the spells that both the forces of Light and Darkness will use at the Armageddon? Such a thing can never be truly destroyed. You did your best when you stood upon those mountain peaks and watched your armies battle to destroy it. But in the end, someone only buried it here—among the bodies and bones of those who fought for and against you."

Kipling guided his mare carefully to one side. "I'm out of my league here, aren't I?" he muttered as he regarded the two women.

Frost ignored her companion. "I have never fought here," she protested, "nor commanded armies! The book is just a legend!"

For a moment, Death's wife actually looked sympathetic. "Blame my husband," she said. "Death and resurrection sometimes play hell with mortal memories. Yours are wonderfully scrambled." She turned grim again. "Nevertheless, you once carried the Book of the Last Battle across three nations. You defended it with blood and sweat, and you did, for a time, keep it safe. That you remember none of this is irrelevant. You have a bond with the book, and it will come to you if you just seek it."

Frost tried to think, but her head reeled. It couldn't be true! Death's wife was trying to trick her. She squeezed her eyes shut, trying to remember. It was almost her undoing. Kipling cried out, and the horses whinnied. When she opened her eyes, the black dust was flowing across the grass like a surging wave. The black stallion reared and threw her from the saddle. Kipling reached out to catch her, and his mare bolted from under him.

The dust surrounded them. Frost smelled the death in the black soil, felt the stirring of old and angry souls in the ashes and bone. Reaching out for Kipling, she yanked him to his feet and pulled him close as armies of ghosts lined up behind the Queen of Hell.

"Find me the book! Bring it to me!"

Her jeweled dagger began to scream in the presence of magic. Demonfang, the blade was called, and well-named. Frost drew her sword as Kipling drew his. But she didn't rely on steel alone. As the ghost horde charged, she unleashed her own magic and called lightning from the dark sky. Death's wife screamed as one of the skulls on her shoulder exploded.

"Whore!" the angry goddess shouted. "You dare!'

Kipling swung his blade in wide-eyed desperation as a trio of warrior ghosts surrounded him. One of those spirits, struck a lucky blow by the boy, screamed and vanished in smoke. The once-shattered sword still bore a residue of magic in its restored steel.

But the sword could not keep Death's wife at bay. She extended a gnarled hand, and Kipling froze. His sword fell from suddenly numbed fingers. He shot a look of question and surprise before his eyes glazed over. Deathly hands rose up from the dust around his feet and dragged him down. The dust surged over him, and he was gone.

Frost screamed. Again, she hurled lightning, but Death's wife waved the bolt away. The ghosts surrounded her. They pressed close with hideous faces. Rotted hands tried to grab her. Quickly, she drew a circle in the dust with the point of her blade and muttered an incantation. Then, with both hands, she drove her sword deep into the ground.

No spirit would get past her barrier.

"Well done," Death's wife complimented. "I can see why you captured my husband's attention and, almost, his heart. But your spell will not save the boy's life. His soul will join the rest, locked forever in this blasted ground. Only the Book of the Last Battle can save him."

"But I don't know how to find it!" Frost shouted. With the toe of her boot, she kicked dust in the face of Death's wife. "Don't you understand that?" The ghosts pressed against her barrier, rained blows upon it with ancient weapons, screamed insults at her.

Death's wife wiped her face with a sleeve and spoke calmly. "The witches of Esgaria were renowned," she said. "You have their blood in your veins and power you don't even realize—power to call the book." She took the remaining skull from her shoulder and held it out to Frost. "Wander across this battlefield where you once walked. This skull will light your way."

The skull's eyes sockets blazed. The ghosts drifted back, but no more than a pace. Their rage did not lessen.

"Don't take too long" Death's wife warned, "or the boy may not come back."

"You bitch!" Frost yanked her sword from the ground and reached out to snatch the skull. She needed its strange light. "I can see why your husband threw you over!"

Death's wife only smiled. "Good luck," she said. "You may still have to fight these spirits. They remember you even if you don't remember them."

Holding the skull high, she strode past Death's wife, but before she got far, she felt a nudge at her back and turned to find her black stallion. The animal nickered and shook its mane, and the glow from the skull reflected in its large eyes almost as if they, too, were filled with flame. "Good boy," she whispered, sheathing her sword. Then, still holding the arcane skull, she climbed into the saddle.

She didn't get far before the ghosts rose up against her. Her dagger screamed a warning as the things flew up out of the dust. Hands, like claws, grasped her legs and tried to drag her down. Still others emerged from the dust-filled air to fly with dizzying speed around her. A pair of them tried to seize the skull, her only light. She might have drawn her sword in panic.

Instead, she drew Demonfang.

The dagger screamed a higher note as she slashed a spectral hand. Impossibly, gray blood spurted. The wounded creature exploded into black ash. She cut a second creature and stabbed a third. Both burst into smoke and ash. The rest abandoned their attack and fell back, their hatred rising to a new level. She wondered what she had done to earn such enmity, but there wasn't time to dwell on it.

Lightning continued to flicker over the plain. Among the grotesque shapes of dead trees and twisted limbs, she rode, sometimes with her shadow stretching before her, sometimes beside or behind at the lightning's whim. By a low outcropping of boulders, she stopped the stallion and looked around. A sighing sound caught her attention.

On the ashen ground, crawling on their bellies in the darkness, waves of ghosts advanced upon her. Throwing one leg over the saddle, Frost dropped to the ground and drew a circle around the stallion and herself. Muttering the incantation, she drove her sword into the ground. With her barrier in place, she contemplated her next move—finding the book.

Call to it, Death's wife had said, and that was as good a plan as any for the moment. She dared to close her eyes, to clear her mind of Kipling and the danger around her. She visualized a book. Visualized it flying through time or space to her outstretched hands. She recalled everything Death's wife had told her, how she had once carried the book, how she had a bond. Frost sent her mind outward.

But how did one call a book? It wasn't a horse or a dog.

Then, without warning, a blast of lightning rocked the sky, and a twisting snake of white fire touched the pommel of her sword. The air crackled, and the sword exploded. The force hurled Frost backward through the air, and the skull went spinning away.

Bereft of vision or hearing, Frost felt the ghosts upon her. They tore at her garments, bit her and beat her. She felt herself dragged down into the dust just as Kipling had been.

But she still grasped Demonfang in her fist. Indeed, she could not yet open her hand. She lashed out blindly, and the dagger sang horrible notes each time it touched one of the spirits. The hands released her, and again the spirits retreated.

For what seemed like a long time, she lay on the ground waiting for sensation to return. Hearing came back first. Close by, her stallion snorted and shook its mane. The wind sighed over the rocks, and the dead trees rattled as her dagger, satiated for the moment, purred. Still blind, she stumbled to her feet, her heart hammering. The stallion came to her, and she leaned upon the saddle, wondering how she could go on,

What had she done here? Why couldn't she remember? Did it matter?

It did to her. Kipling mattered, too. Aching in every joint and muscle, she put a foot in the stirrup and climbed back into the saddle. The dagger fell silent, and little by little, vision returned.

A sort of vision, at least. She saw the world through a misty veil full of indistinct shapes and drifting smoke. The ghosts hung back, but now they were curious more than angry. She heard them, too. They called out their names in the night as if they wanted her to remember.

They called another name, too, the name of this wasteland—*Demonium*.

She touched her stallion with her knees, and the animal stopped. Something important had happened here, on this very spot. She strained to see through the haze over her eyes. She could barely make out shapes: men, wizards, gods, all fighting and dying.

For the Book of the Last Battle.

Suddenly, deep in her brain, she saw the book. Worn, nondescript leather covers, unimpressive in size, locked with enchantments older than time, itself.

With a gasp of shock, she remembered everything. A dying wizard pressing the book upon her, charging her to bring it to this place. Armies arrayed to seize it. Armies arrayed to defend it. Gods of Light and Darkness advancing with covetous intentions.

To stop them all, she alone had opened the book, cutting the leather binding with the unnatural dagger she still held. With Demonfang. She, alone, had read the spells that turned back darkness and when it all was over passed the book into the keeping of a trusting god.

Who had buried it on the battlefield.

Frost swung down to the familiar ground, knelt, and put her hand upon the dust. An energy hummed beneath her fingertips, and through still-fogged eyes she saw thin, red lines of power, like lacework traceries, that ran all the way to the mountains.

She put a hand to her stallion's cheek, stroked him and murmured reassuring words. Then, she walked some paces away. The ghosts gathered closer, but they did not attack.

"Give Kipling back to me," she told them, "and I will give peace to your souls. You have been bound here long enough." Waving a hand, she dismissed them.

"You've found it, haven't you? You know where the book is!"

Death's wife stood behind her, two skulls leering from her shoulders again, but the wedding dress was gone. She wore shining black armor instead with inlaid designs and elaborate skull tracings in gold and silver, and in one hand she held a sword. "Give the book to me," she snarled. "I will use it to unseat my husband, and then I will rule Hell alone!"

The lightning crackled overhead, and another voice spoke on the electric air. "This was your grand motivation?" the voice said. "Petty jealousy? Spousal revenge?"

The night shifted and coalesced into a shape, a tall and painfully beautiful figure that Frost knew too well. The Lord of Hell strode through the dust toward them in armor almost identical to his wife's. He raised his hand, and a sword of fire formed in his gloved fist. "Did you think I wouldn't notice your absence?"

Death's wife shot out a hand toward Frost. "If you think those ghosts can give you back your boy, think again. He is my prisoner. Only I can return him to you, and only if you give me the book! Defy me and he dies forever!"

"I died once," Frost answered in defiance.

The Lord of Death turned a lingering gaze upon her. "And I returned you to life. Your presence in my court..." he hesitated, then looked upon his wife. "Her presence disturbs me."

His wife shrieked. "Hypocrite! You fell in love with her!" She ran at her husband, sword upraised.

Death anticipated the attack. He swung his own fiery blade. When the two weapons met, the sky shattered with thunder, and lightning scorched the air. His wife reeled from his blow, fell backward, then attacked again. Across the plain, dead trees and limbs that were already little more than ash burst into flames.

It was not the first time gods had fought on this battlefield. Yet, these were no ordinary deities. Death-bringers both, they had power to kill the world. Frost shouted for them to stop, but both ignored her.

Squeezing her eyes shut, she recalled the lines of energy in the dust. In her mind, she followed those lines until they stopped at the base of the mountains. The book lay there, quiescent, waiting. With all her magic strength, drawing upon the bond she felt, she called to the book. It answered with her true name.

The mountains shook, and the land split open with a quaking

that knocked Death and his wife off their feet. Startled, they turned to stare at her. The Queen of Hell shrieked with glee.

With a surge of power, Frost held out her hands and rose into the air. Lightning tore open the night, but it didn't touch her. She controlled it now.

Like something alive, the book rose up from the cavern where it had lain and flew through air. Straight for Frost it came, answering a summons.

But Death's wife was not yet done. She, too, rose into the air to intercept the book. "It must be mine!"

Death grew larger, taller, and seized his wife by one ankle. He slammed her to the ground. Furious, she rose up from the resulting crater, thrust with her sword, and stabbed him in the belly. He roared in anger and pain.

Frost ignored them. She held out her hand, and the book appeared on her palm. It spoke to her, reminding her of their bond, telling her that she belonged to it and it belonged to her. Flashes of lightning tore her clothes to tatters, and the wind stripped the tatters away. Naked, she floated in the air.

The Book of the Last Battle opened as the two Deaths continued to fight. The first page ripped itself out of the book. All the letters and symbols flew up from the page. They swirled around Frost, then pressed into her skin like tattoos. The second page ripped free and fluttered up like a bird on the wind. Strange glyphs and markings branded Frost. Her head snapped back as she accepted them.

One by one, in rapid order, the pages tore free. Spells and incantations in languages unremembered by any man or God sprang off the paper. When every inch of Frost's flesh was inked, the ink absorbed into her to make room for more information. Page by page, the book destroyed itself, and the blank sheets erupted into flame.

Death and his wife stopped fighting, lowered their swords, and turned to watch the spectacle. One stood silently, almost proud. The other screamed and stamped her foot with rage. "All my ambitions!" she cried, unable to grasp the scope of her failure. "Give me the Book of the Last Battle!"

Frost called back as the last pages bled into her flesh and burst into flame. Then, the leather covers also burned away. "I am the Book of the Last Battle," she said. All the ghosts of Demonium rose up again at those words, some from the dust, some on the wind. Laughing, weeping, finally free, they wafted away on the night wind, and their voices, like music, faded forever.

"You bitch! You whore!"

With barely a glance toward his wife, Death swung his sword and cut off her head. He shrugged, as he looked up at Frost. "It's only a temporary solution."

Frost lowered herself gently to the ground. She felt different. She *was* different. She remembered everything now, including her time in hell, her time in Death's bed. She didn't approach him, though. He didn't want her close. She disturbed him.

"Things can grow here again," she said with a sigh.

He chuckled. "You're speaking of new life to the Lord of Death." He regarded her for a long moment, and she felt the power of his lust. At least, he told her it was only lust. When he spoke again, she doubted him.

"I know men have called you the Woman Who Loved Death without really knowing what that meant." He paused, and waved a hand over his wife's corpse and head. Both disappeared. "You could be the Queen of Death."

"Death cannot afford emotion," she reminded him gently. "But think of me once in a while as I think of you."

Death looked down upon her and winced. "You have more power than you know now. Both men and gods will try to use you. Be careful, my love."

His words both chilled and warmed her. "You will have my back," she answered.

He shook his great head and drew the night about his shoulders like a cloak. "Not I," he said as he vanished. "But another will."

Kipling came walking through the dust as the lightning weakened. He looked lost and bewildered, yet unafraid. She wondered what the boy had seen, what he remembered of this night. An orphan like herself, she felt closer to him than ever.

"I love your new look," he said. His gaze roamed up and down her naked body, but when he reached out, he only lifted a strand of her once-black hair. The lightning strike had turned it white. "Now you really look like frost."

She hugged him, glad for his return. "Take off your shirt," she told him.

He raised an eyebrow. "Has it come to that already?"

"Imp!" She gave him a little slap. "I want you to carry something for me."

Kipling looked at her as he removed the garment. "What is it?" he asked.

"A key," she answered. "A very important key."

A single symbol appeared on her breast. Glowing, it detached from her body, fluttered around in the air, and then attached itself to Kipling right between his shoulder blades. "It will protect you," she told him, "and it will protect me."

"I can't see it!" he protested as he contorted himself and tried to see over his shoulder.

"No matter," she answered. "A key should be where you can find it."

He looked at her strangely. He didn't understand yet. He would in time.

READING THE FUTURE

by Laura Davy

There are many methods of fortune telling. Some of them can also be used for other things; I knew one author who used tarot cards to make up her characters. There is, however, ample evidence in history—from the Oracle of Delphi on—that the method used doesn't matter as much as the understanding of the results.

Laura Davy lives in California with her husband and two cats. She wrote her first story when she was in Elementary School and, despite the fact that the plot didn't make sense, she kept on writing. Her fiction has been published in Apex Magazine, Escape Pod, Plasma Frequency, *and others. You can learn more about her at www.lauradavy.com.*

The tea was bitter and burned the roof of her mouth, but Aurelia finished it with a practiced ease. She swirled the cup three times, flipped it onto a plate, and let three heartbeats pass before lifting it back up. Finally, she passed the cup over to the fortune teller.

The woman gazed at the teacup with youthful brown eyes, a contrast against her gray hair and wrinkles. The dim lighting and incense smoke made it hard to see so Aurelia doubted many people noticed that the fortune teller was wearing a wig and her wrinkles were drawn on. Did she disguise herself because people trusted wise old witches more? Maybe the woman just wanted to separate her work life with her personal life. If only living a new life was as easy as taking off a wig.

The two were alone in her tiny store, but Aurelia imagined she could hear Valeria's footsteps as she paced outside. Valeria had always been impatient, but she had said she would wait.

The fortune teller's wrinkle-free fingers caressed the cup's ceramic lid as she inspected the remaining tealeaves. When she abruptly stopped moving and let out a sharp gasp Aurelia knew the reading was done. Aurelia put a gold coin on the table. Five times what the woman had asked for.

"I've never seen this before." The fortune teller's fear and awe were apparent despite the disguise. "You will be the main figure in an upcoming battle! The battle for our very souls! May the Gods protect us all!"

"Thank you for your time," Aurelia replied.

"You are the Foreseen One. You alone will save us all or we will be doomed."

"I know," Aurelia said.

Aurelia left the shop and started to walk away. Valeria following after her, looking both annoyed and relieved that the reading was over.

"That was another waste of time and money," Valeria said. "You need to stop requesting readings. It's a sick game."

"You have to admit, it's a little funny."

"It's not. You scare them and then leave. Even known frauds give a true reading when it comes to your destiny."

When Aurelia's future was foretold back when she was ten-years-old, the priests, swordmasters, witches, wizards, spear masters, trackers, and everyone else who had taken an interest in the girl, had all agreed she was the Foreseen One. She had been trained by the best masters and told to stay on the move, to never let herself get tied down. Maybe that would make sense if she knew what or who she would be fighting, but details were lacking. All that they agreed on was that only she could save everyone. Her alone.

"Want to go get a beer?" Aurelia asked. "I'll pay."

"You're just changing the subject."

"You can think of it as apology beer and I'll think of it as normal beer. That way we'll both be happy."

They entered an alehouse and Valeria flagged down a barmaid and ordered.

Aurelia studied the lines around Valeria's mouth. Were they deepening because of age or because she was frowning more? They had been traveling together for since they trained under the same swordmaster six years ago, but Valeria was bound to leave her at some point. The prophecy never mentioned the Foreseen One's Friend.

The beers arrived as a young man in a black robe entered the bar and sat down at a corner table. He put a deck of fortune cards in front of him, waiting for people who would want to know if they would be lucky in dice that night.

Valeria looked over to see what Aurelia was looking at. "No. Not here. You'll cause a scene."

Aurelia left and sat down across from the fortune teller without saying a word.

The fortune teller looked even younger close up, with a patchy beard that didn't hide his pimples.

"Have you come to have your fortune read?" the boy asked.

"Yes," Aurelia answered.

"Would you like your entire future or this night only?" the boy asked as he passed the deck of cards to Aurelia who began to shuffle.

"The entire," Aurelia said. She placed the cards face down.

The boy dealt the cards face up on the table. All of the usual cards appeared: Dragon, Death, The Child, and every major God. With 79 cards in the deck, Aurelia got all the important ones. Another obviously dire reading.

The boy tapped the Dragon card.

"Do you see this card? This means you'll have a big trial ahead. Judging from how it's next to the Death card, most would believe it's dangerous. But, since it's upside down it will be just a normal ordeal, maybe something to do with work."

The boy tapped The Child card. "Responsibly. Maybe a marriage. And the next card shows prosperity."

He went through each card explaining away every terrible meaning giving Aurelia a normal life.

Aurelia began to laugh until she started to sob.

"What's wrong?" The boy asked.

"No. No, everything's perfect." Aurelia put her head down on the table. The wood had been smoothed away with years of use and it felt cool against her forehead. When her eyes were dry she stood up and put every coin she had left in her money pouch on the table.

There was a hitch in Aurelia's voice as she said, "Thank you."

Aurelia walked back to Valeria as the boy scrambled to put the money away before anyone saw it.

The two friends left the bar together with Aurelia walking slightly apart. As always.

ABOUT SWORD AND SORCERESS

by Elisabeth Waters

The *Sword and Sorceress* anthology series started in 1983, when Marion Zimmer Bradley, complaining that she was sick and tired of sword & sorcery stories where the female character was "a bad-conduct prize" for the male protagonist, persuaded Donald A. Wollheim of DAW Books to buy an anthology of sword & sorcery with strong female characters. The book was published in 1984.

The original title, *Swords and Sorceresses*, was changed during the production process when it was discovered that nobody could pronounce it in a conversation. So the first book was titled simply *Sword and Sorceress*. It was a success, so the following year we got *Sword and Sorceress II*.

It is my personal belief that if either Marion or Don had realized how successful this series was going to be, they would not have used Roman numerals, but they did, and DAW published the series through *Sword and Sorceress XXI*. (That's #21, for the non-Romans among us.)

Norilana Books picked up the series with volume 22, and because Marion was no longer alive to edit it, Vera entitled the book *Marion Zimmer Bradley's Sword and Sorceress XXII*. This led to five titles that were listed on the royalty reports as "Marion Zimmer Bradley's" with the only thing different being the ISBN.

We finally reissued volumes 22 through 27 as *Sword and Sorceress 22* through *Sword and Sorceress 27*, and we have been using Arabic numbers every since. We hope that our readers find this less confusing. We know that we do.

Made in the USA
Middletown, DE
22 December 2016